DEMONS OF
THE NIGHT

Edited and with
Nine New Translations by
Joan C. Kessler

DEMONS OF THE NIGHT

Tales of the Fantastic,
Madness, and the
Supernatural from
Nineteenth-Century
France

The University of Chicago Press | Chicago & London

Joan C. Kessler is associate professor of French in the
Department of Foreign Languages at the State University of
New York at New Paltz.

The University of Chicago Press, Chicago 60637
The University of Chicago Press, Ltd., London
© 1995 by The University of Chicago
All rights reserved. Published 1995
Printed in the United States of America
04 03 02 01 00 99 98 97 96 95   1 2 3 4 5

ISBN: 0-226-43207-6 (cloth)
0-226-43208-4 (paper)

Library of Congress Cataloging-in-Publication Data

Demons of the night : tales of the fantastic, madness, and the
supernatural from nineteenth-century France / edited and with nine
new translations by Joan C. Kessler.
    p.   cm.
Includes bibliographical references.
1. Fantastic fiction, French—Translations into English.
2. French fiction—19th century—Translations into English.
3. Mentally ill—Fiction.   4. Supernatural—Fiction.   I. Kessler,
Joan C.
PQ1278.D46   1995
843'.087660807—dc20   94-29819
                                                             CIP

The paper used in this publication meets the minimum requirements
of the American National Standard for Information Sciences—
Permanence of Paper for Printed Library Materials,
ANSI Z39.48-1984.

Illustrations by Julia Robling Griest.

For my parents

Note on Translations

Mérimée's "The Venus of Ille" was translated by Jean Kimber; Villiers de l'Isle-Adam's "The Sign" and "Véra" were translated by Robert Baldick; Schwob's "The Veiled Man" was translated by Iain White. All other translations are by Joan C. Kessler.

Minor changes—such as Americanization of spelling, etc.—have been made with permission to the four previously published translations.

The Notes to all thirteen tales have been added by Joan C. Kessler.

Contents

Acknowledgments

I am grateful for the generous support given me by New York
State United University Professors in the form of a Dr. Nuala
McGann Drescher Affirmative Action Leave for Spring 1990.
I wish to thank Corinne Nyquist, Margaret Hallstead, and Jim
Tyler, as well as the staff at Sojourner Truth Library at SUNY,
New Paltz, and Cornell University's Olin Library, for their most
helpful assistance.

Professors Victor Brombert and Suzanne Nash of Princeton
University and Professor Frank Paul Bowman of the University
of Pennsylvania read parts of my manuscript and gave encouragement. Warmest thanks go to Rob Thorne and Richard Halpern for
their invaluable assistance with computer technology at various
stages in the preparation of the manuscript. I owe thanks also to
Judith Maillard, and to Professors Pietro Pucci, Icky Hohendahl,
Dora Polachek, and L. Pearce Williams at Cornell University.
Nathan Glick and Isa Kapp gave valuable criticism and
encouragement.

I want to express my gratitude to Howard Aldendorff for his
interest and support, and for his valuable help and suggestions.

My greatest debt is to my father, for his conscientious reading of the manuscript, and scrupulous detective work for some of
the endnotes.

Finally, special thanks to my mother, who not only has
been encouraging and supportive throughout, but who first stimulated my love for the written word and for tales of mystery and
imagination.

Introduction

English-speaking readers who are well acquainted with the fantastic tales of Poe, Hoffmann, and Gogol are generally less familiar with the nineteenth-century French offerings in the genre. Although the fantastic mode challenged the imagination and craftsmanship of many of the best French writers of the last century—Romantics, Realists, and Symbolists alike—no selection of such stories in English translation has been made available thus far. A volume gathering some of the most outstanding of these seems long overdue.

The fantastic tale was enormously popular in France from the time of Charles Nodier and Prosper Mérimée. There were several reasons for its wide appeal among fiction writers. The fantastic was, in the early years of the century, a largely uncharted genre and one that promised fresh imaginative resources. It was, moreover, linked to the fashionable, pseudoscientific vogue of mesmerism as well as to various forms of occultism and spiritualism. More profoundly appealing was its rich symbolic and psychological potential: the fantastic would provide an invaluable vehicle for probing the dark side of the human mind, for delving into unexplored spiritual territory and articulating forbidden themes.

A number of literary critics and historians have viewed the emergence of the fantastic tale as a belated response to the rationalist doctrines of the Enlightenment. Throughout earlier centuries—in the magic forests of medieval romance, in the poetry of the Renaissance, vitalized by classical mythology, in the epic fables of the seventeenth-century "marvelous,"[1] and in the vast repertory of European legend and folklore—natural and supernatural had coexisted. Common people and uncommon writers had shared the belief that an otherworldly dimension pervaded and illumined daily life. But the increasingly scientific vision of a world governed by natural laws made such an outlook problematical. In the late seventeenth century and continuing throughout the next, the French novel moved steadily away from realms of the fabulous and fanciful toward greater verisimilitude and social realism. In the eighteenth century, such genres as the *conte oriental, conte philosophique,* and *voyage imaginaire* were the last bastions of the "marvelous," albeit reduced to a purely conventional form as a vehicle for satire and allegory.

Yet not surprisingly, the new scientific mentality, with its materialistic skepticism and scorn for popular superstition, called forth a reaction. The intellectual climate for the emergence of the literary fantastic was prepared, in an important sense, by the Age of Reason, in which unquestioning acceptance of the supernatural had become both intellectually and aesthetically suspect. Within the framework of this new genre, wildly strange occurrences would be experienced as disquieting anomalies, which signal some manner of breach or rupture in the rationalistic fabric of "normal" existence. In a characteristic feature of much fantastic narrative, protagonist and reader alike hesitate whether to believe or disbelieve, whether to hold out for a "rational" explanation or to accept some manner of magical or supranatural conclusion.[2]

The appearance of phenomena which defy the accepted post-Enlightenment view of the world has the effect of triggering in the reader of the fantastic tale the thrill of the mysterious and unknown. The fantastic is, notably, a genre of dread, angst, and ontological doubt. It is also a highly symbolic mode of fiction. For it is precisely when the supernatural ceases to be an object of unproblematic faith that it is able to assume a more psychological and aesthetic dimension.

Jacques Cazotte's *Le Diable amoureux* (*The Devil in Love*), 1772, is generally accepted as the earliest precursor of the nineteenth-century French fantastic tale.[3] Since the Middle Ages, there had been no shortage of written accounts detailing alleged instances of temptation by the Devil; Cazotte's novel, however, adapted this theme to a narrative filled with ambiguity and psychological verisimilitude. In the mind of the reader as well as the protagonist Alvare, the beguiling temptress Biondetta is both Satan in human form and a compellingly natural, real-life woman, depicted (like another eighteenth-century femme fatale, Manon Lescaut) in all her charm and human frailty. Cazotte's tale of desire and seduction never moves entirely beyond the realm of moral allegory, yet it anticipates the nineteenth-century fantastic in its exploration of the psychology of evil—a theme that will assume increasing importance in the aftermath of the French Revolution.

The French public of the late 1790s thrilled to the English Gothic novels of Anne Radcliffe and "Monk" Lewis, replete with medieval crypts and hidden passageways, infernal villains and innocent victims. The marquis de Sade, asserting that only a literature of cruelty and the horrific could hold the attention of readers jaded by the gruesome real-life spectacle of the Revolution, offered this as explanation for the popularity, in France, of the fiction of gothic horror.[4] But this is an oversimplification. The new literary mode responded not merely to a predilection for raw sensationalism but to a heightened consciousness of man's susceptibility to madness and evil, and to a desire to probe the subterranean depths of the unconscious.

During the final years of the eighteenth century, the French reading public was presented with myriad imitations and adaptations (often quite mediocre) of what came to be known as the "roman terrifiant" or "roman noir." By the start of the nineteenth century, this vogue entered a period of decline; under the Empire, Napoleon promoted a return to classicism in the arts, and the Gothic entered a period of dormancy, only to emerge with renewed vigor after 1815, with the development of French Romanticism. The Romantic infatuation with all things medieval corresponded to a growing disillusionment with the rationalist and skeptical Enlightenment worldview which was seen as having paved the way for the Revolution and the Terror. Theoreticians of the new school advocated the enrichment of French literature through exposure to the English and German Romantics: Byron, Scott, Maturin, Goethe, Schiller. The so-called frenetic genre, which reached its apogee around 1819–1820, was marked by a taste for the violent and the monstrous, and for motifs from the realm of popular superstition, such as phantoms, ghouls, and vampires. Victor Hugo, for one, briefly indulged in this wilder phase of French Romanticism (in his early novels *Bug-Jargal* and *Han d'Islande*) before going on to the more renowned portion of his literary career.

■ ■ ■

Charles Nodier (1780–1844), twenty years Hugo's senior, was already a well-respected writer by the time the second vogue of vampirism and horror swept through France in the decade following 1816. The author of several novels *à la Werther*, and a Schilleresque tale of the noble outlaw (*Jean Sbogar*), Nodier was also the leading theorist of the early French Romantic movement. He was one of the first to urge the rehabilitation of Shakespeare, the adoption of English and German models, the rediscovery of the French medieval heritage, and a more positive assessment of the fantastic and the marvelous. Although Nodier's excursion into the frenetic genre was primarily a concession to the taste of the times (he adapted Maturin's drama, *Bertram*, and Polidori's tale, *The Vampire*, for the French theater, and published a collection of macabre tales entitled *Infernalia*), his brief "vampire" phase also bequeathed to posterity a work which, in depth and artistry, ranks with the best of his later fiction: *Smarra, ou Les Démons de la nuit* (*Smarra, or The Demons of the Night*), 1821. Some critics consider it his masterpiece.

Smarra's poor reception by a public that had hoped for merely another sensational melodrama is indicative of the extent to which it differed from the bulk of vampire fiction of its time. Hovering on the periphery of the frenetic genre, Nodier's bizarre tale goes beyond the excesses of that mode to introduce a major theme of mature Romanticism—the dark, secret poetry of dream. In the most literal sense, *Smarra* is a narrative of nightmare. The winding, labyrinthine structure that so unsettled contemporary audiences was a result of Nodier's attempt to follow the meanderings, digressions, and subliminal threads of association that characterize actual dream experience. *Smarra* was ahead of its time: it was not until 1829 that French readers were exposed to the newly translated tales of the German writer E. T. A. Hoffmann, whose protagonists' lives were inextricably entwined with the realm of vision and madness. The preoccupation with dream, both in sleep and as a state of consciousness that can permeate everyday, waking existence, was to be a central feature of the French fantastic tale from its origins throughout the nineteenth century.

Nodier's major body of work, including most of his *contes fantastiques*, depicts dream as the triumph of the imagination over a prosaic and brutally utilitarian "real world." His typical protagonists, childlike innocents and gentle seers whom society labels "idiots" and even "madmen," take refuge from harsh reality in a universe of fantasy. Yet in *Smarra*, Nodier offers a darker, more complex vision of dream—one which anticipates the later insights of Freudian psychology—as a composite creation reflective of the mysterious, elusive logic of the unconscious mind.

The concentrically layered tale-within-a-tale, a convention employed in the eighteenth-century *conte oriental*, affords Nodier the ingenious means of an exploratory descent into the psyche. The frame narrative has as its setting an island in modern Italy where the protagonist Lorenzo lies in bed with Lisidis, his bride of eight days. In the second layer (parts 2 and 4) of the tale, the dreaming Lorenzo, transported back centuries in time, has assumed the identity of Lucius, the hero of Apuleius's *The Golden Ass*. Lorenzo/Lucius's increasingly nightmarish account of his adventures in ancient Athens and Thessaly encloses, in turn, the innermost narrative, recounted by Lucius's friend Polémon. Polémon tells how he was seduced by an evil sorceress, Méroé, only to suffer horrible nightmares at the hands of Méroé and her vampiric consort Smarra. In effect, Lorenzo has two dream surrogates or doubles (each, moreover, with his own female partner), who act out the guilty desires and fears that he has repressed from waking consciousness.

In the author's first preface, he introduces his story as a native product of vampire-haunted Illyria, informing his readers (in this case quite accurately) that *smarra* is a Slavic word denoting the evil spirit of nightmare. In Nodier's tale, not only is Nightmare personified as a vampire, but, as Polémon's narrative reveals, the nightmare victim himself comes to share in this identity. In an 1831 essay entitled "De Quelques Phénomènes du sommeil" (On some phenomena of sleep), the author returns with force to the theme of gruesome compulsions unleashed in nocturnal fantasy. Here, he goes so far as to propose that sleep pathology can explain the phenomena of vampirism, werewolfism, and necrophagy.

When a propensity to both nightmare and somnambulism exists in one individual, Nodier suggests, he may be driven to commit heinous crimes that are entirely unsanctioned by his conscious will. It is evident from this essay that what intrigues Nodier most about the Eastern European vampire legend are the very themes that surface in his 1821 dream narrative. Chief among them is a sense of helpless passivity and agonizing guilt, often for acts that the criminal does not remember having committed. An important concomitant of the "passivity" theme is the experience of nightmarish paralysis that can impede a witness of vampiric violence from coming to the victim's aid. Indeed, the special appeal of Book 1 of *The Golden Ass*, for the author of *Smarra*, owes much to Apuleius's use of this very motif; Aristomenes, rendered powerless by a spell, is forced to look on as the lamia Méroé and her accomplice tear out his friend's heart.

The nightmare element in both Lucius's and Polémon's dream narratives arises, then, from a combination of what might be termed "active" and "passive" complicity with evil. Polémon is forced to watch helplessly as Méroé destroys her infant victims; soon he too will participate in acts of demonic ritual. As for Lucius, there is considerable ambiguity as to the degree of his responsibility for his friend's death. We are given several images of Polémon's death in the course of the tale: (1) sacrificing his life for Lucius on the field of battle, (2) mysteriously "murdered" by Lucius, (3) dragged before the guillotine, and (4) victimized by vampiric lamiae. This symbolic convergence (as Nodier would have us believe, in the dreamer's unconscious) has the effect of blurring three distinct categories of guilt: the guilt of the criminal, who experiences his crime as a passive yielding to compulsion, the guilt of the impotent witness, and the guilt of the survivor.

In this there is considerable power of suggestion, as well as possible clues to the ways in which the author's private obsessions helped weave the fabric of his dream tale. The guillotine was an *idée fixe* for Charles Nodier, carrying with it memories of a childhood marked by the events and passions of the French Revolution. As an adolescent, Nodier witnessed firsthand a number of executions during the Terror, several of which had been ordered by his father, a judge in the Revolutionary tribunal at Ornans and Besançon. At about this same time, the young Charles was re-

cruited to serve the Revolutionary cause by delivering several
rousing speeches before the Besançon Jacobins' Club. There is a
measure of irony in the fact that some of *Smarra*'s nightmare imagery was presaged by the rhetoric of Nodier's early Robespierr-
esque oratory:

> We have caused the criminal heads of our last tyrants to fall
> upon the scaffold. . . . [W]e shall make [your blood] flow. . . .
> We will tear the loathsome entrails from your breast . . .
> [and] toss the bloody scraps to the birds of prey. . . . [5]

Long after Nodier's political enthusiasms had been transformed (by stages) into a position of extreme conservatism, he
would have recourse to similar images to express his horror of
Revolutionary violence. One such telling evocation, in *Souvenirs
et portraits de la Révolution française* (Memories and portraits of the
French Revolution), 1829, is of the Strasbourg Public Prosecutor's
infamous pilgrimages with a "nomad scaffold" through the Alsa-
tian countryside: "[Those were journeys] that one might willingly
relegate to the realm of vampires and ghouls."[6]

Of the various political figures with whom young Charles
came into contact during the Revolutionary era, it was this public
prosecutor, Euloge Schneider, who was to have perhaps the most
lasting impact upon him. The notorious Jacobin was a close family
friend of the Nodiers—a man whom the adolescent Charles evidently admired enough to correspond with, and into whose care
the thirteen-year-old was entrusted during a visit to Strasbourg in
1793. Lucius's vision, in part 2 of *Smarra*, of the nightmare victims
pacing the circumference of the town square like figures on an astronomical clock (an image reminiscent of the famous clock figures of Strasbourg Cathedral) forms a link in a larger chain of
association. In *Souvenirs et portraits de la Révolution française*, Nodier
describes how, shortly after his arrival in Strasbourg, he witnessed
the destruction of the cathedral statues, recently decreed by the
Revolutionary authorities. He uses this alleged memory, several
pages later, as the point of departure for a suggestive metaphor:

> One must be older than eleven to comprehend how weak-
> ness can forge an involuntary solidarity with frenzy, how
> timidity can become an auxiliary of madness or an accom-

plice in crime. I am reminded of those stone saints of the cathedral, mutilated by the populace, even as they furnished it new weapons with which to stone its victims. Several saints of flesh and blood would also become instruments of death in the fearful clutch of the revolution.[7]

This is perhaps Nodier's most explicit elaboration, in the Revolutionary context, of a theme which pervades all of his writings on vampirism and nightmare—that of weakness and innocence inexplicably drawn into complicity with the demonic.

The haunting sense of sullied purity, associated with memories of the Revolution, is only part of the psychological backdrop to Nodier's fantastic tale. As one might infer from the dream permutation of the original couple (Lorenzo-Lisidis) into two quite different sets of male-female relationships, the theme of love and the sexes is at the heart of the tale. (There is, of course, a significant interrelation here, inasmuch as Nodier associated Revolutionary energies with the irrational violence of the sexual impulse.) Long before Freud, the author of *Smarra* displayed a keen awareness of the mechanisms of sexual repression and regression and the role they play in dream experience. One contemporary critic, Laurence M. Porter, has discussed the work in the light of Jungian theories of dream analysis.[8] From this perspective, the protagonist's dream can be read as part of an attempt to overcome conflicts and tensions generated by his recent marriage—conflicts centering around his fear of domination as well as his own desire to dominate. Lorenzo's nocturnal fantasy can be seen to reactivate earlier psychic states embodied in the adolescent, pleasure-seeking Lucius (in love with the slave-girl Myrthé) and the helpless, child-like Polémon, prey to the "devouring" seductress Méroé (a figure of the feared and desired other).

To view Nodier as a writer with Freudian intuitions naturally raises several implications for the vampire theme. The insect-vampire Smarra bears close resemblance to the legendary Incubus, the lewd demon that from ancient times was believed to lie oppressively upon the chests of people in their sleep, sapping their vital fluids and giving rise to the experience of Nightmare. There are hints that Polémon's relation with his vampiric tormentor, Smarra, may be a symbolic transposition of his relationship with the incubus-like femme fatale, Méroé, who is associated with similar uneasy sensations during Polémon's night in her palace. Ernest Jones's classic Freudian study, *On the Nightmare*[9] (1931), describes such nocturnal sensations as arising when desire is repressed, sexual longing accompanied by fear and dread, and the normal features of an erotic dream disguised in nightmare. Jones's theory that such nightmares lie at the root of the incubus, werewolf, and vampire superstitions is almost identical to that which the author of *Smarra* had formulated in poeticosymbolic terms more than a century earlier.

Part of the force behind Nodier's evocation of the demons of the subconscious mind stems from his own troubled vision of sexuality. Throughout his work, his depiction of the male-female relationship betrays a nostalgia for lost innocence and a longing to transcend the realm of the senses. Nodier's tormented sense of the body-soul dichotomy, which reaches back to his early youth, was heightened by his contracting gonorrhea at the age of twenty from a Paris prostitute. The question of whether he was ever completely cured, and to what extent certain of his lifelong ailments (including chronic kidney disease) may be traceable to this venereal disease, is a subject for conjecture. Undeniably, this painful ordeal must have contributed to his enduring vision of the degrading, soulless, even nightmarish aspect of sexuality, and to his fascination with images of vampire predators who devour the internal organs of their victims.

Furthermore, it is plausible that Nodier's repressed anxiety and guilt could have been reawakened by the deaths of his two sons in their infancy, in 1816 and 1821—the latter being the year of *Smarra*'s composition. One particular symbolic association may have facilitated the process whereby several distinct traumatisms, some extending as far back as the period of the Terror, were reactivated in the writer's psyche. Nodier was familiar with the popular superstition in southeastern Europe ascribing the sickness and death of infants to the debilitating effects of vampirism. The vampire motif in *Smarra* may thus be seen as adroitly linking various troubling strands of personal association and memory. In the dark insights of ancient legend, those preyed upon by vampires become vampires in their turn. In Nodier's vision, the nocturnal malady of "smarra" was the nightmare par excellence because it

forced its victims into a complicity and collusion with evil. For
the author of *Smarra*, vampirism was much more than a stock formula; it was the emblem of an irrevocable fall from innocence.

■ ■ ■

More than a decade after the first publication of *Smarra*, the
tale was republished as part of Nodier's collected works (1832).
In the author's introduction, he claims to have located the source
of the "fantastique vraisemblable ou vrai" (the "true-to-life," "authentic" fantastic) in the mysterious inner world of dream experience. It was only natural that he should wish to stress his originality in this regard: since *Smarra's* original publication in 1821,
the French public had discovered the tales of Hoffmann and
had come to consider them synonymous with the "fantastique
intérieur." The extraordinary success of Hoffmann's tales, following their translation by Loeve-Veimars in 1829, was the stimulus
that launched the vogue of the fantastic in France. Literati and
ordinary readers alike saw in Hoffmann a fresh and novel strain
of the imagination, capable of replacing the outmoded "frenetic"
conventions with a more compellingly psychological dimension
of the uncanny.

Within a realistic contemporary setting, Hoffmann's typical
protagonists—artists, dreamers, eccentrics, oversensitive souls
verging on madness—confront a variety of bizarre and often sinister phenomena, hinting at mysterious realms, divine or diabolical, within man and the universe. Throughout his work, Hoffmann made powerful use of the motif of the double to suggest the
divided ego or subconscious self, and he articulated the theme of
inner fatality, which would be central to the nineteenth-century
fantastic:

If there is a dark power which treacherously attaches a
thread to our heart to drag us along a perilous and ruinous
path that we would not otherwise have trod; if there is such
a power, it must form inside us, from part of us, must be
identical with ourselves; only in this way can we believe in
it and give it the opportunity it needs if it is to accomplish
its secret work.[10]

Another theme first exploited by Hoffmann, and which was
to assume various forms in the work of French fantastic writers

from Balzac to Maupassant and beyond, revolved around the phenomenon of "mesmerism" or "animal magnetism." Mesmerism was launched upon the French cultural scene in the late 1770s when Anton Mesmer, a Viennese physician, arrived in Paris to set up a specialized clinic. Mesmer's "cures" were founded on the theory of an invisible, superfine fluid that circulated through the human body as well as through the universe; illness was allegedly caused by obstacles to its flow, and could be overcome by manipulating magnetic currents. In the hands of French disciples such as Puységur, who replaced Mesmer's magnetic tubs and wands with spoken commands that induced somnambulistic trances or "magnetic sleep," mesmerism began to evolve into what later would be termed "hypnotism" and "power of suggestion," and the notion of a physical, universal fluid was increasingly subordinated to the hypnotizer's own force of will. Mesmerism, which was all the rage in Paris in the decade leading up to the French Revolution, would undergo an impressive revival in the post-Revolutionary era as it merged with various currents of nineteenth-century spiritualism and occultism.[11] One of its central tenets was the power of the spirit to defy the laws of time and space, to fathom the future, and to exert preternatural influence by projecting magnetic fluid through the eyes. Many of Hoffmann's tales revolve around these mysterious psychic phenomena. Interestingly, it was Dr. Koreff, the mesmerist physician responsible for fostering Hoffmann's interest in animal magnetism, who was decisive in launching the vogue of Hoffmann in France. Dr. Koreff moved to Paris from Berlin in 1822, the year of Hoffmann's death, and spread the word of his genius through the salons of the 1820s; it was Koreff's friend, Loeve-Veimars, who undertook to translate Hoffmann into French.

■ ■ ■

Around the year 1830, a host of imitations began to appear in the French periodicals, aiming to duplicate the Hoffmannesque atmosphere and effects yet for the most part lacking in depth and originality. It was not long, however, before writers of talent and even genius would discern the new genre's literary and psychological potential. One of the first was Honoré de Balzac (1799–1850). "L'Auberge rouge" ("The Red Inn"), 1831, arose out of an idea upon which the author had meditated since his youth, and which was to form the core of much of his later fiction: the occult power of thought, will, and desire. In his lifelong exploration of this mysterious force, Balzac was inspired by mesmerist notions, by contemporary medical debates regarding the interrelationship of body and soul, and by the writings of the eighteenth-century Swedish mystic, Swedenborg. The thinkers who most intrigued Balzac were at one in positing the existence of a pulsating, intangible, vital fluid or energy, similar in nature to electricity, which according to physiologists could bring about powerful effects within the human system, and according to mesmerists and spiritualists could act in various ways upon the external world. In the celebrated formula of Mesmer's disciple Puységur, "Believe and will; that is the key to mesmerism."[12] Balzac's *Comédie humaine* abounds in examples not only of how obsessive ideas and passions can deplete an individual's supply of vital force, but of how mental energies can be concentrated and projected outward to exert influence and mastery over weaker wills. For Balzac, the ability of man's incorporeal self to disengage itself entirely from his physical being makes possible a host of scientifically inexplicable phenomena.

"Our actions," postulated the author of "The Red Inn," "are but the manifestation of acts already accomplished in our mind."[13] At the heart of Balzac's tale is a crime committed by one man in thought and another in deed. It is in the mysterious relationship between the one's idea and the other's execution that the "fantastic" element of this story resides.

Inasmuch as one character pays the penalty for the other's act while the real criminal escapes retribution, this tale can be seen to articulate Balzac's recurrent theme of hidden crimes, unpursued by justice, which lie behind many a "respectable" worldly career. Yet in presenting the facts of the case, both external and psychological, Balzac refuses us any unequivocal conclusion about the protagonist's guilt or innocence, and it is in this ambivalence that the power of the tale resides. Its potential to unnerve is not contingent upon one's literal belief in mesmerism or thought transference. The modern reader intuits that human psychology, rather than metapsychology, is of the essence here: an individual's imaginative life, with its darkest impulses and most secret desires, is perhaps more truly his "self" than that expressed to the world through words, gesture, or action. It is perhaps no surprise that the author of "The Red Inn" had read and admired Nodier's *Smarra*. In writing his tale, he was also influenced by Nodier's recently published "De Quelques Phénomènes du sommeil," and its provocative excursions into the realm of nightmare and somnambulism. (Included in Nodier's essay was an account of the Italian painter who insisted that his traveling companion tie him to his bed, for fear that he would commit vampirism in his sleep.) The literary influence was, as it happened, reciprocal: Nodier would later adapt the central episode of Balzac's tale to the murder-in-the-inn scene in his novel *La Fée aux miettes* (The crumb fairy), 1832.

There is another dimension, perhaps, to Balzac's mesmerist vision. In the preface to his novel *La Peau de chagrin* (*The Wild Ass' Skin*), 1831, he finds in the creative imagination a consummate example of the autonomy of the inner life:

> [I]n poets or in truly philosophical writers, there occurs an inexplicable, unheard-of, spiritual phenomenon. . . . It is a kind of second sight . . . or better still, a mysterious force which carries them wherever they will themselves to be. . . .
>
> Do men have the power to gather the universe into their mind, or is their mind a talisman with which they nullify the laws of time and space?[14]

It was Balzac's belief that the artist must, in some sense, duplicate within himself the soul of even his darkest characters: "[T]he writer must have . . . embraced all customs, . . . experienced all passions, before writing a book. . . . In composing *Lara* [a poem by Byron], he is criminal, imagining or meditating upon crime."[15] This suggestive formulation anticipates the disquieting analogy sketched by the American writer Nathaniel Hawthorne in his *Twice-told tales*:

> A scheme of guilt, till it be put in execution, greatly resembles a train of incidents in a projected tale. . . . Thus a novel-writer, or a dramatist, in creating a villain of romance, and fitting him with evil deeds, and the villain of actual life, in projecting crimes that will be perpetrated, may almost meet each other, half-way between reality and fancy. . . . In

truth, there is no such thing in man's nature, as a settled and full resolve, either for good or evil, except at the very moment of execution.[16]

Considered from this perspective, Balzac's "The Red Inn" can be seen to raise equally troubling questions about the relationship between thought and action, plot and execution, and to explore the dark, inscrutable power of the human imagination.

■ ■ ■

Many critics consider "La Vénus d'Ille ("The Venus of Ille"), 1837, by Prosper Mérimée (1803–1870) to be his masterpiece, as did the author himself.[17] Mérimée's story draws upon an antithesis between the prosaic, philistine values of nineteenth-century France and a darkly primitive force which returns out of the pagan past with the force of something long repressed. The supernatural in "The Venus of Ille" assumes the aspect of the femme fatale or Eternal Feminine—represented, in this case, by a resurrected effigy of Venus. In Mérimée's tale, as one critic has observed, the vigorous spirit of the past protests against the paltriness of the present, art (indignant at being reduced to the status of an archeological object) utters its dark oracle, and the goddess of love takes revenge upon those who profane her with mercenary motives.[18]

Mérimée's vision of passion, however, is a somber and sinister one. His black, blindly staring, maleficent Venus embodies Eros in its most violent, cruel, and even diabolical aspect: she is an agent of death and disaster, as invincible and all-consuming as destiny. This darker vision of human love was later to find expression in Mérimée's tragic masterpiece, *Carmen*.

The plot of Mérimée's tale has its source in the centuries-old legend of Venus and the Ring.[19] Dating back to the early Christian era, it is thought to have originally represented the conflict and tension between paganism and the new religion of Christianity. The earliest recorded version of the legend appears in a twelfth-century chronicle by the Anglo-Norman William of Malmesbury. He tells of a young Roman, who, wishing to play a game of ball with his friends on the evening of his wedding, leaves his ring on the finger of a nearby statue, later to discover that the finger has curved inward, making the ring impossible to remove. That night, as the young man is preparing to sleep with his bride, a misty form interposes itself between them, and a voice enjoins him: "Embrace me, you are my betrothed; I am Venus, upon whose finger you attached your ring, and I have it and will keep it."[20]

There existed many versions of this legend in medieval and Renaissance Europe. The Romantic revival of the theme inspired several works by German writers, yet in France, prior to Mérimée, it had only once been given artistic expression (in Louis Hérold's opera-comique, *Zampa*, 1831). Mérimée was the first to transpose the legend of Venus and the Ring into a story with a modern setting, to present it as an account by a first-person witness, and to shape it into a truly "fantastic" narrative by rendering the supernatural element ambiguous and problematic.

In 1834, while touring the region of the Pyrenees as inspector of historical monuments, Mérimée had visited the village of Ille. The authentic use of local color in his tale does much to facilitate the reader's suspension of disbelief. The author later observed, "One must not forget that when recounting something supernatural, one can never supply too many details of material reality. That is the great art of Hoffmann in his fantastic tales."[21] In Mérimée's article on Gogol, he is equally explicit: "The transition from what is strange to what is marvellous is imperceptible, and the reader will find himself surrounded by the fantastic before he realizes that the real world has been left far behind."[22] As one critic has pointed out, it is not by chance that two of the great nineteenth-century masters of literary realism, Mérimée and Maupassant, were also masters of the fantastic tale.[23]

The imperceptible heightening of the uncanny in "The Venus of Ille" owes much to the tale's narration. Mérimée deliberately created a narrator with whose perspective and judgment his readers could identify: a Parisian archeologist and visitor to the Pyrenees, whose sophistication and skepticism sets him apart from the naively superstitious local inhabitants. As might be anticipated, this character is reluctant to interpret the series of bizarre events as evidence of the statue's supernatural powers, and Mérimée artfully supplies a possible rational explanation for each perplexing episode. Yet the narrator—and subsequently the reader—is increasingly troubled by suspicions which logic and reason are powerless to quell; as the tale progresses, these ripen into a deeper malaise and, finally, into irrational terror.

There has been much critical speculation as to the significance of the supernatural in Mérimée's fiction. The son of a Voltairean mother, Mérimée was himself an avowed unbeliever. Yet the fascination, beginning in his early youth, with magic, the occult, demonology, vampirism, and all manner of superstition was to endure throughout his life. In his literary creation, the supernatural is introduced with the calculated effect of a master storyteller who delights in illusion and the mystification of his audience. Yet as Frank Paul Bowman has observed, "[T]he fear of the supernatural is not merely a literary device. . . . [Mérimée] realized that reason had its limits and that the incomprehensible existed. He was aware of the irrational aspects of human experience, and expressed these aspects in literature through the supernatural."[24] Mérimée's coolly stoical persona masked a deeper unease, a morbid disquietude in the face of seemingly malevolent forces working beneath the surface of societal and personal relations. His inexorable, cruelly enigmatic Venus of Ille embodies just such a force, which human reason is powerless to defy or, indeed, to fully comprehend.

■ ■ ■

Like those of Mérimée, the fantastic tales of Théophile Gautier (1811–1872) dramatize a confrontation between the passionless, repressive, prosaic spirit of his age and an all-powerful instinctual force, frequently associated with a pre-Christian mentality. With his fellow-Romantic, Balzac, Gautier shares a fascination with the mind's ability to defy the laws of the material world. "Love is stronger than death," declares Clarimonde, the heroine of "La Morte amoureuse" ("The Dead in Love"), 1836, describing how through will alone she was able to journey from beyond the grave to join Romuald, a young novitiate priest. Octavian, the protagonist of "Arria Marcella" (1852), is mesmerized, when visiting the museum in Pompeii, by the sight of the molded contour of a breast faithfully preserved by the ancient catastrophe; the violence of his "retrospective" passion is so great as to transport him back two millennia, to the love of the very woman who had perished and left her trace in the ashes of the volcano.

Although Clarimonde is revealed to be a vampire, and although, in a richly symbolic moment, Arria Marcella sips "dark purple wine, like coagulated blood," the vampirism motif in these tales is associated not with nightmare and compulsion but, instead, with the essence of the Romantic ideal. For Gautier, the "dead in love" (or "love-in-death") corresponds to a longed-for absolute: a condition in which Time, with its power of erosion, no longer exists, freeing the soul to embrace an archetype of Beauty not to be found among the appearances of this mortal existence. In Gautier's otherworldly femmes fatales, as in Goethe's "eternal feminine," there is a considerable component of Romantic platonism: these heroines, with their classical, painterly allure, embody that transcendent "beyond" of art and pure form to which Octavian alludes when he declares, "I knew that I would love only beyond the confines of time and space." For Gautier, the appeal of the fantastic genre stems in part from its ability to make a timeless and therefore impossible object of desire appear to take on a physical, flesh-and-blood reality. The possibility of transgression, of crossing the limits prescribed by human mortality, is at the heart of his most successful fantastic tales.

The magical resurrection, in "Arria Marcella," of a long-buried age reflects the Romantic obsession with vanished civilizations, with archeology and the imaginative reconstruction of the past. More specifically, as Georges Poulet has illustrated,[25] Gautier's sense of the past as an invisible realm of perpetual forms, which continue to transmit mesmeric vibrations through the temporal universe, was heightened by his reading of part 2 of Goethe's *Faust* (translated in 1840 by his friend and fellow author, Gérard de Nerval). In the "Realm of the Mothers" episode, Faust discovers the existence of a mystical corner of the universe in which "powerful goddesses reign in solitude. Around them exists neither space nor time."[26] Here, all that has ever existed endures in perennial movement and vitality. By the force of desire alone (and, Goethe intimates, the poet's power of suggestion), Faust is able to carry away Helen of Troy, the archetype of female beauty. There are audible echoes of this Faustian episode in "Arria Marcella," as the narrator affirms:

> . . . [I]ndeed, nothing dies, but all exists perpetually; that which was once, no power can annihilate. Every act, every word, every shape, every thought which has fallen into the universal ocean of being forms widening circles that go on expanding to the far reaches of eternity. . . . In

some unknown region of space, Paris is still carrying Helen away, and Cleopatra's galley still spreads its silken sails upon the azure stretches of an ideal Cydnus. Passionate minds, powerful wills, have succeded in summoning forth ostensibly vanished centuries and in resurrecting human beings from the dead.

The poet Baudelaire, a great admirer of Gautier, would later honor this faculty of the creative imagination with the celebrated phrase, "evocative witchcraft."[27]

Octavian's journey toward the fulfillment of his desire opens, moreover, not merely onto an ideal realm beyond time but onto a more primitive region of his own being. His return to pagan antiquity makes possible the discovery of his deeply instinctual nature. In both "Arria Marcella" and "The Dead in Love," the protagonists' newly found joy and sensuality is threatened by the repressive, life-denying strictures of a religion of guilt and sin. For Gautier, ancient Greek vitality and delight in physical beauty was a welcome antidote to the inhibiting element in Christianity, and—in a larger sense—to the entire nineteenth century. His Romantic temperament responded to the impulse to escape from a utilitarian age through poetry, imagination, and the instinctual life.

In "The Dead in Love," the notion of the unconscious finds expression in the theme of the double: "Two spirals, one inside the other, inextricably bound together without ever touching, could quite aptly represent my monstrous double existence." In "Arria Marcella," it is elaborated in archeological terms. In a metaphor much exploited in the nineteenth century, to "unearth" the historical past is to uncover the most buried strata of the psyche, long hidden beneath layers of civilization.[28] Octavian's journey into his unconscious corresponds to a descent into subterranean depths and a reunion with the Eternal Feminine. That Goethe should have designated his timeless center of the universe as the realm of "the Mothers" is telling. In both of Gautier's tales, the heroine is the object of forbidden desire. The scene in "The Dead in Love" in which Romuald succumbs to his ardor while contemplating his beloved on her deathbed draws its unsettling effect from its portrayal of an emotion bordering on necrophilia. Gautier's enduring obsession with death is part of a complex psychological mechanism of attraction-repulsion. In a compelling paradox, the death wish itself (as evidenced in his heroes' longing for union beyond the grave) is symptomatic of a deeper impulse to challenge and ultimately defy time and human mortality.

■ ■ ■

The possibility of communication between the living and the dead is also the dominant theme in *Les Mille et un Fantômes* (The thousand and one phantoms), 1849, by the elder Alexandre Dumas (1802–1870). But there is otherwise little similarity between Dumas's often lurid and melodramatic treatment of fantastic themes and the more symbolic and metaphysical approach taken by Gautier.

Dumas's excursion into the phantasmal at the time that he was writing his most famous and popular novels suggests an experimental diversion. Yet his collection of tales is far from hackneyed or conventional; indeed, the closer one looks, the more these tales come to suggest about certain permanent features of the author's vision.

The title of the volume playfully recalls one of the favorite books of Dumas's childhood, *The Thousand and One Nights* (or the *Arabian Nights*). The narrator of Dumas's frame story, while traveling on the outskirts of Paris, is one of several witnesses to a confession of murder. Later, he joins the other witnesses at the house of a local magistrate; the odd assortment of dinner guests discuss the macabre aspect of the crime and whether or not the victim's severed head could have attacked the murderer and bitten his hand. Each of those gathered recounts a story that has some bearing on the subject at issue.

The first tale, told by the mayor, Monsieur Ledru, is in three parts, and spans the chapters of Dumas's text entitled "The Slap of Charlotte Corday," "Solange," and "Albert." In this story, as in most of Dumas's work, historical elements are loosely woven into the fictional plot. Ledru, who happens to be the son of the physician to Louis XVI and Marie-Antoinette, tells how he observed the execution of Charlotte Corday, the young girl who was put to death for assassinating Marat. Ledru's account of the bizarre phenomenon that he witnessed that day near the guillotine serves as prelude to the story of how he met, rescued, and fell in love with the daughter of a French aristocrat, Solange, only to have their liaison terminated by the harrowing events that conclude his tale.

The story's central motif—the continuance of life in a decapitated head in the moments following separation from the body—is naturally rich with fantastic possibilities. Yet, preternatural as it may appear to a twentieth-century reader, what one might call Dumas's "fantastique de la guillotine" has its source in a "scientific" debate that sprang up in the wake of the Revolution and the Terror. The fictional guests around Ledru's table refer, in their discussion, to several members of the medical community who figured prominently in this debate (Sömmering, Sue, and Oesler), all of whom argued for the continuance of sensation after the moment of execution. Their adversary, the physiologist and philosopher Cabanis (1757–1808), rebutted their physiological assertions in his "Note sur le supplice de la guillotine" (Note on execution by the guillotine), 1795: "Among the facts which [they] judge favorable to [their] conclusion, they particularly invoke that of Charlotte Corday, whom they suppose to have blushed from indignation or shame at the moment when the executioner, in a vile and craven act, slapped her while holding the bloody head before the people: in this blush, they discern a moral response which could only have occurred given full and entire consciousness."[29]

Apart from the physiological debate, it was the haunting image of the guillotine itself which intrigued Dumas. His "Femme au collier de velours" ("The Woman with the Velvet Necklace"), 1851, has as protagonist a fictionalized E. T. A. Hoffmann, in Paris during the Terror and in love with Danton's mistress. After Danton's death, he discovers the young woman at the foot of a scaffold; she agrees to accompany him to his hotel; the next morning he awakens beside a corpse. A doctor, called to the scene, removes the dead woman's velvet collar, and her head rolls on the floor: Hoffmann had made love to a victim of the guillotine. This tale was not of the author's own invention: its basic elements, present in Washington Irving's "The Adventures of the German Student" (*Tales of a Traveller*, 1824), and adapted by Petrus Borel in "Gottfried Wolfgang" (1843), found their way to Dumas very probably via his friend Charles Nodier. The fact that Dumas was inspired to recast this story hints at the power which the thematic constellation of Love, Death, and Revolution held for him. *Les Mille et un Fantômes* may offer some clues as to the symbolic value of the guillotine in Dumas's imagination.

At one point in Ledru's narrative, he makes reference to "poor Marie-Antoinette, whom I met a dozen times [as a child], and who more than once . . . took my hands in hers and kissed me." What on first reading seems a purely parenthetical allusion assumes greater importance as the tale progresses. We learn that as a young man Ledru had friends among the Jacobins and was even acquainted with Marat. It is because he was trusted by the men of the Revolution that he was initially able to rescue Solange and facilitate her father's escape to England. Yet there is mysterious significance in the fact that Ledru will later lose his beloved mistress to the scaffold on the very day on which Marie-Antoinette is executed. Could it be, as one critic suggests, that the man who was kissed by the Queen as a child and later embraced the Revolutionary cause is "punished" by a morbid, perverse justice, and that this is perhaps the meaning of the narrator's cryptic remark: "Strange how events work one upon the other!"[30]

The image of the Queen of France, guillotined by the Revolution, was a central and indeed obsessive one for Dumas. Not only does Marie-Antoinette dominate the historical romances that he penned between 1846 and 1852, among them *Joseph Balsamo* and *Le Collier de la reine* (*The Queen's Necklace*), but the other female protagonists in this cycle, in the words of one critic, "all lead to the Queen, of whom they are so many doubles."[31] As for the male protagonists, "they all die, in reality as in metaphor, . . . around her and because of her. Because of the desire—the romantic desire—[that] she awakens as one who is fated to death and the object of an impossible love."[32] In comparison with the Marie-Antoinette cycle, Dumas's fantastic tale renders this theme much more obliquely, yet also with greater hypnotic intensity.

On the purely historical level, the tale reflects its author's lifelong ambivalence toward revolution. Born in 1802, Dumas was the grandson of a marquis and the son of a Napoleonic general. Like many French writers of his generation (Hugo is another), his regard for the principles of the French Revolution was alloyed with a revulsion for the bloody excesses of the Terror. Although Dumas supported the republican cause in 1848, he was nevertheless receptive to the equation linking the populace with irrational violence and destruction. The character whose crime serves as pretext for Dumas's collection of tales is introduced as one of a vast population of stone quarriers who inhabit the "subterranean galleries" of Montrouge:

> Living in darkness, they have some of the instincts of night animals. . . .
> Whenever there is an insurrection, it is rare that [they] do not have a hand in it.[33]

In another striking detail, Dumas notes that the stoneworker's murder weapon was a sword that the criminal admitted having taken from the Artillery Museum during the July Revolution.[34] This point acquires particular significance in light of the fact that, during the Revolution of 1830, Dumas had himself witnessed the pillage of the museum by the mob and had managed to save several of the weapons in its collection.[35]

Yet beyond the shadows of history, Dumas's collection of tales has another dimension. The idea of communication between the living and the dead is associated with the revival of the author's own cherished "phantoms" through the magical processes of memory.[36] The setting for his frame narrative is the region of Ile-de-France (surrounding Paris), where the author grew up. The connection between the "frenetic" theme of the dead-returned-to-life and the resurrection of a vanished past is in this case far from theoretical or abstract, as the subject of revenants and vampires is itself linked with nostalgic memories of Dumas's youth. The writer devotes some famous pages of his memoirs to the story of his first meeting with Charles Nodier during a performance of Nodier's melodrama, *Le Vampire*. Dumas recalls how, having recently arrived in Paris as a naive young man of twenty-one, he was seated next to the older writer without being aware of his identity, and was regaled with Nodier's tales of having witnessed an actual vampire in Illyria, the region bordering Transylvania.[37] Several years later, Nodier invited Dumas to join the artistic and literary gatherings at his Salon de l'Arsenal, and it was thus that he met and befriended the major Romantic writers of his time. It is perhaps not by chance that the frame narrative of *Les Mille et un Fantômes* describes an evening spent in intelligent and congenial conversation around a dinner table. Dumas's wistful nostalgia for the friendships of his youth finds very suggestive expression in his memoirs, as he "summons to life" the shades of several departed friends:

> [W]ho would have known, beloved departed, that I, youth-
> ful still, would survive you. . . .
> It is midnight, . . . the hour of evocations from the
> tomb. . . . Come, brothers! Come! Tell me . . . [your stories]
> in the language of the dead. . . .[38]

Placed in this context, certain lines from Dumas's preface to *Les Mille et un Fantômes* take on their fullest meaning, and cast a dreamy, pensive, melancholy aura upon the tales in his fantastic collection:

> [E]ach day we take another step toward Liberty,
> Equality, Fraternity, three great words which the Revo-
> lution . . . has hurled into the midst of our modern
> civilization. . . .
> . . . God keep me from preaching immobility! Immo-
> bility is death. But I move like one of those men of whom
> Dante speaks, whose feet point forward . . . but whose
> heads face in the direction of their heels.
> And what I look for above all, what I long for above all,
> what my retrospective glance searches for in the past, is
> the society that is evaporating, vanishing, like one of those
> phantoms in my tale.[39]

■ ■ ■

Aurélia ou Le Rêve et la vie (*Aurélia, or Dream and Life*), 1855, was conceived and written largely while its author, Gérard de Nerval (1808 – 1855), was confined in psychiatric clinics. Nerval's auto-biographical tale has been given an important place in every his-tory of the fantastic genre, despite the fact that the "fantastic" elements in the story can be explained by reference to specific psychic phenomena (In this case, hallucination and madness). A great admirer of Hoffmann, Nodier, and Gautier, Nerval elabo-rated in his own tale a number of themes associated specifically with the fantastic tradition. His treatment of these themes was to provide an important transition between the work of such early writers and the later fiction of Guy de Maupassant.

The evolution of the fantastic genre in the nineteenth cen-tury is characterized by an increasing accommodation of the evolving theories of modern psychiatry.[40] Fantastic fiction was to become more oriented toward psychopathology—a development culminating in such masterpieces as Maupassant's "The Horla" (1887). The distance between Maupassant and Nerval, however, in terms of their treatment of the clinical phenomena of hallucination and delirium, is considerable. Nerval, inspired by German Romantics such as Novalis, Ludwig Tieck, Achim von Arnim, and E. T. A. Hoffmann, as well as by his French precursor, Nodier, viewed madness as having an essentially spiritual and visionary dimension. Yet indebted as he was to this tradition, Nerval was also influenced by developments in the field of medicine.

During the 1820s and 1830s, a number of essays began to appear in French medical journals on the subject of hallucinations. An increasing number of psychiatric treatises, moreover, drew attention to aspects of the religious and visionary tradition that could be interpreted as instances of clinically diagnosable psychopathology. During the 1840s and 1850s, medical researchers pursued the study of hallucinations with increased vigor, in an attempt to choose between a physiological and a purely psychical explanation for insanity. Brierre de Boismont's *Des Hallucinations, ou Histoire raisonnée des apparitions, des visions, des songes, de l'extase, du magnétisme et du somnambulisme* (1845)[41] was an especially popular work and one which Nerval read with interest. In a study that appeared in the same year, the psychiatrist Jacques Moreau de Tours drew conclusions about the character of mental disorder from his own experiments with hallucinogens, theorizing that the psychological modifications of madness were "absolutely identical to [those of] the dream state."[42] A decade later, he would affirm: "Madness is the waking man's dream. . . . I do not know of a better definition."[43] Moreau de Tours is known to have been quite impressed with *Aurélia* as a medical case study. In *La Psychologie morbide* (Morbid psychology), 1859, he quoted Nerval's description of his protagonist's experience ("the overflowing of dream into real life") as illustrative of his own clinical hypotheses.[44]

Nerval's *Aurélia* is, however, something other than a clinical document on the dissolution, dispersion, and rupture of mental processes, as expounded by the psychiatrists of the day. While the author makes certain rhetorical concessions to the perspective of psychopathology, he locates the true models for his experience in the visionary tradition. At the outset, he invokes Swedenborg,

Apuleius, and Dante as literary predecessors, who treat dream experience as an opening onto the spiritual unknown. The concluding sentences of the tale reflect Nerval's merging of these two disparate perspectives:

> The care that I had received had already restored me to the affection of family and friends, and I was able to judge more sanely the world of illusions in which I had lived for a time. Nevertheless, I feel happy about the convictions that I have acquired, and I liken this series of trials I have undergone to that which the ancients represented as a descent into the underworld.

This notion of an initiatory descent into the underworld is at the center of Nerval's spiritual drama. The narrator-protagonist's plunge into madness is depicted as a journey into the self (viewed as embracing not only the individual psyche but the collective unconscious of the race). In several dream passages, the hero penetrates the chasm of lost time, voyaging back into his own childhood, into a spiritual communion with his forebears, and even into mythic prehistory. His glimpses of a primordial paradise before the fall give way to visions of chaos, monsters, and awesome natural cataclysms. In the mythopoetic framework of this tale, the hero's gropings toward redemption are mirrored in the struggles of man and nature to transcend Evil and Death.

The descent into hell is, moreover, linked thematically to the notion of the Eternal Feminine. Orpheus's journey into the underworld in search of his lost Euridice was associated in Nerval's imagination with the episode in part 2 of Goethe's *Faust* in which the hero retrieves Helen of Troy from the timeless realm of the Mothers. Nerval's quest for the Eternal Feminine, no less than Gautier's, is both a descent into the abyss of the past, a search for an elusive and timeless love, and an urge to escape the prison house of mortality.

Volumes have been written about Nerval's source material. For the general reader of his work, it is useful to keep in mind certain ideas which he drew from the occultist and illuminist tradition. A common denominator in this tradition, going back to Gnosticism and the Cabala, was the idea that universal creation was the result of emanation from God and represented a falling away from original wholeness and unity. The goal of those who

subscribed to these beliefs—this would include the followers of
Boehme, Swedenborg, and Saint-Martin—was to make possible
man's reintegration with the divine Oneness through a series of ar-
cane studies, exercises, and sacred rituals, many of which draw on
magical numerology and astrology. Nerval was likewise fascinated
with the centuries-old doctrine of the alchemists who, aside from
attempting to turn base metals into gold, often aspired to a more
spiritual objective: to liberate the soul from its surrounding "dross"
of matter.

The title character in Nerval's tale,[45] though playing a
broadly mythical role, does contain a kernel of biographical actu-
ality. For years Nerval had been in love with the actress Jenny
Colon, before briefly becoming involved with her in 1837. For
the rupture which followed, he held himself personally responsible. After Jenny's marriage in 1838, and in the years following
her untimely death in 1841, Nerval progressively transformed her
into a mystical ideal.

The process by which the beloved merged with various
mythic embodiments of the Eternal Feminine or Great Mother
was all the more natural for Nerval as his bereavement reenacted
the tragic loss of his mother in early childhood. In one of his visions, the protagonist hears the goddess Isis declare, "I am the
same as Mary, the same as your mother, the same as the one you
have always loved in all her forms. At each of your trials, I have
dropped one of the masks with which I veil my features, and soon
you shall see me as I really am." In nineteenth-century illuminist
thought as well as the ancient mystery religions, the Egyptian
nature goddess Isis functions as a mediating figure, helping man
to move toward union with the divine. A vital thread running
through Nerval's spiritual drama is the narrator's haunting sense of
culpability and remorse, associated on one level with his personal
loss ("Condemned by the woman I loved, guilty of a wrong for
which I could no longer hope to be forgiven"), and on another
with the fallen condition of humanity and nature. The hero's quest
for Aurélia's forgiveness parallels, for Nerval, the movement of all
of creation toward redemption and universal pardon.

■ ■ ■

Maître Zacharius (*Master Zacharius*) is one of the earliest tales
written by Jules Verne (1828–1905). It dates from 1854, almost

a decade before Verne's meeting and collaboration with the publisher Hetzel would launch him on his celebrated series of science-fiction romances. In this early Hoffmannesque work, one discerns various thematic elements common to Verne's mature fiction. In mood and outlook, however, it anticipates not the optimistic positivism of the novels of the 1860s and 1870s, for which he is best known, but the more somber and skeptical vision of his later years.

Like many of the author's protagonists, Master Zacharius is a genius-inventor, whose Promethean striving for technological mastery isolates him from humanity and tempts him into a blasphemous rivalry with the Creator. Although he is not the modern scientist-adventurer, contriver of futuristic machines, with whom Verne's readers are most familiar, this late fifteenth- or early sixteenth-century Genevan clockmaker plays an analogous role within the writer's fictional universe. By making his hero the inventor of the escapement, the mechanical device which makes possible the exact and continuous measurement of time, Verne is in effect placing him in a crucial position, at the origins of modern science.

The foremost literary influences on the tale were E. T. A. Hoffmann and the American writer Edgar Allan Poe, two masters of the fantastic whom Verne much admired. The theme of Faustian temptation, much exploited by Hoffmann, is central to Verne's tale: in *Master Zacharius*, the satanic power takes the form of a fantastic gnome, the living personification of a mechanical clock. This grotesque creature, Pittonaccio, bears some likeness to the mechanical doll in Hoffmann's "The Sandman," who walks with a step so "peculiarly measured" that "all of her movements seem to stem from some kind of clockwork."[46] In Verne's tale, the clock-demon is a fitting Mephisto for the inventor who has come to posit an intimate relationship between God's human creation and his own created machines: for Master Zacharius, in his smugness and pride, life is "but an ingenious mechanism." Indeed, the protagonist himself, who is introduced as one who "did not live . . . [but] oscillated, like the pendulums of his clocks," manifests much of the same mechanistic soullessness that is taken to a symbolic extreme in the fantastic Pittonaccio. Master Zacharius's blasphemous analogy between man and machine is ironically actualized in his own person—to his own mortal peril, as the ebb and flow of his own vitality is found to be in mysterious correlation with the functioning of his mechanical timepieces. This particular element in the plot is evidence for the inspiration Verne derived from Edgar Allan Poe's tale "The Masque of the Red Death," in which "the life of the ebony clock" goes out simultaneously with that of the last of the plague-infested revelers at the masked ball.

The human/machine analogy is a recurrent motif in Verne's later work, although without the disturbing Hoffmannesque and Poe-esque aspect it had assumed in *Master Zacharius*. Phileas Fogg, the phlegmatic and punctual hero of *Le Tour du monde en quatre-vingts jours* (*Around the World in Eighty Days*), 1873, is an individual "as perfect as a Leroy or Earnshaw chronometer," with a "regular step which beat the second like the pendulum of an astronomical clock."[47] Yet these familiar features are here devoid of the negative, even diabolical overtones that they conveyed in *Master Zacharius*. Instead, Fogg's urge to chronometric exactness is related to the noble and heroic nature of his project—to conquer time and contingency in his race around the globe. Clocks, maps, and myriad other instruments of precise scientific measurement abound in Verne's work, and in his middle period are linked to a positivist faith in man's ability to master his natural environment through technological ingenuity. By contrast, the novels of Verne's later years are increasingly inhabited by arrogant, mad scientists, whose will to power leads them to violate both human and divine law and to place themselves as well as mankind in mortal peril. Such, for example, is Robur in *Maître du monde* (*Master of the World*), 1904: in the novel's climactic ending, he flies his monstrous apparatus into the heart of a lightning storm, only to be struck down for his transgression like the mythological Icarus. Each of the protagonists of the later, darker Verne—tragic spokesmen of science's power, not to liberate or redeem, but to corrupt and destroy—are spiritual descendants of his doomed fantastic hero, Master Zacharius.

■ ■ ■

In the hands of its nineteenth-century practitioners, the *conte fantastique* both accommodated and reacted against the increased prestige of science and the vision of a world ever more subject to systematic analysis. As the century progressed, and the positivist faith grew ever more pervasive, metaphysics as well as the supernatural were increasingly swept aside as antiquated fictions. Villiers de l'Isle-Adam (1838–1889) and other writers of the burgeoning Symbolist movement countered the prevailing worldview with their own mystical idealism. Unlike Mallarmé and Verlaine, Villiers devoted himself primarily to prose fiction. He was one of the most ideologically aggressive of Symbolist writers, and many of his works conduct a literary offensive against the dominant ideas of his time. His fantastic tales aim to undermine one's complacent faith in rational, scientific, and materialist certitudes, and to open the reader's eyes to the disquieting possibility of supernatural mystery.

The narrator of "L'Intersigne" ("The Sign"), 1867–1868, attempts to rationalize and dismiss certain disconcerting phenomena, but is increasingly beset by foreboding and apprehension. This use of fear as a literary device is reminiscent of the narrative technique of Edgar Allan Poe. Along with an entire generation of French readers, Villiers was captivated by Baudelaire's masterful translation of Poe's fantastic tales, published in the late 1850s. Poe's cult of Beauty, his morbid, death-haunted spirituality, his scorn for the religion of progress in the utilitarian age, and his "anti-Romantic" literary aesthetic which stressed the effects to be attained by logical rigor and control, inspired many writers of the Symbolist and Decadent generation in France. Villiers particularly admired Poe's consummate tales of terror, and often read or recited them to friends. The influence of the American author upon his own work was such as to earn him the appellation of the French "Edgar Poe."

The reader will likely recognize several Poe-like elements in "The Sign," although, far from being naively derivative, it is a highly original work in its own right. The narrator, overly susceptible to the debilitating effects of "spleen," is endowed with a hereditary hypersensitivity which predisposes him to hallucinatory and visionary experience. Like the narrator of Poe's story, "The Fall of the House of Usher," Villiers's protagonist is a visitor to a friend's desolate country mansion; upon his arrival, he has a lugubrious vision which imparts to the house the aura of death and the tomb. The otherworldly significance of his increasingly terrifying premonitions is confirmed by the story's denouement, as both narrator and reader confront one of those "extraordinary, amazing, mysterious coincidences" that, Villiers suggests, are not really coincidences but messages from the beyond. At one point in the tale, Villiers appears to employ the French word "correspondance"[48] in its mystical Swedenborgian sense of an accordance between the physical and the spiritual realms, a notion which was given broad currency by Baudelaire. Thus, in the sense of "prefiguration" or premonitory warning, Villiers's "sign" confirms the mysterious interpenetration of two parallel but disparate worlds.

"Véra" (1876) echoes the Poe-esque theme of the inconsolable husband who imagines his beloved wife to have returned from beyond the tomb. Yet unlike Poe's typical protagonist, with his pale, ethereal bride, Villiers's Count and Countess d'Athol are priest and priestess of a passionately sensual religion of Love. After the Countess departs this life, the force of will and imagination sustains her husband in the illusion of her continued presence and, on the anniversary of her death, effects her magical reappearance. "Love is stronger than Death," comments Villiers, attributing the words to the biblical Solomon. This is, interestingly, the very line pronounced by Clarimonde, the woman returned from the tomb in Gautier's "The Dead in Love." (The precise quotation from Solomon is "love is strong as death.")[49] Villiers seems also to have drawn inspiration from Poe's "Ligeia," the epigraph of which is a quotation by the seventeenth-century English philosopher Joseph Glanvill: "Who knoweth the mysteries of the will . . . ? . . . Man doth not yield himself to the angels, nor unto death utterly, save only through the weakness of his feeble will."[50]

In mid-nineteenth-century France, such ideas were at the core of spiritualist thinking, as expounded, for example, in the influential writings of the famous mage and cabalist Eliphas Lévi. Many of the Romantic storytellers were impressed and creatively stimulated by Lévi's doctrine that a person, through a willful transmission of spiritual force, can circumvent the laws of the physical world and actually alter that world. In *Dogme et rituel de la haute magie* (Dogma and ritual of high magic),[51] 1856, Lévi states:

> Man is the miracle-worker of the earth, and in his word, that is, in his intelligent speech, he has at his command the forces of destiny. He radiates and attracts like the stars; he can cure by a touch, by a sign, by an act of his will. This is what Mesmer, before us, came to reveal to the world, this is the terrible secret. . . . What do man's alleged miracles

prove, if not the force of his will and the potency of his
magnetism? . . . [I]t is to the science of the ancient magi
that one must turn for the secrets of man's deliverance. . . .[52]

Lévi goes on to supply detailed ritual instructions for summoning
a loved one from beyond the grave—some of which appear to
have been utilized by Villiers's love-obsessed protagonist.[53]

Villiers's first version of "Véra" (1874) may be read as an almost literal illustration of such an occultist thesis, for it ends with
nothing less than the miraculous resurrection of the Countess
d'Athol and a fusion of the two lovers. The 1876 version is more
ambivalent. As soon as the Count begins to falter in his conviction, Véra vanishes like a modern Euridice. Yet the husband's final
discovery, in his marriage bed, of the mausoleum key that he had
tossed into Véra's tomb paradoxically confirms the "reality" of his
imaginative vision.

Villiers's central theme of reality and illusion testifies to the
ongoing and vital influence of German idealist philosophy upon
his fiction. Villiers was familiar with Hegel's work in French translation as well as through an exposition of his thought written by
the Hegelian scholar, A. Véra. (Villiers doubtless played upon the
resonances in his heroine's name, which is linked etymologically
to the Latin word for "true.") The interest of Hegelian philosophy
for Villiers, as well as for many of his French contemporaries, lay,
as A. W. Raitt has observed, not so much in the dialectical character of his thought as in those ideas which he shared with the German Idealist school (Kant, Fichte, Schelling)—in particular, the
notion that Spirit alone is real and has ascendency over the so-
called real world of matter and the senses.[54] "Ideas are living beings!" Villiers's narrator triumphantly affirms: the assertion reflects
Villiers's fanatical embrace of a system that he dubbed "illusion-
ism," according to which mind, empowered by will and imagination, can actually triumph over the tyranny of the established
physical universe. The episode of the key in "Véra," like the final
paragraph of "The Sign," provides Villiers with an effective means
of suggesting that his protagonist's subjective experience may indeed reach beyond mere solipsism.

It has been said that the passionate aspiration expressed by
the character Edison in Villiers's *L'Eve future* (The future Eve)[55]
articulated the author's own: "I will compel . . . the very Ideal to

reveal itself, for the first time, to your senses, in PALPABLE, AU-DIBLE and MATERIAL form. . . .[56] To the extent this is true, Villiers may indeed be close, as Picard suggests, to compromising the delicate equilibrium of the fantastic genre. Yet was it really his intention to persuade his readers with incontrovertible *proof* of the spiritual realm? Is not his aim better expressed in the words of another of his fictional characters, the skeptic and materialist Tribulat Bonhomet, faced with unsettling evidence he had so long denied: "As for the veracity of my narrative, no one, I would wager, would make undue sport of it. For even granting that the facts . . . be radically false, the merest notion of their possibility is just as unnerving as their established certainty could be."[57]

■ ■ ■

For Villiers, the possibility that there might exist a dimension to life other than that postulated by science and reason represents a spiritual victory over the seemingly inexorable laws of nature. The emotional response of his characters, when confronted with inexplicable phenomena, is analogous to a sensation of awe before an inscrutable enigma. In the fantastic tales of Guy de Maupassant (1850–1893), the emotion of fear is alloyed with an almost existential sense of the absurd, a pervading sensation of nausea, panic, and horror. The fantastic dimension appears as something profoundly ominous, which threatens to rob the protagonist of his spiritual liberty by enslaving him to a will not his own. Most of Maupassant's fantastic tales follow a general pattern: along with the hero's increasing awareness of this malevolent force comes a progressive disordering of his mental faculties and alienation from self, a slow, agonizing descent into madness.

The theme of the Invisible Being, most fully developed in "Le Horla" ("The Horla"), 1887, epitomizes Maupassant's preoccupation with the "other side" of the positivist coin: a nagging disquietude about the invisible, intangible dimension of reality that remains inaccessible to empirical investigation. This brooding concern would explain the writer's obsession with the phenomena of magnetism and hypnosis, which suggest the existence of forces hovering just beyond human understanding. The narrator of "Lettre d'un fou" ("Letter from a Madman") proposes that "half-glimpsed mysteries such as electricity, hypnotic sleep, the trans-

mission of will, telepathy, and all manner of mesmerist phenomena remain hidden to us only because nature did not endow
us with the organ or organs necessary to grasp them."[58] Throughout the centuries, as the hypnotist Docteur Parent remarks to the
narrator of "The Horla," man's fear of what lay beyond his senses
took the form of a superstitious belief in the supernatural, until
"Mesmer . . . opened up for us an unexpected path, and, during
the last four or five years in particular, we have . . . arrived at some
remarkable results."

The "results" that the doctor alludes to, and which were to
stir considerable interest during the 1880s, stemmed from the
contemporary adaptation of mesmerist ideas and techniques to
the domain of psychopathology. The hypnotism research of
Charcot in Paris and Liébault and Bernheim in Nancy lent the
quasi-occultist phenomena of mesmerism a pragmatic basis in experimental neuropsychiatry. In a process of mutual exchange,
spiritism and psychic research increased in credibility as a result
of scientific developments, while Charcot's "Tuesday lessons" in
the hypnotic treatment of hysteria at the mental institution of La
Salpêtrière were invested with a mysterious, almost supernatural
aura.[59] Maupassant attended Charcot's classes during the mid-
1880s (as did Sigmund Freud in the following decade), and his
fantastic tales contain references to the psychiatrists of La Salpêtrière and Nancy. When, in "The Horla," Docteur Parent cites the
experimental findings of the latter school, he confers a degree of
scientific plausibility upon the mysterious phenomena that the
narrator witnesses in his office—and, by extension, upon the narrator's personal encounters with the Invisible Being. Some of the
less than salutary, indeed ominous, implications of mesmerism are
set forth by the narrator of Maupassant's earlier tale, "Un Fou?" ("A
Madman?"):

Magnetism! Do you know what it is? No, no one
knows. Yet it has been observed. It has been identified, even
our doctors practice it; one of the most eminent of these,
M. Charcot, professes it; without a doubt, therefore, it
exists.
A man, a living being, has the frightening, inexplicable
power to hypnotize another being by the very force of his

will, and, as he sleeps, to steal his thought as one would
steal a purse. To steal his thought, that is to say, his soul—
the soul, that inner sanctuary, that mystery of the ego . . .[60]

Such is the psychic vampirism to which the protagonist of
"The Horla" imagines himself to have fallen victim. He uncovers ever more disturbing evidence that an intangible something
haunts his house and garden, drinking not only the liquids he
leaves upon his bedside table but, metaphorically, his very soul.
Maupassant's own mesmerist vision was in striking contrast to that
of Villiers de l'Isle-Adam, who deemed Mesmer to have heralded
man's spiritual emancipation. The intangible yet irresistible Horla
is in many ways analogous to the Schopenhauerian "will," the
blindly impersonal force working in, upon, and through all living
creatures. The German philosopher's view of life as a ceaseless, instinctual striving of the vital force, his denial of any recourse to
the idealistic and humanitarian illusions by which man habitually
seeks to give meaning to existence, found many adherents following the failure of the European revolutions of 1848, and in France
especially after her 1870 defeat in the Franco-Prussian War. By
the 1880s, a Schopenhauerian vogue had set in in France, and the
philosopher's ideas were increasingly popularized for the general
reading public. Adding to the prevailing climate of pessimism was
a growing familiarity with Darwinian ideas. In their simplified and
vulgarized form, these underscored man's animal nature, his en-
slavement to the dictates of material fatality, and the absence of
spiritual transcendance. The impact of popularized Darwinism
upon Maupassant is evidenced by the author's suggestion in "The
Horla" that the ominous Invisible Being may belong to a new race
or species, more perfect than man in the evolutionary chain and
destined to supplant him. For Maupassant, whose inveterately
cynical and gloomy temperament had grown more radically pessi-
mistic under the influence of the novelist Flaubert, contemporary
philosophy and science provided additional grounds for the sadness and horror with which he viewed human existence.

A book that attracted a sizable audience in the last decades
of the century in France was Eduard von Hartmann's *Philosophie des
Unbewussten* (1868; French translation in 1877).[61] The term "unconscious," in Hartmann's usage, has a metaphysical as well as biologi-
cal dimension. Like the Schopenhauerian "will," it designates the

impersonal force of nature which compels individuals to obey instinctual drives (while often cloaking them in idealistic disguise)
in order to advance the larger goals of the species. Although Sigmund Freud was later to give it a more "scientific" and systematic
treatment in the context of human psychology, it is nonetheless
true that by the 1870s and 1880s, the general notion of the unconscious had become a commonplace in Europe. Maupassant was
one of the writers in late nineteenth-century France who would
give this theme powerfully compelling literary form.

The phantasm that ensnares the hapless protagonist of "The
Horla" is a force which—*within us*—is both *us* and *not us*, a force
which makes us a stranger to ourselves. Maupassant's narrator ex-
presses a striking intuition:

> [W]ithout knowing it, I was living that mysterious double
> life that makes us wonder if there are two beings within us,
> or if an alien being, invisible and unknowable, momentarily
> animates (when our soul is benumbed) our captive body
> which obeys the other as it does our own self, more than
> our own self.

The metaphor of the unknown visitor, who takes over not
only a person's house and home but his entire being, is linked thematically with the mirror symbolism in Maupassant's tale: the protagonist, unable to perceive himself in the glass, is convinced that
the Horla is hiding his reflection. In a metaphor familiar to German romanticism, losing one's reflection is equivalent to losing
one's soul. Maupassant's use of this troubling motif only reinforces
the reader's impression of a man who has become radically alien-
ated from his own self: in a concrete and explicit fashion, his "self"
has become "other." For the author, it was the gradual onset of
madness which brought this sense of alienation to a harrowing
pitch of intensity. Maupassant confided to his friend Paul Bourget
that often, upon returning home, he would fall prey to a hallucinatory encounter with his double, seated in his own chair.[62] Elsewhere he recounts a terrifying experience of self-estrangement
which has a mirror as its focal point:

> Do you know that when I stare for a while at my own image
> reflected in a mirror, I have sometimes felt myself losing the
> notion of the ego? At these moments everything grows con-

fused in my mind and I find it strange to be looking at a face
that is no longer familiar to me. Then it seems peculiar that
I should be what I am. . . . And I feel that if this condition
were to last a minute longer, I would go completely mad.
Little by little, all thought would empty out of my brain.[63]

The plot of "Qui sait?" ("Who Knows?"), 1890, is superficially,
at least, quite different from that of "The Horla." The hero of this
story is confronted not with evidence of an Invisible Being but
rather with the bizarre spectacle of his beloved furniture stamped-
ing out of his house one moonlit night, of its own accord. Yet the
two tales are surprisingly parallel in mood and thematic suggestion. Like his earlier counterpart, the narrator of "Who Knows?"
has lived a solitary and tranquil existence, until the mysterious
events occur that are to shatter his illusion of a benevolent universe. These events will force upon his stunned consciousness the
vision of a sinister perversity and malevolence in the world and in
things.

As the narrator observes, some people are extroverted, gifted
for living "outside themselves" ("en dehors"), others for living
"within." In "Who Knows?" this metaphor is literalized: the protagonist's house reflects the reclusive inner sanctum of his own
mind. "My house has become—had become—a world in which I
pursued a solitary . . . existence." The stage is now set for a symbolic vampirism—an emptying out of the very soul of the house,
the furniture. (The French word *déménager*, meaning "to move"
[furniture or people from one place to another] also has a collo-
quial usage, "to go mad.") Maupassant's architectural metaphor for
the human reason, threatened by impending demise, is reminiscent of Edgar Allan Poe's "The Fall of the House of Usher," in
which the ill-fated house is literally rent asunder, its fragments
collapsing into the abyss. "The Haunted Palace," a poem placed
midway in Poe's tale, evokes a radiant edifice "in . . . Thought's
dominion" where "evil things, in robes of sorrow, / Assailed the
monarch's high estate . . ."

> And travellers now within that valley,
> Through the red-litten windows see
> Vast forms that move fantastically
> To a discordant melody;

While, like a rapid ghastly river,
Through the pale door,
A hideous throng rush out forever,
And laugh—but smile no more.[64]

There is additional suggestion in the fact that the narrator's
furniture reappears in an ancient alleyway in medieval Rouen,
inside an antique shop filled with objects "which have outlived
their original owners . . . [and] their century." Maupassant intimates that the fateful, irrational energies which ravaged the hero's
peaceful existence arose out of the depths of the past—once
again analogous to the blind Schopenhauerian will working in and
through each generation while outlasting them all. The antique
dealer, hinted to be somehow responsible for the spiriting away of
the furniture as well as for its unforeseen return, is a disquieting
figure, possibly because he embodies an ominous, impersonal
force larger than any individual existence. Near the end of the
tale, when the antique dealer disappears without a trace, the narrator, who has come to fear him as he would a "ferocious beast,"
exclaims, "Undiscoverable! He is undiscoverable, this monster
with the moon-shaped skull! They will never catch him. . . . I am
the only one who could find him, and I don't want to." Like the
protagonist's confrontation in "The Horla," with the double who
veils his reflection in the mirror, this much-dreaded showdown
represents the hero's potential encounter with the most foreign
and least "humanized" region of the self: the Schopenhauerian
will, the Hartmannian unconscious, the Freudian id. The hereditary insanity which haunted generations of the writer's own family
offered him a particularly brutal image of this blind, irrational
force, originating in the past of the race and making a nightmare
travesty of man's sovereignty and spiritual freedom.

■ ■ ■

Like the tales of Maupassant, those of the fin-de-siècle writer
Marcel Schwob (1867–1905) explore the reality of human alienation and inner fatality. From his childhood, Schwob was an admirer of Edgar Allan Poe, and in his youth was drawn to Greek
philosophy and drama, Schopenhauer, and Shakespeare (*Hamlet* in
particular). The protagonist of "Le Roi au masque d'or" ("The King

in the Golden Mask"), one of Schwob's best known works of fiction, uncovers the dreadful truth about who he really is beneath the disguises that conceal him from himself and from others. "L'Homme voilé" ("The Veiled Man"), a fantastic tale included in the collection *Cœur double* (Double heart), 1891, also deals compellingly with the problem of identity and the theme of the double.

One critic suggests that Schwob's heightened awareness of the double self may stem in part from his own experience of dual identity as a Frenchman and as a Jew, whose family upheld a separate religious and cultural tradition in a society increasingly plagued by antisemitic sentiment.[65] Another critic considers the problem of "doubleness" to reflect, in part, the coexistence within the author of two separate entities: the scholar-critic and the creative artist.[66] Schwob was much respected for his linguistic and philological studies and for his scholarship on the fifteenth-century poet, François Villon. Yet the patient researcher who spent hours poring over old texts was the same person who, in his works of fiction, wove tales of murder, suicide, plague, and leprosy. It was, perhaps, a similar combination of qualities which attracted Schwob to the bookish and adventure-loving Robert Louis Stevenson, upon whose "double personality" Schwob himself commented. One might note, too, that the twentieth-century Argentinian writer, Jorge Luis Borges (who was very likely influenced by Schwob) shared his peculiar blend of personality and interests: as Schwob's translator, Iain White, has observed, "Both are enormously and curiously erudite men of the library, fascinated by the mechanics of storytelling, who are also fascinated by murderers, pirates, outcasts and heretics."[67]

The author of *Cœur double* remains a deeply enigmatic figure. A successful writer much esteemed by the literary world of the 1890s, he was nonetheless plagued by a deeply rooted sense of unworthiness and culpability. In a letter to the writer Anatole France, who had admired his work, Schwob referred to the fact that praise triggered in him an intense discomfort: "I remember with terror the moment when I heard [myself proclaimed] first in my class: I felt as if I had become a criminal. . . ."[68] In another letter, addressed to his wife Marguerite Moréno, Schwob revealed, "I feel that I could be an assassin, a thief, an incendiary. And I am afraid, I am afraid, because I do not feel worthy of you."[69] Schwob published six volumes of tales in his early-to-late twen-

ties, but in 1895–1896 a breakdown in his health (requiring a series of operations that would leave him in a partly invalided condition until his death in 1905, at age thirty-eight) brought an end
to his most creative period of fiction writing. Monique Jutrin hints
at the possible similarities between Schwob's ill health and the illness which destroyed Franz Kafka: "Kafka wrote to [his fiancée]
that his illness, 'externally' tuberculosis, was 'internally' an army
gathered by himself, against himself."[70]

"The Veiled Man" offers the reader all the modulations of the
sinister and uncanny, as they shade imperceptibly into the ghastly
and horrific. Like the central drama of Balzac's "The Red Inn," it
has as its setting an enclosed space momentarily tenanted by three
individuals: the protagonist, the murderer, and the victim. But
whereas Balzac's German inn afforded the perfect backdrop for
a fantastic tale in the Hoffmannesque tradition, Schwob's setting—a moving railway carriage—immediately sets the tone of
late nineteenth-century modernity.

Schwob (again much like Balzac) explores the theme of the
dark, inner self, and the relationship between desire and action,
will and execution. Both writers, or so it might initially appear,
dramatize the mysterious power of fascination that one human
will can exert upon another. Yet while Balzac's tale, a product of
the author's mystico-philosophical speculation, may raise troubling questions in the mind of the reader, one could not say that it
has the power to chill or terrify. Balzac's protagonist may have en-
tertained and come perilously close to committing the act that his
traveling companion actually performs, yet on a literal level at
least he is wrongly accused of the crime. "The Veiled Man" is
more disturbing in its power of suggestion. The emotions of dread
and horror that it arouses have a twofold source. On the one
hand, there is the reader's identification with the protagonist, convinced that a murder is to be committed by the mysterious man
under the speckled cover, yet powerless to prevent it. On the
other, there is the reader's growing suspicion that this gruesome
murder, like the obsessive mental refrain born of the repetitive
song of the train's wheels upon the rails, is in fact ripening in the
protagonist's disturbed brain. In this tale, the narrator's numbed
entrancement in the presence of a will which "annihilated [his]
own" is to be read not in the context of mesmerism or thought
transference but rather of criminal psychopathology.

As in much of Schwob's fiction, the mask image plays an important role in "The Veiled Man." It is introduced as the narrator glances over at his traveling companion who has risen to shade the lamp: "In this operation I should have been able to see his face—*and I did not see it*. I caught a glimpse of a confused blur, the color of a human face, but of which I could not distinguish the least feature." Later, in a kind of swoon, the narrator feels himself endowed with the power to see through the spotted traveling rug: "Thus I *knew* that I was looking through a leopard skin, and through a flesh-colored silken mask, a *crépon* covering a swarthy face." Following Georges Buraud, the critic George Trembley has noted the symbolic relationship between the mask and the notion of instinct. "Static, fixed, the mask is incapable of translating the infinite variety of emotions, the fleeting nuances of sentiment; it fixes a passion, simplifying it. . . . The forces by which fatality operates are also simple forces: these are the primitive instincts, common to all men. [A]t certain moments [they] totally overpower our being. . . . It is then that we speak of 'possession.' . . ."[71] That the mask is an "instrument of magic, of fascination and terror, [suggestive of] those mysterious powers over which we have no control" is indeed a compelling hypothesis.[72]

■ ■ ■

It could be said that, as a genre, the fantastic deals precisely with those aspects of human existence that are perpetually both revealed and concealed. Concealed by the confidence in scientific certitudes, by the predictable, dependable nature of everyday reality, by the sheer force of habit; revealed in momentary glimpses, premonitions, hints of an abyss that yawns just beneath the seemingly solid surface of things. It is this intuition, or intimation, that is at the root of each of the following tales.

The fantastic tale was, from its earliest beginnings, an exploration into the mysterious and elusive human psyche. The writers of these stories were astute psychologists, and their insights are the more forceful for being articulated on an imaginative level rather than in terms that are empirical and systematic. Their works repeatedly probe the subject of the unconscious, often through the metaphor of the divided self or the landscape of dream and madness. As they gravitate toward those areas of experience inaccessible to rational understanding, they actually lead us to a more complete notion of our own minds, with their web of tangled, contradictory motivations and impulses.

In the "postmodern" world, where so much has been logically charted and explained, the allure of the fantastic is as potent as ever—today most often via the genre of science fiction. Human beings continue to suspect, in a prerational, purely intuitive manner, that many elusive phenomena play a significant role in their lives. It is this dimension of mystery—at times exhilarating and liberating, at times fearsome and ominous—which the writers represented here evoke in their tales, and to which readers of any age can respond with a thrill of recognition.

Joan C. Kessler

Charles Nodier

SMARRA,
or
THE DEMONS
OF THE NIGHT

PROLOGUE

Somnia fallaci ludunt temeraria nocte,
Et pavidas mentes falsa timere jubent.

> *Catullus* [1]

The isle is full of noises,
Sounds, and sweet airs, that give delight and hurt not:
Sometimes a thousand twangling instruments
Will hum about mine ears; and sometime voices,
That, if I then had waked after long sleep,
Will make me sleep again—and then, in dreaming,
The clouds methought would open, and show riches
Ready to drop upon me, that when I waked
I cried to dream again.

> *Shakespeare* [2]

Ah, how sweet, my Lisidis, when the last chimes of the midnight bells are fading among the towers of Arona,[3] how sweet to come to you, to share your solitary bed that for a year has filled my dreams!

You are mine, Lisidis, and the evil spirits that removed Lorenzo from your gentle slumbers can no longer frighten me with their magic!

Some have said, and rightfully, that those nocturnal terrors which assailed my soul in its hours of repose were but a natural result of my too fervent study of ancient poetry, and the im-

1

pression that several of Apuleius's fantastic fables had left upon me—for the first book of Apuleius[4] grips the imagination so sharply and so painfully that I would do anything to keep it from your eyes.

But speak no more now of Apuleius and his visions, speak no more of the Greeks and Latins, nor of the dazzling caprices of their genius! Are you not for me, Lisidis, a poem more beautiful than poetry, and richer in divine enchantments than all of nature?

But you are sleeping, my child, and do not hear me! You danced too long tonight at the ball on Isola Bella![5] . . . You danced too long, especially when you were not dancing with me, and you are now weary as a rose that has swayed all day in the breeze and must await the first light of morning to arise, glowing vermilion on its pendulous stem.

Sleep then by my side, resting your forehead on my shoulder and warming me with your perfumed breath. Sleep overcomes me also, but it now descends upon my eyelids almost as gently as one of your kisses. Sleep, Lisidis, sleep.

. . . .

. . . .

. . . .

There is a moment when the mind, suspended in nebulous mists of thought . . . Peace! . . . Night is upon the earth. No longer do you hear the footsteps of the homebound townsman echoing on the sonorous pavement, nor the hoofbeats of the iron-shod mules returning to their evening shelter. The sound of the wind whistling or moaning between the poorly joined sashes of the casement is all that remains of the familiar impressions of your senses, and after some moments you begin to imagine that this murmur too is within you. It becomes a voice of your soul, the echo of an indefinable yet fixed idea that blends with the first sensations of sleep. You are entering that nocturnal life that unfolds (O miracle!) in ever new and uncharted worlds, amid innumerable beings conceived but unrealized by the Great Spirit, and dispersed as protean and mysterious phantoms through the boundless universe of dreams. The Sylphs, giddy with the sounds of evening, swirl humming and buzzing around you. With the dull beating of their moth wings they sweep across your heavy eyelids, releasing a transparent, multicolored powder that you see suspended a while in the darkness like a tiny luminous cloud in a deadened sky. They throng, press, merge together, anxious to renew the magical conversation of past nights, and to recount the extraordinary events which appear to your mind in the guise of wondrous reminiscence. Gradually their voices fade, or rather, reach you only by means of some unknown agency that transforms their tales into *tableaux vivants*, making you an involuntary actor in the scenes they have prepared—for the imagination of the sleeper, in the strength of his free and sovereign soul, partakes of the perfection of the spirits. It soars with them, and carried miraculously amid the aerial choir of dreams, it wings its way from surprise to surprise until the morning bird's song alerts the adventurous company to daylight's return. Startled by the premonitory cry, they gather like a swarm of bees at the first rumbling of thunder, when heavy raindrops weigh down the petals of flowers beneath the swallow's fluttering wing. They fall, rebound, ascend, crisscross like atoms driven by opposing forces, and disappear in confusion in a ray of the sun.

NARRATIVE

... O rebus meis
Non infideles arbitrae,
Nox, et Diana, quae silentium regis,
Arcana cum fiunt sacra;
Nunc, nunc adeste ... [6]

His spirits hear me,
And yet I needs must curse ...
But they'll nor pinch,
Fright me with urchin-shows, pitch me i'th' mire,
Nor lead me, like a firebrand, in the dark
Out of my way, unless he bid 'em; but
For every trifle are they set upon me—
Sometime like apes, that mow and chatter at me,
And after bite me: then like hedgehogs which
Lie tumbling in my barefoot way, and mount
Their pricks at my footfall ...
Shakespeare[7]

I had just finished my studies at the school of philosophy in Athens and, eager to taste the beauties of Greece, I was visiting poetical Thessaly[8] for the first time. My slaves awaited me at Larissa,[9] in a palace which had been readied for my arrival. It had been my desire to travel alone—and in the solemn hours of the night—through that forest renowned for sorceresses' magic, which extends its long green curtain of trees along the banks of the Peneus. The shadows were thickening under the immense canopy of woods, and scarcely a trembling ray of pale starlight, girdled by fog, made its way through the sparser branches of trees where a partial clearing had been made by the woodcutter's axe. My heavy lids were drooping, my eyes tired of straining after the whitish trace of the path that faded into the thicket, and I resisted sleep only by focusing with a painful effort on the sound of my horse's hoofs falling now on sand and now on dry grass. If he occasionally halted, I would be roused by the pause, and in weariness and impatience would call out to him sharply to hasten his pace. At times, surprised by some strange obstacle, he would bound ahead, whinnying and snorting violently through his nostrils, then rear back and recoil in alarm as sparks flashed from the broken stones beneath our feet. . . .

"Phlégon, Phlégon," I said, letting my weary head droop upon his neck that was taut with fear, "O dear Phlégon! Are we not nearly at Larissa, where pleasures and sweet sleep await us? Just a little more courage, and you will lie upon a bed of cut flowers— for the golden straw gathered for Ceres' oxen is not fresh enough for you! . . ."

"Do you not see, do you not see," he said, trembling, "the torches that they brandish before us are devouring the heath, filling the air I breathe with deadly vapors. . . . How am I to pass through their magic circles, through their frightful dances that would make even the Sun's horses recoil in fear?"

And yet the cadenced step of my horse continued to echo in my ear, and a deep sleep suspended all anxiety. Only, now and then, queer glimmering flames would dance before my eyes . . . , some grotesque spirit, in the form of a maimed man or a beggar, would seize hold of my leg and drag along behind me with hideous glee, or else some ghastly old man, whose features mingled senile decrepitude with the ugliness of crime, would spring up behind me and clasp me with arms fleshless as Death.

"Onward, Phlégon!" I would cry, "onward, fairest of Mount Ida's steeds, brave the deadly terrors that grip your soul! These demons are but vain phantoms. My sword, as it circles about your head, cuts through their illusory forms that dissolve like a cloud. When the morning fog, touched by the sun's rays, hangs below the mountaintops like a translucent girdle, the truncated peaks seem suspended in the heavens by an invisible hand. Thus, Phlé-gon, are the sorceresses of Thessaly rent by the edge of my sword. Do you not hear in the distance the cries of pleasure rising from Larissa's walls? . . . Here—here are the lofty towers of the city of Thessaly, haven of sensual delight; and that music floating in the air is the song of its young maidens!"

Which of you, seductive dreams that lull the drunken soul with ineffable memories of pleasure, which of you can bring back to me the song of the young maidens of Thessaly and the volup-tuous nights of Larissa? Amid columns of translucent marble, be-neath twelve brilliant domes whose gold and crystal reflect the light of ten thousand torches, the young maidens of Thessaly, bathed in the colored vapor emanating from countless perfumes, appear blurred and charmingly nebulous to the eye, as if on the verge of fading away. The wondrous cloud hovers about them and its light plays fitfully on their enchanting forms, conjuring the fresh hues of the rose, the shimmer of dawn, the clashing irides-cence of capricious opal. Now droplets of pearl rain down their light tunics; now from their golden hair-clasps flash sparks of flame. Be not alarmed to see them paler than the other maidens of Greece. They scarcely belong to this world, and seem to be awakening from a former existence. They are melancholy, too, whether because in their old world they have forsaken the love of a Spirit or a God, or because in a woman's heart just opening to passion there is a great desire for suffering.

But listen. These are the songs of the young maidens of Thes-saly, the music that rises, rises into the air and, passing like a me-lodious cloud, animates the solitary vestiges of stained glass in ruins beloved of poets. Listen! They clasp their ivory lyres, and strum the sonorous strings which respond, vibrate a moment, and come to rest, sustaining an ineffable, unending harmony that the soul absorbs through all the senses. This melody is as pure as the sweetest thought of a gladdened soul, as the first kiss of love be-fore love is understood, as the caressing glance of a mother at her child in the cradle, the child whose death she had envisioned in a dream, and who has just been brought to her, beautiful and tran-quil in his sleep. The music fades like the last sigh of a cithera, abandoned to the breezes, lost amid echoes, suspended in the silence of the lake, or dying with the waves at the foot of the stolid rock, the last sigh of a cithera plucked by a woman weeping for the lover who did not appear. The singers glance at each other, bend to confer together, cross their elegant arms, mingle their flowing hair, dance so that the nymphs swoon with envy, and send forth flashing from beneath their feet a fiery dust which hangs in the air, grows pale, and then, extinguished, descends in silvery ashes. And their harmonious song flows ever onward like a river of honey, like the gentle stream that adorns with its dulcet murmur the sunlit shores full of secret meanderings, cool shaded bays, flowers and butterflies. They sing. . . .

Only one, perhaps . . . tall, immobile, pensive . . . My God, how somber and troubled she is, standing behind her companions; what does she want from me? Ah, do not haunt my thoughts, imperfect semblance of the beloved who is no more, do not darken my charmed evenings with your dreadful reproach! Be gone, for I have mourned you seven years; let me forget the tears that still scald my cheeks in the innocent delights of fairy music and the sylphids' dance. You see they draw near, you see them gathering, swelling, in wafting, shifting festoons that advance, recede, ebb and flow like the tides, unfurling upon their fleeting waves all the colors of the rainbow which after the storm joins earth to heaven, when it drops the end of its immense arc upon the ship's prow.

But what, to me, are the dangers of the sea and the curious cares of the sailor? A boon from heaven—which perhaps, in a former existence, was man's birthright—grants me (sweet bounty of sleep) to escape all perils at will. Scarcely have my eyes closed, and the entrancing melody faded away, when, if the author of nocturnal magic opens up before me a yawning abyss, a mysterious gulf where all earthly forms, sounds, and lights vanish, if across a seething and ravenous torrent he casts a steep, narrow, treacherous bridge that seems without end, if he flings me to the extremity of a tremulous plank above chasms too fearful for the eye to fathom—tranquil, I stamp upon the compliant ground with a foot accustomed to command. It yields, responds; I'm off, and happy to leave humankind, I see receding in my effortless flight the blue rivers of continents, the somber wastes of ocean, the variegated crests of forests mottled in spring green, the purple and

gold of autumn, the dull bronze and drab violet of brittle winter
leaves. If the rapidly fluttering wings of some errant bird rustle in
my ear, I soar higher, ascending toward unknown worlds. The
river is now no more than a thread fading into the dark green
vegetation, the mountains no more than a vague point, each summit vanishing into its base, the Ocean but a dark blot in some
larger mass, adrift in space, which revolves more rapidly than the
six-sided knucklebone toy that the children of Athens spin on its
pointed axis, along the flagstoned galleries surrounding the
Ceramicus.[10]

Have you ever seen along the walls of the Ceramicus, as they
are lit by the first regenerating rays of the new year, a long line of
pale, gaunt, immobile figures, with cheeks hollowed by want, and
dull, staring eyes?—some squatting like beasts, others standing
but leaning against the columns and sagging under the weight of
their tired frames. Have you seen them, their mouths half-open
to inhale once more the tonic air, to drink in with sullen pleasure
the tepid warmth of spring? You might have seen the same sight
within the walls of Larissa, for the wretched are everywhere: yet
here misfortune bears the mark of a singular fatality, more degrading than poverty, keener than hunger, more oppressive than despair. These hapless creatures slowly advance one behind the
other, with long pauses after each step, like those fantastical figures ingeniously arranged around a wheel that revolves with the
hours. Twelve hours elapse as the silent procession follows the circuit of the public square, although its dimensions are so small that
a lover at one end could learn from his mistress's fingers at the
other the hour of the longed-for rendezvous. These living ghosts
have little left that is human. Their skin is like blanched parch-
ment stretched taut over bones. Not a glimmer of soul emanates
from the sockets of their eyes. Their pale lips quiver from anxiety
and terror, or, more frightful still, there hovers upon them a wild,
scornful smile, like the last thought of a condemned man as he
goes resolutely to his death. Most are shaken by slight yet continual convulsions, and tremble like the iron tongue of that sonorous instrument that children vibrate between their teeth.[11] The
most pitiful of all, vanquished by destiny, are forever doomed to
frighten passers-by with the repulsive deformity of their knotted
limbs and rigid attitudes. Yet this recurrent phase of their existence, between two periods of sleep, is for them a temporary re-

prieve from their most dreaded agonies. Victims of the vengeful sorceresses of Thessaly, they fall prey to torments that no tongue can express, once the sun, slipping below the western horizon, has ceased to defend them against the formidable rulers of darkness. That is why they follow its too rapid course, their eyes ever fixed upon its compass in the hope, forever thwarted, that it might for once forget its azure bed and remain suspended in the golden clouds of the west. Hardly has the night returned to disabuse them, unfurling its wings of crepe on which not a trace remains of the pale gleam dying away upon the treetops, hardly has the last glimmer of reflected light vanished from the polished metal high upon the rooftops—like a piece of coal still aglow in an extinguished furnace, slowly growing pale amid the ashes and soon no longer distinguishable from the depths of the deserted hearth—when a fearsome murmur arises among them, their teeth chatter in rage and despair, they press together, then shrink apart, as if they saw sorceresses and phantoms everywhere. Night has fallen! . . . And once again before them yawns the abyss of Hell!

There was one whose every utterance was like the squeal of worn-out springs, and from whose chest came a sound more hoarse and muffled than the grinding of a rusty screw. Yet several shreds of rich embroidery that still hung from his cloak, an expression full of sadness and grace that now and then illumined his languid and despondent features, I know not what unimaginable mixture of degradation and pride which recalled the despair of a panther subjugated by the hunter's searing muzzle, caused him to stand out from his wretched companions; women sighed when he passed them. His blond hair fell in loose curls upon his shoulders, which rose pure and white like a cluster of lilies from his purple tunic. Yet his neck bore the stamp of blood, the triangular scar left by the head of a spear, the mark of the wound which took Polémon from me at the siege of Corinth,[12] when this faithful friend rushed to shield me from the unbridled fury of a warrior already triumphant but eager to add another corpse to the field of battle. It was that Polémon whom I so long had mourned, and who so often appears in my slumber to remind me, with a kiss of ice, that we must meet again in the everlasting realm of death. It was Polémon, living still, but preserved for such a horrible existence that the larval phantoms of Hell take comfort in recounting his sufferings, Polémon fallen under the sway of the sorceresses of Thessaly and the demons that attend them in the ceremonies, the inexplicable ceremonies of their nocturnal feasts. He paused, perplexed, struggling long to connect my features with some memory, then came toward me with an anxious and measured step, extended his trembling hands to mine, and having clasped me in a sudden embrace that filled me with alarm, and fixed me with a pale gleam from his dimmed eyes, like the last flash of a torch disappearing through the trapdoor of a cell: "Lucius! Lucius!" he cried, with a hideous laugh.

"Polémon, dear Polémon, Lucius's friend and savior! . . ."

"In another world," he said in a muted voice, "I remember . . . it was in another world, in a life not ruled by the phantoms of sleep. . . ."

"You speak of phantoms? . . ."

"Look!" he answered, pointing into the dusk. . . . "They are coming."

"Oh, surrender not, unhappy youth, to night's disquietude! When the mountain shadows lengthen, their immense pyramids meeting and merging in silence upon the darkened plain, when the fantastical patterns of the clouds expand, blend together, and disappear like furtive lovers beneath the protective veil of night, when the mourning birds begin to cry in the woods, and the reptiles sing in a broken monotone by the marsh's edge . . . then, dear Polémon, do not let your tortured imagination yield to the illusions of darkness and solitude. Shun the hidden paths where specters gather, plotting darkly against man's repose, the graveyards where the dead, wrapped in their shrouds, meet in mysterious council before a tribunal[13] among the tombs; shun the open meadow where a circle of grass turns black and withered beneath the sorceresses' cadenced tread. Trust in me, Polémon. As the light wanes, alarmed by the evil spirits' approach, let us rekindle its magic in opulent feasts and voluptuous revels. Do I ever lack for gold? Do the richest mines have a hidden vein that denies me its treasure? The very sand in the riverbeds is transformed beneath my hands into precious stones that could embellish the crowns of kings. Trust in me, Polémon. In vain shall the sun grow dim, so long as the fires it has kindled for the use of man still sparkle in festival lamps, or in the softer lights that adorn the delicious vigils of love. You know that the demons fear the sweet, balmy vapors of oil and wax glowing gently in alabaster, or pouring rose-colored shadows across our thick silken tapestries. They shudder at the sight of polished marble, lit by chandeliers whose trembling pendants of crystal flash forth a long spray of diamonds like a waterfall caught in the last light of the setting sun. Never has dark lamia [14] or fleshless ghoul dared show its hideous features at the banquets of Thessaly. The very moon that they invoke frightens them when it sends down upon them one of those fleeting rays which give to all that they touch the wan pallor of tin. They slip away more quickly than the grass snake fleeing the sound of a footstep upon the sand. Fear not that they will surprise you amid the lamps that glitter in my palace, shining forth from all sides in the dazzling steel of the mirrors. See rather, Polémon, how deftly they have avoided us since we have been walking among my servants' torches, in galleries adorned with statuary, inimitable masterpieces of Greek genius. Did one of these statues reveal by some threatening gesture the presence of those fantastical spirits that inhabit them at times, when the last glimmer leaves the last lamp, rises and dies away? The stillness of their forms, the purity of their features, the calm of their ever-unchanging bearing would reassure fear itself. If you are startled by some strange sound, O cherished brother of my soul, it is that of the thoughtful nymph who pours the treasures of her crystal urn upon your weary limbs, mingling there perfumes hitherto unknown to Larissa: a limpid amber that I gathered by the shores of seas that wash upon the cradle of the sun, the essence of a flower a thousand times sweeter than the rose, which grows only in the dense shades of dark Corcyra, [15] the teardrops of a plant beloved of Apollo and his son, [16] which unfurls upon the rocks of Epidaurus [17] its bouquets of purple cymbals trembling under the weight of the dew. And how could the sorceresses' charms cloud the purity of the waters that lull you with their silvery waves? Myrthé, lovely fair-haired Myrthé, youngest and dearest of my slaves, she whom you saw bowing as you passed, for she loves all that I love . . . she possesses magic known only to her and to the spirit that grants it to her in the mysteries of sleep. She flits now like a shadow round the baths, where the healing water slowly rises; she runs, singing airs that drive away the demons, now and then brushing the strings of a wandering harp that docile genies never fail to offer her before her eyes can convey her soul's desire. She skips along, and the harp skips, singing, beneath her fingers. Listen to the sonorous voice of the harp, the voice of Myrthé's harp: it is a full, deep, solemn sound which banishes all earthly ideas, and, sustained and prolonged, fills the soul like contemplation. It soars, recedes, vanishes, returns; and the airs of Myrthé's harp (bewitching magic of night!), the airs of Myrthé's harp which soar, recede, vanish, and again return—how they soar, the airs of Myrthé's harp, the airs that drive away the demons! . . . Listen, Polémon, do you hear them?

"Truly I have known all the illusions of dream, and what would have become of me then without the aid of Myrthé's harp, without the aid of her voice breaking through my doleful and tormented slumber? . . . How often in my sleep have I bent over the clear, still waters, where my altered features are mirrored only too well—my hair standing up in terror, my gaze fixed and sullen like tearless despair! . . . How often have I trembled to see the pale trace of blood about my lips, to feel my teeth dislodge from their sockets, my nails loosen and fall! How often, frightened by my nakedness, by my shameful nakedness, have I anxiously surrendered to the irony of the mob, wearing a tunic more slight and transparent than that of a courtesan upon the brazen bed of debauchery! Oh, how often dreams more hideous still, dreams that Polémon himself has never known . . . And what would have become of me then, what would have become of me without the aid of Myrthé's harp, without the aid of her voice and the harmonies that she teaches to her sisters, when they gather dutifully round her, to charm away the terrors of the unhappy sleeper, filling his ears with melodies from afar, like the breeze gliding between sails—melodies that merge and commingle, and lull to rest the heart's tempestuous dreams.

"Here now are Myrthé's sisters, who have prepared the feast. Théis stands out among all the maidens of Thessaly, though nearly all the maidens of Thessaly have black hair that falls on shoulders whiter than alabaster; none can boast such soft and sensuous black curls as Théis. It is she who tilts a precious clay vessel over a hot cup of boiling wine, letting fall drop by drop, like liquid topaz, the sweetest honey ever gathered from Sicilian elm. The honeybee, deprived of her treasure, moves anxiously among the flowers, and hangs upon the solitary branches of the abandoned tree, offering an entreaty to the winds. She murmurs in sorrow, for her young will no more find shelter in any of the myriad five-walled palaces that she built for them with a light and trans-

parent wax,[18] and will not taste the honey that she had gathered
for them in the perfumed thickets of Mount Hybla. It is Théis
who pours into the boiling wine honey stolen from the bees of
Sicily; her other sisters, those with the dark hair—for only
Myrthé is blond—bustle obediently, eagerly, tenderly, with a du-
tiful smile, around the preparations for the banquet. They strew
pomegranate flowers or rose leaves upon the frothy milk, or else
they stir the fires of amber and incense that burn beneath the hot
cup of boiling wine—flames that curl upward about the circular
rim, mingling, skimming its lips of gold, and finally blending with
the white- and blue-tongued flames rising from the wine. The
flames soar, descend, shift fitfully like that fantastical demon of
solitude who gazes at his reflection in pools. Who can count how
often the cup made the rounds of the feast table, how often it was
drained and refilled to the brim with new nectar? Maidens, spare
neither the wine nor the mead. The sun sends rays of undying
splendor through the dark leaves of vine branches winding their
garlands among the mulberry trees of Tempe,[19] and ceaselessly
swells the young grapes that hang brightly in clusters. Another
draught, to drive away the demons of the night! For my part,
I see only the joyful genii of intoxication which dart forth, all
a-sparkle, from the quivering foam, chase one another through
the air like fiery gnats, or come to dazzle my eyes with the beating of their radiant wings. They resemble those agile insects that
nature has adorned with an innocent flame,[20] and that often, in
the cool stillness of a short summer's night, one sees bursting in
swarms from amid a cluster of foliage, like a shower of sparks
from beneath the blacksmith's hammer. They drift, carried by a
light passing breeze or enticed by some sweet perfume in the ca-
lyx of the rose. The luminous cloud floats, sways fitfully, turns
briefly on its axis, and descends upon the summit of a young pine,
which it illuminates like a pyramid at a festival, or upon the lower
branch of a huge oak to which it gives the appearance of a luminous garland readied for the forest vigil. See how they gambol
round you, how they quiver in the flowers, how they sparkle and
gleam upon the polished vases: these demons are not our enemies.
They dance, they are merry, they have the brilliant abandon of
madness. If at times they trouble men's repose, it is merely to satisfy a giddy, childish caprice. They roll mischievously in the flax
of an old shepherdess's spindle, twisting and tangling the stray

threads, multiplying the knots and rendering her efforts futile. When a lost traveler scours the night horizon in search of some glimmer of a haven, they make him wander from path to path, lured by a deceptive light, or the imagined sound of a voice or distant barking of a dog ranging like a sentinel around a lonely farm. Thus they beguile the poor traveler until, moved to pity at his fatigue, they suddenly reveal an unforeseen shelter, hitherto unnoticed in the wilderness. Sometimes he is amazed to find on his arrival a crackling hearth, the very sight of which makes him jolly, some rare and delicate dishes fortuitously procured from fisherman or poacher, and a maiden, lovely as the Graces, who serves him without raising her eyes, for she feels that to behold this stranger would be perilous. The next day, surprised that so short a rest should have restored all his strength, he awakens happily to the song of the lark greeting a clear sky; he learns that his propitious error has shortened his route by twenty and a half *stadia*,[21] and his horse, with wide-open nostrils, glossy coat, and a sleek and brilliant mane, whinnies in impatience, stamping thrice upon the ground to signal departure. The imp capers from the rump to the head of the traveler's horse, runs his dexterous fingers through the ample mane, kneads it into waves. Exultant, he sets off to make merry at the plight of a sleeping man who, parched with thirst, sees a cool, refreshing drink dwindle and vanish before his extended lips—who fruitlessly drains the cup with his gaze, fruitlessly inhales the spurious liquid, and then awakens to find the vessel filled with Syracuse wine, which the mischievous sprite had pressed from choice grapes as he chuckled over his victim's restless slumber. Here you may drink, speak, or sleep without fear, for the sprites are our friends. Only satisfy the impatient curiosity of Théis and Myrthé, the even more avid curiosity of Thélaïre, who has not taken her shining eyes from you, her large black eyes that move like auspicious stars in a sky bathed with softest azure. Tell us, Polémon, of the agonies you endured under the sorceresses' sway—or thought you endured, for the torments with which they haunt our imagination are but the illusion of a dream that vanishes with the first rays of dawn. Théis, Thélaïre, and Myrthé are attentive. . . . They are listening. . . . Speak . . . tell us your fears, your despairs, and the mad delusions of the night; and you, Théis, pour some wine; and you, Thélaïre, smile at his tale to comfort his soul; and you, Myrthé, if you should see him, overcome by these memories of madness, sliding into new illusions, sing and pluck the strings of the magic harp. . . . Ask for notes of solace, notes to drive away the evil spirits. . . . It is thus that we free the somber hours of the night from the stormy dominion of dreams, and, flitting from pleasure to pleasure, shake off the sinister spells that fill the earth during the absence of the sun."

EPISODE

Hanc ego de caelo ducentem sidera vidi:
Fluminis haec rapidi carmine vertit iter.
Haec cantu finditque solum, manesque sepulchris
Elicit, et tepido devocat ossa rogo.
Quum libet, haec tristi depellit nubila caelo;
Quum libet, aestivo convocat orbe nives.

Tibullus [22]

For this, be sure, to-night thou shalt have cramps,
Side-stitches that shall pen thy breath up—urchins
Shall, for that vast of night that they may work,
All exercise on thee: thou shalt be pinched
As thick as honeycomb, each pinch more stinging
Than bees that made 'em.

Shakespeare [23]

"Which of you, O young maidens, does not know the sweet caprices of women?" said Polémon, warming. "You have loved, no doubt, and know how the heart of a pensive widow, who lets her lonely memories stray along the shady banks of the Peneus, can be captured by the dark-skinned soldier whose eyes flash with the fire of war and whose breast is blazoned with a noble scar. He strides proudly and tenderly among the fair like a tamed lion who, yearning for the wilds, seeks oblivion in the pleasures of servitude. Thus does the soldier delight in winning women's hearts when the bugle no longer summons him to battle and the perils of war no longer tempt his eager ambition. Smiling, he basks in the maidens' gaze, and seems to be saying: 'Love me!' . . .

"You know too, for you are from Thessaly, that no woman has ever equaled in beauty noble Méroé, who since her widowhood wears long, trailing, white robes embroidered with silver—Méroé, fairest of Thessaly's fair. She is as majestic as a goddess, and yet in

her eyes are deadly flames that embolden the claims of love. Oh,
how often have I flung myself in her wake, into the dust stirred by
her tread, into the happy shadow that follows her! . . . How often
have I dashed ahead to catch a gleam from her eyes, a breath from
her mouth, an atom from the eddy of air that caresses her every
motion; how often (Thélaïre, will you forgive me?) have I sought
the ardent bliss of feeling one of the folds of her dress brush
against my tunic, or of culling one of the spangles of her embroidery from Larissa's garden paths! When she passed, all the clouds
would darken as at the approach of a storm; I would hear a whistling in my ears, a film would come over my eyes, my heart would
nearly burst under the weight of an unendurable delight. She
was there! I worshipped the shadows that had drifted over her,
I breathed in the air that had touched her; I called to all the
trees upon the shore: 'Have you seen Méroé?' If she had lain upon
a bed of flowers, how jealously I would gather up the blossoms
she had crushed: the white petals infused with crimson that adorn
the bending brow of the anemone, the brilliant darts that spring
from the golden disc of the daisy, the veil of chaste gauze that
envelops a young lily before it opens to the sun; and if I dared
press myself upon this couch of fresh green with a sacrilegious
embrace, she would make me burn with a flame sharper than that
of death as it licks the night garments of a fevered man. Méroé
could not help but notice me. I was everywhere. One day, at the
approach of sundown, our eyes met: she was smiling; she had
overtaken me, and slowed down. I was alone behind her, and I
saw her turn round. The air was calm and had not disturbed her
hair, yet her hand was raised as if to repair its disorder. I followed
her, Lucius, to the palace, to the temple of the princess of Thessaly, and night descended upon us, night of bliss and terror! . . .
Would that it had been my last, and that it had come sooner to
a close!

"Have you ever endured, with a resignation mingled with impatience and tenderness, the weight of a sleeping mistress's body
upon your extended arm as she sinks into sleep, oblivious of your
suffering? Have you ever struggled against the shudder that
gradually overcomes you, against the numbness that grips your
helpless muscles, wrestled with the death that threatens to envelop your very soul![24] It was thus, Lucius, that a painful throbbing passed swiftly through my nerves, sending sudden tremors

through them as the sharp metal of the *plectrum* sends dissonance through the strings of the lyre in the hands of an unskilled musician. My flesh burned like a dried membrane brought near a flame. My chest was near to bursting, and breaking the iron bonds that fettered it, when Méroé, suddenly seated at my side, gazed deeply into my eyes, laid her hand on my heart to make sure it had stopped, rested it there awhile, heavy and cold, and darted off as swiftly as an arrow thrust from a quivering crossbow. She ran across the marble floors of the palace, intoning the melodies of the old shepherdesses of Syracuse who charm the moon in its clouds of silver and pearl; she spun through the immense spaces of the hall, now and then crying out, in a horrible burst of gaiety, a summons to companions as yet unknown to me.

"I watched in terror as an endless throng of misty phantoms glided along the walls, crowded beneath the porticos, swung through the archways. Each was distinct from the others, yet with only the semblance of life and form, with voices as faint as the sound of the stillest pool in a calm night, and transparent figures which took on the hue of whatever objects they floated past. . . . Suddenly the sparkling bluish flame shot up from all the cauldrons at once, and formidable Méroé rushed from one to the other, murmuring confused words:

"'Here, some flowering verbena . . . here, three sprigs of sage culled at midnight near the graves of those who died by the sword . . . here, the veil of the beloved, beneath which her lover hid his pallor and desolation after he had slaughtered her sleeping husband to make free with her love . . . and here, the tears of a tigress exhausted by hunger, inconsolable at having devoured one of her young!'

"And her stunned features expressed such horror and suffering that she almost inspired pity. Anxious lest her spells be cut short by some unforeseen obstacle, she leaped up in rage, disappeared, and returned armed with two long ivory wands, the ends of which were tied by a braid of thirteen hairs pulled from the neck of a stately white mare by the thief who had murdered its master. With this supple braid she sent the ebony *rhombus*,[25] with its hollow, echoing globes, screeching through the air; spinning round and round, it returned with a dull rumble, spun some more, still rumbling, then slowed and fell. The flames of the cauldrons stood erect like grass snakes' tongues, and the shades were appeased.

'Come, come,' cried Méroé, 'the demons of the night must be pacified, and the dead must rejoice. Bring me flowering verbena, sage culled at midnight, and four-leaf clover; offer harvests of plucked flowers to Saga[26] and the demons of the night.' Then, turning a wondering eye upon the golden asp that coiled about her naked arm, upon the precious bracelet crafted by the most skillful artisan of Thessaly, who had spared neither materials nor craft—the silver was inlaid in delicate scales, the whiteness of each set off by a dazzling ruby or soft, translucent, sky-blue sapphire—she unfastens it, muses dreamily, invokes the snake with whispered, cryptic words, and the quickened creature uncoils and slithers off with a hiss of joy, like a liberated slave. And the *rhombus* is still spinning, still spinning and rumbling, rumbling like distant thunder that groans amid windswept clouds and then subsides with the passing storm. But now all the vaults of the sky open, vast celestial spaces are unfurled, all the stars descend, all the clouds flatten around the threshold of the heavens like a hall of darkness. The bloodstained moon is like the iron shield that bears home the body of a young Spartan, slaughtered by the enemy. Spinning, it crushes me with the weight of its livid disc, still clouded with smoke from the smoldering cauldrons. Méroé is still darting about; lightning bolts flash from her fingers, striking the myriad columns of the palace, and each column dividing under Méroé's fingers discloses an immense colonnade thronged with phantoms, and each of these phantoms in turn strikes a column which exposes new colonnades, and there is not one column that does not bear witness to the sacrifice of a newborn child torn from the arms of its mother. 'Have mercy, have mercy,' I cried, 'on the unhappy mother in her struggle against death!' But this prayer was stifled upon my lips like the last breath of a dying man who whispers 'Adieu!'—and dissolved upon my mouth in inarticulate stammers. It died away like the cry of a drowning man who tries in vain to impart to the silent waters one last entreaty of despair. The indifferent ocean smothers his voice; dark and cold, it envelops him; it swallows his moans; never will it carry them to the shore.

"While I wrestled with the terror that gripped me, endeavoring to wring from my breast some curse that might call forth vengeance from the gods in heaven, . . . 'Miserable wretch!' cried Méroé, 'be forever punished for your brazen curiosity! . . . Ah, you

dare violate sleep's magic spell. . . . You speak, you shout, you
see. . . . Well then, you shall speak no more, save in moans; you
shall shout no more, save to implore pity from deaf ears; you shall
see no more, save scenes of horror that will chill your soul. . . .'
And speaking thus, with a voice shriller and more piercing than
that of a wounded hyena still raging against the huntsmen, she
slipped off her iridescent turquoise ring that flashed like the colors
of the rainbow, like the leaping waves at high tide which as they
roll mirror the light of the rising sun. With her finger she presses
a secret spring that raises the wondrous stone on its invisible
hinge, revealing in a golden case a formless, colorless monster
who springs up, howls, leaps, and descends, squatting, on the sorceress's breast. 'Here you are,' she declares, 'beloved Smarra, sole
object of my amorous desire, handpicked by Heaven among all its
treasures for mankind's despair. Away, I command you, charming,
delusive, or frightful phantom, torment the victim whom I have
surrendered to you; let him suffer tortures as various as those of
the hell that begot you, as cruel, as implacable as my wrath. Go,
sate yourself upon the anguish of his throbbing heart, count the
palpitations of his pulse that races and stops . . . behold his bitter
agony and suspend it only to begin it anew. . . . In return for this,
loyal slave of love, you may at the flight of dreams return to your
mistress's fragrant pillow and clasp in your loving arms the queen
of nocturnal terror. . . .' She speaks, and the monster springs from
her scalding hand like the round quoit of the discus thrower, spins
round in the air as swiftly as ships' flares, spreads his oddly scal-
loped wings, soars, descends, swells, contracts, and—gleeful, misshapen dwarf whose nails, sharper than steel, can penetrate flesh
without tearing it, and suck a man's blood like insidious leeches—
fastens upon my heart, bloats and swells, lifts his enormous head
to guffaw. Stricken with terror, my eyes cast about in vain for
some object to reassure me; a thousand demons of the night escort the frightful demon of the turquoise ring: stunted women
with drunken stares, red and violet serpents whose mouths dart
flames, lizards lifting their humanoid faces from a lake of slime
and blood, heads newly severed by the soldier's axe, but which
stare at me with living eyes and bound away on reptile toes. . . .

"Since that fatal night, O Lucius, I have known no nights of
peace. The young maidens' perfumed couch, opening only onto
sensuous reveries, the roving tent of the traveler, pitched every

night under a different tree, the very sanctuary of the temple is an unsafe haven from the demons of the night. Scarcely have my eyelids closed, weary of fighting dreaded sleep, when all the monsters are there, just as when I saw them leaping with Smarra from Méroé's magic ring. They run in a circle around me, deafen me with their cries, frighten me with their lust, and defile my quivering lips with their harpies' caresses. Méroé takes the lead and soars above them, loosening her long hair from which flash sparks of pale blue. Only yesterday . . . She was much taller than she had once seemed to me. . . . The figure and features were the same, yet beneath their seductive mien I discerned with fright, as through a thin, transparent gauze, the sorceress's leaden-hued complexion and sulphur-colored limbs: her hollow, staring eyes were shot with blood, tears of blood furrowed her sunken cheeks, and her hand, as she brandished it in space, left a bloody trace imprinted in the air. . . .

"'Come,' she said, scarcely brushing me with a gesture of her finger, which would have annihilated me had it touched me, 'come visit the dominion I accord to my spouse, for I wish you to know all the realms of terror and despair. . . .' And speaking thus, she flew before me, her feet barely off the ground, fluttering up and down like the flame of a guttering torch. Oh, frightful in every way was the road down which we sped! The sorceress herself seemed avid to reach the end of it! Imagine the sepulchral vault where they pile the remnants of all their innocent victims of sacrifice, where among the most mangled of these remains there is not one that has not retained a voice, moans, and tears! . . . Imagine living, moving walls closing in before you from both sides, and slowly enveloping all your limbs in a narrow, icy prison. . . . Your constricted chest shudders and heaves, in the effort to inhale life-giving air amid the dust of ruins, the smoke of torches, the dampness of catacombs, the poisonous exhalations of the dead . . . and all the demons of the night are screeching, hissing, howling, or roaring into your terrified ears: 'You will never breathe again!'

"And as I walked, an insect a thousand times smaller than that whose impuissant tooth attacks the delicate rose petal, a miserable atom that advances but one step in a thousand years upon the celestial sphere whose surface is a thousand times harder than diamond . . . it too walked onward, and the stubborn trace of its plodding footsteps had divided that immutable globe at its axis.

"After traveling—so rapid was our flight—a distance for which human languages have no expression, I saw several rays of white light flash from an aperture, as near as the most distant star. Eagerly, Méroé darted off; I followed her, swept on by an irresistible power. The path down which we had come, indistinguishable as the void and endless as eternity, had just closed behind me, so irrevocably as to defy human endurance. Already between us and Larissa there stretched the remains of countless worlds that had preceded our own in the trials of creation, since the beginning of time—most of which exceed the earth no less in immensity than the earth exceeds, in its prodigious expanse, the invisible nest of a gnat. The cavernous doorway which received us, or rather drew us, out of this abyss opened onto a horizonless, barren field. In a remote corner of the sky, one could barely distinguish the vague outline of a dark, motionless star, more motionless than air and darker than the gloom reigning in this desolate wasteland. It was the corpse of the most ancient sun, lying in the shadowy depths of the firmament like a sunken vessel in a lake swollen with melted snow. The pale light I had just seen did not emanate from there. It would appear to have no origin and to be a mere shade of the night, unless it came from the conflagration of some distant world, the ashes of which were burning still.

"Then—can you believe it—came all the sorceresses of Thessaly, escorted by those gnomes of the earth who work in the mines, who have coppery faces and hair as blue as silver in the forge, and by strangely colored, long-legged salamanders with flattened, oar-like tails, who emerge nimbly from the flames like black lizards from a fiery dust; they were followed by the Aspioles,[27] whose so frail, so slender bodies are surmounted by misshapen yet smiling heads, and who sway upon the stalks of their spindly, hollow legs like dry straw stirred by the wind; the Achrones,[28] who have no limbs, no voice, no face, no age, and who, weeping, leap about upon the moaning earth like goatskins filled with air; the Psylles,[29] who suck bitter venom and who, avid for poison, dance round in a circle, hissing shrilly so as to arouse the serpents, to awaken them in their hidden sanctuary, in the serpents' winding abode. And there were even the Morphoses[30] whom you have loved so well, who are as beautiful as Psyche, who frolic like the Graces, who weave harmonies like the Muses, and whose seductive glance, more penetrating and more deadly than the viper's tooth, will set your blood on fire and boil the marrow within your charred bones. You have surely seen them, wrapped in their purple shrouds, trailing clouds more brilliant than the East, more fragrant than Arabian incense, more melodious than the first sigh of a virgin melted by love—whose intoxicating vapor transfixes the soul so as to destroy it. Now their eyes send forth moist flames that charm and consume, now they bow their heads with unrivaled grace, entreating your naive confidence with a tender smile— the smile of a treacherous living mask that conceals the thrill of crime and the horror of death. How shall I tell you? Borne along by the whirlwind of spirits that floated like a cloud,—like the blood-red smoke descending from a burning city, —like the liquid lava that flows, weaving its fiery streams upon a landscape of ashes . . . I came . . . I came. . . . All the tombs were unsealed . . . all the dead were exhumed . . . all the ghouls,[31] pale, eager, ravenous, were at hand; they smashed the boards of the coffins, rent the sacred garments, the last garments of the corpse, divided the hideous remains with the most ghastly delight, and, with an irresistible hand, for I was, alas! as helpless and feeble as an infant in its cradle, they forced me to join them . . . O terror! . . . in their execrable feast! . . ."

With these words, Polémon raised himself upon his bed, and trembling, frantic, his hair standing on end, and with a fixed and frightful gaze, he called to us in an inhuman voice. But already the airs of Myrthé's harp were filling the air; the demons were appeased, the silence was as serene as the thoughts of an innocent man who drifts into slumber on the eve of his sentence. Polémon was sleeping peacefully to the sweet sounds of Myrthé's harp.

EPODE

Ergo exercentur poenis, veterumque malorum
Supplicia expendunt; aliae panduntur inanes
Suspensae ad ventos, aliis sub gurgite vasto
Infectum eluitur scelus, aut exuritur igni.
  Virgil[32]

. . . 'tis a custom with him
I'th'afternoon to sleep: there thou mayst brain him,
Having first seized his books: or with a log

Batter his skull, or paunch him with a stake,
Or cut his wezand with thy knife . . .
Shakespeare[33]

The vapors of wine and pleasure had made me giddy, and I
could not help but see the ghosts of Polémon's imagination chasing each other in the dimmer recesses of the banquet hall. He had
already fallen into a deep sleep upon the flower-strewn bed, beside his overturned cup, and my young slaves, overcome by a
sweeter fatigue, had let their heavy heads sink down upon their
harps. Myrthé's golden tresses fell across her face like a long veil
amid the paler gold of the harp strings, and her gentle breath,
passing over the tuneful strings as she slept, produced an indescribably voluptuous tone that died away in my ear. Yet the
ghosts had not disappeared; they were still dancing in the shadows of the columns and in the smoke of the torches. Weary of the
specious magic of wine, I drew the fresh branches of protective
ivy over my head, and forcibly shut my eyes to the painful illusions of the light. Then I heard a strange noise, in which I could
distinguish voices alternately grave and menacing or insulting and
ironic. One of them was tediously reciting to me some verses of a
scene from Aeschylus;[34] another, the last advice that my grandfather had given me on his deathbed; now and then, like a gust of
wind whistling through dead branches and dry leaves in a storm,
I heard someone close to me break out in laughter, and felt his
breath upon my cheek before he moved away, still laughing. This
vision was followed by others, strange and horrible. I seemed to
discern, through a cloud of blood, all the objects that I had last
seen before closing my eyes: they hovered before me, taunting me
with horrible gestures and accusatory moans. Polémon, still lying
next to his empty cup, and Myrthé, still leaning over her idle
harp, were uttering furious imprecations against me, calling me to
account for I know not what murder. Just as I was sitting up to
answer them, extending my arms across the couch wet with copi-
ous libations of liqueurs and perfumes, something cold chilled the
joints of my trembling hands: it was an iron fetter, which at that
very moment fell across my numb feet, and I found myself standing between two close ranks of pale-faced soldiers, whose glowing
spears were like a long line of candelabra. Then I began to walk,
my eyes searching the sky for the migrating dove, that I might at

least, before the dreadful moment that I knew awaited me, confide to her the secret of a hidden love that she could one day reveal, as she flew over a pretty white house near the bay of Corcyra; but the dove was weeping upon her nest, because the vulture had just stolen the most precious of her brood, and I stumbled painfully on toward the goal of this tragic procession, amid a dreadful murmur of joy that ran through the crowd as I passed—the murmur of the gaping populace, starved for pain, whose bloodthirsty curiosity laps up from afar all the victim's tears that will be thrown them by the executioner.

"There he is," they were all crying, "there he is! . . ."

"I saw him on a battlefield," said an old soldier, "but he was not pale as a ghost then, and he seemed brave in combat."

"How puny he is, that Lucius whom they made out to be an Achilles or a Hercules!" added a dwarf whom I had not noticed among the others. "It is terror, no doubt, that saps his strength and makes his knees buckle."

"Are you quite sure that a human heart could have housed such ferocity?" said an old man with white hair, whose suspicion chilled my blood. He resembled my father.

"It is he!" came the voice of a woman whose features expressed such gentleness. . . . "He!" she repeated, shielding her eyes from me in horror with her veil. . . . "The murderer of Polémon and the fair Myrthé! . . ."

"I think the monster is staring at me," said a woman of the people. "Shut your lizard's eye, viper, may Heaven curse you!"

Meanwhile the towers, the roads, the entire city was vanishing behind me like a port abandoned by an adventurous vessel bound for the open sea. There remained only a splendid, vast, symmetrical, newly built square filled with stately edifices and thronged with citizens of all classes, who were sacrificing their duties to the lure of piquant pleasure. The windows were filled with avid onlookers, among whom one could see young men contending with their mothers or their mistresses for a turn at the narrow openings. The obelisks rising above fountains, the bricklayers' unsteady scaffolds, the flimsy stages of wandering players, all held spectators. Men breathless with impatience and lust hung from the cornices of buildings and, clinging with their knees to the angles of the walls, repeated with inordinate glee, "There he is!" A little girl in a crumpled blue tunic, with spangles in her blond hair and wild eyes portending madness, was singing the story of my travail. She was proclaiming my death and the confession of my heinous deeds, and her cruel lament revealed to my horrified soul such mysteries of crime as crime itself could not conceive. The focus of the whole scene was myself, another man who accompanied me, and some planks raised on posts, upon which carpenters had placed a crude seat and a poorly squared block of wood projecting several feet beyond. I climbed up a dozen steps and sat down; I cast my eyes over the crowd, hoping to glimpse some kindly face, to find, in the guarded glance of an ignominious farewell, some flicker of hope or sorrow; but I saw only Myrthé who was awakening upon her harp and touching it laughingly, only Polémon who was lifting his empty cup and, half giddy with the vapors of wine, filling it again with an unsteady hand. Calmer now, I offered my head to the cold, keen sword of the officer of death. Never did such a chill run through a human spine; it was as piercing as the last kiss that fever bestows upon the neck of a dying man, as sharp as burnished steel, as consuming as melted lead. I was roused from this agony only by a dreadful commotion: my head had fallen. . . . It had bounced upon the hideous parvis of the scaffold, and just as it was about to fall, battered and bruised, into the hands of the children, the pretty children of Larissa, who play with dead men's skulls, it had fastened its mouth to a jutting plank, and as if with teeth of iron, was biting into it in furious agony. From there my eyes turned toward the crowd, which was dispersing, silent but assuaged. A man had just died before the people. They drifted off, with murmurs of admiration for the one who had not missed his stroke, and horror for the murderer of Polémon and the fair Myrthé.

"Myrthé! Myrthé!" I bellowed, without letting go of my board.

"Lucius! Lucius!" she replied, half-drowsing, "will you never sleep in peace when you have drunk one too many! May the infernal gods forgive you—trouble my rest no more. I would sooner sleep to the sound of my father's hammer, beating copper in his shop, than among the nocturnal terrors of your palace."

And as she spoke, I stubbornly bit down upon the wood, moistened with my freshly shed blood, and I rejoiced to feel the dark wings of Death slowly unfurling beneath my truncated neck. All the bats of dusk were brushing caressingly past me, calling,

"Take wing! . . ." and with an effort, I began to flap the tattered shreds that barely supported me. But I suddenly experienced a comforting illusion. Ten times I beat upon the lugubrious planks with the nearly lifeless membrane that I dragged alongside me like the pliant legs of a reptile as it rolls on the sandy brink of a spring; ten times I rebounded, testing my skill, into the dank fog. How black and chill it was! And how bleak are the deserts of darkness! I ascended at last to the height of the tallest buildings, and circled above the solitary platform, the platform that my lips had brushed in death with a smile and a kiss of farewell. All the onlookers had disappeared, all the noises had ceased, all the stars were shrouded, all the lights had faded away. The air was still, the sky a lusterless sea-green, dull and cold as sheet iron. Nothing remained upon the earth of what I had seen or imagined, and my soul, filled with terror at being alive, shrank horrified from a solitude more vast, a darkness more profound, than the solitude and darkness of the void. But I did not find the haven I sought. I soared like the night butterfly that has thrown off its mysterious swaddling clothes to display the futile splendor of its purple, blue, and gold finery. If it spies from afar the casement of the scholar, who sits writing long into the night by the light of a dim lamp, or that of a young wife whose husband has tarried at the hunt, it flies up, endeavors to alight, flutters against the window pane, flies off, returns, spins, buzzes, and falls, leaving the dust of its delicate wings upon the transparent surface. So I, with the sad wings bequeathed me by death, beat upon the inexorable vault of the sky which answered with only a hollow echo; I drifted down, circling round the solitary platform, the platform that my lips had brushed in death with a smile and a kiss of farewell. It was no longer empty. Another man had just laid his head there; it was thrown back, and on his neck I could see the trace of the wound, the triangular scar left by the head of the spear which took Polémon from me at the siege of Corinth. His flowing hair fell in golden curls around the bloody block: but Polémon, calm and with lowered eyelids, appeared to be sleeping peacefully. A sort of smile, which was not one of terror, played upon his radiant lips, and seemed to be calling for more of Myrthé's songs or Thélaïre's caresses. In the pale light which had begun to spread through my palace, I could make out the still shadowy forms of columns and corridors where in the night I had seen the evil spirits assemble for their dance of death. I looked about for Myrthé, but she had abandoned her harp, and, motionless between Thélaïre and Théis, was gazing darkly, pitilessly upon the sleeping warrior. Suddenly into their midst burst Méroé: the golden asp that she had loosed from her arm slithered, hissing, beneath the archways; the rumble of the spinning *rhombus* resounded in the air; Smarra, summoned at the flight of dreams, was there to claim his promised reward from the queen of nocturnal terror, and hovered close to her, quivering with a hideous love, and fluttering his wings so rapidly that they made scarcely a blur in the pellucid air. Théis, Thélaïre, and Myrthé were dancing wildly and uttering howls of glee. Near me, horrible white-haired children with wrinkled faces and luster-less eyes amused themselves by tying me to my bed with the deli-cate netting of the spider that casts its perfidious web between two walls to snare a poor stray butterfly. Some of them gathered up this silky white fiber, so light that it slips from the fairies' won-drous spindle, and let it fall with all the weight of a leaden chain upon my worn and aching limbs. "Get up," they said, laughing brazenly, and rained blows upon my constricted chest with a straw, broken in the form of a flail, that they had stolen from the sheaf of a gleaner. Meanwhile I tried to free my hands from the fragile bonds which held them fast—my hands which had often meted out the blows of a practiced pugilist at the cruel Thessalian games, and these formidable hands that had once worn a deadly iron cestus grew limp before the unarmed breast of a fantastical dwarf, like the storm-battered sponge at the foot of a stolid rock pounded by the sea since the dawn of time. Thus does that many-colored globe, that dazzling, evanescent plaything set in flight by the breath of a child, vanish without a trace as it floats in mid-air.

Blood was gushing from Polémon's scar, and Méroé, drunk with lustful pleasure, was holding aloft before her avid compan-ions the mangled heart she had just snatched from the soldier's breast. She vied for the torn remains with the maidens of Larissa, thirsty for blood. Smarra, with rapidly beating wings and threat-ening hisses, shielded the dreadful booty for the queen of noc-turnal terror. Scarcely did he pause to caress Polémon's bloody heart, so as to quench his own thirst, with the end of his probos-cis that spiraled out like a spring; and Méroé, beautiful Méroé, smiled at his love and vigilance.

The bonds that held me had finally given way; and I landed

on my feet, awake, at the foot of Polémon's bed, while far from
me fled all the demons, all the sorceresses, and all the illusions
of the night. My very palace, and the young slaves who adorned
it—fleeting fortune of dreams—had given way to the tent of a
wounded warrior beneath the walls of Corinth, and to the dismal
procession of the officers of death. The torches of mourning were
beginning to pale before the rays of the rising sun; the sorrowful
chants were beginning to echo beneath the subterranean vaults
of the tomb. And Polémon . . . O despair! My trembling hand
searched his breast in vain for the faintest movement. His heart
beat no more. His breast was empty.

EPILOGUE

Hic umbrarum tenui stridore volantum
Flebilis auditur questus, simulacra coloni
Pallida, defunctasque vident migrare figuras.
> *Claudius* [35]

. . . I never may believe
These antic fables, nor these fairy toys.
Lovers and madmen have such seething brains,
Such shaping fantasies, that apprehend
More than cool reason ever comprehends.
> *Shakespeare* [36]

"Ah, who will come to break their swords? Who will stanch
my brother's blood and call him back to life? Oh, what have I
come here to find? Eternal sorrow! Larissa, Thessaly, Tempe, ab-
horred waters of the Peneus! O Polémon, dear Polémon! . . ."

"What are you saying, in the name of our good angel, why do
you speak of swords and blood? Who makes you keep stammering confused words and uttering stifled moans like a traveler murdered in his sleep and awakened by death? . . . Lorenzo, my dear
Lorenzo! . . ."

"Lisidis, Lisidis, is it you who spoke? Indeed I thought I heard
your voice, and the shades seemed to recede. Why did you leave
me while, in my palace at Larissa, Polémon was breathing his last
before my eyes, among the sorceresses dancing with glee? See,
see how they dance with glee. . . ."

"Alas, I know nothing of Polémon, nor Larissa, nor the horrible glee of the sorceresses of Thessaly. I know only Lorenzo, my dear Lorenzo. It was yesterday—have you so soon forgotten?—that marked our first week of marriage. . . . Look, look at the daylight, at Arona, at the lake and sky of Lombardy . . ."

"Shadowy figures come and go, angry and menacing; they speak of Lisidis, of a pretty little house at the water's edge, and of a dream I dreamed upon a distant shore. . . . They are swelling, menacing, calling. . . ."

"With what new reproach would you torment me, thankless and jealous heart? Ah, well I know that you trifle with my pain, and seek only to excuse some infidelity or find a strange pretext for a rift planned in advance. . . . I will speak to you no more."

"Where is Théis, where is Myrthé, where are the harps of Thessaly? Lisidis, Lisidis, if I have not imagined your voice, your sweet voice, you must be here, close by. . . . You alone can deliver me from Méroé's vengeful magic. . . . Deliver me from Théis, from Myrthé, even from Thélaïre. . . ."

"It is you, cruel one, who carry revenge too far, and who would punish me for dancing too long with another at the ball on Isola Bella; but if he had dared to talk to me of love, if he had talked to me of love . . ."

"By Saint Charles of Arona,[37] may God forever keep him from that! . . . Could it be, my Lisidis, that we returned from Isola Bella to the sweet sound of your guitar, returned to our pretty house at Arona,—from Larissa, from Thessaly, to the sweet sound of your harp and the waters of the Peneus?"

"Leave Thessaly, Lorenzo, awake! . . . See the rays of the rising sun striking the colossal head of Saint Charles. Listen to the sound of the waves lapping on the shore, below our little house in Arona. Inhale the morning breezes that carry upon their cool wings all the fragrances of the islands and gardens, all the murmurs of the newborn day. The Peneus flows far from here."

"You will never know what I suffered last night upon its shores. May that river be accursed by nature, and cursed, too, be the deadly malady that led my soul astray during hours longer than life, in scenes of false delights and cruel terrors! . . . It has made my hair show ten years of added age!"

"I swear it is not white . . . but next time I shall be more careful; I shall clasp one of my hands in yours, and slip the other among your curls; all night I shall hang on the breath from your lips, and fight against deep sleep so that I might wake you before the evil that torments you can reach your heart. . . . Are you sleeping?"

1 8 2 1

Translated by Joan C. Kessler

For a recent French edition of this work, see Charles Nodier, *Smarra, ou Les Démons de la nuit*, in *Contes* (Paris: Editions Garnier Frères, 1961).

Honoré de Balzac

THE RED INN

To Monsieur le Marquis de Custine[1]

S ome years ago—I forget exactly when—a Parisian banker,
who had very extensive business relations in Germany, was
holding a dinner party in honor of one of those friends whom
merchants acquire here and there through correspondence, although they may personally have never met. This friend, the
head of some prominent firm in Nuremberg, was a stout, hearty
German, a man of taste and erudition, above all a man of the
pipe, who had a broad, handsome Nuremberg face and an ample,
square forehead, embellished with a few stray fair hairs. He was
the very image of the children of that pure and noble Germany,
so prolific of honorable natures, and whose peaceable instincts
have never failed them, even after seven invasions. The stranger
laughed unaffectedly, listened attentively, and drank considerably,
appearing perhaps quite as fond of the French champagne as of
the pale wines of Johannisberg.[2] His name was Hermann, like almost all the Germans in literature. Like a man who does not know
how to do anything lightly, he sat solidly in his chair at the banker's table, eating with that Teutonic appetite which is so renowned
in Europe, and bidding a conscientious farewell to the cuisine of
the great Carême.[3]

In honor of his guest, the master of the house had invited
several intimate friends, capitalists or merchants, as well as a
few attractive and congenial women, whose amiable chatter and
straightforward air accorded well with German cordiality. Truly, if
you could have seen, as I had the pleasure of seeing, this jovial

30

assemblage of people who had drawn in their commercial claws to speculate upon the pleasures of life, you would not have found it in you to begrudge usurious rates of interest or to curse bankruptcies. Man cannot always be doing evil. Even pirates have their hours of repose, when, upon their sinister vessel, you might fancy yourself rocking as gently as in a swing.

"Before the evening's out, I hope that Monsieur Hermann will tell us another spine-chilling German tale."

These words were uttered over dessert by a pale, fair-haired young woman who had doubtless read the tales of Hoffmann and the novels of Sir Walter Scott. She was the banker's only daughter, a charming young creature who was completing her education at the *Gymnase dramatique*,[4] and who was enthusiastic about the plays they performed there. The dinner guests were all happily basking in the state of lethargy and silence that ensues after a splendid meal, when we have rather overestimated our powers of digestion. Each guest was leaning back in his chair, and with his wrist resting lightly on the table edge, playing idly with the gilded blade of his dessert knife. When a dinner has reached this ebb, some fiddle with a pear seed, others roll a crumb between thumb and forefinger, lovers shape unintelligible initials with their fruit rinds, and misers count the pits on their plates, arranging them as a playwright does his walk-ons backstage. These are minor gastronomical pleasures which Brillat-Savarin[5] has not noted in his book, exhaustive as he may otherwise be.

The servants had disappeared. The dessert was like a squadron after a battle, in disarray, pillaged, desolate. The dishes were strewn across the table, despite the efforts of the mistress of the house to keep them in order. Some of the guests stared at the Swiss landscapes symmetrically arranged on the gray walls of the dining room. Not one of them was bored. We have never known a man to be prey to ennui during the digestion of a good dinner. Rather, one is content to bask in an indefinable calm, a happy medium between the reverie of the thinker and the satisfaction of the ruminating beasts, which might be termed the physical melancholy of gastronomy.

So the party turned spontaneously toward the good German, all delighted to have a tale to listen to, even if it should be a dull one. During this blessed pause, the voice of a storyteller is always soothing to our languid senses and conducive to their passive pleasure. As a seeker after pictorial effect, I gazed admiringly at these faces brightened with smiles, illumined by candles, and flushed from the good meal; their various expressions yielded striking effects amid the candelabra, the vessels of porcelain, the fruit and the crystal.

My imagination was suddenly captured by the face of the guest seated just opposite me. He was a man of medium stature, rather stout, jovial-looking, with the bearing and manners of a stockbroker, and who appeared to have been endowed with no more than a very ordinary mind. Up to that point I had not noticed him, but at that moment his face, doubtless obscured by a deceptive light, seemed to me to have undergone a transformation; it had taken on an ashen hue and was streaked with purple. One might have taken it for the cadaverous head of a man in his death agony. Motionless as the painted figures in a diorama,[6] he was staring dazedly at the sparkling facets of a crystal decanter stopper, but unheeding, appeared sunk in some fantastical vision of past or future. When I had lengthily scrutinized this dubious-looking countenance, I began to ponder: "Is he ill? Has he drunk too much wine? Has he been ruined by a drop in the market? Is he scheming to defraud his creditors?"

"Look!" I remarked to the lady next to me, as I drew her attention to the stranger's face. "Would you not say that was a budding bankruptcy?"

"Oh, no," she replied, "he would be more cheerful." Then, with a graceful toss of the head, she added, "If that man ever goes bankrupt, I'll shout it from the rooftops myself! He owns a million in real estate! He's an interesting character; he used to be a contractor to the imperial armies. He married a second time as a business speculation, but he makes his wife very happy nonetheless. He has a pretty daughter whom for a long time he refused to recognize; but when his son was killed tragically in a duel, he was forced to accept her, since he could not hope to have any more children. So all at once the poor girl became one of the richest heiresses in Paris. The loss of his only son threw the dear man into bitter grief, which from time to time still reappears."

At that moment the contractor raised his eyes and looked at me; so dark and troubled was his gaze that it made me shudder. Surely an entire lifetime was contained within that glance. But then suddenly his face grew cheerful; he reached for the crystal stopper, placed it, with an involuntary motion, in a carafe of water beside his plate, and turned toward Monsieur Hermann with a smile. This man, positively beaming with the pleasures of digestion, had, no doubt, scarcely an idea in his head, and was thinking of nothing at all. So I was somewhat ashamed of expending my divinatory talent upon the *anima vili*[7] of a thick-headed financier. While I was wasting my time in phrenological observations, the good German had fortified his nose with a pinch of snuff and was beginning his story. I would be hard-pressed to repeat it in his own words, with his frequent interruptions and wordy digressions. So I have written it down in my own style, leaving out the Nuremberger's errors, and helping myself to whatever is poetic and interesting in it, with the modesty of those writers who forget to add to their title pages: *translated from the German.*

THE IDEA AND THE DEED

"Toward the end of *Vendémiaire*, in the year VII of the Republican era, which in the current denomination corresponds to October 20, 1799,[8] two young men, who had set out that morning from Bonn, were approaching at nightfall the outskirts of Andernach, a little town on the left bank of the Rhine, a few leagues from Coblenz. The French army, commanded by General Augereau,[9] was at that time engaged in maneuvers within sight of the Austrians, who occupied the right bank of the river. The headquarters of the Republican division were at Coblenz, and one of the demi-brigades belonging to Augereau's corps was stationed at Andernach.

"The two travelers were Frenchmen. By their blue and white uniforms with red velvet trimmings, their sabres, and especially their caps, covered with green oilcloth and adorned with a tricolor plume, even the German peasants would have recognized them as military surgeons, men of science and merit who were widely esteemed not only within their own army but also in the territories occupied by our troops. At that time many sons of good families, forced by General Jourdan's conscription law to abandon their medical studies, had naturally preferred to continue them on the field of battle rather than to enter into compulsory service within the ranks, a life little in keeping with their early education and their peaceable ambitions. Men of science, peace-

loving and eager to serve, these young people were able to perform some good amid so much misery, and found kindred spirits
among the learned elite of the various regions overrun by the
ruthless civilization of the Republic.

"Equipped with road maps and with assistant-surgeons' com-
missions signed by Coste and Bernadotte, these two young men
were on their way to join the demi-brigade to which they were
attached. Both belonged to middle-class families of Beauvais, only
moderately well-to-do, but whose traditions of gentle breeding
and provincial loyalty had been part of their birthright. Drawn to
the theater of war, by a curiosity altogether natural to the young,
before the time designated for entrance into their duties, they had
traveled by stagecoach as far as Strasbourg. Although maternal
prudence had entrusted them with no more than a meager sum,
they felt rich in the few louis they possessed, a veritable treasure
at a time when assignats [10] had reached the lowest point of depre-
ciation and when gold was at a high premium.

"The two assistant surgeons, who were no more than twenty
years of age, entered into the romance of their situation with all
the enthusiasm of youth. Between Strasbourg and Bonn, they had
toured the Electorate [11] and the banks of the Rhine in the capacity
of artists, philosophers, and observers. At that age, when we are
destined for a career of science, we are truly multiple beings. Even
when traveling or making love, an assistant surgeon should be
laying the foundations of his future fame and fortune. The two
young men had thus given themselves up to the profound awe
which every educated man feels upon beholding the banks of the
Rhine and the Swabian landscape, [12] between Mainz and Cologne—a vigorous, fertile land, exceedingly hilly, brimming with
reminders of a feudal age, richly verdant, but everywhere scarred
by fire and sword. Louis XIV and Turenne [13] have turned that
beautiful country to ashes. Here and there, scattered ruins bear
witness to the pride, or perhaps the foresight, of the king of Versailles, who wrought destruction upon the magnificent castles
which once adorned this part of Germany. To glimpse this marvelous land, covered with forests, and in which the picturesque
charm of the Middle Ages abounds, albeit in ruins, is to begin to
comprehend the genius of the German mind, with its penchant
for mysticism and reverie.

"The two friends had a twofold purpose in visiting Bonn,

work and pleasure. The main hospital of the Gallo-Batavian army
and of Augereau's division was located in the Elector's palace itself.
The new assistant surgeons had stopped there to visit comrades,
to present letters of recommendation to their chiefs, and to famil-
iarize themselves with the rudiments of their new profession. Yet
also, there as elsewhere, they discarded some of those long-held
prejudices that make us prize exclusively the natural and architectural beauties of our native land. They marveled at the sight of the
marble columns that adorn the Electoral palace, admired the grandeur of German architecture, and discovered new treasures, ancient and modern, at every turn.

"Now and then, in the course of their wanderings toward Andernach, their path would lead them to the peak of an especially
high granite mountain. There, through a clearing in the forest,
through a cleft in the rocks, they would catch a glimpse of the
Rhine, framed by sandstone cliffs or festooned with luxuriant
vegetation. The valleys, the paths, the trees exuded that autumnal
aroma that induces one to reverie; the treetops were turning
golden, taking on the warm, brown hues of old age; the leaves
were falling, but the sky was still a lovely blue, and the dry roads
stood out like yellow lines in the landscape, lit by the slanting
rays of the setting sun.

"Half a league from Andernach, the two friends walked along
amid a silence as profound as if there were no war ravaging that
beautiful land, following a goat trail along the cliff walls of bluish
granite that tower above the swirling waters of the Rhine. Soon
they descended one of the sides of the ravine toward the little
town which, nestling coyly on the river bank, offers a quaint harbor for boatmen.

"'Germany is a beautiful country!' cried one of the two young
men, Prosper Magnan by name, as he caught sight of the painted
houses of Andernach, clustered together like eggs in a basket,
separated by trees and flower gardens. Then he gazed admiringly
for a moment at the high-pitched roofs with their projecting
beams, the balconies and wooden staircases of a host of peaceful dwellings, and the boats in the harbor, gently rocked by the
waves. . . .'"

At the moment when Monsieur Hermann uttered the name of
Prosper Magnan, the contractor seized the decanter, poured some
water into his glass, and emptied it with one gulp. The motion

having attracted my attention, I thought I detected a slight trembling in his hands and moisture on his brow.

"What is the former contractor's name?" I inquired of my gracious neighbor.

"Taillefer," she replied.

"Are you feeling ill?" I exclaimed, seeing this singular individual turn pale.

"Not at all," he answered, thanking me with a courteous gesture. "I am listening," he added, with a nod to the other guests, for all eyes were suddenly upon him.

"I have forgotten," said Monsieur Hermann, "the other young man's name. But I know from what Prosper Magnan later told me that his companion was dark, rather thin, and of a jolly disposition. If you have no objection, I will call him Wilhelm,[14] to lend greater clarity to my tale."

And the good German resumed his narrative after having thus—without the slightest regard for romanticism and local color—baptized the French assistant surgeon with a German name.

"When the two young men reached Andernach, it was past nightfall. Concluding that they would lose too much time in seeking out their superiors, making themselves known, and obtaining billets in a town already crowded with soldiers, they had decided to spend their last night of freedom at an inn just outside the town. They had caught a glimpse of it earlier, from the top of the cliffs, and had admired its rich coloring, heightened by the glow of the setting sun. Painted entirely in red, this inn produced a striking effect in the landscape, whether standing out against the general background of the town, or contrasting its crimson curtain with the green shades of foliage, its brilliant hue with the grayish tones of the water. Since time immemorial, the house owed its name to the exterior decoration which, doubtless, had been imposed upon it by the whim of its builder. A quite natural mercantile superstition among the various owners of the establishment, which had a reputation among the Rhenish boatmen, had caused this custom to be scrupulously preserved.

"At the sound of horses' hoofs, the proprietor of the Red Inn appeared upon the threshold. 'Good heavens, gentlemen!' he cried, 'a little later and you would have to sleep outside, like the rest of your fellow countrymen encamped at the other end of Andernach. Every room in my inn is full! If you want to sleep in a good bed, I have only my own room to offer you. As for your horses, I'll go and put down some hay for them in a corner of the yard. My stable is full of Christians today. . . . —You gentlemen are from France?' he added after a brief pause.

"'From Bonn,' cried Prosper. 'And we have eaten nothing since this morning.'

"'Oh, as to the food!' said the innkeeper, wagging his head. 'Wedding parties come to the Red Inn from ten leagues around! You shall have a meal fit for a prince—fish from the Rhine! I need say no more.'

"Having entrusted their tired horses to the care of their host, who was shouting in vain for his servants, the assistant surgeons entered the public room of the inn. The thick clouds of white smoke, discharged from a multitude of pipes, made it at first impossible for them to distinguish the people they were to have as company; but when they had taken their seats at a table, with the pragmatic patience of philosophical travelers who know when it is futile to make a fuss, they made out through the tobacco fumes the inevitable accessories of a German inn: stove, clock, tables, beer mugs and long pipes, an assortment of motley faces, Jews, Germans, a few rugged-looking boatmen. The epaulettes of several French officers glittered in the smoky haze, and there was a continual clinking of spurs and sabres upon the tiled floor. Some of the guests were playing cards, some were arguing, others were sitting in silence, eating, drinking, or strolling about. A stout little woman with black velvet cap, braided hair, silver-trimmed blue bodice, ball of wool, and keys on a silver clasp, all the earmarks of the typical mistress of a German inn—reproduced too exactly in a host of engravings to warrant further description—the innkeeper's wife, as I say, succeeded with remarkable skill in both provoking and allaying the impatience of the two friends.

"Gradually the hubbub abated, the guests retired to bed, and the cloud of tobacco smoke melted away. By the time the table had been laid for the assistant surgeons, and the classic Rhine carp had been laid before them, the clock was striking eleven, and the room was empty. Amid the silence of the night they could faintly hear the horses eating or stamping their hoofs, the murmur of the Rhine, and all of those vague indefinable sounds that fill a crowded inn when everyone is preparing for bed. Doors and windows opened and closed, there was an indistinct murmur of voices, and now and then the sound of people calling to one another from inside their rooms. During this interval of silence and commotion, the two Frenchmen—as well as their host, who was busy extolling Andernach, the meal, his Rhine wine, the republican army, and his wife—listened with some interest to the hoarse shouts of boatmen and the clatter of a boat drawing alongside the quay. The innkeeper, doubtless familiar with the boatmen's guttural inflections, hurried out. He soon returned, accompanied by a stout little man behind whom walked two boatmen carrying a heavy valise and several bundles. When these were deposited on the floor, the little man picked up his valise himself and kept it beside him as he seated himself without ceremony at the table, opposite the assistant surgeons.

"'You can sleep on board,' he told the boatmen. 'The inn is full. All things considered, that is the best plan.'

"'Monsieur,' said the host to the newcomer, 'here is all the food I have left. And he pointed to the supper that had been served to the two Frenchmen. 'I haven't a crust of bread, not so much as a bone.'

"'And no sauerkraut?'

"'Not so much as would fill my wife's thimble! As I had the honor of telling you just now, the only bed I can offer you is the chair you're sitting in, and no other room but this one.' At these words, the little man cast an anxious glance at the innkeeper, the room, and the two Frenchmen. In his eyes caution and alarm were equally discernible.

"At this point I ought to mention," said Monsieur Hermann, interrupting himself, "that we never found out either the stranger's real name or his history, but his papers showed that he came from Aix-la-Chapelle; he had taken the name of Walhenfer, and owned a rather sizable pin factory near Neuwied. Like all the other manufacturers of that region, he wore a plain cloth frock coat, a waistcoat and breeches of dark green velvet, top boots, and a wide leather belt. His face was perfectly round, his manner straightforward and cordial, but that evening he could not entirely disguise certain secret apprehensions, perhaps cruel anxieties. The innkeeper has always maintained that this German merchant was fleeing his country. I later learned that his factory had been destroyed by fire in one of those accidents which are unfortunately so frequent in time of war. Despite his generally anxious expression, his countenance suggested extreme good nature. He had fine features, in particular a large neck, the whiteness of which was heightened by a black cravat to which Wilhelm jokingly drew Prosper's attention. . . ."

At this point, Monsieur Taillefer drank another glass of water.

"Prosper courteously invited the merchant to share their supper, and Walhenfer accepted without ceremony, as one who was confident of being able to return the favor; he set his valise down on the floor, put his feet upon it, removed his hat, drew up his chair, and laid down his gloves, together with a pair of pistols that he carried in his belt. The host having quickly laid another cover, the three guests began to satisfy their appetite in silence. The room was so warm and the flies so numerous that Prosper asked the landlord to open the window opening onto the gate to let in some fresh air. This window was barricaded by an iron bar, the ends of which fitted into holes on either side of the window frame. For greater security, there were two bolts on each shutter. By pure chance, Prosper happened to observe how the host went about unfastening the window.

"But since I am describing the locale," said Monsieur Hermann, "I should explain the layout of the inn, since to appreciate this story one must have an exact idea of the place. The room where my three characters were sitting had two doors. One opened onto the main road to Andernach, which runs along the Rhine. There, in front of the inn, as might be expected, was a small wharf where the merchant's rented boat was moored. The other door opened onto the courtyard of the inn. This courtyard was girded by high walls and filled, for the moment, with cattle and horses, the stables being occupied by people. The main entrance had been so carefully bolted and barred that, to save time, the host had admitted the merchant and the two boatmen through the street door. Now, after opening the window at Prosper Magnan's request, he proceeded to secure the door, sliding the bars into their sockets and screwing the nuts on the bolts.

"The innkeeper's bedroom, where the two assistant surgeons were to sleep, adjoined the public room and was separated by only a thin partition from the kitchen, where the host and hostess would probably spend the night. The maidservant had just gone out to find a nook in some manger or in the corner of a hayloft. It

will be readily understood that the public room, the host's bedroom, and the kitchen were all isolated, in a sense, from the re-
mainder of the inn. In the courtyard were two large dogs, whose
deep barking indicated two very vigilant and excitable sentries.

"'What silence! And what a lovely night!' said Wilhelm, looking out at the sky, when the innkeeper had finished fastening the
door. The lapping of the waves was the only sound to be heard.

"'Messieurs,' said the merchant to the two Frenchmen, 'permit
me to offer you a bottle or two of wine to wash down the carp.
We'll relax from the exertions of the day while we drink. From the
look of you and the state of your clothes, I see that like myself
you've come a good way today.'

"The two friends accepted, and the innkeeper went out
through the kitchen door on his way to the cellar, which was evidently located beneath that part of the building. When five venerable bottles were set upon the table, his wife finished serving the
meal. She cast a hostess's glance upon the room and the dishes;
then, confident that she had made provision for all the travelers'
needs, she returned to the kitchen.

"The four companions—for the innkeeper had been invited
to partake of the wine—did not hear her go to bed; but later, during the intervals of silence between their talk, certain very pronounced snores, made more sonorous still by the hollow partition
of the loft where she slept, made the friends and especially the
innkeeper himself smile. Toward midnight, when nothing was left
on the table but crackers, cheese, dry fruit, and good wine, the
guests—in particular, the two young Frenchmen—grew loqua-
cious. They spoke of their native land, their studies, and the war.
At last the conversation grew animated. Prosper Magnan brought
tears to the fugitive merchant's eyes when, with Picardian frankness and the naiveté of a kind and affectionate soul, he imagined
what his mother was likely doing at that moment, while he was
here on the banks of the Rhine. 'I can see her now,' said he, 'saying
her bedtime prayers! I know she hasn't forgotten me, and she must
be wondering, "Where is my poor Prosper now?" But if she has
won a few sous at cards from her neighbor—from your mother,
perhaps,' he added, nudging Wilhelm's elbow—'she'll go and put
them in the big red earthen pot where she's saving up money to
buy the thirty acres enclosed within her little estate at Lescheville.
Those thirty acres are worth about sixty thousand francs, at least.

Such fine fields! Ah, if I were to own them some day, I would spend the rest of my life at Lescheville without any other ambition! How my father used to long for those thirty acres and the pretty little brook that winds along through those meadows! But he died before he could buy them. I have played there many a time!'

"'Monsieur Walhenfer, haven't you also your *hoc erat in votis?*' [15] asked Wilhelm.

"'Yes, Monsieur, yes! But it came to pass, and now . . .' He was silent, leaving his sentence unfinished.

"'As for me,' said the innkeeper, whose face had grown slightly flushed, 'last year I purchased a field that I had wanted to own for the last ten years.'

"They went on chatting as men do when their tongues have been loosened by wine, and felt for one another that passing friendship with which we are so lavish when traveling, so that when it was time to retire for the night, Wilhelm offered the merchant his bed.

"'You may accept it the more freely,' he told him, 'since I can sleep with Prosper. It will not be the first time, nor the last. You are our elder; we must honor age!'

"'Bah!' said the innkeeper, 'my wife's bed has several mattresses; you can put one on the floor.'

"And he went to shut the window, making the clatter that usually accompanies this prudent operation.

"'I accept your offer,' said the merchant. 'I confess,' he went on, lowering his voice and looking at the two friends, 'that I do so readily. My boatmen seem rather suspicious to me. For tonight I am not displeased to be in the company of two honest and decent young men, French soldiers! I have a hundred thousand francs in gold and diamonds in my bag!'

"The kind discretion with which this imprudent confidence was received by the two young men reassured the good German. The innkeeper helped his guests make one of the beds ready, and when everything was arranged as comfortably as possible, he bid them good night and went to bed.

"The merchant and the assistant surgeons joked with one another about the state of their pillows. Prosper put his instrument case, along with Wilhelm's, underneath his mattress, so as to raise it up and take the place of the bolster that was missing, just as

Walhenfer, out of precaution, was placing his bag beneath his pillow.

"'We shall both sleep on our fortune: you on your gold, I on my instrument case! It remains to be seen whether my instruments will bring me as much gold as you have made.'

"'You may hope so,' said the merchant. 'Honesty and hard work will accomplish all; only have patience.'

"Walhenfer and Wilhelm were soon asleep. Whether because his bed was too hard, or because of insomnia brought on by extreme fatigue, or perhaps owing to a fateful frame of mind, Prosper Magnan was unable to sleep. Imperceptibly, his thoughts began to take an ominous turn. He could think of nothing but the hundred thousand francs that lay beneath the merchant's pillow. For him, a hundred thousand francs was a vast and ready-made fortune. He began by parceling it out in a hundred different ways, building castles in the air as we are all so happily prone to do in the moments preceding sleep, when confused images are born in our minds and when, in the silence of the night, thought often assumes a magical potency. He gratified his mother's every wish and desire, he bought the thirty acres of meadowland, he married a young lady of Beauvais to whom the disparity of their fortunes presently forbade him to aspire. With this sum he mapped out a lifetime of felicity, and envisioned himself the happy head of a family, rich, respected in his province, and perhaps mayor of Beauvais.

"His Picardian brain took fire, and he cast about for means of turning these fictions into realities. With extraordinary ardor, he began to devise a theoretical crime. As he fantasized the death of the merchant, gold and diamonds danced before his eyes. He was bedazzled by them. His heart was pounding. The deliberation was itself, undoubtedly, a crime. Mesmerized by that mass of gold, he grew mentally intoxicated by means of sanguinary logic. He asked himself if there was really any need for that poor German to live, and imagined that he had never existed. In short, he plotted the crime in such a way as to ensure himself impunity. The opposite bank of the Rhine was occupied by the Austrians; beneath the windows lay a boat and boatmen; he could slit the man's throat, throw the body into the Rhine, escape through the window with the bag, bribe the boatmen with gold, and cross over into Austria. He went so far as to calculate the degree of skill he had acquired in the use of his surgical instruments, so as to sever the head of his victim before he could utter a cry. . . ."

Here Monsieur Taillefer wiped his forehead and drank a little more water.

"Prosper slowly got out of bed without making a sound. Certain of having awakened no one, he dressed and went into the public room; then, with that fatal intelligence that men suddenly find themselves to possess, with that willpower and poise which never fails prisoners or criminals in the execution of their schemes, he unscrewed the iron bars, slipped them from their sockets without the slightest noise, lay them against the wall, and opened the shutters, pressing the hinges to keep them from creaking. The moon, casting its pale light upon the scene, enabled him vaguely to distinguish the objects in the room where Wilhelm and Walhenfer were sleeping. There, he told me, he paused for a moment. The beating of his heart was so rapid, so violent, so loud, that he was almost overcome. He began to fear for his composure; his hands trembled, and the soles of his feet seemed to rest on red-hot coals. But so much good fortune hung upon the execution of his plan that he fancied he saw a kind of predestination in this gift of fate. He opened the window, returned to the bedroom, took out his case, and selected the instrument most suitable for carrying out his crime.

"'When I reached the bed,' he told me, 'I automatically commended myself to God.'

"At the moment when, summoning all his strength, he raised his arm, he heard a sort of voice within him, and thought he saw a light. He flung the instrument on his bed, escaped into the other room, and stood in front of the window. There, he was seized with the utmost horror at himself; feeling nonetheless his virtue faltering, fearing that he might still succumb to the spell that was upon him, he jumped quickly down to the road and began walking along the bank of the Rhine, pacing like a sentinel in front of the inn. Again and again he went as far as Andernach in his headlong rovings; often, too, his feet led him to the foot of the slope he had descended on his way to the inn; but the night was so still, and he had such faith in the watchdogs, that now and then he lost sight of the window he had left open. His goal was to exhaust himself and hasten the approach of sleep.

"But as he wandered beneath a cloudless sky, admiring the

stars, stirred perhaps too by the pure night air and the melancholy lapping of the waves, he fell into a reverie which led him back by degrees to moral sanity. Reason was at last able to dissipate entirely his momentary madness. His education, the precepts of his religion, and most of all, he told me, the images of the modest life he had hitherto led under his father's roof, prevailed over his evil thoughts. He told me that when he returned to the inn, after a lengthy spell of meditation to which he had surrendered while leaning upon a large rock at the edge of the Rhine, he felt he could have kept watch all night beside a billion in gold. As his virtue rose proud and vigorous from the struggle, he fell to his knees, overcome with blissful ecstasy, and thanked God; he felt as lighthearted and content as on the day of his first communion, when he had thought himself worthy of the angels for spending one day without sinning in thought, word, or deed.

"He returned to the inn, closed the window without fear of making a noise, and went immediately to bed. His mental and physical exhaustion made him defenseless against sleep. Soon after laying his head upon his mattress, he fell into that first fantastical somnolence which always precedes deep slumber. It is then that the senses are dulled, and life and vitality gradually ebb away; thought is inchoate, and the last vibrations of sense are like a kind of reverie.

"'How heavy the air is,' thought Prosper. 'It feels as though I am breathing a damp vapor.'

"He explained this atmospheric effect vaguely to himself as the difference between the temperature of the room and the pure country air outside. Soon, however, he became aware of a noise at regular intervals, like the steady drip of water from the stopcock of a fountain. Surrendering to a moment of panic, he was about to get out of bed and call the innkeeper, or awaken Wilhelm or the merchant, but suddenly—alas, to his misfortune—he remembered the wooden clock, and fancying he recognized the sound of the pendulum, he fell asleep, lulled by this vague and indistinct sensation."

"Do you want some water, Monsieur Taillefer?" said the master of the house, observing the banker mechanically take hold of the decanter.

It was empty.

After the slight pause occasioned by this interruption, Monsieur Hermann resumed his tale.

"The next morning, Prosper Magnan was awakened by a loud noise. He thought he had heard piercing screams, and he felt that violent shudder of the nerves which overcomes us when we awake to a painful sensation begun during our slumber. A physiological phenomenon takes place within us, a start, to borrow the common expression, which has not yet been sufficiently analyzed, although it presents elements of interest to science. This terrible agony, caused perhaps by an overly abrupt conjunction of our two natures, which are almost always distinct during sleep, is usually of brief duration, but it persisted and even increased in the case of the unfortunate young surgeon, causing him a convulsive shudder when he beheld a pool of blood between his own mattress and Walhenfer's bed. The poor German's head lay on the floor; the body was still on the bed. All the blood had gushed out at the neck. When he saw the eyes still open and staring, when he saw the blood which had stained his sheets and even his hands, when he recognized his own surgical instrument on the bed, Prosper Magnan fell in a swoon into Walhenfer's blood.

"'It was,' he told me, 'a punishment for my thoughts.'

"Upon regaining consciousness, he found himself in the public room. He was sitting on a chair, surrounded by French soldiers, and facing an intent and curious crowd. He stared in dull bewilderment at a republican officer who was busy taking the testimony of several witnesses, and doubtless drafting a report. He recognized the innkeeper and his wife, the two boatmen and the maidservant. The surgical instrument used by the murderer . . ."

Here Monsieur Taillefer coughed, took out his handkerchief to blow his nose, and wiped his forehead. These perfectly natural motions were observed by no one but myself; all the guests had their eyes fixed on Monsieur Hermann and were listening to him avidly. The contractor leaned his elbow on the table, rested his head in his right hand, and gazed fixedly at Hermann. From that moment he showed no further sign of interest or emotion, but his features remained grave and sallow-hued, as when I first saw him playing with the decanter stopper.

"The surgical instrument used by the murderer lay on the table, alongside Prosper's instrument case, wallet, and papers. The crowd gave its attention by turns to this damaging testimony and to the young man himself, who appeared to be nearly lifeless, and whose glazed eyes seemed to see nothing. The confused murmur that could be heard outside indicated that a crowd had gathered in front of the inn, drawn by the news of the crime, and perhaps too by the desire to catch a glimpse of the murderer. The pacing of the sentries posted outside the windows, the rattle of their muskets, could be heard above the clamor of the populace. The inn itself was shut up, the courtyard silent and deserted. Unable to endure the gaze of the officer who was drawing up the report, Prosper Magnan suddenly felt the pressure of a man's hand upon his own and looked up to see who his protector could be amid that hostile crowd. He recognized by his uniform the surgeon-major of the demi-brigade stationed in Andernach. So stern and piercing was his gaze that the poor young man shuddered and let his head fall onto the back of his chair. A soldier gave him some vinegar to inhale, and he at once regained consciousness. But his wild eyes seemed so devoid of life and intelligence that the surgeon, after feeling Prosper's pulse, said to the officer, 'Captain, it is impossible to question this man just now.'

"'Very well! Take him away,' snapped the captain, interrupting the surgeon and addressing a corporal who stood behind the assistant surgeon's chair.

"'Damned coward!' said the soldier in a low voice, 'try at least to hold your head up before these German swine, and save the honor of the Republic.'

"This appeal awakened Prosper Magnan from his torpor; he rose, and took several steps forward. But when the door opened, and he felt the fresh air and saw the crowd surging toward him, his strength failed him; he staggered, and his knees gave way.

"'This confounded sawbones deserves death twice over! Get moving!' said the two soldiers, who were holding him up.

"'Oh! The scoundrel! Here he is! Here he comes!'

"These words seemed to him to be uttered by a single voice, the tumultuous voice of the crowd that followed him, flinging insults, and growing larger at each step. On the way from the inn to the prison, the clamor of the soldiers and the mob, the murmur of many voices, the sight of the sky and the coolness of the air, the view of Andernach and the rippling of the waters of the Rhine—all this reached the young man's soul as vague, confused, and dull impressions, like all the sensations he had experienced since waking. There were moments, he told me, when he imagined he had ceased to exist.

"I was then in prison," said Monsieur Hermann, interrupting his narrative. "With the enthusiasm we all feel at the age of twenty, I had wished to defend my country, and was commanding a volunteer company which I had organized in the vicinity of Andernach. Several nights before this, I had fallen into the hands of a French detachment of eight hundred men. We numbered two hundred at the most. My spies had betrayed me. I was thrown into the prison at Andernach. At that time the plan was to have me shot, so as to set a daunting example for the country. The French were also talking of reprisals, but the murder for which the republicans sought vengeance had been committed outside the Electorate. My father had obtained a three-day reprieve, so that he might go before General Augereau and ask for my pardon, which was granted. Thus it happened that I saw Prosper Magnan when he arrived at Andernach prison, and the sight of him filled me with the deepest pity. Pale, haggard, bloodstained though he was, there was a candidness and innocence in his features which moved me deeply. It was as if Germany herself stood there before me, in his long blond hair, in his blue eyes. The very embodiment of my humbled fatherland, he appeared to me as a victim and not a murderer. As he passed beneath my window, a bitter, melancholy smile hovered for a moment upon his lips, the smile of a madman who has recovered a fleeting glimmer of reason. That smile was not that of a murderer. When I saw the jailer, I questioned him about his new prisoner.

"'He has not spoken a word since he went into his cell. He sits with his head between his hands, sleeping, or brooding over his predicament. The French say he will be sentenced tomorrow morning, and shot within twenty-four hours.'

"That evening I paused beneath the prisoner's window during the short time allotted me for exercise in the prison yard. We talked together, and he candidly related his experience to me, responding with frankness to my various questions. After that first conversation, I had no more doubt of his innocence. I asked and obtained permission to spend several hours with him. I saw him in this way several times, and the poor child opened his heart to me. In his own mind, he was both innocent and guilty. Remembering the horrible temptation that he had found strength to resist, he feared that he might have committed in his sleep, in a fit of somnambulism, the crime he had fantasized while awake.

"'But what about your companion?' I said.

"'Oh,' he cried fervently, 'Wilhelm is incapable . . .' He did not even finish the sentence. At that warm declaration, full of youth and virtue, I clasped his hand.

"'When he awoke,' he went on, 'he must have been terrified and lost his head; no doubt he ran away.'

"'Without waking you,' I said. 'Why then your defense is easy, since Walhenfer's valise will not have been stolen.'

"All at once he burst into tears. 'Oh yes, I am innocent!' he cried. 'I have killed no one. I remember my dreams. I was playing prisoners' base with my friends at school. I could not have cut off a man's head while dreaming that I was playing!'

"Yet in spite of these gleams of hope which intermittently restored some of his calm, he still felt weighed down with remorse. He had clearly raised his arm to sever the merchant's head. He was his own judge, and concluded that his heart was no longer pure after having committed the crime in his mind.

"'And yet, I am good! he cried. 'Oh, my poor mother! At this very moment, perhaps, she is playing happily at cards with her neighbors in her little tapestried sitting room. If she knew that I had so much as raised my hand to kill a man . . . oh, it would kill her! And I am in prison, accused of a crime! Even if I did not kill that man, I shall certainly kill my mother!'

"As he uttered these words, he did not weep, but seized by one of those wild fits of frenzy not uncommon among the men of Picardy, he rushed toward the wall, and if I had not restrained him, would have dashed his head against it.

"'Wait until you are tried,' I said. 'You will be acquitted, you are innocent. And your mother . . .'

"'My mother,' he cried in a passion, 'she will learn of the charge against me first. It is always like that in small towns; the poor woman will die of grief. Besides, I am not innocent. Do you want to know the whole truth? I feel I have lost the virginity of my conscience.'

"With these terrible words, he sat down, folded his arms across his chest, bowed his head, and stared gloomily at the floor. Just then the turnkey came to ask me to return to my room, but reluctant to leave my companion alone at a moment of blackest despondency, I clasped him in a warm embrace.

"'Have patience,' I said. 'All may yet go well. If the words of an honest man can still your doubts, let me tell you that I respect and admire you. Accept my friendship, and rest upon my heart, if you cannot find peace in your own.'

"The next day, about nine o'clock, a corporal and four riflemen came to take the assistant surgeon away. At the sound of the soldiers' approach, I went to the window. As the young man crossed the courtyard, he looked up at me. Never shall I forget that look, filled with forebodings, resignation, and an indescribably sad and melancholy grace. It was a sort of unspoken but eloquent last testament in which a man bequeathed his lost life to his only friend. The night must have been terribly hard, terribly lonely for him; yet perhaps, too, the pallor of his features revealed a stoicism drawn from a newly acquired self-respect. Perhaps he had been purified by remorse, and felt his sin to have been washed away by his anguish and shame. He walked with a firm stride; he had also washed away the blood with which he had accidentally been stained.

"'I must have wet my hands in it while I slept; I always was a restless sleeper,' he had told me the night before, with a dreadful despair in his voice.

"I learned that he was to appear before a court-martial. The division was to move on in two days' time, and the brigade commander did not wish to leave Andernach without passing judgment on the crime in the place where it had been committed.

"While that court-martial was proceeding, I was in a state of mortal anguish. Finally, about noon, Prosper Magnan was brought back to the prison. I was taking my usual walk; he saw me, and threw himself into my arms.

"'Lost!' he said. 'I am lost beyond hope! Here, in the eyes of everyone, I am a murderer.' He lifted his head proudly. 'This injustice has wholly restored my innocence. My life would have been forever destroyed, but my death shall be without reproach. But, is there anything beyond?'

"The entire eighteenth century was contained in that sudden question. He remained immersed in thought.

"'But what did you tell them?' I said. 'What did they ask you? Did you not relate the simple truth as you told it to me?'

"He stared at me a moment, and after an awesome pause, answered me in a feverish rush of words:

"'First of all they asked me, "Did you leave the inn during the night?" "Yes," I told them. "By which exit?" I blushed, and answered, "Through the window." "You opened the window, then?" "Yes," I said. "You must have taken great care with it; the innkeeper heard nothing!" I was stupefied. The boatmen testified that they had seen me walking, sometimes toward Andernach, sometimes toward the forest. I went back and forth many times, they said. I buried the gold and diamonds. And the valise has not been found! Besides, I was still struggling with my remorse. Whenever I tried to speak, a pitiless voice cried out within me, "You meant to commit the crime!" Everything was against me, even myself! . . . They questioned me about my companion, and I categorically defended him. Then they told me, "One of you must be the guilty party— you, your companion, the innkeeper or his wife! This morning all the windows and doors to the inn were found shut!" On hearing these words, I had no more voice, nor strength, nor soul left in me. Being more certain of my friend than of myself, I could not accuse him. I saw that they thought us both equally guilty of the murder, and that I was regarded as the clumsier of the two! I tried to explain the crime by somnambulism, and in so doing clear my friend, but I lost my train of thought. I am lost. I read my sentence in the judges' eyes, in their incredulous smiles. All is over. No more uncertainty. Tomorrow I shall be shot. —I think no longer of myself,' he went on after a pause, 'but only of my poor mother!' He broke off and, tearless, looked toward heaven. His dry eyes worked convulsively. 'Frédéric!'

"Ah, Frédéric! The other was called Frédéric! Yes, that was the name!" exclaimed Monsieur Hermann triumphantly.

My neighbor touched my foot, and motioned to me to look at Monsieur Taillefer. The contractor had nonchalantly let one hand fall across his eyes, but through the fingers we thought we saw them smoldering somberly.

"Well?" she whispered in my ear. "What if his name were Frédéric?"

I answered her with a sidelong glance as if to say, "Be quiet!"

Hermann resumed his tale:

"'Frédéric,' cried the young surgeon, 'Frédéric has abandoned me like a coward. He must have been afraid. Perhaps he is hiding in the inn, for both our horses were still in the courtyard this morning. —What an impenetrable mystery!' he added, after a pause. 'Somnambulism, somnambulism! I have only had one attack of it in my life, and that was when I was six years old. —Must I leave this earth,' he went on, stamping his foot on the ground, 'and take with me all the friendship there is in this world? Must I die a double death, doubting the friendship that began when we were only five and continued throughout our years at school and university? Where is Frédéric?'

"He began to weep. We are more attached to certain sentiments than to life itself.

"'Let us go in,' he said, 'I would rather be in my cell. I want no one to see me weeping. I will go bravely to my death, but I cannot play the hero out of season, and I confess that I mourn my beautiful lost youth. I could not sleep last night; my memory brought back scenes of my childhood, and I saw myself romping in those fields, the memory of which, perhaps, led to my ruin. —I had a future,' he said, interrupting his own words. 'And now, a dozen men, a sublieutenant shouting "Ready, aim, fire," a roll of drums, and infamy! That is my future now. Oh, there is a God, or all this would be too absurd.'

"Then he took me in his arms and clasped me to him in a tight embrace.

"'Ah, you are the last man to whom I can pour forth my soul. You will be free again, you will see your mother! I know not if you are rich or poor, but no matter; you are all the world to me. They will not fight forever. When peace is declared, go to Beauvais. If my mother survives the fatal news of my death, you will find her there. Bring her these consoling words: "He was innocent!" —She will believe you,' he went on. 'I shall write to her; but you will be the bearer of my last glance, you will tell her that you were the last person I pressed to my heart. Ah! Ah, how she will love you, poor woman, you who were my last friend on earth!' There was a moment's pause, during which he seemed crushed beneath the weight of his memories. 'Here,' he went on, 'officers and soldiers alike are strangers to me, and they all look upon me with horror. If not for you, my innocence would be a secret between myself and Heaven.'

"I swore I would faithfully carry out his last wishes. My words and expressions of emotion touched him deeply. A short time later, the soldiers returned to take him again before the court-martial. He was condemned to death.

"I know nothing of the formalities which accompanied or followed this judgment; I know not if the young surgeon made any attempts at appeal; but he prepared to go to his death on the following morning, and spent the night writing to his mother.

"'We shall both be free,' he said with a smile, when I went to see him the next day; 'I am told that the general has signed your pardon.'

"I was silent, and gazed at him as if to etch his features into my memory. Then an expression of disgust came over his face, and he said: 'I have been a miserable coward! All night long I have been begging the very walls for mercy.' And he pointed to the sides of his cell.

"'Yes, yes,' he went on, 'I howled with despair, my entire being revolted, I endured the most dreadful mental agony. —I was alone! Now, I am thinking of what others will say of me. . . . Courage is a garment that we put on. I must go decently to my death. . . . And so . . .'"

TWO KINDS OF JUSTICE

"Oh, stop!" cried the young lady who had requested the story, abruptly breaking in upon the Nuremberger's tale. "I would rather remain in suspense and imagine he was saved. If I were to learn that they shot him, I would not sleep a wink tonight. You can tell me the rest tomorrow."

We rose from the table. As the woman next to me took Monsieur Hermann's arm, she asked: "They shot him, didn't they?"

"Yes. I witnessed the execution."

"What, Monsieur!" she said. "You were able . . ."

"It was his wish, Madame. There is something dreadful about following the funeral procession of a living man, a man you love, an innocent man! The poor fellow did not take his eyes from my face. He seemed to live only in me! He wanted me, he said, to bear his last dying breath to his mother."

"And did you?"

"After the Peace of Amiens,[16] I went to France to bring the mother these noble words: 'He was innocent.' I had undertaken that pilgrimage like a sacred charge. But Madame Magnan was dead; she had died of consumption. It was not without deep emotion that I burned the letter that had been entrusted to me. You will smile at me, perhaps, for my exalted German imagination, but I glimpsed a sublime and melancholy drama in the eternal silence that had swallowed those farewells cast in vain between two tombs, unheeded by all of creation, like the cry of a traveler in a desert surprised by a beast of prey."

"And what if," I interrupted, "what if you were brought face to face with one of the men in this room, and told: 'There is the murderer!' Would that not be yet another drama? And what would you do?"

Monsieur Hermann took up his hat and went out.

"You are behaving like a boy, and very irresponsibly," said my neighbor. "Look at Taillefer there, sitting in the wing chair by the fireplace. Mademoiselle Fanny is handing him a cup of coffee. He is smiling. Could a murderer, to whom this tale must have been torture, display such calm? Does he not look quite patriarchal?"

"Yes, but go and ask him if he was in Germany during the war," I exclaimed.

"Why not?"

And with that audacity which is seldom lacking in women when they are tempted by some undertaking, or swayed by curiosity, my neighbor went over to the contractor.

"Were you ever in Germany?" she asked him.

Taillefer nearly dropped his saucer.

"I, Madame? No, never."

"What is that you're saying, Taillefer!" interrupted the banker, "were you not in supplies and provisions during the Wagram campaign?"[17]

"Ah, yes!" replied Monsieur Taillefer, "I was there at that time."

"You are mistaken, he is a good man," said my neighbor when she returned.

"Very well," I exclaimed. "Before the evening is over I will drive the murderer out of the mire in which he is hiding."

Every day, an amazingly profound psychological phenomenon, yet one too simple to be noticed, takes place before our eyes. If two men should meet in a drawing room, one of whom has cause to detest the other, whether because he knows the other's secret shame, or because he is plotting revenge, these two men will see through each other, and glimpse the abyss that divides or will come to divide them. Furtively they observe each other; some imperceptible emanation of their thought seems to issue from each look and gesture; there is a magnet between them. I do not know which exerts the greater attraction, crime or vengeance, insult or hate. Like a priest who cannot consecrate the host in the presence of the evil spirit, both are suspicious and ill at ease; one is polite, the other sullen; one blushes or turns pale, the other trembles. Often the avenger is as much a coward as the victim. Few men have the courage to do harm even when it is necessary, and many hold their peace or forgive through sheer aversion to commotion, or through fear of a tragic outcome.

This mutual susceptibility of mind and feeling gave rise to a mysterious struggle between the contractor and myself. Since the first question I had put to him during Monsieur Hermann's narrative, he had avoided my gaze. It may be that he had done the same with all the guests! He was chatting now with the young and inexperienced Fanny, the banker's daughter; doubtless, like all criminals, he longed to fraternize with innocence, hoping it would bring him peace. Although I was at some distance from him, I listened to all he said, and my piercing gaze mesmerized him. When he thought he could watch me unobserved, his eyes met mine, and his lids dropped instantly. Weary of this torture, Taillefer hastened to put an end to it by sitting down at a card table. I at once went to bet on his opponent, hoping to lose my money. My wish was granted. The player left the table and I took his place, finding myself face to face with the murderer. . . .

"Monsieur," I said as he dealt the cards, "would you be so kind as to *begin a fresh score?*"

He rather hastily pushed his counters from left to right. The lady who had been my neighbor at dinner had come to stand nearby; I gave her a meaningful glance.

"Are you," I asked, addressing the contractor, "Monsieur Frédéric Taillefer, whose family I knew very well at Beauvais?"

"Yes, Monsieur," he replied.

He dropped his cards, turned pale, covered his face with his hands, asked one of his backers to take over his game, and rose from his chair.

"It is too hot in here," he exclaimed. "I fear . . ."

He did not finish his sentence. An expression of horrible suffering suddenly came over his features, and he rushed out of the room. The master of the house followed Taillefer with an appearance of great concern. My neighbor and I looked at each other, but I observed that a trace of bitter melancholy had come over her countenance.

"Is your conduct merciful?" she asked, drawing me aside to the window as I left the card table a loser. "Would you want the power to read into every heart? Why not leave things to human and divine justice? We may escape the one, but we can never escape the other! Do you really envy the prerogatives of a president of a court of assizes? You have all but done the work of the executioner."

"After sharing and stimulating my curiosity, you lecture me on morality!"

"You have made me think twice," she replied.

"So, it is to be peace to the wicked and woe to the unfortunate, is it? Let us worship gold! But we'll drop the matter," I added, with a laugh. "Do you see that young lady who is just entering the room?"

"Well?"

"I met her three days ago at the Neopolitan ambassador's ball, and fell madly in love with her. For pity's sake, tell me who she is. No one could tell me. . . ."

"That is Mademoiselle Victorine Taillefer!"

My head began to swim.

"Her stepmother," said my neighbor, whose voice I could scarcely hear, "has recently brought her home from the convent where she rather belatedly completed her education. For a long time her father refused to recognize her. She comes here today for the first time. She is very beautiful, and very rich."

A sardonic smile accompanied these words. At that very moment we heard violent but stifled cries. They seemed to issue from an adjoining room, and echoed faintly through the gardens.

"Is that not Monsieur Taillefer's voice?" I exclaimed.

We listened intently to the sound, and a dreadful moaning reached our ears. The banker's wife hurried toward us and closed the window.

"Let us avoid a scene," she said. "If Mademoiselle Taillefer were to hear her father, she might well have a fit of hysteria!"

The banker reentered the drawing room, looked around for

Victorine, and said a few words to her in an undertone. The girl uttered a cry, dashed toward the door, and disappeared. This incident produced a great sensation. The card games broke up. Everyone turned for explanation to his neighbor. The murmur of voices swelled, and people congregated into groups.

"Has Monsieur Taillefer . . ." I began.

"Killed himself?" my neighbor scoffed. "You would wear mourning for him cheerfully, I suppose!"

"But what has happened to him?"

"The poor man," replied the mistress of the house, "suffers from a disease—I forget the name of it, although Monsieur Brousson has told me often enough—, and he has just had a seizure."

"What is the nature of the disease?" asked an examining magistrate suddenly.

"Oh, it is something dreadful, Monsieur," she replied. "The doctors know of no remedy. The agony, it seems, is excruciating. One day, while the poor man was staying with us in the country, he had a seizure, and I had to go to a neighbor's house so as not to hear him. He shrieks terribly, and tries to kill himself; his daughter had to have him put into a straitjacket and tied down to his bed. The poor man insists there are live animals in his head, gnawing at his brain: he has a horrible, stabbing, sawing pain that shoots through every nerve. The pain in his head is so intense that he could not feel the moxas[18] that they used to apply to distract him; but Monsieur Brousson, his doctor, forbade them, insisting that it was a nervous condition, an inflammation of the nerves, which required leeches to be applied to the neck and opium to the head. And in fact, the attacks have become less frequent, and only come on now once a year, toward the end of autumn. When he recovers, Taillefer keeps repeating that he would rather be broken on the wheel than endure such agony."

"Then he must suffer terribly," said a stockbroker, the wit of the salon.

"Why, last year," she replied, "he nearly died. He had gone alone to his country estate on urgent business; perhaps because there was no one to help him, he lay twenty-two hours flat on the ground, stiff as a corpse. A scalding hot bath was all that saved him."

"Is it some kind of tetanus, then?" asked the broker.

"I don't know," she replied. "He has had this disease for nearly thirty years now, since he was in the army. He says that he got a splinter of wood in his head from falling in a boat; but Brousson hopes to cure him. They say the English have discovered a safe way of treating this disease, with prussic acid."

Just then a cry more piercing than the others echoed through the house, chilling us with horror.

"There, that is what I listened to continually," said the banker's wife. "It made me jump out of my skin, and set all my nerves on edge. But the extraordinary thing is that poor Taillefer, though he suffers untold agony, is never in any danger of dying. He eats and drinks as usual whenever he has a respite from that torture (nature is so bizarre!). A German doctor told him it was a kind of gout in the head; that pretty much accords with Brousson's opinion."

I left the group which had gathered around the mistress of the house, and went out with Mademoiselle Taillefer, who had been summoned by a servant.

"Oh, my God, my God!" she cried, weeping. "What has my father ever done to deserve such suffering? . . . Such a good man!"

I accompanied her downstairs, and as I was helping her into her carriage, I saw her father inside, bent almost double. Mademoiselle Taillefer tried to stifle her father's moans by putting her handkerchief to his mouth; unfortunately, he saw me, his face seemed to become even more distorted, a convulsive scream rent the air, he gave me a dreadful look, and the carriage started off.

That dinner and the evening that followed were to exert a bitter influence upon my life and emotions. I loved Mademoiselle Taillefer, precisely, perhaps, because honor and scruple forbade me to marry into the family of a murderer, however good a husband and father he might be. A remarkable fatality drew me to visit those houses where I knew I would find Victorine. Often, after having pledged to myself that I would never see her again, that very evening would find me by her side. My ecstasy was unbounded. My legitimate affection, colored by a wild, romantic remorse, took on the complexion of an illicit passion. I despised myself for bowing to Taillefer when by chance he was with his daughter, but I bowed to him all the same!

Alas, Victorine is not only a lovely girl, she is also well educated, full of talent and charm, without the slightest pretentiousness or affectation. She has a certain reserve, and a melancholy grace that is irresistible; she loves me, or at least she allows me to think so; she has a certain smile that she saves for me alone, and for me her voice grows gentler than ever. Oh, she loves me! But she worships her father; she extols his kindness, his gentleness, his rare and admirable qualities. All her praises are like so many daggers thrust into my heart.

One day, I nearly found myself an accessory to the crime which had laid the foundation for the Taillefer fortune: I was on the verge of asking for Victorine's hand. It was then that I fled; I traveled abroad, I went to Germany, to Andernach. But I returned. I found Victorine grown pale and thin! If I had found her in good health and spirits, I should have been saved! But my passion for her burst forth again with exceptional violence. Afraid lest my scruples should degenerate into monomania, I resolved to convene a Sanhedrin [19] of spotless consciences in order to throw some light upon this problem of ethics and philosophy. The matter had been further complicated since my return.

Therefore, the day before yesterday, I gathered together several of my friends whom I know to possess the greatest integrity, scruples, and honor. I had invited two Englishmen, an ambassadorial secretary and a Puritan; a former minister, in the full maturity of his political wisdom; several young men still under the spell of innocence; an elderly priest; my former guardian and trustee, an ingenuous creature who gave me the best account of his management that ever was filed at the Palais de Justice; a lawyer; a notary; a judge;—in short, representatives of all varieties of social opinion and practical virtue. We began with a good dinner and lively conversation; then, over dessert, I candidly related my tale and asked for some sound advice, concealing the name of my intended.

"Instruct me, my friends," I concluded. "Consider the question at length, as if it were a draft of a law. The urn and billiard balls will be brought round, and you will vote for or against my marriage, by secret ballot!"

A profound silence suddenly fell over the company. The notary declined to vote, saying, "I have a contract to draw up."

Wine had reduced my former guardian to silence, and it was necessary to put him into the care of a guardian, in order that he might get home safely.

"I see!" I cried. "By not giving an opinion, you are telling me emphatically what I ought to do."

A ripple went through the company.

A landowner, who had contributed to General Foy's tombstone[20] and to a fund providing for his children, exclaimed:

Like virtue, crime has its degrees![21]

"Babbler!" said the former minister in a low voice, nudging me with his elbow.

"What is the problem?" asked a duke, whose fortune consisted of lands confiscated from Protestants after the revocation of the Edict of Nantes.[22]

The lawyer rose. "As a matter of law," cried the mouthpiece of justice, "the *case* before us would not present the least difficulty. Monsieur le duc is right! Is there not a statute of limitations? Where would we all be if we had to delve into the origins of every fortune! This is a matter of conscience. If you insist on taking the case before a tribunal, take it to the confessional."

Having had his say, the personification of the Law sat down and drank a glass of champagne. The good priest, the man entrusted with the interpretation of the Gospel, rose next.

"God created us frail and weak," he said firmly. "If you love the heiress of that crime, marry her, but make do with her mother's property and give her father's money to the poor."

"But," cried one of those pitiless cavilers whom one meets so often in society, "perhaps the father made a good match only because he was rich himself. Therefore, is not the least of his good fortune still the fruit of his crime?"

"The discussion is itself a verdict! There are some things upon which a man does not deliberate," exclaimed my former guardian, thinking to enlighten the company by this drunken sally.

"True!" said the embassy secretary.

"True!" cried the priest.

Each of these two men meant something very different.

A *doctrinaire*,[23] who had missed being elected by a mere hundred and fifty votes out of a hundred and fifty-five, rose next.

"Gentlemen, this phenomenal accident of intellectual nature is one of those which depart most markedly from the normal condition of society," said he. "Therefore, the decision to be made must be an extemporaneous act of our conscience, a sudden conception, an illuminating judgment, a fleeting nuance of our innermost consciousness, not unlike those flashes of perception in matters of taste. Let us vote."

"Let us vote!" cried my other guests.

Each was given two billiard balls, one white, the other red. White, the color of virginity, was to count against the marriage; red to count in favor of it. I myself abstained from voting as a matter of scruple. My friends numbered seventeen; nine was therefore a majority. Each put his ball into the narrow-necked wicker basket used to hold the numbered balls when the players draw for turns at pool, and we were stirred by keen curiosity, for there was something decidedly original in this secret ballot of purified morality. When the votes were counted, there were nine white balls! That did not surprise me, but it occurred to me to count the number of young men of my own age whom I had included among my judges. These casuists numbered exactly nine; they had all had the same thought.

"Aha," I said to myself, "there is a secret unanimity in favor of the marriage, and equal unanimity against it! How shall I get out of this dilemma?"

"Where does the father-in-law live?" thoughtlessly inquired one of my schoolmates, less crafty than the rest.

"There is no more father-in-law," I cried. "At one time my conscience spoke plainly enough to make your verdict superfluous. And if its voice is weaker today, here are the grounds for my cowardice. I received, two months ago, this seductive letter."

I showed them the following invitation, which I drew from my wallet.

YOU ARE INVITED TO BE PRESENT AT THE FUNERAL PROCESSION AND BURIAL OF MONSIEUR JEAN-FRÉDÉRIC TAILLEFER, OF THE FIRM OF TAILLEFER AND COMPANY, FORMER CONTRACTOR FOR SUPPLIES AND PROVISIONS, IN HIS LIFETIME CHEVALIER OF THE LEGION OF HONOR AND OF THE GOLDEN SPUR, CAPTAIN OF THE FIRST COMPANY OF GRENADIERS OF THE SECOND LEGION OF THE NATIONAL GUARD OF PARIS, DECEASED ON MAY 1,

AT HIS RESIDENCE AT RUE JOUBERT. SERVICES WILL
BE AT . . . , etc.
On behalf of . . . , etc.

"What am I to do now?" I continued. "I will put the question
crudely to you. There is undeniably a pool of blood on Mademoiselle Taillefer's estates; her inheritance from her father is one vast
hacelma.[24] That I know. But Prosper Magnan left no heirs, and I
could not find any trace of the family of the pin manufacturer
who was murdered at Andernach. To whom should the fortune be
returned? And should it be returned in its entirety? Have I the
right to disclose the secret I have discovered, to add a severed
head to an innocent girl's dowry, to give her bad dreams, to destroy her noble illusions, to kill her father a second time by informing her: 'All your gold is stained with blood?' I borrowed the
Dictionary of Cases of Conscience[25] from an old priest but can find no
resolution for my doubts. Shall I establish a religious foundation
for the souls of Prosper Magnan, Walhenfer, and Taillefer? Here
we are, in the middle of the nineteenth century. Shall I endow a
hospice, or award a prize for virtue? The prize would only fall to
scoundrels. And as for most of our hospices, it seems to me that
these days they have become the custodians of vice!

"Moreover, would such investments, more or less in the service of vanity, constitute reparation? And is it my place to make
any? Besides, I am in love, and passionately in love. My love is my
life! If I suggest, for no apparent motive, to a girl accustomed to
elegance, luxury, and a life rich with the pleasures of the arts, to a
girl who lazily enjoys the music of Rossini at the comic opera, if
to her I propose that she give up fifteen hundred thousand francs
for the benefit of senile old men or some imaginary scabious pau-
pers, she would laugh and turn away, or her confidante would take
me for a joker! If, in an ecstasy of passion, I extol the charms of
a modest life in my little house on the banks of the Loire, if I ask
her to sacrifice her life in Paris in the name of our love, it would
be a virtuous lie to begin with, and besides, it would probably end
badly for me; I might lose the heart of this girl, who loves dancing, fine dresses, and me, for the moment. Some smart, spruce officer with a well-curled moustache, who plays the piano, gushes
over Lord Byron, and mounts a horse gracefully, will spirit her

away from me. What shall I do? Gentlemen, for Heaven's sake, some advice!"

The honorable man whom I have already mentioned, and who thus far had not spoken a word, that Puritan not unlike the father of Jenny Deans,[26] shrugged his shoulders. "Idiot," he said, "why did you ask him if he came from Beauvais!"

1831

Translated by Joan C. Kessler

For a recent French edition of this work, see Honoré de Balzac, "L'Auberge rouge," in *La Comédie humaine*, vol. 11 (Paris: Editions Gallimard, Bibliothèque de la Pléiade, 1980).

Prosper Mérimée

THE VENUS
OF ILLE

Ἵλεως, ἦν δ᾽ ἐγώ, ἔστω ὁ ἀνδριὰς
χαὶ ἤπιος οὕτως ἀνδρεῖος ὤν.
ΛΟΥΚΙΑΝΟΥ ΦΙΛΟΨΕΥΔΗΣ [1]

I was going down the last slope of the Canigou,[2] and, although
the sun had already set, I could distinguish on the plain the
houses of the little town of Ille, toward which I was making.

"You know, no doubt," I said to the Catalan who had been my
guide since the previous day, "where Monsieur de Peyrehorade
lives?"

"Do I know where?" he exclaimed. "I know his house as well
as I know my own; and if it wasn't so dark I would point it out
to you. It is the prettiest in Ille. Monsieur de Peyrehorade is a
rich man; and he is marrying his son to a lady even richer than
himself."

"Is the marriage to take place soon?" I asked.

"Very soon; indeed, the fiddlers may already have been ordered for the wedding. Perhaps it will be tonight, or tomorrow, or
the day after, for all I know. It'll be at Puygarrig; for the son is to
marry Mademoiselle de Puygarrig. Oh, it'll be a very grand affair!"

I had been recommended to call on Monsieur de Peyrehorade
by my friend Monsieur de P., who told me he was a very learned
antiquarian and extremely good-natured. He would be delighted
to show me all the ruins for miles around. So I had been looking
forward to visiting with him the district surrounding Ille, which
I knew to be rich in monuments both of ancient times and the
Middle Ages. This wedding, of which I now heard for the first
time, would upset all my plans.

I said to myself that I was going to be a killjoy; but I was expected, and as Monsieur de P. had written to say I was coming, I should have to present myself.

"I'll bet you, Monsieur," said my guide, when we were already in the plain—"I'll bet you a cigar that I can guess why you're going to Monsieur de Peyrehorade's."

"But that is not a difficult thing to guess," I replied, offering him a cigar. "At this hour, after traveling six leagues on the Canigou hills, the main thing is to have supper."

"Yes, but tomorrow? . . . I'll bet that you have come to Ille to see the idol. I guessed that when I saw you drawing pictures of the Saints at Serrabona."[3]

"The idol! What idol?" The word had aroused my curiosity.

"What! Did nobody tell you at Perpignan that Monsieur de Peyrehorade had found an idol in the earth?"

"Do you mean a statue in terracotta, in clay?"

"No, I don't. It's made of copper, and there's enough of it to make hundreds of coins. It weighs as much as a church bell. It was a good way down, at the foot of an olive tree, that we dug it up."

"So you were present at the find?"

"Yes, sir. Monsieur de Peyrehorade told Jean Coll and me, a fortnight ago, to uproot an old olive tree which had been killed by the frost last year, for there was a very hard frost, you'll remember. Well, then, while he was working at it with all his might, Jean Coll gave a blow with his pickaxe, and I heard a ting, just as if he had hit a bell. 'What's that?' I said. We went on picking away, and a black hand appeared, which looked like the hand of a dead man coming out of the ground. I felt frightened; I went up to Monsieur and I said to him: 'There's dead folk, master, under the olive tree; you'll have to send for the priest.' 'What dead folk?' he asked. He came along, and he'd no sooner seen the hand than he cried out: 'An antique statue! An antique statue!' You might have thought he'd found buried treasure. And then he set to with a pickax and hands, as if his life depended on it, and did almost as much work as the two of us together."

"And what did you find in the end?"

"A huge black woman, more than half naked, saving your presence, sir, all in copper, and Monsieur de Peyrehorade told us it was an idol of pagan times . . . you know, when Charlemagne was alive."

"I see what it is . . . a statue of the Virgin in bronze which belonged to a convent that has been destroyed."

"The Blessed Virgin? Not on your life! . . . I'd have known straightaway if it had been the Blessed Virgin. I tell you it's an idol; you can see from her appearance. She looks straight at you with her great white eyes. . . . Anybody'd think she was trying to stare you out, because you daren't look her in the eyes."

"White eyes, were they? No doubt they are inlaid in the bronze; it might be a Roman statue."

"Roman! That's it! Monsieur de Peyrehorade said that it was Roman. Ah! I can see that you're a learned man like him."

"Is it whole and in good condition?"

"Oh, it's all there, Monsieur. It's much more beautiful and better finished than the painted plaster bust of Louis-Philippe in the town hall. But for all that, I don't fancy the idol's face. She looks wicked . . . and she is wicked, too."

"Wicked! What harm has she done you?"

"None to me exactly; but you can judge for yourself. We had gone down on all fours to raise her up on end, and Monsieur de Peyrehorade, too, was tugging at the rope, although he's no stronger than a chicken, the dear man! After a lot of trouble we got her upright. I was picking up a tile to prop her up, when— bang!—she fell slap on her back. 'Look out!' I yelled, but I wasn't quick enough, for Jean Coll didn't have time to pull his leg away."

"And was he injured?"

"His poor leg was broken as clean as a whistle. By heavens, when I saw it I was furious. I wanted to break up the idol with my pickax, but Monsieur de Peyrehorade wouldn't let me. He gave some money to Jean Coll, but all the same, he's been in bed the whole fortnight since it happened, and the doctor says he'll never walk with that leg again as well as with the other. It's a crying shame; he was our best runner and, after Monsieur de Peyrehorade's son, our best tennis player too. Monsieur Alphonse de Peyrehorade was terribly upset, for he always played against Coll. It was a treat to see them sending the balls back and forth. Biff! Biff! They never touched the ground."

Chatting like this, we reached Ille, and I soon found myself in the presence of Monsieur de Peyrehorade. He was a little old man, still spry and active; he had powdered hair, a red nose, and a jovial, bantering manner. Before opening Monsieur de P.'s letter he had installed me at a well-appointed table and presented me to his wife and son as a famous archaeologist, who was going to raise the province of Roussillon from the obscurity in which it had been left by the neglect of the learned.

While I was eating with a good appetite—for nothing makes one so hungry as mountain air—I examined my hosts. I have said a word or two about Monsieur de Peyrehorade; I should add that he was vivacity itself. He talked and ate, got up, ran to his library, brought me books, showed me engravings, and poured out drinks for me; he was never still for two minutes at a time. His wife was rather too stout, like most Catalan women over forty, and she seemed to me an out-and-out provincial, completely taken up with the cares of her household. Although the supper was ample for six people at least, she ran to the kitchen, had pigeons killed and cornmeal cakes fried, and opened heaven knows how many pots of preserves. In a trice the table was littered with dishes and bottles, and I should undoubtedly have died of indigestion if I had so much as tasted all that was offered me. However, at each dish that I refused there were fresh apologies. They were afraid I would be very badly off at Ille—they had so few resources in the provinces, and Parisians were so hard to please!

Monsieur Alphonse de Peyrehorade stirred no more than a boundary stone[4] in the midst of his parents' comings and goings. He was a tall young man of twenty-six, with handsome, regular features, but which were lacking in expression. His figure and his athletic build fully justified the reputation he had enjoyed in the region as an indefatigable tennis player. That evening he was exquisitely dressed, just like the latest fashion plate. But he seemed to me to be ill at ease in his garments; he was as stiff as a post in his velvet collar, and did not turn round unless all of a piece. His large sunburnt hands, with their short nails, contrasted strangely with his costume. They were the hands of a ploughman poking out of the sleeves of a dandy. For the rest, although he studied me from head to foot very inquisitively in my capacity as a Parisian, he spoke to me only once in the whole evening, and that was to ask me where I had bought my watch chain.

"Ah, now, my honored guest," Monsieur de Peyrehorade said to me when supper was drawing to its conclusion, "you belong to me. You are in my house and I shall not give you any peace until you have seen everything of any interest among our mountains. You must learn to know our Roussillon and to do it justice. You have no idea what we can show you—Phoenician, Celtic, Roman, Arab, and Byzantine monuments. You shall see them all—lock, stock, and barrel.[5] I shall take you everywhere, and I shan't spare you a single stone."

A fit of coughing compelled him to stop. I took advantage of it to tell him I should be greatly distressed if I disturbed him during the important event about to take place in his family. If he would be so kind as to give me the benefit of his valuable advice about the outings I ought to go on, then without putting him to the inconvenience of accompanying me, I would be able to . . .

"Ah, you're referring to this young fellow's marriage!" he exclaimed, interrupting me. "That's nothing. It takes place the day after tomorrow. You shall celebrate the wedding with us; it will be a quiet affair, for the bride is in mourning for an aunt, whose heiress she is. So there won't be any festivities, and there won't be a ball. . . . That's a pity. . . . You would have seen our Catalan women dance. . . . They're very pretty, and you might have been tempted to follow Alphonse's example. One marriage, they say, leads to others. . . . On Saturday, after the young people are married, I shall be at liberty, and we'll set out. I must apologize for boring you with a provincial wedding. To a Parisian who has had his fill of festivities . . . And a wedding without a ball too! However, you will see a bride . . . a bride . . . who will take your breath away. . . . But you are a serious man, and you are no longer interested in women. I have better things to show you. I'm going to give you something to feast your eyes on! I've a fine surprise in store for you tomorrow."

"Ah," I replied, "it isn't easy to have a treasure in your house without the public knowing about it. I think I can guess the surprise you have in store for me. If it's your statue you're talking about, I'm quite prepared to admire it, for my guide's description of it has whetted my curiosity."

"Ah, so he's told you about the idol, for that is what they call my beautiful Venus Tur—but I refuse to say another word. Tomorrow, as soon as it is daylight, you shall see her, and you shall tell me if I am not right in considering her a masterpiece. Upon my word, you couldn't have arrived at a better time! There are inscriptions which I in my ignorance explain as best I can . . . but a scholar from Paris! . . . You'll probably laugh at my interpretation, for I have written a treatise on it. . . . I—an old provincial anti-quarian—I've been so bold . . . I want to set the press groaning. If you would be so good as to read and correct it, I might hope . . . For example, I would very much like to know how you would translate this inscription on the pedestal: 'CAVE . . .' But I don't want to ask you anything yet! Tomorrow, tomorrow! Not a word about the Venus today."

"You're quite right, Peyrehorade," said his wife, "to stop talk-ing about your idol. You ought to see that you're preventing our guest from eating. Why, he has seen far more beautiful statues in Paris than yours. There are dozens of them in the Tuileries, and in bronze too."

"Now there's ignorance for you—the blessed ignorance of the provinces!" interrupted Monsieur de Peyrehorade. "Fancy comparing a splendid antique statute to the mediocre figures of Coustou![6]

> How irreverently of the gods
> My wife is pleased to talk![7]

"Do you know my wife wanted me to have my statue melted down to make a bell for our church? She would have been its god-mother. A masterpiece of Myron's,[8] Monsieur!"

"A masterpiece! A masterpiece! A fine masterpiece it is to break a man's leg!"

"Look here, wife," said Monsieur de Peyrehorade in a deter-mined voice, as he stretched his right leg out towards her, clad in a shadowed silk stocking, "if my Venus had broken this leg I wouldn't have complained."

"Good gracious! Peyrehorade, how can you say a thing like that? Fortunately, the man is getting better . . . All the same, I can't bring myself to look at a statue which did a dreadful thing like that. Poor Jean Coll!"

"Wounded by Venus, Monsieur," said Monsieur de Peyre-horade, laughing loudly. "The rascal complains of being wounded by Venus!

> Veneris nec praemia nôris.[9]

Who hasn't been wounded by Venus in his time?"

Monsieur Alphonse, who understood French better than

Latin, gave a knowing wink, and looked at me as if to say: "Do you understand that, you Parisian?"

Supper came to an end. For an hour I had not been able to eat any more. I was tired, and I could not manage to hide my frequent yawns. Madame de Peyrehorade was the first to notice and said that it was time to retire. Then began fresh apologies for the poor bed I was going to have. I would not be as comfortable as I was in Paris; in the country things were so inferior. I must make allowances for the people of Roussillon. It was in vain I protested that after a journey among the mountains a bundle of straw would seem a wonderful bed: they still begged me to pardon poor country folk if they did not treat me as well as they would have wished. At last, accompanied by Monsieur de Peyrehorade, I reached the room prepared for me. The staircase, the top steps of which were of wood, led to the center of a corridor, off which several rooms opened.

"To the right," said my host, "is the set of rooms I intend for the future Madame Alphonse. Your room is at the other end of the corridor. You will understand," he added, with a look which he meant to be sly, "you will readily understand that newly married people have to be isolated. You are at one end of the house and they at the other."

We entered a handsomely furnished room, where the first object which met my eye was a bed seven feet long, six feet wide, and so high that one needed a stool to get into it. My host pointed out the position of the bell, and after making sure that the sugar bowl was full and the bottles of eau de cologne in their proper places on the dressing-table, and asking me several times if I had all I wanted, wished me good night and left me alone.

The windows were shut. Before undressing, I opened one to breathe the cool night air, which was delicious after such a lengthy supper. In front of me was the Canigou, which is always a wonderful sight, but which that night struck me as the most beautiful mountain in the world, lighted up as it was by a splendid moon. I stood for a few minutes contemplating its marvelous outline, and I was just going to close my window when, lowering my gaze, I saw the statue on a pedestal about forty yards from the house. It had been placed at a corner of the quickset hedge which separated a little garden from a large, perfectly level, square plot which, I learned later, was the town tennis court. This ground had been Monsieur de Peyrehorade's property, but he had given it to the public at his son's urgent request.

From where I was, it was difficult for me to make out the posture of the statue; I could only judge its height, which I guessed was about six feet. At that moment two town rowdies passed along the tennis court, close to the hedge, whistling the pretty Roussillon tune, *Montagnes régalades*. They stopped to look at the statue, and one of them even apostrophized her in a loud voice. He spoke the Catalan dialect, but I had been long enough in the province of Roussillon to be able to understand nearly all that he said.

"So there you are, you hussy!" (The Catalan expression was more forcible than that.) "There you are," he said. "So it was you as broke Jean Coll's leg! If you belonged to me I'd break your neck."

"Bah! What with?" asked the other. "She's made of copper, and so hard that Etienne broke his file on her, trying to cut into her. It's copper from pagan times, and harder than anything I can think of."

"If I had my cold chisel" (apparently he was a locksmith's apprentice), "I'd soon knock out her big white eyes; it would be like getting a couple of almonds out of their shells. There's over five francs' worth of silver in them."

They moved a few paces farther off.

"I must wish the idol good night," said the taller of the apprentices, stopping suddenly.

He stooped, and probably picked up a stone. I saw him stretch out his arm and throw something, and immediately after, I heard a loud noise come from the bronze. At the same moment the apprentice raised his hand to his head and cried out in pain.

"She's thrown it back at me!" he exclaimed.

And the two scamps took to their heels as fast as they could. The stone had obviously rebounded from the metal, and had punished the rascal for the outrage done to the goddess.

I shut the window, laughing heartily.

"Yet another vandal punished by Venus! Would that all destroyers of our ancient monuments could have their heads broken like that!"

And with this charitable wish I fell asleep.

It was broad daylight when I awoke. On one side of the bed

stood Monsieur de Peyrehorade in a dressing-gown; on the other, a servant sent by his wife with a cup of chocolate in his hand.

"Come now, Parisian, get up! How lazy you people from the capital are!" said my host, while I hurriedly dressed. "It's eight o'clock and here you are, still in bed. I've been up since six o'clock. I've been upstairs three times; I've tiptoed up to your door; but there was no sign of life at all. It is bad for you to sleep too much at your age. And my Venus waiting to be seen! Come along, drink this cup of Barcelona chocolate as fast as you can. . . . It's real contraband. You can't get chocolate like this in Paris. Take in all the nourishment you can, for when you see my Venus, no one will be able to tear you away."

I was ready in five minutes, that is to say, I was only half shaved, carelessly buttoned, and scalded by the chocolate which I had swallowed boiling hot. I went down into the garden and soon found myself in front of an admirable statue.

It was indeed a Venus, and one of extraordinary beauty. The upper part of her body was bare, just as the ancients usually depicted their great deities; her right hand, raised to the level of her breast, was turned palm inwards, the thumb and two first fingers extended, while the other two were slightly curved. The other hand was near the hips, and held up the drapery which covered the lower part of the body. The attitude of this statue reminded me of that of the Morra player,[10] which, for some reason or other, goes by the name of Germanicus. Perhaps the sculptor wished to depict the goddess playing the game of Morra.

However that might be, it is impossible to imagine anything more perfect than the body of that Venus; nothing could be more harmonious or more voluptuous than her outlines, nothing more graceful or dignified than her drapery. I had expected some work of the Later Empire, and I was confronted with a masterpiece of the most perfect period of sculpture. What struck me most of all was the exquisite truth of form, which might have led one to suppose that it had been modeled upon nature herself, if nature ever produced such perfect specimens.

The hair, which was raised off the forehead, looked as if it had been gilded at some time. The head was small, like those of nearly all Greek statues, and bent slightly forward. As for the face, I should never be able to express its strange character; it was of quite a different type from that of any other antique statue I could remember. It was not at all the calm and austere beauty of the Greek sculptors, whose rule was to give a majestic immobility to every feature. Here, on the contrary, I noticed with astonishment that the artist had deliberately set out to express ill-nature raised to the level of wickedness. Every feature was slightly contracted: the eyes were rather slanted, the mouth turned up at the corners, and the nostrils somewhat distended. Disdain, irony, cruelty, could be distinguished in that face which was, notwithstanding, of incredible beauty. Indeed, the longer one looked at that wonderful statue, the more distress one felt at the thought that such a marvelous beauty could be united with an utter absence of goodness.

"If the model ever existed," I said to Monsieur de Peyrehorade, "and I doubt if Heaven ever produced such a woman, how I pity her lovers! She must have delighted in making them die of despair. There is something ferocious in her expression, and yet I have never seen anything so beautiful."

"Venus with all her might has fastened on her prey!"[11]

exclaimed Monsieur de Peyrehorade, pleased with my enthusiasm.

That expression of fiendish scorn was perhaps enhanced by the contrast offered by her eyes, which were encrusted with silver and shone brightly, with the greenish-black patina which time had given to the whole statue. Those bright eyes produced a kind of illusion which recalled real life. I remembered what my guide had said, that she made those who looked at her lower their eyes. That was almost true, and I could hardly restrain an impulse of anger with myself for feeling rather ill at ease before that bronze face.

"Now that you have admired it in detail, my dear colleague in antiquarian research," said my host, "let us, by your leave, open a scientific conference. What do you think about this inscription, which you haven't noticed yet?"

He showed me the pedestal of the statue, and I read on it these words:

CAVE AMANTEM [12]

"*Quid dicis, doctissime?*"[13] he asked me, rubbing his hands together. "Let us see if we agree on the meaning of this *cave amantem.*"

"But," I answered, "it has two meanings. It can be translated: 'Beware of him who loves thee; mistrust thy lovers.' But in that sense I don't know whether *cave amantem* would be good Latin. Looking at the lady's diabolical expression, I would rather think that the artist intended to put the spectator on his guard against her terrible beauty; I would therefore translate it: 'Beware if *she* loves thee.'"

"Humph!" said Monsieur de Peyrehorade; "yes, that is an admissible interpretation; but, with all respect, I prefer the first translation, which I will nevertheless expand upon. You know who Venus's lover was?"

"There were several."

"Yes, but the chief one was Vulcan. Didn't the sculptor mean: 'In spite of all thy beauty and thy scornful expression, thou shalt have for thy lover a blacksmith, an ugly cripple?' What a profound lesson, Monsieur, for flirts!"

I could hardly help smiling at this farfetched explanation.

"Latin is a difficult tongue, because of its conciseness," I remarked, to avoid contradicting my antiquarian friend outright; and I stepped back a few paces to see the statue better.

"One moment, colleague," said Monsieur de Peyrehorade, seizing me by the arm, "you haven't seen everything. There is another inscription. Climb up on the pedestal and look at the right arm." And saying this, he helped me up.

I held on rather unceremoniously to the Venus's neck, and began to make myself better acquainted with her. I even looked at her *right in the face* for a moment, and found her even more spiteful and beautiful at close quarters. Then I discovered that there were some written characters, in what seemed to me an ancient, running hand, engraved on the arm. With the help of my spectacles [14] I spelt out the following, while Monsieur de Peyrehorade repeated every word as soon as I uttered it, with approving gestures and voice. It read thus:

VENERI TVRBVL . . .
EVTYCHES MYRO
IMPERIO FECIT. [15]

After the word *TVRBVL* in the first line, I thought that there were some letters which had been effaced; but *TVRBVL* was perfectly legible.

"What does that mean?" asked my gleeful host, mischievously smiling, for he knew very well that I would not find it easy to make much of this *TVRBVL*.

"There is one thing which I cannot explain yet," I said to him; "all the rest is easy. Eutyches Myron made this offering to Venus by her order."

"Good. But what do you make of *TVRBVL*? What is *TVRBVL*?"

"*TVRBVL* puzzles me greatly; I cannot think of any epithet normally applied to Venus which might assist me. Let us see: what would you say to *TVRBVLENTA*? Venus who troubles and disturbs. . . . You notice I am still preoccupied with her spiteful expression. *TVRBVLENTA* is not at all a bad epithet for Venus," I added modestly, for I myself was not quite satisfied with my explanation.

"Venus the turbulent! Venus the disturber! Ah! So you think that my Venus is a Venus of the pothouse? Nothing of the sort, Monsieur. She is a Venus of good society. And now I will explain this *TVRBVL* to you. You will at least promise not to divulge my discovery before my treatise is published. I am rather proud, you see, of this find. . . . You really must leave us poor provincial devils a few ears to glean. You Parisian savants are rich enough!"

From the top of the pedestal, where I was still perched, I solemnly promised that I would never be so dishonorable as to steal his discovery.

"For *TVRBVL*, Monsieur," he said, coming nearer and lowering his voice for fear that anyone else but myself might hear, "read *TVRBVLNERAE*."

"I don't understand any better."

"Listen carefully. A league from here, at the foot of the mountain, there is a village called Boulternère. That is a corruption of the Latin word *TVRBVLNERA*. Nothing is commoner than such an inversion. Boulternère, Monsieur, was a Roman town. I had always thought so, but I had never had any proof of it. The proof lies here. This Venus was the local goddess of the city of Boulternère; and this word Boulternère, which I have just shown to be of ancient origin, proves a still more curious thing, namely, that Boulternère, before becoming a Roman town, was a Phoenician one!"

He stopped a minute to take breath and to enjoy my surprise. I had to repress a strong inclination to laugh.

"Indeed," he went on, "*TVRBVLNERA* is pure Phoenician. *TVR* can be pronounced *TOUR*. . . . *TOUR* and *SOUR* are the same word, are they not? *SOUR* is the Phoenician name for Tyre. I need not remind you of its meaning. *BVL* is Baal, Bâl, Bel, Bul, slight differences in pronunciation. As for *NERA*, that gives me some trouble. I am tempted to think, for want of a Phoenician word, that it comes from the Greek νηρός—damp, marshy. That would make it a hybrid word. To justify νηρός I will show you at Boulternère how the mountain streams there form foul pools. On the other hand, the ending *NERA* might have been added much later, in honor of Nera Pivesuvia, the wife of Tetricus, who may have rendered some service to the city of Turbul. But, on account of the pools, I prefer the derivation from νηρός."

He took a pinch of snuff with a satisfied air.

"But let us leave the Phoenicians and return to the inscription. I translate, then: 'To the Venus of Boulternère Myron dedicates at her command this statue, the work of his hand.'"

I took good care not to criticize his etymology, but I wanted, in my turn, to give some proof of perspicacity, so I said to him:

"Wait a bit, Monsieur. Myron dedicated something, but I don't in the least see that it was this statue."

"What!" he exclaimed. "Wasn't Myron a famous Greek sculptor? The talent would pass on to his descendants; and one of them made this statue. Nothing can be clearer."

"But," I replied, "I see a little hole in the arm. I fancy it has been used to fasten something, perhaps a bracelet, which this Myron gave to Venus as an expiatory offering, for Myron was an unlucky lover. Venus was angry with him, and he appeased her by consecrating a golden bracelet. You must remember that *fecit* is often used for *consecravit*. The terms are synonymous. I could show you more than one instance if I had access to Gruter or, better still, Orelli.[16] It is natural that a lover should see Venus in his dreams, and that he should imagine that she ordered him to give her statue a golden bracelet. Myron consecrated a bracelet to her. . . . Then the barbarians, or perhaps some sacrilegious thief . . ."

"Ah, it's easy to see that you have written some novels!" exclaimed my host, helping me down. "No, Monsieur, it is a work of Myron's school. Just look at the workmanship, and you'll agree."

Having made it a rule never to contradict pigheaded antiquarians outright, I bowed my head as if convinced, and said: "It's a splendid piece of work."

"Good gracious!" exclaimed Monsieur de Peyrehorade, "here's another piece of vandalism! Someone has thrown a stone at my statue!"

He had just noticed a white mark a little above the breast of the Venus. I saw a similar mark on the fingers of the right hand, which I then supposed had been touched by the stone in passing, or else a fragment of it might have been broken off by the shock and hit the hand. I told my host about the insult I had witnessed and the prompt punishment which had followed. He laughed heartily, and compared the apprentice to Diomedes, expressing the hope that he would see all his comrades changed into white birds, as the Greek hero did.[17]

The breakfast bell interrupted this classical conversation; and, as on the previous evening, I was forced to eat as much as four people. Then Monsieur de Peyrehorade's tenants came to see him, and, while he was giving them audience, his son took me to see a carriage which he had bought for his fiancée at Toulouse, and which I naturally admired. After that I went with him to the stables, where he kept me for half an hour praising his horses, telling me their pedigrees, and listing the prizes he had won at the country races. At last he spoke of his future bride, in connection with a gray mare which he intended to give her.

"We shall see her today. I don't know if you will think her pretty. You are so hard to please in Paris; but everybody here and at Perpignan thinks her lovely. The best of it is she's very rich. Her aunt, who lived at Prades, left her all her money. Oh, I'm going to be ever so happy!"

I was deeply shocked to see a young man appear more affected by the dowry than by the beauty of his bride-to-be.

"Do you know anything about jewelry?" continued Monsieur Alphonse. "What do you think of this ring which I'm going to give her tomorrow?"

As he said this, he drew from the first joint of his little finger a large ring blazing with diamonds and formed with two clasped hands: a most poetic conceit, I thought. It was of ancient work-

manship, but I guessed that it had been retouched when the diamonds were set. Inside the ring was engraved in gothic letters:
"Sempr' ab ti" ("Ever thine").

"It is a pretty ring," I said, but added: "The diamonds have de-
tracted slightly from its original character."

"Oh, it's much prettier as it is now," he replied with a smile.
"There are one thousand two hundred francs' worth of diamonds
in it. My mother gave it to me. It was an old family ring . . . from
the days of chivalry. It was worn by my grandmother, who had it
from her grandmother. Goodness knows when it was made!"

"The custom in Paris," I said, "is to give a perfectly plain ring,
usually made of two different metals, such as gold and platinum.
For instance, the other ring which you have on that finger would
be most suitable. This one is so large, with its diamonds and its
hands in relief, that no glove would go over it."

"Oh, Madame Alphonse can do as she likes. I think that she
will be glad to have it in any case. Twelve hundred francs on one's
finger is very pleasing. That little ring," he added, looking with a
satisfied expression at the plain ring which he was holding, "was
given me one Shrove Tuesday by a woman in Paris. Ah, what a
time I had when I was staying there two years ago. That's the
place to enjoy oneself, and no mistake! . . ." And he sighed
regretfully.

We were to dine at Puygarrig that day, at the house of the
bride's parents; we drove over to the château, which was about a
league and a half from Ille. I was introduced and received as a
friend of the family. I will not talk of the dinner, nor of the conversation which followed, and in which I took little part. Monsieur Alphonse, who was seated next to his future bride, whispered in her ear every quarter of an hour. As for her, she hardly
raised her eyes, and blushed modestly every time her intended
spoke to her, though she replied without embarrassment.

Mademoiselle de Puygarrig was eighteen years old, and her
lithe, delicate figure was a great contrast to the bony frame of her
sturdy fiancé. She was not just beautiful: she was enchanting. I admired the perfect naturalness of all her replies. Her expression was
kindly, but nevertheless was not devoid of a slight touch of mali-
ciousness which reminded me, in spite of myself, of my host's Venus. While making this comparison to myself, I wondered if the
superior beauty which the statue undoubtedly possessed was not

largely due to her tigerish expression, for strength, even in the evil passions, always arouses wonder and a sort of involuntary admiration.

What a pity, I reflected, as we left Puygarrig, that such a charming person should be so rich, and that her dowry should be the cause of her being courted by a man unworthy of her!

On the way back to Ille, not knowing what to talk about to Madame de Peyrehorade, but thinking I ought to speak to her, I said:

"You are very skeptical folk here in Roussillon, to have a wedding on a Friday! In Paris, we are more superstitious; nobody would dare to get married on that day."

"Oh, please don't talk about it," she said; "if it had depended only on me, I would certainly have chosen another day. But Peyrehorade wanted it, and I had to give in to him. It worries me, though. Suppose some misfortune should happen? There must be something in it, or else why should everybody be afraid of a Friday?"

"Friday," her husband exclaimed, "is the day dedicated to Venus. An excellent day for a wedding! You will notice, my dear colleague, that I think of nothing but my Venus. Naturally, it was on her account that I chose a Friday. Tomorrow, if you are willing, we will offer her a small sacrifice before the ceremony—two ringdoves and, if I can find any, some incense . . ."

"For shame, Peyrehorade!" interrupted his wife, who was deeply shocked. "Offer incense to an idol! It would be an outrage! What would people say about us round here?"

"At all events," said Monsieur de Peyrehorade, "you will let me put a wreath of roses and lilies on her head.

Manibus date lilia plenis.[18]

You see, Monsieur, the Charter is a vain thing. We have no religious freedom."[19]

The arrangements for the next day were made in the following manner. Everyone had to be ready and dressed for the wedding at ten o'clock sharp. After taking chocolate we were to drive over to Puygarrig. The civil marriage was to take place at the village registry, and the religious ceremony in the château chapel. After that there would be a luncheon. Then we would be able to spend the time as we liked until seven o'clock, when we were all

to return to Monsieur de Peyrehorade's house, where the two
families would have supper together. The rest followed naturally.
Since there could be no dancing, it had been decided to have as
much eating as possible.

As early as eight o'clock, I was sitting in front of the Venus,
pencil in hand, beginning again for the twentieth time the statue's
head, without being able to seize the expression. Monsieur de
Peyrehorade bustled about, giving me advice and repeating his
Phoenician derivations. Then he placed some Bengal roses on the
pedestal of the statue and addressed to it, in a tragicomical voice,
supplications for the couple who were going to live under his
roof. He went in to change about nine o'clock, and at the same
time Monsieur Alphonse appeared, wearing a close-fitting suit,
white gloves, patent-leather shoes, chased buttons, and a rose in
his buttonhole.

"You must do my wife's portrait," he said, leaning over my
drawing; "she is pretty, too."

Just then, on the tennis court which I have already mentioned, a game started that at once attracted Monsieur Alphonse's
attention. I was tired and, despairing of being able to reproduce
that diabolical face, I soon left my drawing to watch the players.
There were among them a few Spanish muleteers who had arrived
the night before. They were men from Aragon and from Navarre,
almost all remarkable players. Although the local players were en-
couraged by the presence and advice of Monsieur Alphonse, they
were very soon beaten by these new champions. The patriotic onlookers were aghast. Monsieur Alphonse looked at his watch. It
was still only half past nine. His mother was not ready yet. He
hesitated no longer, threw off his coat, asked for a jacket, and
challenged the Spaniards. I looked at him with amusement and
in some surprise.

"The honor of our country must be upheld," he said.

At that moment I admired him. His blood was up. His
clothes, which a little earlier had filled his thoughts to the exclu-
sion of everything else, were completely forgotten. A few minutes
before he would not have dared turn his head, for fear of disturbing his cravat. Now he no longer gave a thought to his curled hair
or his beautifully pleated jabot. As for his fiancée, I do believe
that, if necessary, he would have postponed the wedding. I saw
him hastily put on a pair of sandals, roll up his sleeves, and with

a confident air put himself at the head of the defeated side, like
Caesar when he rallied his soldiers at Dyrrachium.[20] I jumped over
the hedge and took up a convenient position in the shade of a
nettle tree in such a way as to be able to see both sides.

Contrary to general expectation, Monsieur Alphonse missed
the first ball; true, it grazed the ground, hit with astonishing force
by one of the players from Aragon, who seemed to be the leader
of the Spaniards.

He was a man of about forty, six feet tall, slim and wiry; and
his olive skin was almost as dark as the bronze of the Venus.

Monsieur Alphonse threw his racquet on the ground in
a rage.

"It's this damned ring," he exclaimed, "which is too tight on
my finger and made me miss a sure thing!"

With some difficulty he took off his diamond ring, and I went
over to him to take it, but he forestalled me, ran to the Venus,
slipped the ring on her third finger, and resumed his position at
the head of his fellow villagers.

He was pale, but calm and determined. From then on he
made no more mistakes, and the Spaniards were soundly beaten.
The enthusiasm of the spectators was a fine sight: some uttered
shrieks of joy and threw their caps in the air; others shook hands
with him and called him the pride of the region. If he had re-
pulsed an invasion I doubt if he would have received heartier or
more sincere congratulations. The disappointment of the vanquished added still more to the splendor of his victory.

"We must have another match, my good fellow," he said to
the muleteer from Aragon in a condescending tone; "but I must
give you points."

I would have preferred Monsieur Alphonse to be more modest, and I was almost sorry for his rival's humiliation.

The Spanish giant felt the insult keenly. I saw him go pale
under his tanned skin. He looked miserably at his racquet and
ground his teeth; then in a choking voice he muttered: "Me lo
pagarás."[21]

The voice of Monsieur de Peyrehorade interrupted his son's
triumph; my host was astonished not to find him superintending
the preparation of the new carriage, and even more astonished to
see him holding a racquet and dripping with sweat. Monsieur Alphonse ran to the house, washed his face and hands, put on his

new coat again and his patent-leather shoes, and five minutes later we were in full trot on the road to Puygarrig. All the tennis players of the town and a large crowd of spectators followed us with shouts of joy. The stout horses which drew us could only just keep ahead of those dauntless Catalans.

We had reached Puygarrig, and the procession was about to set off for the village hall when Monsieur Alphonse suddenly slapped his forehead, and whispered to me:

"What a blunder! I've forgotten the ring! It's on the Venus's finger, damn her! Don't tell my mother, whatever happens. Perhaps she won't notice anything."

"You could send someone for it," I said.

"No. My servant has stayed behind at Ille, and I can't trust these fellows here. There's more than one of them who might be tempted by twelve hundred francs' worth of diamonds. Besides, what would the people here think of my absentmindedness? They'd make fun of me and call me the statue's husband. . . . If only nobody steals it! Fortunately, the idol frightens the young rascals. They daren't go within arm's length of her. Well, it doesn't matter. I have another ring."

The two ceremonies, civil and religious, were performed with suitable pomp. Mademoiselle de Puygarrig received the ring of a Paris milliner, little thinking that her fiancé had sacrificed a love token to her. Then we sat down and drank, ate, and sang for long enough. I felt sorry for the bride, who had to put up with the coarse jollity which was going on all around her; however, she took it better than I would have thought possible, and her embarrassment was neither awkward nor affected.

Perhaps courage comes to people in difficult situations.

The luncheon eventually came to an end, and at four o'clock the men went for a walk in the park, which was a magnificent one, or watched the peasant girls of Puygarrig dance on the château lawn, dressed in their best clothes. We spent a few hours like this. In the meantime the women crowded round the bride, who showed them her wedding presents. Then she changed, and I noticed that she covered up her beautiful hair with a cap and a hat with feathers in it, for women are always in a hurry to don as quickly as possible those adornments which custom forbids them to wear while they are still unmarried.

It was nearly eight o'clock when we made ready to go back to

Ille. But first a pathetic scene took place. Mademoiselle de Puygar-rig's aunt, who had been a mother to her, a lady of advanced age and very religious, was not due to come to Ille with us. On our departure she gave her niece a touching sermon on her wifely du-ties, which resulted in a flood of tears and endless embraces. Mon-sieur de Peyrehorade compared this parting to the Rape of the Sabines.[22] However, we set off at last, and during the journey ev-eryone did their utmost to cheer up the bride and make her laugh, but in vain.

At Ille supper was waiting for us; and what a supper! If the morning's coarse jollity had shocked me, I was even more dis-gusted by the quips and jokes of which bride and bridegroom were the chief butts. The bridegroom, who had disappeared for a moment before sitting down to supper, was as pale and chilly as an iceberg. He kept drinking the old wine of Collioure, which is almost as strong as brandy. I was sitting beside him, and felt I ought to warn him:

"Have a care. They say that wine . . ."

I don't know what nonsense I said to him to put myself in uni-son with the other guests.

He nudged my knee and whispered:

"When we get up from the table I have something to say to you."

His solemn tone surprised me. I looked at him more closely, and noticed a strange alteration in his features.

"Do you feel ill?" I asked.

"No."

And he started drinking again.

In the meantime, in the midst of all the shouting and clap-ping of hands, a child of eleven, who had slipped under the table, showed the company a pretty white and pink ribbon which he had just taken from the bride's ankle. They called it her garter. It was promptly cut and distributed among the young people, who decorated their buttonholes with it, in accordance with a very old custom which is still observed in a few patriarchal families. This made the bride blush to the whites of her eyes. But her confusion reached its height when Monsieur de Peyrehorade, after calling for silence, sang some Catalan verses to her, which he said were impromptu. This is the meaning, so far as I understand it.

"What is the matter with me, my friends? Has the wine I have drunk made me see double? There are two Venuses here. . . ."

The bridegroom turned round suddenly with a frightened expression, which set everybody laughing.

"Yes," continued Monsieur de Peyrehorade, "there are two Venuses under my roof. One I found in the earth, like a truffle; the other came down to us from the heavens to share her girdle with us."

He meant, of course, her garter.

"My son, choose between the Roman and the Catalan Venus. The rascal chooses the Catalan, the better part, for the Roman is black and the Catalan is white; the Roman is cold, and the Catalan sets on fire all who come near her."

This conclusion aroused such an uproar of noisy applause and loud laughter that I thought the roof would fall on our heads. There were only three grave faces at the table—those of the bridal couple and mine. I had a splitting headache; besides, I don't know why, a wedding always makes me feel melancholy. This one disgusted me slightly too.

The last couplets were sung by the deputy mayor, and, I must say, they were very broad; then we went into the drawing room to witness the departure of the bride, who was soon to be conducted to her bedroom, as it was nearly midnight.

Monsieur Alphonse drew me aside into the recess of a window, and, turning his eyes away, said to me:

"You will laugh at me . . . but I don't know what is the matter with me . . . I am bewitched, dammit!"

My first thought was that he fancied he was threatened with some misfortune of the sort referred to by Montaigne and Madame de Sévigné: "The whole realm of love is full of tragic stories."[23]

"I thought that this kind of mishap happened only to men of genius," I said to myself.

"You have drunk too much Collioure wine, my dear Monsieur Alphonse," I said. "I did warn you."

"That may be. But this is something much worse."

His voice was broken, and I thought he was quite drunk.

"You know my ring?" he continued, after a pause.

"Yes. Has it been taken?"

"No."

"In that case you have it?"

"No—I—I could not get it off the finger of that confounded Venus."

"Nonsense! You didn't pull hard enough."

"Yes, I did. . . . But the Venus . . . has clenched her finger."

He looked at me fixedly with a haggard expression, leaning against the window latch to keep himself from falling.

"What a ridiculous tale!" I said. "You pushed the ring too far. Tomorrow you must use pincers, only be careful not to injure the statue."

"No, I tell you. The Venus's finger has contracted and bent up; she has closed her hand, do you hear? . . . She's my wife, apparently, because I gave her my ring. . . . She won't give it back."

I shivered suddenly, and for a moment my blood ran cold. Then a deep sigh he gave sent a breath of wine into my face and all my emotion disappeared.

"The wretch is completely drunk," I thought.

"You are an antiquarian, Monsieur," the bridegroom added in dismal tones; "you know all about such statues. . . . There may be some spring, some devilish trick, I don't know about. If you would go and see . . ."

"Willingly," I said. "Come with me."

"No, I would rather you went by yourself."

I left the drawing room.

The weather had changed during supper, and rain was beginning to fall heavily. I was going to ask for an umbrella, when I stopped short and reflected. "I should be a fool," I said to myself, "to go and verify the tale of a man who is drunk! Besides, perhaps he intended to play some stupid trick on me to amuse these country people; and the least that could happen to me would be that I should get wet through and catch a bad cold."

I cast a glance at the dripping statue from the door, and went up to my room without returning to the drawing room. I went to bed, but sleep was a long time coming. All the scenes that had occurred during the day returned to my mind. I thought of that beautiful, innocent young girl given up to a drunken brute. "What an odious thing," I said to myself, "is a marriage of convenience! A mayor puts on a tricolor sash, and a priest a stole, and the most innocent of girls may be handed over to the Minotaur. What can two beings who do not love each other say at such a moment, a moment which lovers would buy at the price of life itself? Can a woman ever love a man whom she has once seen behaving in a vulgar way? First impressions can never be obliterated, and I am certain Monsieur Alphonse will deserve to be hated. . . ."

During my monologue, which I have considerably abridged, I had heard much coming and going about the house, doors opening and shutting and carriages driving away; then I thought I could hear the light steps of several women on the stairs going toward the end of the passage opposite my room. It was probably the procession leading the bride to bed. Then they went downstairs again, and Madame de Peyrehorade's door shut. "How unhappy and ill at ease that poor girl! must feel!" I said to myself. I tossed about in my bed in a bad temper. A bachelor cuts a poor figure in a house where there is a wedding going on.

Silence had reigned for some time when it was interrupted by heavy steps coming up the stairs. The wooden stairs creaked loudly.

"What a clumsy lout!" I cried. "I bet he'll fall downstairs."

Then all became quiet again. I took a book to change the course of my thoughts. It was a statistical report on the department, embellished with a memoir by Monsieur de Peyrehorade on the druidical monuments in the arrondissement of Prades. I dozed off at the third page.

I slept badly and awoke several times. It must have been five in the morning, and I had been awake for over twenty minutes, when the cock began to crow. Dawn was about to break. Then I distinctly heard the same heavy steps and the same creaking of the stairs that I had heard before I went to sleep. This struck me as very strange. I tried in the midst of my yawning to guess why Monsieur Alphonse should rise so early; I could not think of any likely reason. I was going to close my eyes again when my attention was aroused once more by a strange stamping noise which was soon mingled with the ringing of bells and the banging of doors, after which I distinguished some confused cries.

"That drunkard must have set fire to the house!" I thought, jumping out of bed.

I dressed rapidly and went into the corridor. Cries and wails were coming from the opposite end, and one piercing cry sounded above all the others: "My son! My son!" Obviously some accident had happened to Monsieur Alphonse. I ran to the bridal chamber; it was full of people. The first sight which met my eyes was the young man, half dressed, stretched across the bed, the wood of which was broken. He was livid and motionless, and his mother was weeping and crying by his side. Monsieur de Peyrehorade was busy rubbing his son's temples with eau de cologne and holding smelling salts under his nose. Alas, his son had been dead a long time. On a couch at the other end of the room, the bride was in the grip of terrible convulsions. She was uttering inarticulate cries, and two strapping servants were having the greatest difficulty in holding her down.

"Good God!" I exclaimed. "What has happened?"

I went to the bedside and raised the body of the unfortunate young man; he was already cold and stiff. His clenched teeth and blackened face denoted the most frightful pain. It was obvious that his death had been violent and his agony terrible. There was, however, no trace of blood on his clothes. I opened his shirt and found a livid mark on his breast which extended down his sides and over his back. It was as if he had been crushed in a band of iron. My foot stepped on something hard which was lying on the rug; I bent down and saw the diamond ring.

I led Monsieur de Peyrehorade and his wife away into their room; then I had the bride carried there.

"You have a daughter left," I said to them; "you must give all your care to her." Then I left them to themselves.

There seemed to me to be no doubt that Monsieur Alphonse had been the victim of a murder, and that the murderers had found some means of entering the bride's room during the night. Those bruises on the chest and their circular direction puzzled me greatly, however, for neither a stick nor an iron bar could have produced them. Suddenly I remembered having heard that in Valencia hired assassins used long leather bags full of fine sand to crush the people whom they had been paid to kill. I immediately recalled the muleteer from Aragon and his threat, though I found it hard to believe that he could have taken such a terrible revenge for a light jest.

I went round the house, looking everywhere for traces of someone having broken in, but I found none whatever. I went down into the garden to see if the murderers had got in from there, but I could not find any definite clue. The previous night's

rain had, moreover, so soaked the ground that it could not have
retained a clear imprint. But I noticed several deep footmarks in
the earth; they were in two contrary directions, but in the same
line, beginning at the corner of the hedge next to the tennis court
and ending at the front door of the house. These might have been
the footmarks made by Monsieur Alphonse when he had gone to
get his ring from the statue's finger. Moreover, the hedge at that
spot was not as thick as it was elsewhere, and it must have been
there that the murderers had got through it. Passing to and fro in
front of the statue, I stopped for a moment to look at it. I must
admit that I could not look at its expression of ironical malice
without fear, and my head was so full of the ghastly scenes I had
just witnessed that I felt as if I were looking at an infernal divinity
gloating over the misfortune which had befallen the house.

I went back to my room and remained there until noon. Then
I went down and asked for news of my host and hostess. They
were a little calmer. Mademoiselle de Puygarrig—or rather Monsieur Alphonse's widow—had regained consciousness; she had
even spoken to the public attorney of Perpignan, then at Ille on an
official visit, and this magistrate had taken down her statement.
He asked me for mine. I told him what I knew, and did not conceal my suspicions regarding the muleteer from Aragon. He gave
orders for him to be arrested immediately.

"Have you learned anything from Madame Alphonse?" I
asked the magistrate, when my statement had been taken down
and signed.

"That unfortunate young lady has gone mad," he said, with a
sad smile. "Mad, completely mad. This is what she told me:

"She had been in bed, she said, for a few minutes with the
curtains drawn, when the bedroom door opened and someone
came in. Madame Alphonse was lying on the inside of the bed,
with her face turned to the wall. She did not stir, convinced that it
was her husband. A moment later the bed creaked as though it
were burdened with an enormous weight. She was terribly frightened, but did not dare to turn round. Five minutes, or perhaps
ten—she could not tell how long—passed. Then she made an involuntary movement, or else the other person in the bed made
one, and she felt the touch of something as cold as ice—those are
her very words. She pressed herself to the wall, trembling in every
limb. Shortly after, the door opened again, and someone entered,

who said: 'Good evening, my little wife,' and a little later the curtains were drawn. She heard a stifled cry. The person who was in
bed beside her sat up, and seemed to stretch out both arms in
front. Then she turned her head . . . and saw, so she says, her husband on his knees by the bed, with his head on a level with the
pillow, in the arms of a sort of greenish giant who was embracing
him with all its might. She said—and she repeated it to me over
and over again, poor woman! —she said that she recognized . . .
can you guess? The bronze Venus, Monsieur de Peyrehorade's
statue. . . . Since it was found here, everybody has been dreaming
about it. But to go on with the story of the poor mad girl, she lost
consciousness at this sight, and probably she had lost her reason
a little earlier. She cannot say how long she remained in a faint.
When she came to, she saw the phantom again—or the statue, as
she persists in calling it—motionless, its legs and the lower half of
its body on the bed, the bust and arms stretched out before it, and
in its arms her lifeless husband. A cock crew, and then the statue
got out of the bed, dropped the dead body, and went out. Madame Alphonse tugged at the bell, and you know the rest."

They brought in the Spaniard; he was calm, and defended
himself with great coolness and presence of mind. He did not attempt to deny the remark I had heard; he explained it by main-
taining that he meant nothing by it, but that on the following day,
when he had had a rest, he would have won a game of tennis
against his victor. I remember that he added:

"A native of Aragon, when he is insulted, does not wait for
the next day to take his revenge. If I had thought that Monsieur
Alphonse meant to insult me, I would have immediately stabbed
him with my knife."

His shoes were compared with the marks in the garden; but
they were much larger than the footprints.

Finally, the innkeeper with whom the man was staying as-
serted that he had spent the whole night rubbing and doctoring
one of his sick mules.

Moreover, this man from Aragon was highly respected and
well known in the district, to which he came annually to do business. He was therefore released with many apologies.

I nearly forgot to mention the deposition of a servant who
had been the last person to see Monsieur Alphonse alive. It had
been just as he was going upstairs to his wife, and he had called

the man and asked him in an anxious manner if he knew where I was. The servant had replied that he had not seen me. Then Monsieur Alphonse had heaved a sigh, and stood there for a moment in silence. Then he had said: *"Well, the devil must have carried him off too!"*

I asked this man if Monsieur Alphonse had had his diamond ring on when he had spoken to him. The servant hesitated before he replied, then he said that he thought not, that at all events he had not paid any attention.

"If he had been wearing that ring," he added, correcting himself, "I should certainly have noticed it, because I thought that he had given it to Madame Alphonse."

While I was questioning this man I felt a little of the superstitious terror that Madame Alphonse's deposition had spread throughout the house. The magistrate looked at me and smiled, and I refrained from pressing the point.

A few hours after Monsieur Alphonse's funeral, I prepared to leave Ille. Monsieur de Peyrehorade's carriage was to take me to Perpignan. In spite of his feeble condition the poor old man insisted on accompanying me to the gate of his garden. We crossed the garden in silence, with him hardly able to drag himself along even with the help of my arm. Just as we were parting, I cast a last glance at the Venus. I could see that my host, although he did not share the terror and hatred which it inspired in the rest of his family, would want to get rid of an object which would otherwise be a constant reminder of a frightful misfortune. I intended to try and persuade him to give it to a museum. I was wondering how to broach the subject when Monsieur de Peyrehorade automatically turned his head in the direction in which he saw me gazing. He saw the statue, and immediately burst into tears. I embraced him and, without daring to say a single word, I got into the carriage.

Since my departure I have not heard of any fresh discovery being made to throw light on that mysterious catastrophe.

Monsieur de Peyrehorade died a few months after his son. In his will he bequeathed me his manuscripts, which some day I may publish. But I have not been able to find among them the treatise relating to the inscription on the Venus.

P.S. My friend Monsieur de P. has just written to me from Perpignan to tell me that the statue no longer exists. After her hus-

band's death, the first thing Madame de Peyrehorade did was to
have it melted down and made into a bell, and in this new form it
is used in the church at Ille. But, adds Monsieur de P., it would
seem that an evil fate pursues those who possess that piece of
bronze. Since that bell began to ring in Ille, the vines have twice
been frost-bitten.

1 8 3 7

Translated by Jean Kimber

THE DEAD
IN LOVE

You ask me, brother, if I have ever loved. I have. It is a strange
and terrible story, and, though I am sixty-six years old, I
hardly dare to stir the ashes of this memory. I would refuse you
nothing, but to a soul less proven than yours I should never relate
such a tale. I can scarcely believe that such extraordinary events
ever happened to me. For more than three years, I was the victim
of a singular and diabolical illusion. I, a poor country priest, lived
each night in my dreams (God grant that they had been only
dreams!) a life of damnation, of worldliness, and debauchery worthy of Sardanapalus.[1] One weak and indulgent glance at a woman
nearly caused the destruction of my soul; but at last, with the help
of God and my patron saint, I was able to cast out the evil spirit
that had taken possession of me. Until then, I lived an utterly divided existence. During the day, I was a priest of the Lord, chaste,
absorbed in prayer and holy things; each night, as soon as I closed
my eyes, I would become a young nobleman, a subtle connoisseur
of women, dogs, and horses, who gave himself up to gambling,
drink, and blasphemy. Upon awakening at dawn, I would imagine
that I was just falling asleep to dream that I was a priest. From this
somnambulistic existence I have retained memories of words and
things against which I am powerless still. Although I have never
been beyond the confines of my presbytery, one would think to
hear me that I was a man jaded and disenchanted with the world,
who has embraced a monk's existence in the hope of finishing out
his too turbulent life in the bosom of the Creator—rather than a

91

humble seminarian who had grown old in an unknown country parish in the depths of the woods, without the slightest contact with the affairs of his century.

Yes, I have loved as no other has ever loved, with a wild and convulsive passion, so violent that I am amazed it did not cause my heart to explode. Ah! What nights! What nights!

Since my earliest years, I had felt a vocation for the priesthood; accordingly, all my studies were directed toward that end, and my life until the age of twenty-four was but a prolonged novitiate. Having completed my theological studies, I progressed through all the minor orders, and in spite of my youth my superiors deemed me worthy to take the last and most formidable step. The day of my ordination was set for Easter week.

I had never set foot in society; for me, the world did not extend beyond the confines of school and seminary. I knew vaguely that there existed something called woman, but I gave it little thought; I was completely innocent. I saw my elderly, invalid mother only twice a year. This was my sole contact with the world outside.

I had no regrets; I felt not the slightest hesitation before this irrevocable engagement; instead I was filled with joy and impatience. Never did a young fiancé count the hours with more feverish ardor. I could not sleep; I dreamed that I was reciting mass; neither the life of king nor poet seemed more wonderful to me than that of a priest. My ambition could conceive of nothing beyond.

I say this only to illustrate that what happened to me should really never have happened, and to show you how inexplicable was the bewitchment to which I fell victim.

The great day having arrived, I set off for the church with so light a step that it seemed as if I were floating on air, or as if I had wings on my shoulders. I felt like an angel, and I was surprised by the somber and distracted features of my companions; for we were several. I had passed the night in prayer and was in a state bordering upon ecstasy. The bishop, a venerable old man, looked like God the Father brooding over eternity, and I thought I saw heaven through the arches of the temple.

You know the details of the ceremony: benediction, communion with bread and wine, the anointing of the palms of the hands with oil, and finally the holy mass led by the priest in conjunction with the bishop. I shall not dwell upon these now. Oh, Job was right; imprudent is he who does not make a covenant with his eyes![2] I chanced to raise my head, which until then had been bowed, and saw before me—so close that I felt I could touch her, although she was actually at some distance, on the other side of the railing—a young woman of rare beauty, dressed with regal magnificence. It was as if scales had fallen from my eyes. I felt like a blind man who had suddenly recovered his sight. The bishop, so radiant a moment ago, suddenly faded away; the candles waned on their golden candlesticks like morning stars, and the church was engulfed in total blackness. The charming creature stood out against this dark background like an angelic revelation; she seemed to be illuminated from within, to be giving off light rather than reflecting it.

I lowered my eyes, determined not to look up again, in order to shield myself against external influence, for a strange confusion was taking hold of me and I hardly knew what I was doing.

A minute later I opened my eyes, for through my lashes I could see her sparkling with all the colors of the spectrum, in a crimson penumbra as when one looks directly at the sun.

Oh, how lovely she was! The greatest painters who, in their heavenly search for ideal beauty, brought back to earth the divine portrait of the Madonna, hardly approach this wondrous reality. Neither poet's verses nor painter's palette can convey the slightest idea of it. She was fairly tall, with the stature and bearing of a goddess; her light blond hair was parted on top and fell in two golden streams over her temples; she resembled a queen with her diadem. Her forehead, of a transparent bluish-white hue, rose broad and serene above the arcs of two nearly brown lashes, adding to the effect of her sea-green eyes with their unendurable brilliance. What eyes! With a flash they could decide a man's destiny; they were filled with a vitality, a limpid clarity, a warmth, and a moist brilliance that I had never beheld in human eyes; they sent forth rays like arrows heading straight for my heart. I know not if the flame which illumined them came from heaven or from hell, but there was no doubt it came from one or the other. This woman was angel or demon, and perhaps both at once; certainly she was not descended from Eve, our common mother. Pearly white teeth glistened between her rosy lips, and little dimples formed in the pink satin of her adorable cheeks at every inflection of her mouth. Her nose was regal and delicate, revealing she was of the noblest origin. A sheen of blue agate played upon the smooth, glossy surface of her half-bared shoulders, and upon her bosom hung strings of large, almost flesh-colored pearls. Now and again she would lift up her head like a strutting peacock, or with the sinuous motion of a snake, sending a light shudder through the embroidered ruff that encircled her neck like a silver trellis.

She wore a dress of light red velvet, and protruding from her wide, fur-cuffed sleeves were two infinitely delicate, noble hands with long, rounded fingers, so ideally diaphanous that light shone through them as through rosy-fingered Dawn.

Every detail is as vivid to me now as if it were yesterday, and although I was in a state of extreme agitation and confusion, nothing escaped me. With astonishing lucidity I absorbed the slightest nuance: the small beauty mark on the side of her chin, the imperceptible down at the corners of her lips, the velvety smoothness of her forehead, the trembling shadow of her eyelashes upon her cheeks.

As I gazed, doors that hitherto had been closed began to open within me. Windows that had been blocked were unplugged, yielding glimpses of unknown vistas; life appeared to me in an entirely different light; I had been reborn to a new order of ideas. A horrible anguish gnawed at my heart; each passing minute seemed at once a second and a century. The ceremony proceeded, however, bearing me ever farther from the world whose entrance my budding desires were now furiously besieging. I gave my assent, even as I longed to refuse, even as all within me revolted and raged against the violence that my voice was doing to my soul: a preternatural force seemed to wrest the words from my throat. That is perhaps why so many young girls go to the altar determined to refuse emphatically the husband forced upon them, and yet not one is able to carry through with her resolve. It is doubtless why so many poor novices take the veil, in spite of their firm intention to tear it to shreds at the moment of their vows. One dares not cause such a scandal before all these people, or disappoint so many expectations; all these wills, all these glances, seem to weigh one down like a leaden cloak. And besides, every detail has been decided in advance, in so plainly irrevocable a manner that one's mind sinks under the weight of it and at last gives way.

The expression of the fair stranger altered as the ceremony progressed. At first tender and affectionate, it came to take on an air of scorn and displeasure, as if of not having been understood.

With an effort that could have moved mountains, I tried to cry out that I did not want to be a priest, but I was unable to finish the sentence; my tongue was glued to my palate, and it was impossible for me to express my will by even the slightest negative sign. I was perfectly awake, but in a state resembling nightmare, when although one's very life may depend upon a certain word, one is incapable of uttering it.

She seemed to be aware of the agony I was suffering, and, as if to encourage me, threw me a glance filled with divine promises. Her eyes were a poem in which each glance formed a separate canto. She said:

"If you will be mine, I will make you happier than God Himself in His heaven; the very angels will envy you. Tear up that funereal winding sheet in which you are about to shroud yourself. I am beauty, youth, life; come to me, and together we shall be love. What could Jehovah offer you in exchange? Our life will glide by like a dream, like an eternal embrace.

"Spill the wine from that chalice, and you are free. I will carry you away toward unknown isles; you will sleep upon my breast, on a bed of solid gold, under a silver canopy—for I love you, and would take you from your God, before whom so many noble hearts pour out floods of love that will never reach Him."

I seemed to hear the infinitely sweet rhythm of these words, for her glance was almost sonorous, and the sentences that radiated from her eyes echoed in the depths of my heart as if an invisible mouth had breathed them into my soul. I felt on the verge of renouncing God, yet my heart mechanically acquiesced in the outward motions of the ceremony. The lovely creature threw me a second glance, so full of entreaty and despair that it was as if sharp blades had pierced my heart; I felt more swords in my breast than the Mater Dolorosa.

It was over; I was a priest.

Never have human features expressed such bitter anguish: the maiden who sees her betrothed suddenly fall down dead beside her, the mother bending over the empty cradle of her child, Eve seated upon the threshold of the gate of paradise, the miser who finds a stone in place of his treasure, the poet whose only manuscript of his most precious work has fallen into the fire—none of these could look more stunned by grief nor more inconsolable. The blood completely drained from her lovely face, and she turned as white as marble; her beautiful arms fell limply to her sides, as if by a slackening of the muscles, and she had to lean against a pillar because her legs were trembling and giving way beneath her. As for myself, deathly pale, I staggered toward the church door, my forehead dripping with a sweat more bloody than that of Calvary. I was suffocating; the vaults seemed to be pressing down upon my shoulders, and I felt as if my head alone bore the entire weight of the dome.

As I was about to step across the threshold, a hand suddenly grasped mine—a woman's hand! I had never touched one before. It was as cold as a serpent's skin, yet it burned like the brand of red-hot iron. It was she. "Unhappy man! Unhappy man! What have you done?" she whispered; then she vanished into the crowd.

The elderly bishop passed me, fixing me with a stern expression. I looked a strange sight indeed, pale, blushing, and turning dizzy. One of my companions took pity upon me and, taking my arm, led me away; I would have been incapable of finding my way back to the seminary alone. At a corner of the road, while the young priest had his head turned, a blackamoor page in strange attire approached me and, without stopping, handed me a small wallet with corners of chased gold, motioning to me to conceal it. I slipped it into my sleeve and hid it until I was alone in my cell. Then I broke open the clasp; it contained only two sheets of paper with the words "Clarimonde, at the Concini Palace." I had had so little experience of the world that, despite Clarimonde's reputation, I had never heard of her, and I was entirely ignorant of the location of the Concini Palace. I made a number of conjectures, each more preposterous than the last; but in truth, it mattered very little to me what she might be, noblewoman or courtesan, so long as I could see her again.

This love, so newly born, had now taken root within me and was ineradicable. I did not even think of trying to conquer it, so convinced was I that it was impossible. This woman had taken complete possession of me; a single glance had sufficed to transform me. She had infused her will into my own; I lived no longer in myself, but in her and through her. I indulged in all manner of absurdities, kissing the place on my hand that she had touched, and repeating her name for hours on end. I had only to close my eyes to see her as clearly as if she were there before me, and I would repeat to myself the words that she had uttered under the church portal: "Unhappy man! Unhappy man! What have you done?" I grasped the full horror of my situation, and saw with utter clarity the funereal ghastliness of the profession I had embraced. To be a priest!—that is, to be chaste, never to love, to make not the slightest distinction of sex or age, to turn one's back upon all beauty, to put out one's eyes, to creep along in the icy darkness of church or cloister, to see only the dying, to watch over unknown corpses, and to shroud oneself in a black cassock as in one's own funeral pall!

And I felt the life force surging within me like an inner lake that swells to overflowing; my blood pulsed wildly in my arteries; my youth, so long restrained, suddenly welled forth like the aloe plant which waits a hundred years before bursting thunderously into bloom.

How would I manage to see Clarimonde again? Knowing no one in the town, I had no pretext for leaving the seminary; in fact, I was to remain there only temporarily, until I could be assigned to a vicarage. I tried to loosen the bars of the window, but it was at an awful height, and having no ladder, escape was unthinkable. Besides, I could exit only by night; and how would I find my way through the inextricable labyrinth of streets? All these problems, which for others would have been of little consequence, were enormous for me, a poor seminarian newly in love, with neither experience, money, nor attire.

Ah! If I had not been a priest, I would have been able to see her every day; I would have been her lover, her husband, I told myself in my blind passion. Instead of being wrapped in my dismal shroud, I would have worn silk and velvet, golden chains, a sword and plumes such as are worn by dashing young gentlemen. My hair, instead of being shaved in an ignominious tonsure, would fall in curls about my neck. I would have a fine waxed moustache, I would be gallant. But a single hour before an altar, several half-articulated words, had cut me off forever from the realm of the living, and I had sealed my own tomb, I had bolted with my own hand the door to my prison!

I went to the window. The sky was marvelously blue, the trees were clothed in spring garments; all of nature flaunted an

ironic joy. The square was thronged with people coming and going; young dandies and youthful beauties, two by two, made their
way toward the garden and the arbor. Some journeymen passed
by, singing drinking songs. There was a feeling of bustle, anima-
tion, and gaiety, which threw into painful relief my mournful solitude. In a doorway, a young mother was playing with her child,
kissing his little pink mouth still beaded with droplets of milk, and
teasing him with a thousand divinely childish frivolities that only
a mother can invent. The father, standing nearby, smiled sweetly
at the engaging pair, his arms folded as if to press his joy to his
heart. I could not endure the sight; closing the window, I threw
myself on my bed with a horrible jealous hatred in my heart, and
bit my hands and gnawed my blanket like a tiger that had been
starved for three days.

I have no idea how long I remained in this state, but at one
point, turning round in a wild spasmodic motion, I saw Father Serapion standing in the middle of the room, eyeing me attentively.
In shame, I let my head fall upon my breast and covered my eyes
with my hands.

"Romuald, my friend, something extraordinary is going on
within you," said Serapion after several moments of silence. "Your
conduct is truly inexplicable! You—so pious, calm, and gentle—
you have been raging in your cell like a wild beast. Beware, my
brother, and heed not the suggestions of the devil. The evil spirit,
angered that you have dedicated your life to the Lord, prowls
around you like a ravening wolf, making one last attempt to lure
you. Rather than losing heart, my dear Romuald, arm yourself
with prayers, make a shield of mortifications, and wrestle valiantly
with the enemy; you will defeat him. Virtue must be put to the
test, and gold emerges finer from the cupel. Do not be frightened,
nor discouraged; the best-guarded and most resolute souls have
had moments like these. Pray, fast, meditate, and the evil spirit
will withdraw."

Father Serapion's words caused me to reflect, and I recovered
some of my calm. "I have come to tell you of your appointment to
the parish of C***. The priest who held it has just died, and his
Lordship the bishop has asked me to induct you into your new
office. Be ready to leave tomorrow." I nodded in reply, and the
priest took his leave. I opened my missal and began to recite some
prayers, but the lines soon started to swim before my eyes; I lost

the thread of the ideas, and the book slipped from my hands
without my noticing it.

Leave tomorrow, without having seen her again? Add still another impossible obstacle to those that already lay between us?
Renounce for all eternity the hope of meeting her again, unless by
a miracle? Should I write to her? Who would deliver the letter?
With the holy office with which I was invested, whom could I
confide in, whom could I trust? I was overcome with a terrible
anxiety. Then I remembered what Father Serapion had told me
about the snares of the devil. The strangeness of the encounter,
Clarimonde's supernatural beauty, the phosphorescent brilliance
of her eyes, the burning touch of her hand, the turmoil and confusion into which she had plunged me, the sudden transformation
which had taken place within me, the abrupt vanishing of all my
piety, all this clearly proved the devil's presence, and that satiny
hand was perhaps only the glove in which he had concealed his
claws. These ideas filled me with alarm; I picked up the missal
which had slipped from my knees onto the floor, and resumed my
prayers.

The next day, Serapion came to fetch me. Two mules, loaded
with our meager baggage, were waiting outside the door; he
mounted one and I managed to climb onto the other. As we rode
through the streets of the town, I searched all the windows and
balconies for Clarimonde, but it was too early, and the town
had not yet awakened from its slumber. My eyes strained to see
through the curtains and blinds of each of the palaces that we
passed. Serapion doubtless attributed this curiosity to my wonder
at the beauty of the architecture, for he slowed his horse to give
me more time to look around me. Finally we passed through the
town gates and began to climb the hill. When I reached the top,
I turned to gaze once more upon the place where Clarimonde
lived. The shadow of a cloud blanketed the entire town; its blue
and red roofs blended into a common half-tone, from which the
morning smoke stood out here and there like white flecks of foam.
A curious optical effect caused one building to stand out among
the rest, gilded by a single ray of sun. Towering over all its neighbors, which were still shrouded in mist and haze, it seemed quite
close, although it was actually more than a league away. I could
make out its slightest details: the turrets, terraces, casement windows, even the dovetailed weathervanes.

"Which palace is that, just over there, that I see lit up by the sun?" I asked Serapion. He looked, shielding his eyes with his hand, and answered, "It is the ancient palace that Prince Concini gave to the courtesan Clarimonde; dreadful things happen there."

At that moment—I am still uncertain if it was reality or illusion—I thought I saw a slender white form glide along the terrace, gleaming for an instant before it disappeared. It was Clarimonde!

Oh, did she know that at that very hour, from the heights of that arduous road which was carrying me far from her and upon which I could never return, I was gazing with feverish longing upon her palace, which a trifling play of light appeared to bring nearer as if to invite me to enter it as a master? Yes, without a doubt she knew, for her soul was too deeply bound to mine not to feel its slightest tremors. It was that intuitive sympathy that had driven her forth, still wrapped in her night garments, onto the terrace in the icy morning dew.

Darkness overspread the palace, and soon it was no more than a motionless sea of roofs and pinnacles, in which nothing was visible but a hilly undulation. Serapion urged on his mule, mine followed, and a bend in the road concealed from me the town of S*** forever—for I would never return. After traveling for three days across the dreary countryside, we saw the weather-cock of the church that I was to serve peeping through the trees. We rode through several winding streets lined with thatched cottages and garden plots, and soon found ourselves facing the church facade, which was not especially magnificent. A porch adorned with several moldings and two or three pillars of roughly hewn sandstone, a tile roof, and buttresses of the same sandstone as the pillars—that was all. To the left was the cemetery over-grown with weeds, with a large iron cross in the center; to the right and in the shadow of the church, the presbytery. The house was simple and plain, and of an almost stark cleanliness. We entered the courtyard. Some hens were pecking at a few grains of oats on the ground; accustomed, apparently, to black ecclesiastical garments, they were unstartled by our presence and hardly stirred to let us pass. We heard a sudden, hoarse bark and saw an old dog running toward us.

It had belonged to my predecessor. It had dull eyes, a gray coat of hair, and every appearance of extreme old age. I patted it

gently, and it immediately trotted beside me with an air of indescribable contentment. A rather elderly woman, who had been the
former priest's housekeeper, came at once to meet us, and having
ushered me into a ground-floor room, asked if I intended to keep
her on. I replied that I would keep her, the dog, the chickens, and
whatever furniture her master had left her at his death. This threw
her into a fit of joy, Father Serapion having immediately given her
the price that she asked.

When I had settled in, Father Serapion returned to the seminary. I was thus left alone, and with no other support than myself.
Thoughts of Clarimonde began again to haunt me, and, strive as I
might to dispel them, I was not always successful. One evening,
while strolling along the box-bordered paths of my little garden,
I thought I saw, through the shrubbery, a female form following
my every movement, and two sea-green eyes glittering amid the
leaves; but it was only an illusion, and crossing to the other side of
the path I could find nothing but a footprint in the sand, so tiny
that it looked like the foot of a child. The garden was encircled
by high walls; I searched their every nook and cranny but found
no one. I have never been able to explain this incident, which,
moreover, was nothing in comparison to the strange occurrences
which would later befall me. I had been living in this way for a
year, scrupulously performing my priestly duties, praying, fasting,
exhorting, ministering to the sick, making the most stringent sac-
rifices in order to give to charity. But my heart was arid and barren, and the sources of grace were closed to me. I did not feel the
happiness that comes from the accomplishment of a holy mission;
my thoughts were elsewhere, and Clarimonde's words would often
come to my lips like an involuntary refrain. Oh brother, ponder
this! For having once looked upon a woman, for such a seemingly
slight offense, I have lived for years on end in the most wretched
turmoil: one moment, and my peace was shattered forever.

I will not dwell any longer upon this succession of defeats
and inner victories which were always followed by greater lapses;
rather, I shall turn immediately to a crucial episode. One night
there was a loud ring at the door. The old housekeeper went to
open it, and in the rays of her lantern there appeared a man with
a coppery complexion, richly attired in foreign garb, and carrying
a long dagger. Barbara's first impulse was one of fright, but the
man reassured her, saying that he had to see me immediately

about a matter concerning my ministry. Barbara showed him upstairs. I was preparing for bed. The man told me that his mistress,
a very great lady, was near death and had asked for a priest. I
replied that I would follow him, and taking with me what was
needed for the rite of extreme unction, I descended in haste. Two
horses, black as night, were stamping in impatience before the
door, breathing forth two long streams of smoke. The man held
the stirrup for me and helped me mount one of them, then leaped
onto the other, with only one hand upon the pommel of the
saddle. He tightened his knees and slackened the reins, and the
beast took off like an arrow. My horse, whose bridle he held,
broke into a gallop and kept perfect pace with him. We flew along
the path; the earth sped by in gray streaks beneath us, and the
black silhouettes of the trees dashed past like a routed army. We
made our way through a forest so dark, so thick, so chill that it
sent shudders of superstitious terror down my spine. The spray of
sparks that our horses' feet sent flying up from the stones left a
flaming trail in our wake, and if anyone had seen us at that hour of
the night, he would have taken us for two specters upon the steed
Nightmare. Now and then, will-o'-the-wisps would cross our path,
jackdaws uttered pitiful shrill cries from the depths of the wood,
and the phosphorescent eyes of wildcats glinted here and there in
the darkness. The horses' manes grew wild and tousled, sweat
streamed down their sides, and their breath came loud and heavy
from their nostrils. But whenever he saw them slackening, their
rider would utter a strange, inhuman, guttural cry, and they would
surge ahead furiously. At last the whirlwind subsided; a black mass
dotted with several points of light suddenly loomed up before us;
the horses' hoofbeats rang out upon an iron pavement, and we entered the dark mouth of an archway that yawned between two
huge towers. Within the palace gates, confusion reigned; servants
carrying torches were crossing the courtyards in every direction,
and there was a continuous movement of lights up and down
between the landings. I caught a confused glimpse of immense
structures—columns, arcades, flights of stairs, balustrades, a
splendid architectural profusion that was utterly regal, and
straight out of a fairy tale. A blackamoor page, whom I instantly
recognized as the one who had handed me Clarimonde's writing
tablets, helped me dismount, and a majordomo, dressed in black
velvet, with a golden chain about his neck and an ivory walking

stick in his hand, came forward to meet me. Tears flowed from his eyes and coursed down his cheeks onto his white beard. "Too late," he cried, shaking his head, "too late, Father; but even though you could not save her soul, come watch over her poor body." He took my arm and led me to the chamber of death; I was weeping as violently as he, for I understood that the dead woman was none other than the Clarimonde I had so madly loved. A prayer stool stood beside the bed. A bluish flame, playing over a bronze vase, sent a fitful, uncertain light throughout the room, here and there causing some jutting angle of furniture or cornice to flicker in the shadows. On the table, a faded white rose stood in a chiseled urn; all but one of its petals had fallen at the foot of the vase like fragrant tears. A broken black mask, a fan, and every manner of disguise were scattered about the armchairs, suggesting that death had entered this sumptuous abode suddenly and without warning. I knelt down, scarcely daring to glance toward the bed, and began fervently to recite the psalms, thanking God that he had placed the grave between me and the idea of this woman, so that I might pronounce her now sanctified name in my prayers. But gradually this burst of enthusiasm subsided, and I fell into reverie. This room was not in the least like a death chamber. Instead of the fetid air of decay that I was accustomed to breathing during these funereal vigils, the languorous scent of Oriental perfumes, mingled with a sensual feminine odor, hung sweetly in the tepid air. The dim illumination seemed more a voluptuous semi-obscurity than the yellow light of a night-lamp flickering beside a corpse. I pondered the strange quirk of chance that had led me to Clarimonde at the very moment when I had lost her forever, and a sigh of grief rose from my chest. I thought I heard someone else sigh just behind me, and I involuntarily turned round. It was an echo. As I turned, my eyes fell upon the ceremonial bed, which until then they had avoided. The red flowered damask curtains had been looped back with golden tassels, revealing the dead woman lying on her back with her hands clasped upon her breast. She was covered with a veil of dazzlingly white linen, set off more strikingly still by the dark purple hangings. So thin was the veil that it scarcely concealed the lovely contours of her body, and allowed one to follow the beautiful supple curves, as undulating as the neck of a swan, that even death had been unable to stiffen. She resembled an alabaster statue carved by some master sculptor for the tomb of a queen, or a sleeping maiden covered with fallen snow.

I could endure it no longer; the intimate atmosphere, the feverish odor of half-withered roses, were intoxicating, and I paced about the room, pausing at each circuit before the raised platform to gaze at the lovely deceased beneath her transparent winding-sheet. Strange thoughts ran through my mind; I imagined that she was not really dead, and that this was merely a ruse that she had employed in order to lure me to her palace and reveal her love. For an instant I even thought I saw her foot stir beneath the whiteness of the veils, disturbing the straight stiff folds of the shroud.

And I wondered, "Is this really Clarimonde? What proof do I have? Couldn't the black page have entered another woman's service? I am surely mad to be so distraught." But my throbbing heart answered, "It is she, it is truly she." I drew nearer to the bed and gazed more attentively at the object of my uncertainty. Must I confess it? This perfection of form, though purified and sanctified by the shadow of death, stirred me more voluptuously than was proper, and her stillness so resembled sleep that one might have thought her alive. Forgetting the priestly duties that had brought me there, I imagined that I was a young husband entering the bedchamber of his bride, who had veiled her features in chaste modesty. Heartbroken with grief, overcome with joy, trembling with fear and pleasure, I leaned toward her and took hold of the corner of the sheet, raising it gently and holding my breath for fear of waking her. My veins were throbbing so violently that I could hear the blood pounding in my temples, and sweat ran down my forehead as though I had just lifted a slab of marble. It was indeed Clarimonde, just as I had seen her in the church on the day of my ordination. She was as lovely as ever; death seemed to have brought but an added coquetry. The pallor of her cheeks, the fainter rose of her lips, her long, lowered eyelashes darkly outlined against the whiteness of her cheeks, gave her an expression of melancholy chastity and pensive suffering that was indescribably seductive. Her long, flowing hair, which still held several little blue flowers, made a pillow for her head and shielded her naked shoulders with its soft curls. Her lovely hands, purer and more diaphanous than the host, were folded in an attitude of pious repose and silent prayer, mitigating the too great seductiveness, even in death, of her exquisitely round, ivory, naked arms, which still wore their bracelets of pearl. I remained absorbed for a long while in mute contemplation, and the longer I gazed, the less I could believe that life had abandoned forever that lovely frame. I am not sure if it was an illusion or a reflection of the lamp, but I would have sworn that beneath that dull pallor the blood had begun to circulate again. Yet she remained perfectly still. I touched her arm lightly; it was cold, though no colder than her hand had been the day it had brushed against mine under the church portal. Again I bent down, with my face close to hers, letting my tears fall like warm dew upon her cheeks. Ah! What bitter helplessness and despair! What agony was this vigil! I wished that I might gather up my entire life and lay it before her, that I might breathe into these icy remains the flames that consumed me. The night was wearing on, and sensing the moment had come when we should be parted forever, I could not refuse myself the sad and supreme pleasure of kissing her lifeless lips—she who had been the sole object of my love. O miracle! A gentle breath mingled with mine, and Clarimonde's lips responded to my pressure. Her eyes opened and recovered some of their sparkle; she sighed, and unfolding her arms, slipped them around my neck with an expression of ineffable rapture. "Ah! It is you, Romuald," she said in a soft, languorous voice, like the last faint vibrations of a harp. "What are you doing? I waited so long for you, that I died of waiting; but now we are betrothed, and I will be able to see you and visit you. Farewell, Romuald, farewell! I love you; that is all I wish to say, and I give back the life that you restored to me for a moment with your kiss; till we meet again."

Her head fell back, but her arms still encircled my neck as if to hold me fast. A furious gust of wind flung open the window and burst into the room; the last white rose petal hung fluttering like a wing on the end of its stalk, then fell off and blew through the open casement, carrying Clarimonde's soul with it. The lamp went out, and I fell in a swoon upon her lovely, lifeless breast.

When I regained consciousness, I was lying on my bed in my tiny room at the presbytery, and the former priest's dog was licking my hand that was stretched out upon the blanket. Barbara was bustling about with the tremulousness of old age, opening and closing drawers or stirring powders in glasses. Upon seeing me open my eyes, the old woman uttered a gasp of joy, the dog yelped and wagged his tail; but I was so weak that I could not utter a word nor make the slightest movement. I later found out that I had been three whole days in that condition, giving no sign of existence other than an almost imperceptible breathing. Those three days do not count as part of my life, and I have no knowledge of where my mind was during that time, having absolutely no memory of it. Barbara told me that the same man with the coppery complexion who had come to fetch me during the night had brought me back the next morning in a covered litter, and had departed immediately. As soon as I could recover my memory, I went over in my mind all the events of that fatal night. At first I supposed that I had been the victim of some magical illusion, but palpable evidence soon nullified this conjecture. I could not imagine that I had been dreaming, since Barbara too had seen the man with the two black horses and could describe in precise detail his appearance and attire. However, no one in the neighborhood knew of any palace like that in which I had seen Clarimonde.

One morning Father Serapion entered my chamber. Barbara had sent word that I was ill, and he had come in haste. Although this eagerness was evidence of his affection and concern, his visit did not bring me the pleasure that it should have. There was in Father Serapion's expression something searching and inquisitorial which troubled me. I felt uneasy and guilty in his presence. He had been the first to discern my inner turmoil, and I resented him for his shrewdness.

Inquiring after my health in a falsely honeyed tone, he fixed his two yellow, lion-like eyes upon me as if to plumb the depths of my soul. Then he asked me some questions about how I was managing my parish, if I enjoyed my work, how I spent my free time, if I had made any acquaintances among the local inhabitants, what my favorite books were, and a number of other such trifles. I answered him as briefly as possible, and even before I had finished my replies he would go on to something else. This conversation had evidently little to do with what he had come to say. Then, without any warning, and as if he had just remembered something that he was afraid of forgetting, he said in a clear, resonant voice that resounded in my ear like the trumpet of doom:

"The famous courtesan Clarimonde recently died, after an orgy that lasted eight days and eight nights. It was infernally magnificent, and recreated the abominations of the feasts of Balthazar and Cleopatra.[3] Good God, what a century is ours! The guests were served by sun-bronzed slaves speaking an unknown tongue, who had every appearance of demons; the livery of the least of them could have served as the festal attire of an emperor. There have always been strange stories going round about this Clarimonde, and every one of her lovers has met a miserable or violent end. It has been said that she was a ghoul, a female vampire, but I am convinced that she was the Devil in person."

He fell silent, observing me more closely than ever in order to gauge the effect of his words. I had not been able to keep from starting upon hearing Clarimonde's name, and the news of her death—apart from the fact of its painfully coinciding with the nocturnal scene that I had witnessed—threw me into a distress and terror which showed upon my face in spite of my efforts to conceal it. Serapion flashed me a stern and anxious glance, then said, "My son, I must warn you, your foot is poised over an abyss; beware or you shall fall. Satan has a long arm, and the grave is not always secure. Clarimonde's tomb should be triply sealed, for they say it is not the first time she has died. May God watch over you, Romuald!"

With these words Serapion walked slowly to the door, and I did not see him again, for he left for S*** almost immediately.

I had entirely recovered and had resumed my normal duties. The memory of Clarimonde and the words of the old priest were ever present to my mind, yet nothing out of the ordinary had occurred to confirm Serapion's dark forebodings, and I was beginning to imagine that his suspicions and my fears had been exaggerated, when one night I had a dream. I had scarcely sipped the first draughts of slumber when I heard my bed curtains opening and the rings sliding noisily along the curtain rods. I raised myself up abruptly on my elbow and saw the shadow of a woman standing before me. At once, I recognized Clarimonde. She held a small lamp in her hand, of the sort placed in tombs, and its light gave her slender fingers a rosy transparency that faded off imperceptibly into the opaque, milky whiteness of her bare arms. She wore only the linen winding-sheet that had covered her as she lay on her ceremonial bed, and she drew its folds to her breast as if ashamed to be so scantily clothed, but her little hand did not suffice; she was so white that in the pale light of the lamp the color of the cloth merged with that of her flesh. Wrapped in this delicate fabric that revealed all the contours of her body, she looked more like an ancient marble statue of a bather than like a living woman. Alive or dead, woman or statue, flesh or shade, her beauty was still the same, save that the green luster of her eyes was slightly dulled, and her once ruby mouth was now only a faint, delicate pink, almost the color of her cheeks. The little blue flowers that I had noticed in her hair had withered and lost most of their petals, yet she was lovely nonetheless, so lovely that in spite of the strangeness of the circumstances and the mysterious manner in which she had appeared, I was not for a moment afraid.

She set the lamp on the table and sat down at the foot of my bed, then leaned toward me and said in a voice that was at once silvery and mellow, a voice that I have heard from no other lips:

"I have made you wait a long time, dearest Romuald, and you must have thought that I had forgotten you. But I have come a long distance, from a place from which no one has ever returned. In that place there is neither moon nor sun; it is but space and shadow; there are no paths or lanes there, no ground for one's feet, no air for wings; yet I have come to you, for love is stronger than death, and will one day conquer it. Ah, what dismal faces, what awful things I saw on my journey! What a struggle it was for my soul, returned to this world by the power of will alone, to find its body and take up its former abode there! What a mighty effort it was to lift the stone slab with which they had covered me! Look! The palms of my poor hands are all bruised. Kiss them and make them better, dearest love!" She laid the cold palms of her hands upon my mouth one after the other; I kissed them again and again, as she watched with a smile of ineffable satisfaction.

To my shame, I confess that I had completely forgotten Father Serapion's warnings, and the office with which I was invested. I had yielded without a struggle, and at the first assault. I had not even tried to fend off the tempter; I felt the coolness of Clarimonde's skin upon my own, and voluptuous shudders ran over my body. Poor child—in spite of all that I know of her, I can still hardly believe that she was a demon; at least she bore no resemblance to one, and never did Satan more deftly conceal his horns and claws. She had drawn her feet underneath her, and was poised on the edge of the bed in a nonchalantly coquettish attitude. Now and then she ran her little hand through my hair, twisting it into curls as if to see how different styles would suit my face. This fondling, to which I acquiesced most shamefully, was accompanied by an engaging stream of chatter. The remarkable thing is that I felt no surprise at this extraordinary experience, and with that facility with which, in a vision, one perceives the most bizarre events as nothing out of the ordinary, I thought it all perfectly natural.

"I loved you long before I saw you, dearest Romuald, and I sought you everywhere. You were my dream, and when I glimpsed you in the church at that fatal moment, I knew instantly: 'It is he!' I cast you a glance that contained all the love I had ever felt and would feel for you, a glance that would have damned a cardinal and made a king kneel at my feet before his entire court. You were unmoved, and chose your God over me.

"Ah, how I envy this God, whom you loved and whom you still love more than me!

"Unhappy, unhappy woman that I am! I shall never call your heart my own, I whom you raised from the dead with a kiss, Clarimonde the dead, who for your sake has forced open the doors of the tomb and who has come to offer you her life—a life to which she has returned with no other object but your happiness!"

These words were intermingled with intoxicating caresses that made my mind and senses reel, so much so that to comfort her I did not shrink from uttering a dreadful blasphemy: that I loved her as much as God.

Her eyes brightened, and shone like chrysoprases.[4] "Is that true? As much as God?" she cried, clasping me in her lovely arms. "Then you shall come with me, you shall follow me wherever I go. You shall give up your ugly black clothes. You shall be the proudest and most envied of men, you shall be my lover. To be the avowed lover of Clarimonde, who refused the love of a pope—how grand! Ah, the charmed, golden life we shall lead! When do we leave, my lord?"

"Tomorrow! Tomorrow!" I cried, delirious with joy.

"Tomorrow it shall be!" she replied. "It will give me time to change, for this attire is somewhat scanty and not suited for traveling. I must also notify my servants, who believe me to be really dead, and who are deep in mourning. Money, clothes, carriages, all will be ready; I will call for you at this very hour. Farewell, dear heart." And her lips brushed my forehead in a kiss. The lamp went out, the curtains closed, and I saw no more: a deep and dreamless sleep held me in a leaden stupor until morning. I awoke later than usual, and the memory of that strange vision troubled me all day. At last I managed to persuade myself that it had been the mere fever of my overheated imagination. Yet the sensations had been so intense that it was hard to believe that they had not been real, and it was not without some trepidation that I went to bed, after praying God to cast from me all evil thoughts and to watch over the chastity of my slumber.

I was soon sleeping soundly, and my dream continued. The curtains were drawn aside, and I saw Clarimonde: not, as before, pale in her pale shroud, and with the purple hues of death upon her cheeks, but spruce, nimble and merry, with a splendid traveling dress of green velvet trimmed with gold braid and hitched up on the side to reveal a satin petticoat. Her thick blond curls emerged from beneath a broad-brimmed, black felt hat that held a whimsical arrangement of white feathers. In her hand was a small riding whip with a gold whistle on the handle. She touched me gently, saying, "So, fair sleeper, is this the way you get ready? I expected to find you up. Hurry, we have no time to lose." I leaped out of bed.

"Come, put on your clothes and let us go," she said, pointing to a little bundle that she had brought. "The horses are impatient and champing at the bit outside the door. We ought to be ten leagues off by now."

I dressed myself hastily, she herself handing me the different items of clothing, laughing heartily at my awkwardness and correcting me on how they should be worn. She arranged my hair, and when it was done, handed me a little pocket mirror of Venice crystal, trimmed with silver filigree, and said, "Do you like it? Will you take me on as your valet?"

I was no longer the same man, and hardly recognized myself. I was no more like myself than a finished statue is like a block of unhewn stone. My former features seemed but the crude, rough sketch of those reflected in the mirror. I was handsome, and the metamorphosis visibly tickled my vanity. This elegant attire, this richly embroidered jacket, had transformed me, and I marveled at the power of a few yards of cut cloth. The spirit of my garments permeated my skin, as it were, and in the space of ten minutes I had become quite conceited.

I took several turns about the room to give myself more ease. Clarimonde watched with an air of maternal indulgence and seemed quite pleased with her work. "Now that's enough childishness; let us be off, dearest Romuald, or we shall never get there; we have a long way to go." She took my hand and led me out. All the doors opened at her touch, and we passed by the dog without waking him.

At the gate we found Margheritone, the horseman who had previously accompanied me. He was holding three black horses, just like the first, by the reins—one for me, one for himself, and another for Clarimonde. These horses must have been Spanish jennets, born of mares impregnated by Zephyrus, for they ran as swiftly as the wind. The moon, which as we set off had risen to light our way, rolled across the sky like a wheel that had come loose from a cart; we saw it on our right, leaping from tree to tree, breathless from trying to keep up with us. We soon reached a plain where, near a grove of trees, stood a carriage drawn by four sturdy horses. We got in, and the horses started off at a mad gallop. I had one arm around Clarimonde's waist and held one of her hands in mine; she rested her head on my shoulder, and I could feel her half-naked bosom brushing against my arm. Never had I experienced such bliss. I forgot everything in that moment, and had no more recollection of having been a priest than of having been in my mother's womb, so great was the fascination that the evil spirit exerted over me. From that night onward my very being split in two, as it were, and there were two men within me, each of whom was unknown to the other. At times I thought myself a priest who dreamed each night that he was a gentleman, at other times, a gentleman who dreamed that he was a priest. I could no longer distinguish between dreaming and waking, and I was uncertain where illusion ended and reality began. The conceited and dissolute young nobleman scoffed at the priest; the priest loathed the profligacy of the young nobleman. Two spirals, one inside the other, inextricably bound together without ever touching, could quite aptly represent my monstrous double existence. Yet in spite of the strangeness of my situation, I do not believe that I ever for a moment verged on madness. The perceptions of my two alternate lives always remained very clear and distinct. However, there was one phenomenon that was inexplicable: that the consciousness of the same "I" could exist in two so very different beings. I was unable to account for this anomaly, whether I imagined myself to be the village priest of ***, or *il signor Romualdo*, the recognized lover of Clarimonde.

Be that as it may, I resided—at least imagined myself to reside—in Venice; I still have difficulty distinguishing illusion from reality in this bizarre adventure. We lived in a large marble palace on the Canaleio, filled with frescoes and statues, with two Titians of the artist's best period in Clarimonde's bedroom—a palace worthy of a king. We each had our own gondola and gondoliers in our livery, our own music room and personal poet. Clarimonde envisioned life in the grand style, and she had something of Cleopatra in her nature. As for me, I lived like a prince, making as much of a stir as if I were related to one of the twelve apostles or one of the four evangelists of the Most Serene Republic. I would not have stepped aside for the Doge of Venice, and I doubt that since Satan fell from heaven there had been anyone prouder and more insolent than I. I would visit the Ridotto and gamble for high stakes. I consorted with the cream of society—ruined sons of wealthy families, women of the stage, swindlers, parasites, and hired assassins. Yet in spite of the dissipated life I led, I remained faithful to Clarimonde. I loved her madly. She would have awakened satiety itself and changed fickleness into constancy. To possess Clarimonde was to possess twenty mistresses, so mobile and changeable was she, and so dissimilar from herself—a veritable chameleon! She would make you commit with her the infidelity that you might have committed with others, so thoroughly did she assume the nature, appearance, and style of beauty of the woman who had stolen your fancy. She returned my love a hundredfold: the young noblemen, even the ancients of the Council of Ten, made her the most splendid offers, but in vain. One Foscari went so far as to propose to marry her; she refused everything. She had gold enough; all that she now desired was love, a pure, young love that she herself had awakened, and that was both the first and the last. My felicity would have been complete were it not for an accursed nightmare that returned every night, and in which I imagined myself a village priest, mortifying myself and doing penance for the day's excesses. The habit of being with Clarimonde had so reassured me that I no longer gave any thought to the strange manner in which I had come to know her. Nevertheless, what Father Serapion had told me about her came occasionally to my mind and never failed to cause me some anxiety.

For some time Clarimonde's health had been failing; her complexion was becoming duller by the day. The doctors we sent for could find no cause for her illness and were at a loss as to what to do. They prescribed some trifling remedies and never returned. Meanwhile she was visibly paling, and growing colder and colder. She was now nearly as white and as lifeless as on that memorable night in the mysterious palace. I was disconsolate to see her thus slowly wasting away. Moved by my sorrow, she would give me a sweet, melancholy smile, the fateful smile of those who know they are to die.

One morning I was sitting by her bedside, eating my breakfast upon a little table so as not to leave her for a moment. As I was slicing some fruit, I accidentally cut myself with the knife and made a rather deep gash in my finger. The blood flowed instantly from the wound, and several purple drops spurted onto Clarimonde. Her eyes lit up, her features took on an expression of fierce, savage delight that I had never before seen in her. She leaped from the bed with animal agility, with the nimbleness of a cat or monkey, and threw herself upon my wound, which she began sucking with an air of unutterable pleasure. She sipped the blood slowly and with great care, like an epicure savoring a Xeres or Syracuse wine; her green eyes were half closed, and her round pupils had become slits. Now and then she stopped to kiss my hand, then pressed her lips again to the lips of the wound so as to draw out a few more red drops. When she saw that no more blood was flowing, she got up, her eyes shining, her skin rosier than a Spring dawn, her face full, her hands warm and moist—in a perfect state of health and more beautiful than ever.

"I will not die! I will not die!" she exclaimed, half mad with joy, and clinging to my neck, "I will be able to love you a long time. My life is in yours, and all that I am comes from you. A few drops of your rich and noble blood, more precious and potent than all the elixirs in the world, have restored me to life."

This scene haunted me for a long time, and filled me with strange doubts concerning Clarimonde. That very evening, when sleep had taken me back to my presbytery, I found Father Serapion more solemn and anxious than ever. He looked at me attentively and said, "Not content with losing your soul, you would

lose your body also. Hapless young man, into what snare have
you fallen!" I was startled by the tone in which he uttered these
words; but this impression, intense as it was, was soon dispelled
by a hundred other cares and concerns. One evening, however, I
looked in my mirror, the perfidious position of which she had not
reckoned with, and caught a glimpse of Clarimonde who was
pouring some powder into a glass of seasoned wine that she was
in the habit of preparing after dinner. I took the glass, pretended
to sip from it, and then set it down as if to finish it later at my
leisure. Availing myself of a moment when she had her back
turned, I poured out its contents under the table, after which I retired to my room and went to bed, determined not to sleep but
rather to wait and see what would happen. I did not have to wait
long; Clarimonde entered in her nightdress and, having disrobed,
lay down beside me. When she was satisfied that I was asleep, she
bared my arm and drew a gold pin from her hair. Then she began
to whisper:

"One drop, just one little red drop, a touch of red at the end
of my needle! . . . Since you still love me, I must not die. . . . Ah,
poor love, I shall drink your beautiful, brilliant, crimson blood.
Sleep, my only treasure, sleep, my god, my child; I will not hurt
you, I will take of your life only what is absolutely vital to my
own. If I did not love you so, I might bring myself to take other
lovers whose veins I could drain, but since I have known you, all
others fill me with abhorrence . . . Ah—what a lovely arm! How
plump it is! How white! I shall never dare to prick that pretty blue
vein." And as she spoke, she wept, and I felt her tears raining
down upon my arm, which she held between her hands. Finally
she plucked up her resolve, pricked me lightly with her needle
and began to suck up the blood that flowed from it. Then, fearing
to exhaust me although she had swallowed scarcely a few drops,
she carefully wrapped up my arm with a little strip of bandage after having rubbed it with an ointment that immediately closed the
wound.

I could no longer doubt that Father Serapion was right. Yet
despite this certitude, I could not help loving Clarimonde, and I
would gladly have given her all the blood she needed to sustain
her artificial existence. Besides, I was not overly afraid; the woman
made answer for the vampire, and what I had seen and heard put

my mind at ease: my veins' abundant supply would not be so
quickly drained, and I did not begrudge her a few drops of my
life. I would have opened my arm myself and told her, "Drink!
And may my love enter your body with my blood!" I avoided
making the slightest allusion to the narcotic she had given me and
to the pin episode, and we went on living in the most perfect harmony. Yet my priestly qualms of conscience tortured me more
than ever, and I scarcely knew what new inflictions to invent in
order to humble and mortify my flesh. Even though all these visions were involuntary and I had no control over them, I dared
not touch the crucifix with hands so impure and a mind sullied by
such real or imagined debauchery. To avoid falling into these ex-
hausting hallucinations, I would try to keep from falling asleep; I
would hold my eyelids open and stand upright against the wall,
struggling with all my might against sleep. But the sand of somnolence would soon enter my eyes, and realizing that all efforts were
futile, I would let my arms fall in weariness and despair, and the
tide would carry me away toward treacherous shores. Serapion
made the most vehement exhortations, reproaching me severely
for my listlessness and lack of fervor. One day when I had been
more agitated than usual, he told me, "There is only one way to
rid yourself of this obsession, and although it is extreme, we must
resort to it: powerful evils require powerful remedies. I know
where Clarimonde was interred; she must be exhumed, so that
you may see the object of your love in her true, pitiful condition.
You will no longer be tempted to perdition for the sake of a vile
corpse, devoured by worms and about to crumble into dust; this
will surely bring you to your senses." For my part, I was so weary
of this double life that I assented: wishing to find out, once and
for all, whether it was the priest or the nobleman who was the
victim of an illusion, I was resolved to kill one of the two men
within me to save the other—or to kill both, for such a life had
become unendurable. Father Serapion provided a pick, a crowbar,
and a lantern, and at midnight we set off toward the cemetery of
***, the location and layout of which he knew perfectly. After
having cast the dull light of the lantern upon the inscriptions of
several tombs, we finally came to a stone half buried in long grass
and weeds and covered with moss and parasites, on which we de-
ciphered this beginning of an inscription:

Here lies Clarimonde
Who while she lived
Was lovelier than all the world.

. . . .

"This is the place," said Serapion, and setting down his
lantern, he slipped the crowbar into the crack in the stone and
started to raise it up. The stone gave way, and he set to work with
the pick. I stood watching him, somber and silent as the night.
As for him, bent over his lugubrious task, he was dripping with
sweat, and his rapid, heavy breath was like a death rattle. It was
truly a strange spectacle, and anyone who might have seen us
would have taken us for thieves and profaners of the tomb rather
than for priests of God. Serapion's zeal had something savage and
cruel about it that made him resemble a demon more than an
apostle or an angel, and his large, austere features, sharply outlined in the glimmer of the lantern, were far from comforting. I
felt a cold sweat break out in beads upon my limbs, and my hair
stood painfully on end; in the depths of my heart I regarded the
severe Father's action as a heinous sacrilege, and I would have
been glad if from the dark clouds moving heavily above us there
had issued forth a triangle of flame to reduce him to dust. The
owls perched in cypresses, disturbed by the light of the lantern,
beat heavily upon the glass with their dusty wings, uttering plaintive cries; foxes yelped in the distance, and a host of ominous
sounds emanated from the silence. Finally Serapion's pick struck
against the boards of the coffin, which reechoed with a muffled,
sonorous sound, with the dreadful reverberation of the void. He
drew back the lid, and I saw Clarimonde, pale as marble, her
hands clasped, her white shroud enveloping her from head to
foot. A tiny red drop glistened like a rose at the corner of her colorless lips. At this sight, Serapion flew into a fury: "Ah, there you
are, demon, shameless courtesan, devourer of blood and gold!"
And he sprinkled holy water over the body and the coffin, making
the sign of the cross with his sprinkler. Poor Clarimonde had no
sooner been touched by the holy dew than her lovely body fell to
dust, and nothing was left but a hideous, shapeless mass of ashes
and half-charred bones. "Behold your mistress, Lord Romuald,"
said the inexorable priest, pointing to the sad remains. "Will you
be tempted, now, to stroll upon the Lido and at Fusina with your

beauty?" I bowed my head; something had just collapsed into a ruin within me. I returned to my presbytery, and Lord Romuald, lover of Clarimonde, parted at last from the poor priest with whom he had for so long kept such strange company. But the following night, I saw Clarimonde. She said to me, as she had that first time under the church portal, "Unhappy man! Unhappy man! What have you done? Why did you listen to that stupid priest? Were you not happy? And what have I done to you, that you should violate my tomb and lay bare my wretched nothingness? All communication between our souls and our bodies is henceforth broken. Farewell, you shall mourn me." She vanished into the air like smoke, and I never saw her again.

Alas. She spoke the truth: I have mourned her loss more than once, and I mourn her still. The peace of my soul has been very dearly bought. All the love of God was not too much to compensate for her love. There, brother, is the story of my youth. Never look upon a woman, and walk always with your eyes upon the ground, for chaste and sober as you may be, a moment can suffice to make you lose eternity.

1836

Translated by Joan C. Kessler

For a recent French edition of this work, see Théophile Gautier, "La Morte amoureuse," in *Contes fantastiques* (Paris: Librairie J. Corti, 1986).

Théophile Gautier

ARRIA MARCELLA

A year ago, three young men, three friends who were traveling together in Italy, were visiting the Studii Museum in Naples, where there was an exhibit of various ancient artifacts excavated from the ruins of Pompeii and Herculaneum.

They wandered, each according to his whim, through the rooms of the museum, poring over the mosaics, bronzes, and frescoes taken from the walls of the dead city, and whenever one of them came upon something out of the ordinary, he would call out joyfully to his companions, to the dismay of the taciturn Englishmen and staid bourgeois who stood turning the pages of their guidebooks.

But the youngest of the three, who had stopped in front of a glass display case, seemed not to hear the exclamations of his comrades, so absorbed was he in deep contemplation. What he was examining so intently was a fragment of black, coagulated ash containing a hollow impression: it resembled part of a mold which had been broken in the process of casting. An artist's trained eye would easily have recognized the outline of an exquisite breast and the curves of a female form, flawless as a Greek statue. It is well known, as any travel guide can tell you, that this ancient lava had congealed around the body of a woman, preserving thus its graceful contour. Owing to the whims of an eruption which destroyed four cities, this noble form that has been dust for nearly two thousand years has endured into our own time. The contour of a breast has come down through the ages, when many an empire has vanished without a trace! Nothing could efface this seal of beauty, affixed by chance upon the slag of a volcano.

Seeing that Octavian could not tear himself from his contemplation, his two friends went over to him, and Max, touching him on the shoulder, made him start like one taken red-handed. He had been plainly unaware of their approach.

"Come, Octavian," said Max, "don't linger hours over each exhibit, or we'll miss our train, and won't be able to see any of Pompeii."

"What's our friend looking at?" Fabio queried, drawing nearer. "Ah! The impression from the house of Arrius Diomedes." And he darted a queer, quick glance at Octavian.

Octavian blushed slightly, took Max's arm, and their visit concluded without further incident. On leaving the Studii, the three friends got into a corricolo and were driven to the train station. The corricolo, with its large red wheels, its jump seat studded with copper nails, and its thin, spirited horse, harnessed like a Spanish mule, galloping over the broad lava flagstones, is too familiar to warrant further description. Besides, this is not a travel album on Naples but the simple account of a bizarre and scarcely credible—although true—adventure.

The railway line to Pompeii runs for most of its length along the ocean, where, upon sand as black as sifted coal, the waves unfold their sweeping scrolls of foam. The beach is in fact composed entirely of lava flows and volcanic ash, the somber tones of which are in salient contrast to the blue of the sky and water. Amid all this radiance, only the earth seems suffused with darkness.

The villages along the way—Portici, immortalized in Auber's opera,[1] Resina, Torre del Greco, Torre dell'Annunziata—offering, as one passes, glimpses of arcaded houses and terraced roofs, have a plutonian and ferruginous quality about them, like Manchester or Birmingham, in spite of the southern whitewash and the intensity of the sun. Here even the dust in the air is black; an impalpable soot adheres to everything; one cannot but be aware that the forge of Vesuvius is at work, heaving and puffing, only a few paces away.

The three friends alighted at Pompeii, chuckling among themselves at the curious mixture of ancient and modern in the words *Pompeii Station:* a Greco-Roman city, with a railway arrival platform!

They crossed the cotton field, over which a few balls of white fluff were floating, on their way to the site of the excavated city, and found a guide to take them to the *osteria*[2] that stood outside the ancient ramparts—or, more precisely, a guide found them, a mischance which it is difficult to avoid in Italy.

It was one of those halcyon days so common in Naples, when the radiant sunlight and the pellucid air imbue objects with hues that in Northern climes would appear fantastical, and which seem to belong more to the realm of dream than to that of physical reality. Whoever has just once beheld this golden and azure brilliance will carry it back with him into the mist and fog as an incurable nostalgia.

The resurrected city, having thrown off a corner of its ashy shroud, stood out in all its myriad details in the blinding light of the sun. The cone of Vesuvius, with its bands of blue, pink, and violet lava, gilded by the sun, stood vividly outlined against the sky. A faint haze, almost invisible in the sunlight, lay like a cap upon its truncated crest; at first glance one might have mistaken it for one of those clouds which veil the mountain peaks even on the clearest days. On closer examination, one could see small wisps of white vapor emanating from the summit of the mountain as from the holes of an incense burner, then converging in a fine mist. The volcano, in a benevolent mood that day, quietly puffed upon its pipe, and had it not been for the sight of Pompeii buried at its feet, one would not have thought it of any more ferocious a temper than Montmartre. On its far side, lovely hills formed a voluptuously feminine, undulating contour; farther still, the sea, which once brought biremes and triremes below the ramparts of the city, drew across the horizon its placid line of blue.

The appearance of Pompeii is truly astonishing; even the most prosaic and undiscerning of souls would be astonished at this sudden leap backward across nineteen centuries. Two paces are enough to transport you from the ancient world to the modern, from Christianity to paganism. So when the three friends first glimpsed the streets which preserve intact the shape and configuration of a vanished existence, prepared as they were for the sight by books and drawings, they were moved by a sentiment as strange as it was profound. Octavian, especially, seemed struck with amazement, and followed along behind the guide like a som-

nambulist, deaf to the monotonous drone of names which the im-
pudent fellow was reeling off like a schoolboy's lesson.

He stared about him in stunned bewilderment at the ruts
carved by chariot wheels in the cyclopean paving stones, tracks
so sharply imprinted that they seemed to have been made only
yesterday; at the inscriptions traced in red cursive lettering on
the sides of walls: playbills, rental notices, votive formulae, shop
signs, advertisements of all sorts, looking just as odd as would a
poster-plastered bit of wall in Paris to the unknown souls living
two thousand years hence. He stared at houses whose roofs had
fallen in, exposing to a single glance of the eye all their inner
mysteries, domestic details passed over by historians, which civilizations carry with them to the grave; at fountains seemingly only
just run dry; at the Forum, surprised by catastrophe in mid-repair,
whose hewn and sculpted columns and entablatures seem to be
waiting still, in skeletal purity, for someone to fit them in proper
position; at temples consecrated to ancient gods long since passed
into the realm of myth, but who in their day saw not a single unbeliever; market stalls with only the vendors missing; taverns
where the circular stains of drinkers' cups can still be seen on the
marble tabletops; barracks with columns painted in red lead and
ochre, upon which soldiers had scrawled caricatures of combatants; and those twin theaters of song and drama, side by side,
which might well have reopened their doors but for the fact that
the troupes that played there, reduced to clay, were perhaps busy
stopping up a bunghole or a crack in the wall, like the noble dust
of Alexander and Caesar in Hamlet's melancholy meditation.[3]

While Max and Octavian clambered up the rows of seats to
the top, Fabio climbed onto the stage of the Tragic Theater, and
there began to recite, with abundant pantomime, the passages of
verse which came to his mind—to the great dismay of the lizards,
who fled with quivering tails, taking cover within the cracks of
ruined foundations. Although the bronze and earthen vessels that
had served as sounding boards now no longer existed, his voice
rang out nonetheless in sonorous and vibrant tones.

The guide next led them through the cultivated fields that
covered the still unexcavated portions of Pompeii, toward the
amphitheater at the opposite end of the city. They pursued their
way beneath trees whose roots plunged into the roofs of buried

houses, detaching the tiles, cracking the ceilings, fracturing the columns,—and across fields where prosaic vegetables ripened over artistic wonders, material emblems of the oblivion to which time relegates even the most splendid things.

The amphitheater did not surprise them. They had seen the one at Verona, larger and equally well preserved, and they were as familiar with the layout of these ancient stadiums as with that of the bullfight arenas in Spain, which resemble them in all but their architectural solidity and fineness of material.

So they retraced their steps, taking a short cut to the Street of Fortune. They listened distractedly to the cicerone who, as he passed each house, called it by the name given it at its discovery, and which derived from some distinctive feature: the House of the Bronze Bull, the House of the Faun, the House of the Ship, the Temple of Fortune, the House of Meleager, the Tavern of Fortune at the corner of Consular Street, the Academy of Music, the Village Oven, the Pharmacy, the Surgeon's Shop, the Custom House, the House of the Vestals, the Inn of Albinus, the Thermopolium,[4] and so on, until they reached the gate leading to the Way of the Tombs.

This brick doorway, covered with statues, but which had lost all other ornamentation, contains within its inner archway two deep grooves designed to hold a portcullis—the kind of defense one might have expected to find only in a medieval donjon.

"Who would have suspected," said Max to his friends, "that Pompeii, the Greco-Roman city, should have such a romantically Gothic gateway? Can you imagine a Roman knight returning late, and impatiently sounding his horn before the entrance, like a fifteenth-century page, to have the portcullis raised?"

"There is nothing new under the sun," replied Fabio, "not even that axiom, since Solomon invented it."

"Perhaps there may be something new under the moon," Octavian added, with a smile of melancholy irony.

"My dear Octavian," said Max, who during this brief conversation had stopped in front of an inscription traced in red chalk upon the outer wall, "Would you like to watch a contest of gladiators? Here is the announcement: combat and hunt on the fifth of the nones of April[5]—masts will be raised—twenty pairs of gladiators will fight on the nones—and if you fear for your complexion, be reassured, there will be awnings—unless you prefer to arrive at the amphitheater early, for the contestants will cut each other's throats in the morning—*matutini erunt.* [6] How accommodating!"

Conversing thus, the three friends continued down the tomb-lined Way. To our modern mind this would seem a somber thoroughfare for a city, but it did not have this gloomy connotation for the ancients, whose tombs, instead of a hideous corpse, contained but a handful of ashes: the abstract idea of death. Art embellished this final resting place, and, as Goethe has observed, the pagan adorned his urns and sarcophagi with the images of life.

No doubt that was the reason why Max and Fabio were lingering, with a blithe curiosity and cheerful exuberance that they could never have felt in a Christian cemetery, among these sepulchral monuments so richly gilded by the sun, and which, placed as they were right alongside the pathway, seemed still to be part of life, inspiring none of that cold repulsion or fantastic terror which is stirred in us by our lugubrious graveyards. They paused before the tomb of Mammia, the public priestess, not far from which a tree had sprung up, a cypress or poplar; they sat in the semicircular triclinium of funereal repasts, laughing as if they had just come into a fortune; they cracked no end of jokes upon the epitaphs of Naevoleia, Labeon, and the Arria family, while Octavian followed behind, appearing more moved than his carefree companions by the fate of these mortals dead for two thousand years.

They thus came to the villa of Arrius Diomedes, one of the largest residences in Pompeii. Brick steps lead up to a door, flanked by two small columns, and after stepping through, one finds oneself in a courtyard much like the *patio* in the center of Spanish or Moorish houses, to which the ancients gave the name *impluvium* or *cavaedium.* On all four sides, fourteen brick columns coated with stucco form a portico or covered peristyle, like the cloister of a convent, through which one could walk sheltered from the rain. The court is paved with a mosaic of bricks and white marble, the effect of which is soft and pleasing to the eye. In the center there still stands the square marble basin that was used to catch rainwater dripping from the roof of the portico. —It is the strangest sensation to be able thus to step into the life of antiquity, and to tread in patent leather boots upon the stones worn down by the sandals and cothurns[7] of the contemporaries of Augustus and Tiberius.

The cicerone then led them into the exedra or summer sitting room, opening toward the sea with its fresh, cool breezes. This was where visitors were received and where the inhabitants had their siesta during the hours of sweltering heat, when the winds blew in from Africa heavy with languor and storms. He showed them into the basilica, a long open gallery which lighted the series of rooms, and where the visitors and clients would wait until summoned by the usher. He led them onto the white marble terrace, opening out over green gardens and the blue of the sea. Then he showed them the nymphaeum, or bathing hall, with its yellow painted walls, stucco columns, mosaic paving, and marble bath which once held so many lovely bodies, now dissolved like shadows,—and the cubiculum, in which once had floated so many dreams that entered by the gates of ivory, and where the alcoves in the wall were closed off by a conopeum or curtain, the bronze rings of which still lay upon the ground. Then there was the tetrastyle or recreation room, the chapel of the household gods, the archives, the library, the painting gallery, the gynaeceum or women's apartments, composed of small chambers partly in ruins, their walls conserving traces of paintings and arabesques, like cheeks from which the makeup has been imperfectly wiped clean.

Having concluded this portion of their tour, they descended to the floor below, for the ground is much lower on the garden side than on that of the Street of Tombs. They passed through eight rooms painted in *rosso antico*, one of which contained architectural niches like those in the vestibule of the Hall of Ambassadors in the Alhambra, and they came at last to a cellar-like storeroom, the function of which was clearly indicated by eight clay amphoras that stood against the wall and that once must have been fragrant, like Horace's odes, with Cretan, Falernian, and Massican wine.

Through a narrow opening choked by nettles, a bright shaft of light entered, changing the translucent leaves to topaz and emerald—this gladdening touch of nature falling very opportunely into the prevailing gloom.

"It was here," said the cicerone in his nonchalant tone of

voice, which scarcely accorded with the meaning of the words, "that they discovered, among seventeen skeletons, the remains of the lady whose impression is preserved in the Naples Museum. She wore gold rings, and the remnants of her delicate tunic were found still clinging to the compressed ash in which her figure was cast."

The guide's banal utterances touched Octavian deeply. He asked to be shown the exact spot in which these precious remains had been discovered, and if he had not been restrained by his friends' presence, he would have given way to some lyrical effusion. His chest heaved, his eyes were moist with furtive tears: this catastrophe, effaced by twenty centuries of oblivion, moved him as though it were a recent tragedy. The death of a mistress or a dear friend could not have grieved him more; and while Max and Fabio had their backs turned, a tear fell, belated by two thousand years, on the very spot where she who had awakened in him a retrospective love had perished, suffocated in the fiery ash of the volcano.

"Enough archaeology!" Fabio exclaimed. "We shan't be writing a dissertation on a jug or tile of Julius Caesar's time, so as to be elected to some provincial academy; these classical mementos whet my appetite. Let us go and eat, if we can, at that picturesque *osteria*, though I fear they will serve us only fossil steaks and fresh eggs laid before the death of Pliny."[8]

"I shall not quote Boileau and say, 'A fool now and then gives good advice,'[9] laughed Max, "that would be impolite; but your idea is a good one. Though it would have been nicer to banquet here, reclining on a triclinium as was the custom, and served by slaves as were Lucullus and Trimalchio.[10] True, I don't see many oysters from Lake Lucrine, there are no turbots and mullets from the Adriatic, the Apulian boar is absent from the marketplace, and the loaves and honey cakes now sit in the Naples Museum, hard as stones, next to their verdigris-coated molds. Raw macaroni sprinkled with cacciacavallo, revolting as it may be, is still better than Nothing.[11] What does dear Octavian think?"

Octavian, sunk in regret at not having been in Pompeii on the day of Vesuvius's eruption, so that he might have rescued the lady with the golden rings and so earned her love, had heard nothing of this gastronomical conversation. Only Max's last two words had reached him, and as he had little desire to initiate a discussion, he gave a desultory nod of assent, and the three friends started back along the ramparts toward the inn.

The table was set in a sort of open porch which forms a vestibule to the osteria. Its whitewashed walls were decorated with several crude canvases, identified by the host as the work of Salvator Rosa, Spagnoletto, Massimo, and other celebrated painters of the Neapolitan school, whom he felt it his duty to extol.

"Venerable host," said Fabio, "do not waste your eloquence. We are not English, and we prefer young women to old paintings. Why don't you have that handsome velvet-eyed brunette, whom I saw on the stairs, bring us your wine list."

The *palforio*, realizing that his guests were not of the easily deluded species of philistines and bourgeois, left off boasting of his gallery only to glorify his cellar. To begin with, he had every wine of the best vintage: Château-Margaux, Grand-Lafite retour des Indes, Sillery de Moët, Hochmeyer, Scarlat wine, port and stout, ale and ginger beer, red and white Lacryma Christi, Capri, and Falernian.

"What! You have Falernian, you brute, and you put it at the bottom of your list! You put us through an insufferable oenological litany," said Max, leaping at the innkeeper's throat with a display of comic fury, "but have you not the least sense of local color? You are unworthy of living in this ancient habitat! But is your Falernian good at least? Was it put into amphoras under the consulship of Plancus—*consule Planco?*"[12]

"I am not familiar with Consul Plancus, and my wine is not in amphoras, but it is aged and costs ten carlini a bottle," was the host's reply.

Night had fallen, a night transparent and serene, clearer beyond a doubt than noonday in London. There was an unimaginable softness in the shades of blue upon the earth and the silvery reflections in the sky; the air was so still that the flames of the candles upon the table did not even flicker.

A young boy playing a flute drew near and stood beside the table in the attitude of a bas-relief, gazing at the three guests and blowing into his dulcet-toned instrument one of those bewitchingly seductive popular melodies in the minor key.

This boy was, perhaps, a direct descendant of the flute player who walked ahead of Duilius.[13]

"Our meal is assuming quite an ancient aura; we lack only

Gaditan [14] dancers and ivy wreaths," said Fabio, pouring himself a brimming glassful of Falernian wine.

"I feel in the mood to quote some Latin, like a feuilleton of the *Débats*," [15] added Max. "Stanzas of odes keep coming into my mind."

"Keep them to yourself," cried Octavian and Fabio, justly alarmed. "Nothing is so indigestible as Latin at table."

Conversation between young men with cigars in their mouths and elbows on the table, and with a number of empty bottles in front of them, generally turns fairly rapidly, especially if the wine is heady, to the subject of women. Each of the three set forth his personal views, which are here briefly summarized.

Fabio set store by youth and beauty alone. Sensual and down-to-earth, he had no illusions or prejudices in matters of love. A peasant girl was every bit as good as a duchess, provided she was handsome; he cared more for the body than for the dress. He made much fun of several of his friends who had become enamored of a few meters of lace and silk, declaring that it would be more logical to be in love with a dressmaker's display window. These opinions, basically quite sound, and which he did not trouble to conceal, made him pass for an eccentric.

Max, less of an artist than Fabio, cared only for difficult undertakings and complicated intrigues. He was on the lookout for any resistance to conquer, any virtue to seduce; love for him was like a game of chess, with long-meditated moves, delayed outcomes, surprises and stratagems worthy of Polybius. [16] Whenever he entered a drawing room, he would choose as the object of his attack the woman who appeared most lukewarm toward him. To cause her to pass, by subtle gradations, from aversion to love, was for him an exquisite delight; to command the acquiescence of those who spurned him, to break the wills that resisted his potent allure, seemed the sweetest of triumphs. Like the hunter who roams woods and fields in rain, sun, and snow, undaunted by fatigue and with an unrelenting zeal, in search of some scrawny game which more often than not he would scarcely deign to eat, Max had no sooner secured his prey than he lost all interest in it and almost immediately reembarked upon the chase.

As for Octavian, he readily admitted that reality held no great charm for him. Not that he gave himself up to schoolboy dreams, strewn with lilies and roses like a madrigal by Demoustier,[17] but every beautiful woman was surrounded by too many prosaic and disenchanting accessories: too many senile fathers wearing decorations of honor, coquettish mothers with real flowers in their false hair, red-faced cousins silently devising declarations of love, ridiculous aunts with a fancy for little dogs. An aquatint after a painting by Horace Vernet or Delaroche,[18] hanging in a woman's room, was enough to stifle his budding passion. More poetical than amorous, he yearned for a moonlit terrace on Isola Bella, in Lago Maggiore, by way of a backdrop for a rendezvous. He would have liked to bear his love aloft amid the stars, far above the theater of common existence. He had conceived a wild and impossible passion for each of the great embodiments of the feminine immortalized in art and history. Like Faust, he had loved Helen,[19] and his deepest wish was that the undulations of the centuries should bring him one of those sublime incarnations of human dream and desire, whose form, invisible to vulgar eyes, continues to exist in space and time. He had created an ideal seraglio with Semiramis, Aspasia, Cleopatra, Diana of Poitiers, Joan of Aragon.[20] Occasionally, too, he fell in love with statues, and one day, as he passed the Venus de Milo in the Louvre, he had exclaimed, "Oh, who will give you back your arms, that they might press me to your marble breast!" In Rome, the sight of a thick tress of hair exhumed from an ancient tomb had filled him with strange delusions. Tempting the guard with some gold coin, he had obtained two or three strands of the hair, and taken them to a powerful medium in an attempt to summon the shade of the dead woman, but the conductive fluid had evaporated with the lapse of so many years, and the spirit was unable to emerge from eternal night.

As Fabio had surmised when he saw his friend standing before the glass case in the Studii, the cast taken from the cellar of Arrius Diomedes' villa had inflamed Octavian with a mad surge of desire for a retrospective ideal. He yearned for a way to leave time and life behind, and to transport his soul into the age of Titus.[21]

Max and Fabio withdrew to their rooms and, their heads somewhat heavy from the classic vapors of the Falernian, soon fell asleep. Octavian, who as usual had left his glass untouched, disinclined to let a grossly corporeal inebriation disturb the poetic raptures seething within his brain, knew from the commotion of

his nerves that sleep would not come to him that night. With un-
hurried step he left the osteria to cool his brow and compose his
thoughts in the night air.

Instinctively and without his being aware of it, his feet carried him toward the entrance to the dead city. He pushed aside
the wooden bar and stepped in aimlessly among the ruins.

White moonbeams illuminated the ghostly dwellings, dividing the streets into two segments of silvery light and bluish
shadow. This nocturnal light, with its muted tints, disguised the
deteriorated condition of the buildings. The broken columns,
cracked facades, and collapsed roofs were less conspicuous now
than in the glare of the sunlight; the missing portions were filled
in by half-tones, and an unexpected beam, like an evocative touch
in a sketch for a canvas, disclosed an entire ensemble of fallen
ruin. The silent genii of the night seemed to have restored the fossil city for some fantastical, living reenactment.

Occasionally Octavian even fancied he saw shadowy human
forms moving in the darkness, but they vanished as soon as they
reached the lighted patches. Indistinct sounds, faint muffled whispers, drifted through the stillness. Our stroller at first ascribed
them to the blinking of his eyes and the buzzing of his ears; —it
could also be an optical illusion, the sigh of the sea breeze, or the
scurrying of a lizard or grass snake through the nettles, for all is
alive in nature, even death; everything murmurs, even silence.
Nevertheless he felt an involuntary twinge of anxiety, a light
shudder brought on perhaps by the chill night air, and which
made his flesh creep. Several times he turned round; he no longer
felt alone in the deserted town, as he had only a moment before.
Could his friends have had the same idea as he, and were they
searching for him among the ruins? These half-glimpsed forms,
these faint sounds of footsteps—could it be Max and Fabio chatting as they strolled, and disappearing around a corner? Octavian
knew from his emotion that this natural explanation was not the
right one, and all the logical reasoning he could muster failed to
convince him otherwise. The darkness and solitude ·was filled with
invisible beings that his presence had disturbed; he had stumbled
into the midst of an enigma, a mysterious drama that seemed to
await the moment he should leave in order to begin. Such were
the extravagant thoughts that ran through his mind, and that were

made plausible by the place, the hour, and the innumerable minor pretexts for alarm that anyone who has spent a night amid vast ruins will readily appreciate.

Passing in front of a house that he had noticed earlier in the day, and upon which the moon was now shining brightly, he recognized a certain portico that he had previously attempted to reconstruct in his mind, but which now appeared in a state of total restoration. Four Doric columns, fluted half-way up, their shafts covered with a coat of red lead like a purple-crimson drapery, supported a curved molding blazoned with polychrome embellishments, which seemed to have been completed only the day before. On the wall next to the door, a Laconian mastiff painted in encaustic,[22] with the customary inscription, *Cave canem*,[23] bayed with painted ferocity at visitors and at the moon. Upon the mosaic threshold, the word *Ave* in Oscan[24] and Latin welcomed the guests with its cordial syllables. The outer walls, painted in red and yellow ochre, showed not a single crack. The house was higher by one story, and the tile roof, capped with a bronze acroter, threw its intact profile against the pale blue sky with its fading stars.

This singular restoration, executed between afternoon and evening by an unknown architect, unnerved Octavian, who was certain that that very day he had seen this house in a deplorable state of ruin. The mysterious builder had worked very quickly, for each of the neighboring dwellings had the same newly constructed appearance. All the pillars were crowned with their capitals; not a stone, not a brick, not a layer of stucco, not a flake of paint was missing from the gleaming facades, and through the spaces of the colonnade he could see pink and white laurels, myrtles, and pomegranate trees around the marble basin in the *cavaedium*. History was in error—there had never been any volcanic eruption, or else the hand of time had moved back twenty centuries upon the clock face of eternity.

Exceedingly astonished, Octavian wondered if he were half asleep. He asked himself seriously if the hallucinations of madness were not dancing before his eyes, but was compelled to acknowledge that he was neither dreaming nor mad.

The skies had curiously altered. Pale rosy tints were blending, by violet gradations, into the bluish moonbeams; a faint glow was appearing on the horizon; it looked as if day were about to dawn.

Octavian looked at his watch—it was midnight. Thinking it had stopped, he pressed the repeater spring; the mechanism sounded twelve times. It was surely midnight, yet the skies continued to brighten, and the moon dissolved into the ever more radiant blue. The sun was rising.

Octavian, in whose mind the notion of time had become utterly confused, was forced to conclude that he was walking not in a dead Pompeii, the stiffened corpse of a city half unveiled from its shroud, but in a Pompeii that was vital, young, and intact, one that had not yet known the burning mud torrents of Vesuvius.

An inexplicable miracle had just transported him, a Frenchman of the nineteenth century, into the age of Titus, not in spirit but in reality—or else it had reclaimed this ruined city from the depths of time, bringing it back to him with all its vanished inhabitants. For at that very moment a man dressed in ancient garb emerged from a neighboring house.

The man had short hair and was smooth shaven. He had on a brown tunic and a grayish cloak, the bottom of which was drawn up so as not to hamper his stride. He was walking rapidly, almost running, and passed Octavian without noticing him. On his arm he carried a rush basket, and he was heading toward the Forum Nundinarium. No doubt about it, he was a slave, some Davus [25] on his way to market.

There came a rumble of wheels, and an ancient wagon, drawn by white oxen and laden with vegetables, turned into the street. Alongside the oxen walked a driver with bare, suntanned legs, sandals on his feet, and wearing a sort of linen shirt puffed out at the waist. A pointed straw hat, held by a strap, was thrown back to reveal his head, of a type unfamiliar nowadays: a low forehead with several lumpy protuberances, black, tightly curled hair, a straight nose, eyes as fixed and placid as those of his oxen, and the neck of a peasant Hercules. His statuesque pose, as he solemnly touched his animals with the goad, would have made Ingres [26] stare in awe.

He noticed Octavian and appeared surprised, but continued on his way. Once he looked back, no doubt perplexed by this curious figure but, in his placid rustic stupidity, leaving it to those more clever than he to decipher the enigma.

Campanian peasants also passed by, ringing bronze bells and

driving before them donkeys bearing wine in goatskins. Their faces were as different from those of our modern peasants as a coin of precious metal is from a copper penny.

The town was gradually filling with people, like one of the scenes in a diorama[27] which at first appear empty before a change of light makes them come alive with figures hitherto invisible to the eye.

A change had taken place within Octavian. Just a moment before, in the deceiving darkness of night, he had been prey to that unease which plagues even the most intrepid souls when faced with troubling, fantastic phenomena that reason is powerless to explain. His vague alarm had turned to profound astonishment; the clarity of his perceptions made it impossible for him to doubt the evidence of his senses, yet what he beheld was utterly incredible. —Still unconvinced, he began to make mental note of small details in order to prove to himself that he had not fallen victim to a hallucination. —Surely these were not phantoms gliding before his eyes, for the brilliant sunlight imbued them with an unmistakable air of reality, and they cast long morning shadows over the sidewalks and the walls.

Completely at a loss as to what had befallen him, and at heart delighted to see one of his most cherished dreams fulfilled, Octavian yielded himself to the wonder of the adventure without attempting to make any sense of it. Because, he told himself, some mysterious power had granted him to live a few short hours in a vanished age, he would not waste his time brooding over an insoluble mystery. And he continued resolutely on his way, gazing this way and that at a spectacle at once so ancient and so new. Yet into what period in the life of Pompeii had he been transported? From the names of public figures that figured in an aedile's inscription on the wall, he deduced that he must be in the early part of Titus's reign—that is to say, in the year 79 of our era. —A sudden idea flashed into Octavian's mind. The woman at whose preserved impression he had marveled in the Naples Museum must still be alive, since the eruption of Vesuvius, in which she had perished, had occurred on August 24 of that very year. So he could find her, see her, speak to her. . . . The wild desire that had stirred in him at the sight of that ash molded upon those heavenly contours was perhaps to be fulfilled, for nothing could be impossible to a love

powerful enough to reverse the course of time and make an hour
slide twice through the sandglass of eternity.

While Octavian was lost in these reflections, several pretty
young maidens passed on their way to the fountains, supporting
the vessels they balanced on their heads with the tips of their
white fingers. Patricians wearing white, purple-bordered togas
and followed by a retinue of clients were heading toward the forum. Buyers crowded round the tiny shops, each of which was
designated by a carved and painted sign, and which in size and
shape were reminiscent of the Moorish shops in Algiers. Above
most of the stalls was a magnificent, colored terra cotta phallus
bearing the inscription *hic habitat felicitas* [28]—part of a ritual practice of warding off the evil eye. Octavian even noticed an amulet
shop with a display of horns, coral branches, and little golden
Priapi such as still can be found in Naples as defenses against
the *jettatura*. [29] Superstition, he reflected, is more enduring than
religion.

Following the sidewalks that line every street in Pompeii
(thus depriving the English of the smug honor of having invented
them) Octavian came face to face with a handsome young man of
about his own age, wearing a yellow tunic and draped in a mantle
of fine white wool as soft as cashmere. The spectacle of Octavian,
wearing a dreadful modern hat and buttoned into an ugly black
frock coat, his legs constricted by trousers and his feet squeezed
into shiny boots, appeared to amaze the young Pompeian much as
the sight of an Ioway or a Botocudo with his feathers, bear-claw
necklace, and strange tattoos would amaze us on the boulevard de
Gand. Nevertheless, as he was a well-bred young man, he did not
burst out laughing in Octavian's face; rather, taking pity on the
poor barbarian lost in this Greco-Roman city, he addressed him in
a gently modulated voice:

"Advena, salve." [30]

Nothing could be more natural than that an inhabitant of
Pompeii, in the reign of his august majesty, the divine emperor
Titus, should speak in Latin, yet Octavian started upon hearing
this dead language articulated by a living tongue. Then he felt
very pleased at having once been a top student and having won
prizes in the competitions. On this occasion, at least, the Latin
taught at the university served him well, and summoning up his

classroom memories, he replied to the Pompeian's greeting in the style of *De Viris Illustribus* and *Selectae e Profanis*,[31] in a fairly intelligible manner but with a Parisian accent that made the young man smile.

"Perhaps it would be easier for you to speak Greek," said the Pompeian. "I know that language too, for I studied at Athens."

"I know even less Greek than Latin," replied Octavian. "I am from the land of the Gauls—from Paris, from Lutetia."[32]

"I know that country. My grandfather fought in Gaul under the great Julius Caesar. But what curious clothes you are wearing! The Gauls I saw in Rome were not dressed like that."

Octavian tried to make the young Pompeian understand that twenty centuries had elapsed since Julius Caesar's conquest of Gaul and that styles might have changed in the interim, but he became entangled in his Latin, which was meager in any case.[33]

"My name is Rufus Holconius, and my house is yours," said the young man, "unless you prefer the freedom of the tavern. Albinus's inn is quite comfortable, near the Augustus Felix district, as is the inn of Sarinus, son of Publius, near the second tower; but if you like, I would be happy to show you the city, which is so new to you. I rather like you, young barbarian, although you did strain my credulity a bit about the reigning Emperor Titus having been dead two thousand years, and the Nazarene—whose vile followers, coated with pitch, lit up Nero's gardens—ruling as Lord of the heavens in place of the fallen gods. —By Pollux!"[34] he added, glancing at a red inscription above a street corner, "you are just in time: they're performing Plautus's *Casina*,[35] recently restored to the stage. It's an odd, comical drama which should amuse you even if you can't make out much more than the gestures. Follow me, it is about to begin; I'll show you to the seats for the guests and foreigners."

And Rufus Holconius started off toward the little comic theater that the three friends had visited earlier in the day.

The Frenchman and the Pompeian made their way along the Street of the Fountain of Abundance, the Street of Theaters, passed the academy, the Temple of Isis, the Sculptor's Studio, and entered the Odeon or comic theater by a side entrance. Thanks to a word from Holconius, Octavian was seated near the stage. Immediately he was the center of kindly curiosity, and a faint murmur swept through the amphitheater.

The play had not yet begun, and Octavian took advantage of the opportunity to look round the auditorium. The semicircular tiers, each ending in a magnificent lion's paw carved from Vesuvian lava, rose in widening circles from an empty space corresponding to our orchestra pit, but much smaller and paved with a mosaic of Greek marble. At regular intervals, wider tiers formed separate zones, and four staircases corresponding to the entrances and ascending from the base to the summit of the amphitheater divided it into sections, wider at the top than at the bottom. The spectators, whose tickets consisted of small ivory counters on which were marked the number of the section and the row, along with the title of the play to be performed and the name of the author, had no difficulty finding their places. The magistrates, nobles, married men, young men, and soldiers with their gleaming bronze helmets were all seated separately. —It was a marvelous spectacle: the lovely togas and the full, white, beautifully draped mantles spread over the lower steps and contrasting with the varied attire of the women, seated above, and the gray cloaks of the common people, relegated to the upper tiers near the roofed colonnade—through which could be glimpsed a sky as brilliantly blue as the azure field of a Panathenaea.[36] A fine spray of water, scented with saffron, fell in imperceptible droplets from the hangings above the stage, cooling and perfuming the air. Octavian recalled the fetid emanations that poison the atmosphere of our modern theaters, so uncomfortable that they might almost be called places of torture, and reflected that civilization had not greatly advanced.

The curtain, supported by a transverse beam, fell into the depths of the orchestra. The musicians seated themselves on their platform, and Prologue appeared, grotesquely attired and with his head covered with an ugly mask made to fit like a helmet.

After bowing to the audience and calling for applause, Prologue launched into a comical argument. Old plays, he said, were like old wine that improves with age, and *Casina*, beloved by the elders, should be no less dear to the young. It can be enjoyed by everyone, by some because they are familiar with it, by others because it is new to them. The play had, moreover, been meticulously restaged, and the audience should listen with their minds free from cares, without thought of their debts or of their creditors, for one cannot be arrested in a theater. It was a happy day, the weather was fine, and the kingfishers were soaring high above the forum. Then he gave a summary of the comedy which the actors were about to perform, in such detail as to make it evident that suspense was hardly a factor in the ancients' enjoyment of the theater. He explained how the old Stalino, in love with his beautiful slave Casina, plans to marry her to his tenant farmer Olympio, an obliging chap whose place he would then assume on the wedding night; and how Stalino's wife Lycostrata, to thwart her dissolute husband's lust, and to further her son's amours, plans to marry Casina to the riding master Chalinus; finally, how Stalino, duped, mistakes a disguised slave youth for Casina, who, when it is discovered that she is of free birth, marries the young master, whom she loves and who loves her.

Absentmindedly, the young Frenchman watched the actors with their bronze-mouthed masks as they moved about the stage. The slaves ran hither and thither in simulated zeal, the old man wagged his head and held out his tremulous hands, the matron, loud-voiced and with a look of scorn and ill-temper, was putting on airs and scolding her spouse to the great delight of the audience. —The actors entered and exited by three doors in the back wall, leading to the actors' foyer. —Stalino's house occupied one corner of the stage, and opposite was the house of his old friend Alcesimus. The setting, though very well painted, evoked more the idea of the place than the place itself, like the crude stage sets of classical tragedy.

When the nuptial procession escorting the mock Casina made its entrance upon the stage, a great burst of laughter, such as Homer attributes to the gods, ran along all the benches of the amphitheater, and the space echoed with thunderous applause; but Octavian no longer looked nor listened.

For there in the women's rows, he had caught sight of a creature of wondrous beauty. From that moment all the lovely faces which had previously attracted him were eclipsed, as Phoebe [37] eclipsed the stars. Everything vanished, disappearing as if in a dream; a mist obscured the teeming rows of spectators, and the shrill voices of the actors seemed to recede into infinite distance.

An electric shock seemed to pass through his heart, and each time the woman's glance fell upon him it seemed to strike sparks in his breast.

She was dark-haired and pale; her crimped locks, black as

Night, were slightly drawn back on her temples in the Greek fashion, and in her lusterless face shone two soft, dark eyes, with an indefinable expression of voluptuous melancholy and passionate ennui. Her mouth, disdainfully curved at the corners, protested with the lusty vitality of its flaming purple against the serene whiteness of the mask-like features. Her neck had those lovely, pure lines that one finds nowadays only on statues. Her arms were bare to the shoulder, and from the tips of her proud breasts that lifted her violet-pink tunic fell two folds that might have been carved in marble by Phidias or Cleomenes.[38]

The sight of these breasts, so perfectly molded, their outline so firm and pure, mesmerized Octavian. These curves seemed to correspond exactly to the hollow mold in the Naples Museum, which had stirred him to such ardent fantasy, and his heart cried out within him that this was indeed the woman who had perished in Arrius Diomedes' villa amid the ashes of Vesuvius. By what miracle did he now behold her alive, at a performance of Plautus's *Casina?* He did not even attempt to fathom it; how, indeed, did he come to be there himself? He accepted her presence, just as in dreams we see those whom we know to be long dead moving before us with all the appearance of life. Besides, his emotion had completely overpowered his reason. For him, the wheel of time had slipped out of its channel, and his victorious desire had chosen its object among the vanished centuries! He was face to face with his phantom ideal—with the most profoundly unattainable of dreams, a retrospective chimera. In an instant his life had become whole.

As he gazed upon that face, so composed yet so passionate, so cool yet so ardent, so impassive yet so alive, he knew that he beheld his first and his last love, the cup of his ultimate intoxication. The images of all the women he had ever thought he loved seemed to dissolve like pale shadows, and he felt his soul grow pure again, unsullied by any previous emotion. The past vanished.

The beautiful Pompeian girl, her chin resting upon her palm, threw Octavian a velvety glance from her dark eyes, even as she seemed to be watching the stage, and he felt this glance fall upon him like a rush of molten lead. Then she leaned over and whispered to a girl seated by her side.

The performance was over; the crowds streamed out of the theater. Declining the kind offers of his guide Holconius, Octa-

vian made a dash for the nearest exit. He had scarcely reached it
when he felt a hand on his arm and heard a female voice whisper,
in low tones but so distinctly that he did not miss a word:

"I am Tyche Novoleja, serving at the pleasure of Arria Marcella, daughter of Arrius Diomedes. My mistress loves you; follow me."

Arria Marcella had just entered her litter, which was borne by
four sturdy Syrian slaves naked to the waist, their bronze torsos
gleaming in the sun. Then the curtains of the litter were drawn
aside, and a pale hand, studded with rings, made a friendly sign to
Octavian as if to corroborate the servant's words. The purple folds
fell together again, and the litter moved off to the rhythmic tread
of the slaves.

Tyche led Octavian through side streets, at the crossings
treading lightly on the stepping stones between the ruts of the
chariot wheels, and making her way through the labyrinth with
the ease that comes of familiarity. Octavian observed that he was
passing through sections of the city which had not yet been excavated, and which as a result were entirely unknown to him. This
curious detail, amid so many others, did not surprise him. He had
made up his mind to be surprised by nothing. In all this archaic
phantasmagoria, which would be enough to make an antiquarian
swoon with delight, he could see nothing but the deep, dark eyes
of Arria Marcella, and that exquisite breast, victorious over the
centuries, which destruction itself was determined to preserve.

They came to a hidden door that opened and immediately
closed, and Octavian found himself in a courtyard surrounded by
Ionic columns of Greek marble, painted halfway up in a bright
yellow, the capitals set off by red and blue ornaments. A garland
of aristolochia dangled its broad, heart-shaped leaves over the jutting angles of the building like a natural arabesque, and near a basin bordered with plants a pink flamingo stood on one leg, like a
feathered flower among the flowers of the garden.

Frescoed panels representing fanciful architecture or imaginary landscapes adorned the walls. Octavian noted these details
with a rapid glance, as Tyche handed him over to the slaves of the
baths, who despite his impatience made him endure all the ther-
mal refinements of antiquity. After passing through the various
degrees of vaporized heat, suffering through the process of scrap-
ing and rubbing, and being drenched with cosmetics and per-

fumed oils, he was clothed in a white tunic and was met at the last door by Tyche, who took his hand and led him into another richly ornamented room.

On the ceiling were Mars, Venus, and Cupid, painted with a purity of outline, brilliance of color, and stylistic liberty that was the mark, not of a common decorator, but of a great master. A frieze composed of stags, rabbits, and birds frolicking amid foliage ran above the Cipoline marble wainscoting. The mosaic floor, a masterful bit of composition which was perhaps the work of Sosimus of Pergamum,[39] featured reliefs of a banquet executed with artful illusion.

At the far end of the room, on a biclinium or double bed, Arria Marcella leaned upon her elbow in a serene, voluptuous pose that recalled the reclining woman carved by Phidias for the pediment of the Parthenon. Her shoes, embroidered with pearls, lay at the foot of the bed, and her lovely bare feet, purer and whiter than marble, extended from beneath her light silken coverlet.

Two earrings in the shape of scales, with a pearl in each balance, shimmered against her pale cheeks; a necklace of golden balls, from which hung pear-shaped beads, lay upon her bosom, half-revealed by a careless fold of her straw-colored peplos, bordered with black fretting; a black and gold band gleamed in her ebony hair. She had changed her clothes upon returning from the theater, and round her arm, like the asp of Cleopatra, coiled a golden serpent with eyes of precious stones, trying to bite its tail.

A small table supported on griffin's feet and inlaid with ivory, silver, and mother-of-pearl, stood by the double bed, laden with various dishes set out on gold and silver plates or on china enameled with precious paintings. There was a pheasant lying on a bed of feathers, and an assortment of fruits which ripen at different seasons and are rarely seen together.

Everything pointed to an awaited guest: freshly cut flowers were strewn upon the ground, and the wine jugs stood in snow-filled urns.

Arria Marcella signaled to Octavian to lie down beside her on the biclinium and to share in the meal; the young man, half mad with love and surprise, helped himself at random from the dishes held out to him by little Asiatic slaves with short tunics and curly hair. Arria did not eat, but frequently raised to her lips an opalescent myrrhine goblet filled with dark purple wine, like coagulated blood; as she drank, a faint pinkish flush overspread her pale cheeks, rising from the heart which had not beat for so many years. Yet when Octavian, lifting his glass to his lips, brushed her bare arm with his hand, it was as cold as a serpent's skin or the marble of a tomb.

"Oh! When, in the Studii, you stopped to look at the piece of hardened clay that has preserved my form," said Arria Marcella, turning her deep moist eyes upon Octavian, "and your thought came rushing fervently toward me, my soul felt it even in that world where I float invisible to vulgar eyes; as belief creates the god, so love does a woman. One does not truly die until one is no longer loved; your desire has restored me to life, and your heart's all-powerful summons has dissolved the distances that divide us."

This notion of amorous evocation, expressed by the young woman, coincided with some of Octavian's philosophical beliefs—beliefs we are much inclined to share.

For indeed, nothing dies, but all exists perpetually; that which was once, no power can annihilate. Every act, every word, every shape, every thought which has fallen into the universal ocean of being forms widening circles that go on expanding to the far reaches of eternity. Their material outline is invisible only to vulgar eyes; they send forth specters which populate the expanses of the infinite. In some unknown region of space, Paris is still carrying Helen away; Cleopatra's galley still spreads its silken sails upon the azure stretches of an ideal Cydnus.[40] Passionate minds, powerful wills, have succeeded in summoning forth ostensibly vanished centuries and in resurrecting human beings from the dead. Faust took Tyndareus's daughter[41] for his mistress and bore her away to his Gothic castle from the mysterious depths of Hades. So Octavian, too, had lived for a day in the reign of Titus and had been loved by Arria Marcella, Arrius Diomedes' daughter, who at this very moment was reclining beside him upon an ancient couch, in a city that in the eyes of the world was long since destroyed.

"In my aversion to all other women," Octavian began, "in the irresistible reverie that drew me to its radiant archetypes glowing in the depths of the ages like beckoning stars, I knew that I would love only beyond the confines of time and space. It was you I was awaiting, and, through a secret magnetism, that fragile trace pre-

served by human curiosity brought me into contact with your
soul. I know not if you are dream or reality, woman or phantom, if
like Ixion I am clasping a cloud to my breast,[42] or if I have fallen
victim to sorcerers' vile magic, but of this I am certain: that you
are my first and my last love."

"May Eros, son of Aphrodite, hear your vow," said Arria Marcella, leaning her head upon her lover's shoulder as he drew her to
him in a passionate embrace. "Oh, press me to your young breast,
envelop me with your warm breath, I am cold for having been so
long without love." And close to his heart Octavian felt the rise
and fall of her beautiful bosom—at the mold of which he had
gazed that very morning through the glass of a case in the museum. He felt the coolness of her flesh through his tunic; it inflamed him like fire. The gold and black band had slipped from
Arria's head, which she had thrown back in her passion, and her
hair spilled across the blue pillow like a jet-black river.

The slaves had removed the table. Nothing could be heard
but a muffled murmur of kisses and sighs. The tame quails, heed-
less of this amorous scene, chirped as they picked the remains of
the feast from the mosaic floor.

Suddenly the bronze rings of the portiere slid along the rod,
and an old man with stern features and draped in a loose brown
mantle appeared upon the threshold. He wore his gray beard in
two points, like the Nazarenes, and his face seemed furrowed as if
from maceration. A small, black, wooden cross hung around his
neck, leaving no doubt as to his creed: he belonged to the sect,
only recently established, of the disciples of Christ.

Overwhelmed with confusion at the sight of him, Arria Marcella hid her face in a fold of her mantle, as a bird unable to flee
from an enemy hides its head under its wing, so as to shield herself at least from the horror of the sight, while Octavian, leaning
on his elbow, stared at this troublesome individual who had in-
truded so abruptly upon his bliss.

"Arria, Arria," said the stern figure in an admonishing tone,
"was one lifetime not enough for your extravagance, and must
your sordid, infamous loves encroach upon the centuries which
do not belong to you? Can you not leave the living in their own
sphere? Have your ashes not yet cooled since the day you died
unrepentant in a rain of volcanic fire? Two millennia of death

seem not to have quieted you, and your ravenous arms still lure poor fools, enchanted by your philtres, to your heartless marble breast!"

"Have mercy, my father, do not torment me in the name of that gloomy religion which never was my own. I believe in our old gods who loved life, youth, beauty, pleasure. Do not plunge me back into pale nothingness; let me take joy in the life which love has restored to me."

"Silence, blasphemer, speak not to me of your demon gods. Let this man, shackled by your wanton seductions, go free; tempt him no more beyond the circle of the life which God has assigned to him. Be gone to your pagan limbo with your Greek, Roman, and Asiatic loves. Young Christian, flee this larval phantom, who would seem to you more hideous than the Empusae and Phorcides [43] if you could see her as she really is."

Octavian, pale and frozen with horror, tried to speak, but his voice clave to his throat, as in the Virgilian expression. [44]

"Will you obey, Arria?" cried the towering old man, imperiously.

"No, never!" declared Arria, her eyes flashing, her nostrils dilating, her lips quivering as she clasped Octavian in her lovely statue-like arms, cold, hard, and rigid as marble. Her wild beauty, exacerbated by the struggle, shone with a supernal brilliance at this final moment, as if to leave her young lover with an ineluctable memory.

"Well then, wretched creature," returned the old man, "I shall have to resort to drastic measures, to make your nothingness palpable and visible to this spellbound youth." And in a commanding tone, he uttered a formula of exorcism that made Arria's cheeks, flushed from the dark wine in the myrrhine cup, turn deathly pale.

At that moment, a distant church bell from one of the villages near the sea or one of the hamlets that nestled in the folds of the mountain sounded the first chimes of the Angelus.

At the sound, a sigh of anguish was rent from the young woman's breast. Octavian felt the arms that held him grow limp, the draperies that covered her gave way as if the contours that filled them had collapsed, and the unhappy night stroller saw, there at his side on the festal bed, nothing but a handful of ashes and shapeless remains mingled with charred bones among which gleamed bracelets and golden jewels, such as must have been discovered in the excavation of Arrius Diomedes' house.

He uttered a terrible cry and lost consciousness.

The old man had disappeared. The sun was rising, and the hall, a moment before so brilliantly adorned, was now no more than a moldering ruin.

After a heavy sleep brought on by the libations of the previous night, Max and Fabio awakened with a start, and their first thought was to call out to their friend, whose room was adjacent to theirs, with one of those mock rallying cries sometimes adopted by traveling companions. Octavian made no reply, for good reason. Fabio and Max, receiving no answer, proceeded to enter their friend's room, and observed that the bed had not been slept in.

"Most likely he could not make it back to his room," said Fabio, "and fell asleep on a chair, for dear Octavian hasn't a very strong head. He probably got up early and went out to work off the wine in the morning air."

"Yet he hardly drank anything," rejoined Max, reflecting. "The whole thing seems strange to me. Let us look for him."

The two friends, accompanied by the cicerone, searched every street, every lane, every crossroads, every square in Pompeii, entered every quaint and curious house where they suspected Octavian might be copying a painting or noting down an inscription, and at last found him lying in a swoon upon the loose mosaic of a small room that was partly collapsed in ruin. They had difficulty bringing him to his senses; when he finally regained consciousness, he gave no explanation other than that he had been taken by a whim to visit Pompeii by moonlight, and that he had had a fainting fit which was not likely to have any serious consequences.

The little party returned to Naples by train, as they had come, and that evening, in their box at San Carlo, Max and Fabio watched through their opera glasses a swarm of knickered ballet nymphs skipping after Amelia Ferraris, the dancer then in vogue, all of them wearing beneath their gauze skirts hideous drawers of a monstrous green, that made them look like frogs stung by a tarantula. Octavian, pale, weary, with misty eyes, seemed hardly to notice what was happening on stage, so difficult was it after his extraordinary nocturnal adventure to enter once again into the sensation of real life.

From that day onward, Octavian was consumed by a black melancholy, which the joking good humor of his friends did more to aggravate than to relieve. The image of Arria Marcella haunted him constantly, and the unhappy ending of his fantastical love affair did not detract from its charm.

Once, unable to resist the desire, he secretly returned to Pompeii and wandered among the ruins by moonlight as he had that first time, his heart throbbing with a wild, absurd hope; but the hallucination was not renewed. He saw only the lizards scurrying over the stones, and heard only the calls of frightened night birds. His friend Rufus Holconius was not to be seen; Tyche did not come to pose her slender hand upon his arm; Arria Marcella, implacable, remained dust.

As a last resort, Octavian recently married a lovely young English girl, who is madly in love with him. He is a perfect husband, yet a secret, unerring instinct of her heart tells Ellen that he is in love with another. But with whom? The most meticulous sleuthing has failed to provide any indication. Octavian does not keep a ballerina; in society, he honors women with the merest platitudes; he even gave a pointedly cool reception to the advances of a Russian princess known for her beauty and coquetry. A secret drawer, opened during her husband's absence, furnished Ellen with not the slightest proof of infidelity. But how would it ever occur to her to be jealous of Arria Marcella, daughter of Arrius Diomedes, a freedman of Tiberius?

1852

Translated by Joan C. Kessler

For a recent French edition of this work, see Théophile Gautier, "Arria Marcella," in *Contes fantastiques* (Paris: Librairie J. Corti, 1986).

Alexandre Dumas

THE SLAP OF CHARLOTTE CORDAY

L ike everything that belonged to Monsieur Ledru, the dining room table had character.

It was in the shape of a large horseshoe, and was placed up against the garden windows, leaving three quarters of the vast hall clear for the servants. The table could comfortably seat twenty people; Monsieur Ledru dined there regularly, whether he had one, two, four, ten, or twenty guests or whether he ate alone: that day we were only six and occupied scarcely a third of it.

Every Thursday the menu was the same. Monsieur Ledru assumed that during the previous week the guests would have had the opportunity to vary their fare, at home or as the invited guests of others. One was therefore sure to find, every Thursday at the house of Monsieur Ledru, soup, beef, tarragon chicken, roast leg of lamb, green beans, and a salad.

The quantity of chicken doubled or tripled according to the appetite of the guests.

Whether there were few guests, many, or none at all, Monsieur Ledru always sat at one end of the table, facing the courtyard, with his back to the garden. He sat in a large armchair, which during the past ten years had taken root in that spot. There, his gardener Antoine—converted, like a jack-of-all-trades, into a footman—would hand him, in addition to ordinary table wine,

Editor's note: This story is drawn from Dumas's *Les Mille et un Fantômes* (The thousand and one phantoms), and embraces the three chapters entitled "The Slap of Charlotte Corday," "Solange," and "Albert."

several bottles of well-aged Burgundy, which would be proffered with ceremonious reverence, and which Monsieur Ledru would then uncork and pour into his guests' glasses with equal reverence and ceremony.

Eighteen years ago, people still believed in something;[1] ten years hence they will no longer believe in anything, not even in old wine.

After dinner, everyone would go into the drawing room for coffee.

The dinner was spent, as dinners usually are, in extolling the food and the wine. Yet one of the guests, a young woman, ate but a few crumbs of bread, drank but one glass of wine, and spoke not a word. She reminded me of the ghoul in the *Thousand and One Nights* who would sit at table with the others, but only to eat a few grains of rice with a toothpick.[2]

After dinner, as was the custom, everyone went into the drawing room. It naturally fell to me to offer my arm to our silent guest. She came part of the way toward me to accept it. There was always the same indolence in her movements, the same grace of bearing, I would almost say the same ghostly impalpability in her limbs. I led her over to a chaise longue, on which she reclined.

Two people had been shown into the room while we were still at table. They were the doctor and the police inspector.

The inspector had come to have us sign the statement that Jacquemin had already signed in his prison cell.[3] A faint blood-stain was visible upon the paper.

As I signed in my turn, I asked: "What is this stain? Did this blood come from the wife or the husband?"

"It came," replied the inspector, "from the wound on the murderer's hand, which is still bleeding and cannot be stanched."

"Do you realize, Monsieur Ledru," said the doctor, "that that brute still insists that the head of his wife spoke to him?"

"And you believe that to be impossible, do you not, Doctor?"

"Of course!"

"You believe it impossible even for the eyes to have opened?"

"Impossible."

"You do not believe that the blood, interrupted in its flow by the plaster[4] which instantly plugged up all the arteries and blood vessels, could have effected a momentary restoration of life and feeling?"

"I do not."

"Well," said Monsieur Ledru, "I do."

"And I," said Alliette.

"And I," said the abbé Moulle.

"And I," said the chevalier Lenoir.

"And I," said I.

Only the inspector and the pale lady were silent: one, no doubt, because the question held too little interest; the other, perhaps, because it held too much.

"Ah, if you are all against me, you are probably right. Yet, if one of you were a doctor . . ."

"But Doctor," said Monsieur Ledru, "you know that I am, more or less."

"In that case," said the doctor, "you should know that there is no pain where there is no feeling, and that feeling is destroyed by the severing of the spinal column."

"And who told you that?" asked Monsieur Ledru.

"Reason, naturally!"

"Ah, an excellent answer. And was it not also reason that told the judges who condemned Galileo that it was the sun that revolved around the earth? Reason is a fool, my dear Doctor. Have you yourself ever done experiments on severed heads?"

"No, never."

"Have you read Sömmering's treatises? Have you read the reports of Doctor Sue? Have you read Oelcher's declarations?"[5]

"No."

"Then you believe, on the testimony of Monsieur Guillotin,[6] that his machine is the most rapid, most reliable, and least painful method of terminating a life?"

"I do."

"Well, you are wrong, my dear friend, and that is all."

"Oh? Really!"

"Listen; because you have invoked science, Doctor, I shall talk science, and none of us, believe me, is so unfamiliar with this kind of conversation as not to take part."

The doctor made a skeptical gesture.

"No matter; you shall be the only one to understand, then."

We had gathered around Monsieur Ledru, and for my part I was listening avidly, the question of the death penalty as applied by rope, blade, or poison having always been of considerable interest to me as a human issue. I had even pursued some research on my own regarding the various kinds of pain which precede, accompany, and follow the various modes of death.

"Well, go on," said the doctor in an incredulous tone.

"It is easily demonstrated, to whomsoever possesses the least knowledge of our body's structure and vital forces," resumed Monsieur Ledru, "that feeling is not entirely destroyed by the instrument of death, and this claim, Doctor, is founded not on hypotheses but on facts."

"Then show us these facts."

"They are as follows: first, the center of feeling is the brain, is it not?"

"Very likely."

"The processes of consciousness and feeling can survive even when the circulation of blood though the brain is interrupted, weakened, or partially arrested?"

"That is possible."

"If the seat of feeling is, in fact, in the brain, as long as the brain conserves its vital force the victim would retain consciousness of his own existence."

"The proof?"

"As follows. Haller, in his *Elements of Physics*,[7] volume 4, page 35, states: 'A severed head opened its eyes and looked sideways at me, because I had touched its spinal chord with my fingertip.'

"Haller, well and good; but Haller may have been wrong."

"Fair enough, let us say he was wrong. Let us take another. Weycard, *Philosophical Arts*,[8] page 221, states: 'I saw the lips of a decapitated man move.'

"Well and good, but to actually speak . . ."

"Wait, I'm coming to that. Here is Sömmering; his works are here, and you can check for yourself. Sömmering states: 'A number of medical colleagues have alleged to have seen a head that was severed from its body gnash its teeth in pain, and I myself am convinced that if air continued to circulate through the vocal organs, *heads would speak*.' Well, Doctor," continued Monsieur Ledru, turning pale, "I am ahead of Sömmering: I have had a head speak to me."

We all shuddered. The pale lady sat up upon her chaise longue.

"To you?"

"Yes, to me; would you, too, call me mad?"

"Why," said the doctor, "if you are telling me that you yourself . . ."

"Yes, I tell you that it has happened to me. You are too polite, are you not, Doctor, to call me a madman to my face, but you think me one, and it comes to the same thing."

"Well then, tell us the story," said the doctor.

"That is easily said. Do you realize that what you ask me to tell you, I have never told a soul in the thirty-seven years since it occurred; do you realize that I cannot promise not to faint as I tell it, just as I fainted when that head began to speak, with its languid eyes fastened upon mine?"

The discussion was growing ever more intriguing, the situation ever more dramatic.

"Come, Ledru, take heart!" said Alliette, "and tell us the story."

"Tell us the story, my friend," said the abbé Moulle.

"Tell us," said the chevalier Lenoir.

"Monsieur . . ." murmured the pale lady.

I said nothing, but my keen interest showed in my eyes.

"Strange," said Monsieur Ledru as if speaking to himself, "strange how events work one upon the other!" Then, "you know who I am," he said, turning toward me.

"I know, Monsieur," I replied, "that you are a very learned, very witty man, who gives excellent dinners, and who is mayor of Fontenay-aux-Roses."

Monsieur Ledru smiled, with a nod of acknowledgment.

"I am alluding to my origin, my family," he said.

"I know nothing of your origin, Monsieur, and I am not acquainted with your family."

"Listen, and I shall tell you, and then perhaps the story that you wish to hear, and which I fear to relate, will follow after. If it does, well, you shall have it; if it does not, do not press me further: it will mean that I lacked the strength to tell the tale."

Everyone settled comfortably in their seats and prepared to listen.

The drawing room was, indeed, a perfect setting for tales and legends—large, dark, and gloomy, owing to the thick curtains and the waning light; the corners of the room were already lost in shadow, and only the outlines of windows and doors retained a faint luminosity.

In one of the corners sat the pale lady. Her black dress had merged entirely with the darkness. Only her head was visible, white, motionless, leaning back upon the cushion of the sofa.

Monsieur Ledru began:

"I am," he said, "the son of the famous Comus, physician to the King and Queen.[9] My father, whose burlesque nickname placed him among the ranks of conjurers and charlatans, was a distinguished scientist in the tradition of Volta, Galvani, and Mesmer.[10] He was the first in France to dabble in electricity and phantasmagorical effect, holding sessions in mathematics and physics at the royal court.

"Poor Marie-Antoinette, whom I met a dozen times, and who more than once in her early days in France, that is, when I was a child, took my hands in hers and kissed me—Marie-Antoinette was crazy about him. When Joseph II visited the court in 1777, he swore that he had never seen anything more curious than Comus.

"Amidst all this, my father attended to the education of my brother and myself, initiating us into what he knew of the occult sciences, and into a host of galvanic, physical, and mesmeric erudition, which is now within the public domain but which at that time was a well guarded secret, the privilege of a select few. The title of King's Physician led to my father's imprisonment in '93; but owing to several contacts that I had among the *Montagne*,[11] I was able to obtain his release.

"My father then retired to this very house, where he died in 1807 at the age of seventy-six.

"But let me return to myself. I mentioned my ties to the *Montagne*. I was, in fact, friendly with Danton and Camille Desmoulins.[12] I knew Marat[13] more as a doctor than as a friend. Still, I knew him. As a result of this association, brief as it was, on the day when Mademoiselle Corday[14] went to the scaffold, I decided to witness her execution."

"I was just about to support you," I interrupted, "in your dispute with Doctor Robert about the continuance of life, by relating the facts that history has recorded regarding Charlotte Corday."

"I am coming to that," said Monsieur Ledru. "Let me go on. I was a witness; therefore you can believe all I am about to say.

"By two in the afternoon I had taken my position near the statue de la Liberté. It was a hot, sultry July morning; it was cloudy and looked as if it were about to storm.

"At four o'clock the storm broke; it was at that very moment, or so they say, that Charlotte climbed into the wagon.

"They had come to fetch her at the prison just as a young artist was working on her portrait. Jealous Death seemed to want nothing of the girl to survive, not even her image.

"The head had been sketched out on the canvas, and strangely enough, at the moment when the executioner entered, the artist was just painting that part of the neck which the blade of the guillotine was about to sever.

"The rain was falling, there were flashes of lightning and bursts of thunder, but nothing could disperse the eager populace. The river embankments, bridges, squares, were jammed; the rumblings on the ground drowned out the rumblings in the skies. Those women who were called by the graphic epithet of 'guillotine-lickers' were howling imprecations. The roaring resounded in my ears like the noise of a waterfall. Undulations swept through the crowd long before anything could be seen; at last, like a doomed vessel, the wagon appeared, ploughing through the waves, and I could make out the features of the victim whom I had never seen, who was a total stranger to me.

"She was a handsome young girl of twenty-seven, with magnificent eyes, a perfectly contoured nose, and regular, well-formed lips. She stood straight and tall, with her head held high, less from a sense of superiority over the crowd than from physical necessity, as her hands were tied behind her back. The rain had stopped, but as it had been falling upon her for most of the way, it had drenched her woolen clothing all through, revealing the contours of her lovely body: she looked as though she were just emerging from her bath. The red smock that the executioner had given her conferred a strange, eerie splendor upon her head, so dauntless and so proud. At the moment when she arrived upon the square, the rain stopped and a ray of sunlight, breaking through the clouds, played in her hair, illuminating it like a halo. The truth is, and I swear this is the truth, even though behind this girl was a murder—a terrible act, even when it is to avenge humanity—, even though I was appalled by this murder, I could

not have told whether what I beheld was an execution or an apo-
theosis. As she caught sight of the guillotine, she grew pale,
and her pallor was plainly visible, mostly owing to the red smock
which mounted to her neckline; but almost immediately she
strove to master her emotion, and turned, smiling, to face the
scaffold.

"The wagon came to a stop, and without allowing anyone to
help her, Charlotte jumped down; then, as rapidly as her long,
trailing smock and tightly bound arms would permit, she ascended the steps of the scaffold, made slippery by the newly
fallen rain. As she felt the executioner lay his hand upon her
shoulder to remove the kerchief she wore across her neck, she
once more grew pale, but almost instantly a final smile belied this
pallor, and of her own free will, without waiting to be attached to
the infamous machine, in a sublime and almost joyous impulse,
she slipped her head through the hideous aperture. The blade descended; the head, severed from the body, fell bouncing onto the
platform. It was then that one of the executioner's assistants,
named Legros, grabbed hold of the head by its hair, and in a vile
gesture of conciliation to the multitude, gave it a slap. Well, let
me tell you that at that slap the head turned red; I saw it, the
head, not the cheek, mind you, not just the cheek that was
touched but both cheeks alike—because that head still had feelings, and it was indignant at being made to endure a shame that
was not part of the sentence.

"The people, too, saw this blush, and took the side of the
dead against the living, the victim against the executioner. They
demanded, forthwith, vengeance for this shameful act, and forthwith, the scoundrel was handed over to the police and led away to
prison. Wait—" said Monsieur Ledru, seeing that the doctor was
about to speak, "wait, that is not all. I wanted to find out what
emotion could have induced this man to commit such a vile act. I
managed to ascertain his whereabouts and requested permission
to visit the Abbey where he was being held. It was granted, and I
went to see him.

"A ruling of the revolutionary tribunal had just sentenced
him to three months in prison. He did not understand how he
could have been imprisoned for something so *natural* as what he
had done.

"I asked him what could have prompted him to such an act.

"'Ah,' he said, 'a good question! I am a follower of Marat, and having just punished the woman on behalf of the law, I wanted to punish her on my own behalf.'

"'But,' I said to him, 'didn't you understand that it is almost a crime to violate the respect owed to the dead?'

"'Oh, really?' said Legros, fixing me with a stare, 'so you believe they are dead, because they have been beheaded?'

"'Of course.'

"'Well, it's clear you've never looked into the basket when they are all there together; you've never seen them roll their eyes and gnash their teeth for a full five minutes after the execution. We have to change the basket every three months because of the mess they make of it with their teeth. They're a pack of aristocrats' heads, see, that just don't want to die, and I wouldn't be surprised if one day one of them began to shout, "Long live the King!"'

"I had learned what I wished to learn; I took my leave, haunted by the idea that those heads might still be alive—and I resolved to find out."

■ ■ ■

Night had fallen during the course of Monsieur Ledru's tale. The occupants of the drawing room were now no more than shadows, shadows not only mute but motionless, so anxious were they that Monsieur Ledru continue without interruption. For they sensed that behind the terrible tale that he had just recounted lay a tale more terrible still.

Not a breath could be heard. Only the doctor opened his mouth to speak. I took hold of his hand to stop him, and he remained silent.

After several moments, Monsieur Ledru began again.

"I had just left the Abbey, and was crossing the Place Taranne on my way to the rue de Tournon, where I lived, when I heard a woman's voice crying for help.

"It couldn't be robbers: it was barely ten o'clock. I ran toward the corner of the square from where I had heard the cry, and saw, by the light of the moon as it emerged from behind a cloud, a woman struggling in the midst of a patrol of sans-culottes.[15]

"The woman in turn noticed me, and seeing from my clothes that I was not quite a man of the people, she rushed toward me, crying, 'Eh! Look, here's Monsieur Albert—I know him; he can tell you I'm the daughter of old Mother Ledieu, the laundress.'

"And the poor woman, pale and trembling from head to toe, seized my arm and clung to me as a drowning man clings to a sheet anchor.

"'The daughter of old Mother Ledieu, if you like; but you don't have an identification card, my dear girl, and you're going to follow us to the guardroom!'

"The young woman tightened her grip on my arm; in the pressure of her hand I felt all the depths of terror and entreaty. I had understood.

"As she had called me by the first name to come into her head, I too addressed her by the first name I could think of.

"'What! It's you, my poor Solange!' I cried. 'What has happened to you?'

"'There, now you see, gentlemen,' she declared.

"'Shouldn't you say: citizens?'

"'Listen, Sergeant, it's not my fault if I speak like that,' said the girl. 'My mother had high society clientele, and she brought me up to be polite, so that I fell into bad habits, I know, aristocratic habits, but what do you expect, Sergeant, I can't get rid of them.'

"And in this reply, uttered in a trembling voice, there was an imperceptible note of mocking humour that I alone detected. I wondered what sort of woman she could be. It was an unfathomable enigma. The only thing of which I was certain was that she was not a laundress's daughter.

"'What happened to me!' she went on. 'Citizen Albert, here's what happened to me. I went to deliver some laundry, and the lady of the house was out, so I waited for her to come back, in order to be paid. Why, these days being what they are, everybody needs money. Night came on; I decided to return in the daylight. I didn't have my identification card with me; I ran smack into these gentlemen, pardon me, I mean these citizens; they asked to see my card; I told them I didn't have it; they wanted to drag me off to the guardroom. I screamed, you came running, an acquaintance as it happened, so I could breathe a little easier. I said to myself: since Monsieur Albert knows my name is Solange, since he knows I am the daughter of old Mother Ledieu, he will vouch for me, isn't that true, Monsieur Albert?'

"'Certainly I will vouch for you, and I do so.'

"'Good!' said the leader of the patrol. 'And who will vouch for you, Monsieur Coxcomb?'

"'Danton. Is that good enough? Is he enough of a patriot for you?'

"'Ah, if Danton can vouch for you, I have nothing more to say.'

"'Well, the Cordeliers are in session today; let's go.'

"'Let's go,' said the sergeant. 'Citizens and sans-culottes, forward, march!'

"The Cordeliers' Club was housed in the old Cordelier convent, rue de l'Observance; we were there in an instant. When I reached the door, I tore out a page from my wallet, scribbled several words in pencil, and handed it to the sergeant with instructions to deliver it to Danton, while we remained in the hands of the corporal and the patrol.

"The sergeant entered the club, and returned with Danton.

"'What!' he said to me. 'Is it you they're arresting? You, my friend and Camille's? You, one of the best republicans alive? Come now! Citizen sergeant,' he added, turning toward the leader of the sans-culottes, 'I vouch for him. Is that enough for you?'

"'You vouch for him, but do you vouch for her?' pursued the sergeant, stubbornly.

"'Her? Who are you talking about?'

"'That woman, of course!'

"'For him, for her, for anyone with him; are you satisfied?'

"'Yes, I'm satisfied,' said the sergeant, 'especially at having seen you.'

"'Ah, of course, that pleasure is yours for free; look at me as much as you like while you have me.'

"'Thank you. Continue to uphold as you have the cause of the people, and rest assured, the people will be eternally grateful to you.'

"'Oh yes! I am counting on it!' said Danton.

"'Will you shake my hand?' continued the sergeant.

"'Why not?' And Danton gave him his hand.

"'Long live Danton!' cried the sergeant.

"'Long live Danton!' repeated the entire patrol.

"And it marched off, escorted by its leader, who after ten paces turned round and, waving his red bonnet, cried once more, 'Long live Danton,' a cry that was promptly echoed by his men.

"I was about to thank Danton, when we heard his name called out several times from inside the club.

"'Danton! Danton!' cried a number of voices, 'to the podium!'

"'Excuse me,' he said, 'you hear them calling. A handshake, and I'll be off. I gave my right hand to the sergeant, I give you my left. Who knows? Perhaps the worthy patriot had scabies.' And turning round: 'Here I am!' he said in that mighty voice that could both rouse and assuage the stormy passions of the multitudes; 'here I am, wait for me!' And he dashed into the club.

"I remained standing alone at the door with my mysterious companion.

"'Now, Madame,' I said to her, 'where would you like me to take you? I am at your service.'

"'Why, to old Mother Ledieu's,' she replied, laughing, 'you know she's my mother.'

"'But where does old Mother Ledieu live?'

"'24 rue Férou.'

"'To old Mother Ledieu's, then, 24 rue Férou.'

"We went back along the rue des Fossés-Monsieur-le-Prince to the rue des Fossés-Saint-Germain, and from there along the rue du Petit Lion, through the Place Saint-Sulpice to the rue Férou.

"We had gone the whole way without exchanging a word.

"But in the rays of the moon, which was shining in all its splendor, I had been able to observe her at my ease.

"She was a delightful little thing of about twenty or twenty-two, with dark hair and big blue eyes, more full of wit than melancholy, a straight and delicate nose, lips that curled ironically, teeth like pearls, the hands of a queen, the dainty feet of a child. In all this, beneath the crude garments of old Mother Ledieu's daughter, she had preserved an aristocratic bearing that had awakened the suspicions—and rightfully so—of the good sergeant and his militant patrol.

"Upon reaching the door we stopped, and stared at each other for a moment in silence.

"'Well, what do you want, my dear Monsieur Albert?' said my mysterious companion, smiling.

"'I wanted to say, my dear Mademoiselle Solange, that it was not worth the trouble of meeting only to part so quickly.'

"'But I beg your pardon. On the contrary, it was entirely worth it, considering that if I hadn't met you, I would have been taken away to the guardroom, they would have found out that I wasn't the daughter of old Mother Ledieu, that I was an aristocrat, and they would very likely have made me pay with my head.'

"'So you admit that you are an aristocrat?'

"'I don't admit anything.'

"'Come now, you can at least tell me your name.

"'Solange.'

"'You know very well that that name, which I chose at random, is not yours.'

"'No matter! I like it and I will keep it, at least for you.'

"'Why do you need to keep it for me, if I am not to see you again?'

"'I'm not saying that. I'm only saying that if we do see each other again, it is as pointless for you to know my name as it is for me to know yours. I called you "Albert"; keep that name, as I am keeping "Solange."'

"'Very well then, but listen, Solange,' I said to her.

"'I am listening, Albert,' she replied.

"'You are an aristocrat—do you admit it?'

"'Even if I did not admit it, you would guess it, wouldn't you? So my admission is somewhat less to my credit.'

"'And as an aristocrat, you are being hunted down?'

"'Something like that.'

"'And you are in hiding?'

"'24 rue Férou, at old Mother Ledieu's—her husband was my father's coachman. You see I keep no secrets from you.'

"'And your father?'

"'I keep no secrets from you, my dear Monsieur Albert, provided these secrets are my own; but my father's secrets are not mine. My father too is in hiding, awaiting an opportunity to emigrate. That is all I can tell you.'

"'And you, what do you intend to do?'

"'To leave with my father, if it is possible, if not, to let him go alone and join him later.'

"'And this evening, when you were stopped, you had just come from seeing your father?'

"'I had just come from there, yes.'

"'Listen to me, dear Solange!'

"'I am listening.'

"'Did you see what happened tonight?'

"'Yes, and it showed me the extent of your influence.'

"'Oh, my influence isn't great, I'm afraid. But I do have a few friends.'

"'I met one of them tonight.'

"'And as you know, he is not one of the least powerful men of our time.'

"'Do you plan to use his influence to help my father escape?'

"'No, I am saving it for you.'

"'And my father?'

"'For your father, I have another plan.'

"'You have another plan!' cried Solange, grasping my hands and staring at me anxiously.

"'If I rescue your father, will you remember me?'

"'Oh, I will be forever grateful to you.' And she uttered these words with a delightful expression of anticipated gratitude.

"Then, looking at me imploringly, she asked: 'But will that be enough?'

"'Yes.'

"'Now there, I was not wrong; you have a noble heart. I thank you on my father's behalf and on my own, and, even if you should fail in the future, I am no less indebted to you for the past.'

"'When will we see each other again, Solange?'

"'When do you need to see me?'

"'Tomorrow; I hope to have good news for you.'

"'Very well, let us meet tomorrow.'

"'Where?'

"'Here, if you like.'

"'Here, in the street?'

"'Yes! Why, you see it's the safest place; we've been standing here talking a while now without seeing a soul.'

"'Why shouldn't I come in, or why shouldn't you come to my house?'

"'Because if you came in, you would be compromising the good people who are hiding me; and if I went to your house, I would be compromising you.'

"'Very well then; I will take one of my relatives' identification cards and give it to you.'

"'Yes, so that your relative can be guillotined, if by chance I am arrested.'

"'You're right; I'll bring you a card under the name of Solange.'

"'Perfect! You'll see that Solange will become my real name.'

"'The time?'

"'The same as when we met today. Ten o'clock, if you like.'

"'Very well, ten o'clock.'

"'And how are we to meet?'

"'Oh, that's not difficult. At five minutes to ten, you will be at the door; at ten, I will come down.'

"'Until tomorrow at ten, then, dear Solange.'

"'Tomorrow at ten, dear Albert.'

"I tried to kiss her hand; she offered her forehead.

"The next evening, at nine-thirty, I was waiting in the street. At a quarter to ten, Solange opened the door. We were each ahead of time. In a bound I was beside her.

"'I see you bring good news,' she said, smiling.

"'Excellent news; first, here is your card.'

"'First, my father.' And she pushed away my hand.

"'Your father is saved, if he agrees to it.'

"'If he agrees to it, you say? What must he do?'

"'He must have faith in me.'

"'He already does.'

"'You have been to see him?'

"'Yes.'

"'You made yourself vulnerable.'

"'What do you expect? I had to; but God is watching over me!'

"'And you told your father everything?'

"'I told him that yesterday you saved my life, and that tomorrow you may perhaps save his.'

"'Tomorrow, yes, precisely; tomorrow, if he agrees to it, I shall save his life.'

"'How? Come now, tell me. What a fortunate encounter this will have been if all should go well!'

"'Only . . . ' I said, hesitating.

"'Well?'

"'You will not be able to leave with him.'

"'As for that, didn't I tell you I had made up my mind?'

"'Besides, I am certain of getting you a passport later.'

"'Let us speak first of my father, and then of me.'

"'Well, I told you I had friends, didn't I?'

"'Yes.'

"'I went to see one of them today.'

"'And?'

"'A man whose name you know, and whose name attests to his courage, loyalty, and honor.'

"'And this name is . . . '

"'Marceau.'"

"'General Marceau?'[16]

"'Precisely.'

"'You are right; if he makes a promise, he will keep it.'

"'Well then; he promised.'

"'My God, how happy you make me! Come, what did he promise? Tell me!'

"'He promised to help us.'

"'How?'

"'Ah, very easily. Kléber[17] has just appointed him Commander of the Western Army. He leaves tomorrow night.'

"'Tomorrow night? But we won't have time to prepare.'

"'There is nothing to prepare.'

"'I don't understand.'

"'He is taking your father with him.'

"'My father!'

"'Yes, as his secretary. Once in Vendée, your father will pledge his word to Marceau that he will not fight against France; then, one night, he will reach a Vendée camp, and from Vendée, he will head for Brittany, then go on to England. When he is settled in London, he will send news; I will get you a passport, and you will go to join him there.'

"'Tomorrow!' cried Solange. 'My father leaves tomorrow!'

"'But there is no time to lose.'

"'My father has not been informed.'

"'Inform him.'

"'Tonight?'

"'Tonight.'

"'But how, at this hour?'

"'You have a card, and my arm.'

"'You're right. My card?'

"I gave it to her; she slipped it into her dress.

"'Now, your arm.'

"I gave her my arm and we set off. We walked until we came to the Place Taranne, that is, to the spot where we had met the previous day.

"'Wait for me here,' she said.

"I bowed, and waited. She disappeared around the corner of the old Hôtel Matignon; then, after about a quarter of an hour, she returned.

"'Come,' she said, 'my father wishes to see you and thank you.'

"She took my arm and led me along the rue Saint-Guillaume, across from the Hôtel Mortemart. Once there, she took a key from her pocket, opened a little side door, took me by the hand, led me up to the second floor, and signaled with a special knock.

"A man of about forty-eight or fifty opened the door. He was dressed in workers' clothes and appeared to be in the bookbinding business. But at the first words he uttered, at his first expressions of gratitude, the gallant aristocrat was revealed.

"'Monsieur,' he said, 'you have been sent to us by Providence, and I receive you as Providence's envoy. Is it true that you can save me, and above all, that you wish to save me?'

"I told him everything. I told him how Marceau had promised to take him along as his secretary, asking nothing in return but the pledge not to take up arms against France.

"'I make this promise in good faith, and I will reiterate it to him.'

"'I thank you, on his behalf and on mine.'

"'But when does Marceau leave?'

"'Tomorrow.'

"'Must I join him tonight?'

"'When you wish; he will be waiting for you.'

"Father and daughter looked at each other.

"'I think it would be wiser to join him tonight, father,' said Solange.

"'Very well. But if they should arrest me, I have no identification card.'

"'Here is mine.'

"'But you?'

"'Oh, I am known.'

"'Where does Marceau live?'

"'40, rue de l'Université, at the home of his sister, Mademoiselle Dégraviers-Marceau.'

"'Will you accompany me?'

"'I will follow behind, so as to bring Mademoiselle back afterward.'

"'And how will Marceau know I am the man you described to him?'

"'You will give him this tricolor cockade, as a token of gratitude.'

"'What can I do for my liberator?'

"'You will entrust me with the salvation of your daughter, as she has entrusted me with yours.'

"'Let us be off.'

"He put on his hat and extinguished the lights. We made our way downstairs by the gleam of a ray of moonlight filtering through one of the staircase windows. At the door, he took his daughter's arm, headed to the right, and by way of the rue des Saints-Prés, reached the rue de l'Université. I followed about ten feet behind.

"We arrived at number 40 without encountering anyone. I joined them at the door.

"'It's a good sign,' I said. 'Now, would you like me to wait or go up with you?'

"'No, don't compromise yourself further; wait for my daughter here.'

"I bowed.

"'Once again, thank you and farewell,' he said, offering me his hand. 'No words can convey the emotion I feel. I hope that someday God will grant me to express my full debt of gratitude to you.'

"I answered him with a simple handshake.

"He went in. Solange followed him. But she too, before entering, shook my hand.

"After ten minutes had passed, the door opened.

"'Well?' I asked her.

"'Well!' she replied, 'your friend is certainly worthy of your friendship, that is to say, he showed us every kindness. He understands that I wish to stay with my father until he leaves. His sister

made up a bed for me in her room. By three in the afternoon tomorrow, my father will be out of all danger. At ten tomorrow
night, if the gratitude of a daughter who owes you her father's
life is worth the trouble, you can come and find her in the rue
Férou.'

"'Oh, certainly I will come. Did your father not have any
message for me?'

"'He thanks you for your card, which I have here, and asks
you to send me to him as soon as possible.'

"'Whenever you wish, Solange,' I replied, with a sinking
heart.

"'Shouldn't I at least know where to join my father?' she
asked. 'Ah, you are not rid of me yet.'

"I took her hand and clasped it to my breast. But she merely
offered me her forehead as before, saying, 'Till tomorrow.' And
pressing my lips to her forehead, it was no longer just her hand
that I clasped to my breast, it was her trembling bosom and her
leaping heart.

"I went home, my soul filled with a joy I had never felt before.
Was it pleasure in my generous act, or was I already falling in love
with the charming creature?

"I know not whether I slept or woke; I do know that all the
harmonies of nature were singing within me, I know that the
night seemed without end, and boundless the day; I know that
even as I and time moved forward together, I longed for it to
stand still, so as not to lose a minute of the days that remained
before me.

"The next day at nine, I was in the rue Férou. At nine-thirty,
Solange appeared. She came toward me and threw her arms
around my neck.

"'Saved!' she declared. 'My father is saved, and it is to you that
I owe his salvation! Oh! How I love you!'

"Two weeks later, Solange received a letter informing her that
her father was in England. The next day, I brought her a passport.
As she took it from me, she burst into tears.

"'You don't love me, then?' she said.

"'I love you more than my life,' I answered, 'but I gave my
word to your father, and I must honor my word above all.'

"'Then,' she said, 'it is I who shall not honor mine. If you have

the courage to let me go, Albert, I do not have the courage to
leave you!'

"Alas! She stayed."

■ ■ ■

Just as with the first pause in Monsieur Ledru's story, there
followed a moment of silence.

A silence which was even more respectfully observed than
the former, for one sensed that the end of the narrative was near,
and Monsieur Ledru had hinted that he might not have the
strength to complete his tale. But almost immediately he went on:

"Three months had passed since we had spoken of Solange's
departure, and since that evening, we had uttered not a word
about our separation.

"Solange had wished to take lodgings in the rue Taranne. I
found rooms for her under the name 'Solange,' for I did not think
of her as having any other, just as she knew me by no other name
than 'Albert.' I had secured her a position as assistant mistress in a
private school for girls, so as to shield her more effectively from
the pursuit of the revolutionary police, now grown more assidu-
ous than ever.

"We spent every Sunday and Thursday together in the little
apartment in the rue Taranne: from the bedroom window we
could see the square where we had met for the first time.

"Daily we each received a letter, she under the name 'Solange,' and I under the name 'Albert.' Those three months were
the happiest months of my life.

"Still, I had not abandoned the idea that had come to me after
my conversation with the executioner's assistant. I had asked and
obtained permission to conduct experiments on the prolongation
of life after decapitation, and those experiments had established
that the pain continued past the moment of beheading, and was
doubtless excruciating."

"Ah, that is what I dispute!" cried the doctor.

"Come now," Monsieur Ledru went on, "will you deny that
the blade penetrates the most sensitive part of the body, where all
the nerves come together? Will you deny that the neck contains
all the nerves connected to the upper limbs—the sympathetic,
the vagus, the phrenic, and lastly, the spinal chord, which is also
the source of the nerves connected to the lower limbs? Will you

deny that the shattering, the crushing of the spinal column results in the most atrocious suffering that it is possible for a human being to endure?"

"That may be," said the doctor, "but this suffering lasts but a few seconds."

"Oh, that is what *I* dispute!" cried Monsieur Ledru with ardent conviction. "And even if it should last but a few seconds, during those few seconds, *one's feeling, one's personality, one's sense of the 'I'*, remains intact; the head hears, sees, feels, and observes the fragmentation of its very being, and who can say if the limited duration of the suffering can compensate for its horrible intensity." [18]

"Thus, in your opinion, the decree of the Constituent Assembly which substituted the guillotine for the gallows was a philanthropic error, and it was better to be hanged than to be beheaded?"

"There is no question that many have been hanged, or have hanged themselves, and then returned to life. Well, such people have been able to tell us of the sensation they experienced. It is that of a sudden, violent stroke, that is to say, a deep sleep without any pain or any particular feeling of agony, a kind of flame which flashes before one's eyes, and which gradually turns blue, then dark, as when one falls into a faint. And in fact, Doctor, you know this better than anyone. If you apply pressure to a man's brain at the spot where part of his cranium is missing, the man will feel no pain, and simply fall asleep. The same phenomenon occurs when pressure is applied to the brain by a buildup of blood. Now in the case of the hanging victim, the blood builds up in the first place because it enters the brain by the spinal arteries, which cross the bony cavity of the neck; second, because it would tend to rush back into the veins of the neck and would be blocked in its flow."

"Very well," said the doctor, "but let us return to your experiments. I am anxious to hear about that talking head."

I thought I detected something like a sigh escape from Monsieur Ledru's chest. As for his face, it was impossible to make out. It was completely veiled in darkness.

"Yes," he said, "you're right, I am straying from the subject, Doctor. Let us return to my experiments.

"Lamentably, we did not lack for subjects.

"The executions were at their peak; thirty or forty people a day were dying on the guillotine, and so much blood was flowing on the Place de la Révolution that it had been necessary to dig a trench three feet deep around the scaffold.

"This trench was covered with planks. One of these planks flipped over beneath the foot of an eight- or nine-year-old child, who fell into the hideous pit and was drowned.

"Needless to say, I was careful not to tell Solange how I spent my time during the days when I did not see her. Moreover, I must confess that at first these poor human remains filled me with such repugnance that I feared my experiments were only prolonging their death agony. But I told myself, after all, that the research I was engaged in was for the benefit of society as a whole, given that if ever I managed to bring my ideas persuasively before a legislative session, I would perhaps be able to abolish the death penalty.

"I noted down the results of my experiments as they came in. After two months, I had conducted all my preliminary experiments on the prolongation of life after decapitation. I resolved to carry these experiments even further, if possible, with the help of electricity and galvanism.

"I was granted permission to enter Clamart Cemetery and to examine all the heads and corpses of those who had died on the guillotine. A small chapel that stood at one corner of the cemetery had been converted into my laboratory. (As you know, after the kings were banished from their palaces, God was banished from His churches.) There I had an electric machine, and three or four of those instruments called 'stimulators.'

"Around five o'clock, the terrible convoy appeared. The corpses were piled in a heap in the cart, the heads thrown together in a sack. I removed one or two heads and one or two bodies at random; the rest were thrown into a common grave.

"Each day, the heads and bodies upon which I had previously experimented were added to the day's new quota. Almost invariably, my brother aided me in these experiments.

"In the midst of this association with death, my love for Solange grew daily stronger. As for herself, the poor child loved me with all her heart. I thought often of making her my wife, often we envisioned the happiness of such a union; but in order to become my wife, Solange would be obliged to reveal her name, and her name, which was that of an émigré, an aristocrat, an outlaw, carried with it a death sentence.

"Her father had written to her several times in an attempt to hasten her departure, but she had told him of our love. She had asked for his consent to our marriage, which he had given, so in that regard all was going well.

"Yet in the midst of these terrible trials, one more terrible than the rest had saddened us both very deeply. This was the trial of Marie-Antoinette.

"Begun on the fourth of October,[19] this trial was being followed with keen interest: on the fourteenth of October, she had made her appearance before the revolutionary tribunal; on the sixteenth, at four in the morning, she had been sentenced to death; that same day, at eleven, she had ascended the scaffold.

"That morning I had received a letter from Solange, who wrote that such a day must not pass without her seeing me.

"Around two o'clock I arrived at our little apartment in the rue Taranne and found Solange in tears. I too was deeply moved by this execution. The Queen had been so good to me in my youth that her kindness was profoundly etched in my memory.

"Oh, I will always remember that day; it was a Wednesday: there was more than sadness in the city of Paris, there was terror.

"As for me, I was prey to a curious despondency, something like the premonition of a terrible tragedy. I wanted to comfort Solange as she wept in my arms, but I could not find any consoling words, for consolation was not in my heart.

"We spent the night together as usual; this night was even sadder than the day. I remember that a dog, shut up in an apartment below ours, howled until two o'clock in the morning.

"The following day we found out what had happened: his master had gone out, locking the door behind him; he had been arrested in the street and taken to the revolutionary tribunal; sentenced to death at three o'clock, he had been executed at four.

"Then we had to take leave of each other, as Solange's classes began at nine in the morning. Her school was located near the Jardin des Plantes. I hesitated a long while before letting her go. She too could not bring herself to leave me. But to be absent was to expose oneself to inquiries which were invariably perilous for someone in Solange's position.

"I called a carriage, and accompanied her as far as the corner of the rue des Fossés-Saint-Bernard; there I descended and let her go on alone. For the entire way we had held each other without uttering a word, mingling the bitter tears that fell upon our lips with the sweetness of our kisses.

"I descended from the carriage; but instead of continuing on my way, I remained glued to the spot, my eyes fixed upon the retreating carriage. After it had gone several yards, it stopped. Solange stuck her head out of the window, as if she had guessed that I was still there. I ran toward her, climbed back into the carriage, and closed the windows. I folded her once more in my arms. But the bells were striking nine at Saint-Etienne-du-Mont. I dried away her tears, closed her lips with a kiss, and, leaping down from the carriage, dashed hastily away.

"I thought I heard Solange calling to me—but all those tears, all those hesitations might be noticed. I had the fatal courage not to turn back.

"I returned home in despair. I spent the day writing to Solange; that evening, I sent her a very long letter. I had only just come from mailing it when I received one from her.

"She had been sternly reprimanded; they had asked her a score of questions, and had threatened to deny her her first day off. This would have been the following Sunday, but Solange swore to me that no matter what, even at the risk of an altercation with the headmistress, she would see me that day.

"I swore the same; I felt that if I had to go a week without seeing her—which would happen if she did not take her day off—I would go mad. Especially since Solange had expressed a certain anxiety: a letter from her father that had arrived at the school one day appeared to her to have been opened.

"I spent a restless night, and an even more restless next day. As usual, I wrote to Solange, and as it was my day for experiments, I passed by my brother's house around three in order to take him along with me to Clamart. As he was not at home, I set off alone.

"The weather was miserable; nature, disconsolate, had dissolved into rain, that cold torrential rain that signals the onset of winter. All along the way I heard the hoarse voices of the town criers rasping out the names of those sentenced that day to death. They were numerous: men, women, and children. There was an abundant harvest of blood, and I would not lack for subjects for my experiments that evening.

"The days were getting shorter. At four o'clock, I arrived at Clamart; it was almost completely dark. The cemetery had a gloomy and almost hideous aspect, with its enormous, freshly turned graves, and its sparsely planted trees, rattling like skeletons in the wind. Where the earth was not turned, there was grass, thistles, or nettles. Each day the turned earth encroached a little more upon the green.

"Amid all this bloated ground, the daily grave stood wide and gaping, waiting to receive its prey. In readiness for an anticipated increase in the number of victims, the pit was larger than usual.

"I went toward it automatically. The bottom of the pit was full of water; poor, cold, naked corpses that would be flung into that water as cold as they!

"As I drew near the grave, my foot slipped, and I barely escaped falling into it. My hair stood on end. Wet and shivering, I headed for my laboratory.

"It was, as I mentioned, an ancient chapel. I peered about—why, I know not—I peered about to see if on the wall, or on what had once been the altar, there remained any vestige of religious worship; the wall was empty, the altar was razed. In the very spot where the tabernacle—that is to say God, and life—had been, lay a fleshless, hairless skull—that is to say death, and nothingness.

"I lit my candle; I set it on my table alongside all the strangely shaped experimental gadgets that I myself had invented, and I sat down, musing . . . upon what? Upon that poor Queen whom I had seen so beautiful, so happy, so beloved; who only yesterday, amid the curses of an entire nation, had been escorted in a cart to the scaffold, and who now, her head sundered from her body, lay in a pauper's coffin—she who had lain beneath the gilded paneling of the Tuileries, Versailles, and Saint-Cloud.

"While I was sunk in these somber reflections, the rain fell harder and faster, the wind blew in violent gusts, sending its mournful wail through the branches of the trees and among the stalks of grass that quivered as it passed.

"To these sounds there was soon added a noise like the lugubrious roll of thunder, yet this thunder, instead of rumbling in the heavens, was rebounding upon the ground and making it tremble. It was the rumbling of the red cart, returning to Clamart from the Place de la Révolution.

"The door of the little chapel opened and two men, dripping with water, entered carrying a sack. One of them was the same Legros whom I had visited in prison, the other was a gravedigger.

"'Look, Monsieur Ledru,' said the executioner's assistant to me, 'here is what you want; you don't need to hurry tonight, we'll leave you the whole lot; they'll be buried tomorrow, when it's light. They're not going to catch cold after one night in the open air.' And, with a hideous laugh, Death's two hired men set down their sack in front of me, in the corner near where the old altar had been.

"Then they went out again without closing the door, which began to bang against its frame, letting in gusts of wind which made the flame of my candle flicker as it rose pale and dying, as it were, along its blackened wick.

"I heard them unharness the horse, lock the cemetery gates, and depart, leaving the cart filled with corpses.

"I had felt a strong desire to leave with them, but for some mysterious reason I was unable to budge from the spot, and remained there, shivering. I was not afraid, certainly, but the sound of the wind, the lashing of the rain, the groans of the writhing trees, the whistlings in the air that made my flame flicker, all this shook down about my head a vague alarm which, from the wet roots of my hair, spread through my entire body.

"Suddenly I thought I heard a voice at once soft and woeful, a voice emanating from inside the chapel, pronounce the name 'Albert.'

"This time I gave a start. Albert! . . . There was only one person in the world who called me by that name.

"My eyes, staring wildly, peered slowly round the little chapel—small as it was, my candle could not illuminate all of its walls—and came to rest upon the sack that lay in the corner. Its lumpy, blood-soaked canvas revealed only too well its lugubrious contents.

"At the instant that my eyes alighted upon the sack, the same voice, but fainter and more pitiful still, repeated the same name:

"'Albert!'

"I started up in terror: the voice seemed to be coming from inside the sack.

"I pinched myself to ascertain whether I was asleep or awake; then, walking as stiffly as if I had been made of stone, my arms extended before me, I went up to the sack and thrust one of my hands into it.

"Then I thought I felt the pressure of lips, still warm, upon my hand.

"I had reached that pitch of terror where its very excess can restore our courage. I took hold of the head, and returning to my armchair, into which I collapsed, I set it on the table.

"Oh! I gave a terrible cry. This head, whose lips seemed still warm, whose eyes were half closed, was the head of Solange!

"I thought I was going mad.

"I screamed three times.

"'Solange! Solange! Solange!'

"On the third time, the eyes opened, looked at me, let fall two tears, and flashing forth moist flames as though her soul were escaping, closed once more, never to open again.

"I leapt up, delirious, frenzied, mad; I was about to flee when one of my coattails caught on the table. It toppled over, extinguishing the candle as it went, letting the head roll onto the floor, taking even myself, frantic with terror, down with it. Then, as I lay there on the floor, I thought I saw the head sliding toward me down the sloping paving stones: its lips touched my lips, an icy shudder ran through my entire body; I uttered a moan, and fainted away.

"The next morning at six o'clock, the gravediggers found me, cold as the stones on which I lay.

"Solange, identified by her father's letter, had been arrested that very day, sentenced to death that very day, and executed that very day.

"That head that had spoken to me, those eyes that had looked at me, those lips that had kissed my lips, they were the lips, the eyes, the head of Solange.

"You know, Lenoir," Monsieur Ledru continued, turning toward the chevalier, "it was then that I came close to death."

1 8 4 9

Translated by Joan C. Kessler

For a recent French edition of this work, see Alexandre Dumas, *Les Mille et un Fantômes* (Paris and Geneva: Slatkine Reprints, 1980).

Gérard de Nerval

AURÉLIA,
or
DREAM
AND LIFE

PART ONE[1]

I.

D ream is a second life. Never have I been able to pass without
a shudder through those gates of ivory or of horn[2] which
divide us from the invisible world. The first moments of sleep are
the image of death: a hazy torpor overcomes our thoughts, and it
is impossible for us to determine the precise instant when the *I,* in
another form, resumes the creative work of existence. Little by
little an obscure underground cavern grows lighter, and the pale,
solemnly immobile figures that inhabit the realm of limbo emerge
from shadows and darkness. Then the picture takes form, a new
light illumines and sets in motion these odd apparitions: —the
world of Spirits opens before us.

Swedenborg[3] called these visions *Memorabilia;* he owed them
more often to reverie than to sleep; *The Golden Ass* of Apuleius,[4]
Dante's *Divine Comedy,*[5] these are the poetic models of such studies
of the human soul. I shall attempt, following their example, to
transcribe the impressions of a long illness which took place entirely within the mysterious regions of my mind; —and I do not
know why I use the word "illness," since for myself, I have never
felt in better health. At times I thought my strength and energy
were doubled; I seemed to know everything, understand everything; my imagination brought me infinite delight. In recovering
what men call reason, must I mourn the loss of these joys as
well? . . .

This *Vita nuova*[6] had two phases for me. Here are the notes regarding the first. —A woman whom I had long loved, and whom I shall call Aurélia, was lost to me. The circumstances of this event, which was to have so great an impact upon my life, are of little importance. Each of us can search his memory for the most heartrending emotion, the most dreadful blow that fate has inflicted upon his soul; at such moments as these, one must decide whether to live or to die: —I will later explain why I did not choose death. Condemned by the woman I loved, guilty of a wrong for which I could no longer hope to be forgiven, nothing was left for me but to throw myself into vulgar diversions. I affected high spirits and blithe unconcern, I roamed the world, in love with variety and caprice. I was particularly intrigued by the costumes and strange customs of distant peoples, for it seemed that in this way I was altering the terms of good and evil, the terms, as it were, of what for us Frenchmen is *sensibility*.[7] "What madness," I thought, "to go on platonically loving a woman who no longer loves you! My reading is to blame for this; I have taken the fabrications of poets seriously, and have made a Laura or a Beatrice[8] out of an ordinary woman of our own century. . . . Let me turn to new love affairs, and she shall soon be forgotten." The giddy whirl of a merry carnival in an Italian town dispelled all my melancholy thoughts. I was so happy at the relief I experienced that I shared my elation with all my friends, and, in my letters, represented as a permanent condition of mind what was just a feverish state of overstimulation.

One day an illustrious woman arrived in the town. She struck up a friendship with me and, engaging and captivating as she invariably was, drew me effortlessly into the circle of her admirers. After an evening during which she had been perfectly natural, yet radiant with a charm that was felt by everyone, I was so enthralled by her that I could not for a moment refrain from writing to her. I was so happy to feel my heart capable of a new love! . . . In this artificial enthusiam, I adopted the very turns of phrase which I had used, only a short time before, to convey a genuine and long-felt love. As soon as I had sent the letter, I regretted having done so, and went off to brood in solitude over what seemed to me a profanation of my memories.

That evening restored to my new love all the magic of the previous night. I could see that the woman had been touched by what I had written, although she evinced some astonishment at my sudden ardor. In the course of one day, I had passed through several stages of those feelings that one can entertain for a woman with any semblance of sincerity. She confessed that I had surprised her, yet also made her proud. I tried to be convincing, but in spite of all I could think to say to her, I could not recapture in our conversation the tone of my written style, so that ultimately I was obliged to confess to her, in tears, that I had deceived both her and myself. My tearful confidences had, nonetheless, a certain charm, and my vain protestations of affection were succeeded by a friendship more solid for being more temperate.

II.

Later, I met her again in another town, where the lady with whom I was still hopelessly in love was living. By chance, they became acquainted, and the former doubtless took the opportunity of speaking of me to the woman who had exiled me from her heart, and moving her to pity. It thus ensued that one day, finding myself at a gathering of which she was part, I saw her come up to me, holding out her hand. How was I to interpret this overture and the deep sad look which accompanied her greeting? I thought I saw in it forgiveness for the past; the heavenly note of pity gave inexpressible value to the simple words she addressed to me, as though something sacred had mingled with the sweetness of a love hitherto profane, impressing upon it the seal of eternity.

An urgent duty compelled me to return to Paris, but I resolved at once that I would remain there only a few days before hastening to rejoin my two friends. Joy and impatience had thrown me into a state of giddiness, which was intensified by the strain of settling my affairs. One evening, at about midnight, I was returning home through the neighborhood where I lived, when I chanced to raise my eyes and notice the number on a house, lit up by a street lamp. The number was that of my age. Looking down again, I saw before me a woman with a pale complexion and hollow eyes, whose feaures seemed to me to resemble Aurélia's. I thought, "It is a sign either of *her death* or my own!" For some unknown reason, I decided on the latter conjecture, and became obsessed with the idea that it was to happen the next day at that very hour.

That night, I had a dream which confirmed me in this belief. —I was wandering through a vast building made up of a number of rooms, some of which were set aside for study, others for conversation or philosophical discussion. I lingered with interest in one of the former, where I thought I recognized my old masters and fellow students. The lessons on Greek and Latin authors droned on in that monotonous hum that sounds like a prayer to the goddess Mnemosyne. —I went into another room, where philosophical discussions were taking place. I took part in them for a while, then left to try to find my room in a sort of inn with immense staircases, crowded with bustling travelers.

I lost my way several times in the long corridors, and then, as I was crossing one of the central galleries, I came face to face with a curious spectacle. A winged being of enormous proportions— man or woman, I do not know—was fluttering painfully in the space overhead and seemed to be struggling amid thick clouds. Exhausted and out of breath, it fell at last into the center of the dim courtyard, catching and crumpling its wings on the roofs and balustrades. I was able to observe it for a moment. It was colored with shades of bright red, and its wings shimmered with a thousand changing reflections. Clothed in a long gown with classical folds, it resembled Albrecht Dürer's Angel of Melancholy.[9] —I could not keep from calling out in fright, and my cries woke me with a start.

The following day, I hastened to visit all of my friends. Mentally I bid them adieu, and telling them nothing of what was occupying my mind, I animatedly expatiated on mystical themes. I surprised them with my uncommon eloquence; it seemed to me as if I knew everything, and that the mysteries of the world were being revealed to me in these final hours.

That evening, as the fatal hour seemed to be approaching, I was sitting with two friends at a club table, discoursing upon painting and music, expounding my ideas on the generation of colors and the meaning of numbers. One of them, Paul ***,[10] wanted to escort me home, but I told him that I was not going back. "Where are you going?" he asked me. —"*To the East!*" And as he walked along beside me, I began to search the sky for a Star that I thought I knew, as if it had some influence upon my destiny. Having found it, I continued walking, keeping to the streets from which it was visible, walking as it were to meet my destiny, and determined to keep the star within my view until the moment when death would strike me down. Having arrived, however, at a point where three streets converged, I refused to go any further. It seemed to me that my friend was exerting superhuman strength to make me move; to my eyes he was growing larger, and taking on the features of an apostle. I seemed to see the spot on which we were standing rise up and lose its urban aspect; —on a hill, surounded by a vast, desolate wilderness, this place was becoming the scene of combat between two Spirits, like a biblical temptation. "No!" I declared, "I do not belong to your Heaven. In that star are those who are awaiting me. They preceded the revelation that you have made to me. Let me join them, for the one I love is among them, and it is there that we are to meet again!"

III.

Here began for me what I shall call the overflowing of the dream into real life. From that moment, everything took on at times a dual aspect—without my reasoning ever lacking logic, nor my memory losing the slightest details of what was happening to me. It was just that my actions, to all appearances mad, were subject to what human reason would call illusion. . . .

The idea has often occurred to me that, in certain critical moments in life, some Spirit of the outer world is suddenly incarnated in the form of an ordinary person, and brings or attempts to bring its influence to bear upon us, without that person having any awareness or memory of it.

My friend had left me, seeing that his efforts were futile, and doubtless believing me to be prey to some obsession that would be eased by walking. Finding myself alone, I got to my feet with an effort and set off again in the direction of the star, upon which I kept my eyes fixed. As I walked I sang a mysterious hymn, which I thought I recalled from having heard it in some other existence, and which filled me with an ineffable joy. At the same time, I took off my earthly garments and scattered them around me. The road seemed to lead ever upward, and the star to grow larger. Then I stood still, with my arms outstretched, waiting for the moment when my soul would leave my body, drawn magnetically into the rays of the star. A shudder passed through me; nostalgic regret for the earth and for those I loved gripped my heart, and so ardently within myself did I beseech the Spirit who was drawing me to him that it seemed as if I was redescending to the world of men. I was surrounded by a night patrol; I had the idea that I had grown very large and that, flooded with electrical forces, I would strike down all who approached me. There was something comical in the care I took to spare the strength and the lives of the soldiers who had taken me into custody.

If I did not believe that a writer's mission is to analyze with sincerity what he feels and experiences in critical moments of life, and if I did not have in mind what I deem to be a useful purpose, I would stop here, and not attempt to describe what I then experienced in a series of visions, attributable perhaps to madness or to some common illness. . . . Stretched out on a cot, I thought I saw the heavens unveiled, opening before me in a thousand images of incomparable splendor. The destiny of the emancipated Soul seemed to reveal itself to me, as if to fill me with regret for having wished to regain a foothold, with all the strength of my mind, upon the earth that I was about to leave. . . . Immense circles were tracing themselves across the infinite, like the rings made in water when it is disturbed by a falling object; each region, thronged with radiant figures, took on color, moved, and dissolved in its turn, and a goddess, ever the same, smilingly threw off the furtive masks of her various incarnations, and at last vanished, elusive, into the mystic splendors of the Asiatic sky.

Through one of those phenomena which everyone has experienced in certain dreams, this celestial vision did not leave me oblivious to what was going on around me. Lying on a cot, I heard the soldiers talking about some unidentified person who had been taken into custody like me and whose voice had echoed in this very room. Owing to an odd effect of vibration, it seemed to me that his voice was resonating within my chest, and that my soul had as it were divided—distinctly split between vision and reality. For a moment, I thought of trying to turn round to face the person in question, then shuddered as I remembered a popular German superstition which says that every man has a *double*, and that when you see him, death is near. —I closed my eyes and fell into a confused state of mind in which the fantastical or real figures surrounding me seemed to shatter into a thousand fleeting images. There was a moment when I saw, close by, two of my friends who were asking for me; the soldiers pointed me out. Then the door opened and someone of my build, whose face I could not see, went out with my friends, to whom I called in vain. "But there is some mistake!" I cried. "I am the one they came for, and someone else is leaving!" I made so much noise that they put me in a cell.

I remained there for several hours in a sort of stupor; finally, the two friends whom I *thought I had seen* earlier came for me in a carriage. I told them everything that had happened, but they denied having come during the night. I dined with them calmly enough, but as night approached I felt that I had cause to dread the same hour which, the day before, had so nearly been fatal to me. I asked one of them for an oriental ring that he wore on his finger, and which I regarded as an ancient talisman; then, running a scarf through it, I tied it around my neck, taking care to turn the setting, which held a turquoise, toward a place on the nape of my neck where I felt a pain. In my mind, it was through this place that my soul might leave my body at the moment when a certain ray from the star I had seen the evening before would, relative to myself, coincide with the zenith. Whether by chance or as the result of my intense fixation, I fell down as though struck by lightning, at the very same time as on the evening before. I was laid upon a bed, and for a long time I lost all sense of the meaning and interconnection of the images that came into my mind. This state lasted a number of days. I was taken away to an asylum. Many relatives and friends visited me there without my being aware of it. For me the only difference between my waking and sleeping states was that in the former everything was transfigured in my eyes; every person who came near me seemed transformed, material objects had about them a kind of penumbra which altered their form, and the shifting play of light, the combinations of colors, were diffused in such a way as to provide me with a continual series of interwoven impressions, the plausibility of which continued in the dream state, unconstrained as it was by external elements.

IV.

One evening, I was certain that I had been transported to the banks of the Rhine. Before me were sinister rocks, the rough out-

lines of which were visible in the shadows. I entered a cheerful
house; the rays of the setting sun were shining gaily through its
green shutters festooned with vines. It seemed to me that I was
returning to a familiar abode, the home of one of my maternal uncles, a Flemish painter, who had been dead for more than a century. Preliminary sketches of paintings hung here and there; one
of them depicted the familiar fairy of these shores. An old servant, whom I addressed as Marguerite and whom I seemed to
have known since childhood, said to me, "Why don't you go and
lie down on your bed? You've come a long way, and your uncle
won't be back until late. We'll wake you up for supper." I lay down
on a four-poster bed, which had cretonne curtains with a large red
flower pattern. On the wall across from me hung a rustic clock,
and on this clock was a bird who began to talk like a person. And
the idea occurred to me that my grandfather's soul was in that
bird; but I no more marveled at his new form and speech than at
finding myself transported back a century in time. The bird spoke
to me of living relatives and of those who had died at various
times in the past as if they were contemporaneous, and said to
me, "You can see that your uncle took care to paint *her* portrait in
advance. . . . Now, *she* is with us." I glanced over at a painting
which depicted a woman dressed in traditional German garb,
leaning over the river bank, her eyes fixed on a cluster of forget-
me-nots. —Meanwhile, night was gradually falling, and the appearance, sounds, and feeling of the place commingled in my
drowsy mind; I imagined I was falling into an abyss that traversed
the globe. I felt I was being carried painlessly along by a current
of molten metal, and a thousand such streams, of different colors according to their chemical composition, were crisscrossing the bosom of the earth like the vessels and veins that wind
through the lobes of the brain. They were all flowing, circulating,
and pulsating in such a fashion, and I had the feeling that these
currents were made up of living souls, in the molecular state,
which would have been visible to me had it not been for the
speed at which I was traveling. A whitish light gradually filtered
into these channels, and at last I saw, stretching out before me like
a vast dome, a new panorama, dotted with islands surrounded by
luminous waves. I found myself on a shore illumined by this sun-
less daylight, and I saw an old man who was tilling the earth. I
recognized him as the same man who had spoken to me through

the voice of the bird, and whether because he was speaking to me
or because I understood him on an instinctive level, it became
clear to me that our ancestors assume the forms of certain animals
to visit us on earth, and that they are present as silent observers of
the phases of our existence.

The old man left his work and accompanied me to a house
that stood nearby. The surrounding countryside reminded me of
a part of French Flanders where my parents had lived and where
they were buried: the field surrounded by groves of trees at the
edge of the wood, the nearby lake, the river and the washhouse,
the village with its steeply ascending street, the hills of dark sandstone with their clumps of broom and heather—a revitalized image of the places I had loved. Yet the house I entered was not at
all familiar to me. I understood that it had existed in some other
time, and that in this world I was now visiting, the ghosts of inanimate things coexisted with those of human bodies.

I entered an immense hall where many people were gathered.
Everywhere I looked I saw familiar faces. The features of dead
relatives whom I had mourned were reproduced in others who,
clothed in more old-fashioned garb, welcomed me with the same
paternal greeting. They seemed to have assembled for a family
banquet. One of these relatives came up to me and embraced me
tenderly. He wore old-fashioned garb, the colors of which seemed
to have faded, and his smiling face beneath his powdered hair
bore a certain resemblance to mine. He seemed to me more distinctly alive than the others, and, as it were, in more intimate contact with my own spirit. —He was my uncle. He had me sit next
to him, and a kind of communication was established between
us; for I cannot say that I heard his voice, yet, as I focused my
thought on a particular question, the explanation would immediately become clear to me, and images would take shape before my
eyes like animated pictures.

"Then it is true!" I said, transported. "We are immortal, and
preserve here the images of the world we once inhabited. What
happiness to think that everything we have loved will be around
us forever! . . . I was so weary of life!"

"Do not be too quick to rejoice," he said, "for you still belong
to the world above and you have yet to endure hard years of trial.
This dwelling place which so delights you has its own sorrows,

struggles, and dangers. The earth on which we lived is ever the theater where our destinies are twined and untwined; we are the rays of the central fire that sustains it and that has already grown weaker. . . ."

"What!" I exclaimed. "The earth could die, and we could be consumed by nothingness?"

"Nothingness," he replied, "does not exist in the sense it is usually understood; but the earth is itself a material body whose soul is the sum of all the spirits within it. Matter can no more perish than spirit, but it can be altered for good or for evil. Our past and our future are interwoven. We live in our race, and our race lives in us."

This idea immediately became palpable to me, and, as if the walls of the room had opened onto infinite perspectives, I seemed to see an uninterrupted chain of men and women in whom I was and who were myself; the costumes of all peoples, the images of all lands, appeared to me distinctly and simultaneously, as if my faculties of concentration had been multiplied without becoming confused, in a spatial phenomenon analogous to the temporal one which can compress a century of action into a minute of dream. My astonishment grew as I observed that this vast multitude was made up only of the people who were present in the room, and whose shapes I had seen breaking apart and combining in a thousand fleeting images.

"We are seven," I said to my uncle.

"That is, indeed," he said, "the typical number of every human family, and, by extension, seven times seven, and so on."[11]

I cannot hope to make this reply comprehensible; it remains very obscure even for me. Metaphysics provides me no terms for the intuition that then came to me of the relationship between this number of people and universal harmony. One can readily perceive, in father and mother, the analogy with the electrical forces of nature; but how can one establish the individual centers which have emanated from them—from which they emanate, like a composite, living *figuration* whose possible permutations are both multiple and limited? One might as well ask the flower to account for the number of its petals or the number of divisions in its corolla . . . , the earth for the shapes it assumes, the sun for the colors it produces.

V.

Everything around me was changing form. The spirit with
whom I was conversing had no longer the same appearance. He
was now a young man, who received ideas from me rather than
imparting them. . . . Had I ventured too far upon these vertigi-
nous heights? I seemed to understand that these questions were
obscure or dangerous, even for the spirits of the world I was then
perceiving. . . . Perhaps, too, a higher power forbade me these
investigations. I found myself wandering through the streets of
a populous, unfamiliar city. I observed that it was knobbed with
hills and dominated by a mountain which was covered with
houses. Among the inhabitants of this capital city, I could distinguish certain men who seemed to belong to a special nation; their
keen, resolute air and energetic cast of features made me think of
those sovereign, warlike races that live in the mountains or on certain islands almost completely cut off from the outside world; yet
it was within a great city, amid a heterogeneous and ordinary
population, that they were able to maintain their fierce individu-
ality. Who then were these men? My guide took me up steep,
noisy streets where the various sounds of industry could be heard.
We climbed higher by means of long flights of steps, beyond
which the view stretched out before us. Here and there we could
see terraces covered with trellises, small gardens laid out on a few
level patches, roofs, lightly constructed pavilions, painted and
carved with whimsical patience; vistas linked together by long
trails of climbing vegetation enchanted the eye and delighted the
mind like an exquisite oasis, a hidden refuge above the noisy tumult below, which was here no more than a murmur. I have often
heard speak of outlaw nations, living in the shadow of necropo-
lises and catacombs; here, no doubt, was the opposite. A happy
race had made itself this retreat beloved of birds, flowers, pure air,
and light. "These," my guide told me, "are the ancient inhabitants
of this mountain which towers above the city where we now
stand. Since time immemorial they have dwelt here, simple in
their customs, loving and just, preserving the natural virtues of the
first days of creation. Neighboring peoples held them in esteem
and modeled themselves upon them."

I followed my guide down, from the point where I then was,

into one of those high-perched dwellings, the massed roofs of
which presented such a curious appearance. It seemed as if my
feet were sinking into successive layers of buildings of different
ages. These phantom structures were continually giving way to
others, in which I could discern the distinct style of each century;
they resembled the excavations of ancient cities, except for the
fact that everything was airy and full of life, irradiated by a thousand crisscrossing beams of light. At last I found myself in a vast
room where I saw an old man working at a table at some sort of
craft. —Just as I crossed the threshold, a man dressed in white,
whose face I could scarcely make out, brandished at me a weapon
that he held in his hand; but my guide motioned to him to go
away. It appeared that they had wanted to prevent me from penetrating the mystery of these sanctuaries. Without asking anything
of my guide, I intuitively understood that these heights, and these
depths as well, were the retreat of the primordial inhabitants of
the mountain. Forever resisting the advancing tide of new races,
they dwelt there, simple in their customs, loving and just, clever,
steadfast, and resourceful—and peacefully victorious over the
blind masses who had so often encroached upon their heritage.
Indeed, they were neither corrupted, nor destroyed, nor enslaved;
they were pure, despite having conquered ignorance, preserving
in prosperity the virtues of poverty. —A child was playing on the
floor with crystals, shells, and carved stones, doubtless turning its
lesson into a game. An elderly yet still beautiful woman was busy
with the household chores. At that moment several young people
entered noisily, as if returning from work. I marveled to see them
all dressed in white, but it seems this was an optical illusion; to
make this apparent to me, my guide began to draw their costumes, tinting them with bright colors, giving me to understand
that this was the way they were in reality. The whiteness that had
surprised me was due perhaps to a special brilliance, to a play of
light in which the ordinary colors of the spectrum blended and
merged. I left the room and found myself on a terrace which was
laid out as a flower garden. There, some young girls and children
were strolling about and playing. Their clothes appeared to me to
be white like the others, but were set off with pink embroidery.
These young people were so beautiful, their features so full of
grace, and the radiance of their souls shone so vividly through

their delicate forms that they all awakened in me a kind of love without partiality and without desire, encapsulating all the intoxication of the vague passions of youth.

I cannot convey the emotion I felt among these charming creatures, who were dear to me even without my knowing them. They were like a primordial, heavenly family, whose smiling eyes sought mine with a gentle compassion. I began to weep a flood of tears, as if at the memory of a lost paradise. There, I sensed poignantly that I was only a wayfarer in this strange yet beloved land, and I trembled at the thought of having to return to life. In vain, the women and children pressed round me as if to keep me there. Already their enchanting forms were dissolving into a nebulous mist; those lovely faces were fading away, and those strong features and sparkling eyes were vanishing into a shadowy obscurity where there still gleamed the last flicker of a smile. . . .

Such was this vision, or such at least were the main details that I can remember. The cataleptic state that I had been in for some days was explained to me in scientific terms, and the accounts of those who had seen me in that condition caused me some irritation when I saw that they attributed to mental aberration certain words and actions coinciding with the various phases of what was for me a succession of logical events. I felt more affection than ever for those of my friends who, out of patient indulgence or because they held ideas similar to my own, asked me for lengthy descriptions of the things I had seen in my mind. One of them said to me, in tears, "There really is a God, isn't there?" —"Yes!" I replied with emotion. And we embraced like two brothers from that mystic homeland I had caught a glimpse of. —What happiness I found at first in that conviction! Thus that eternal doubt about the immortality of the soul, which besets the best of minds, had been dispelled for me. No more death, no more sadness, no more anxiety. Those I loved, relatives and friends, were giving me indisputable signs of their eternal existence, and I was separated from them only by the hours of the day. I awaited those of the night with a sweet melancholy.

VI.

Another dream confirmed me in this belief. I suddenly found myself in one of the rooms of my grandfather's house. Yet it appeared to have grown larger. The old furniture gleamed with a marvelous polish, the carpets and curtains were like new, a light three times brighter than natural daylight was coming in through the window and the door, and in the air was the freshness and fragrance of the first mild mornings of spring. Three women were working in this room, and corresponded—without exactly resembling them—to certain relatives and friends of my youth. It seemed that each possessed the features of several such people. The contours of their faces kept shifting like the flame of a lamp, and all the while something of one would pass into the other; smile, voice, color of eyes and hair, stature, familiar gestures, all these were mutually interchanged as if they had lived the same life, and each was thus a composite of all, analogous to those types that painters distill from a number of models in order to create perfect beauty.

The eldest one spoke to me in a vibrant, melodious voice that I recognized as having heard in my childhood, and something she was saying—what, I am not sure—struck me with its profound aptness. But she drew my attention to myself, and I saw that I was wearing a little, old-fashioned, brown suit, entirely woven with a needle, from threads as fine as those of a spider's web. It was smart, graceful, and imbued with a sweet fragrance. I felt much younger and quite spruce in this garment fashioned by their fairy fingers, and I blushingly thanked them, as if I had been but a small boy in the presence of fine ladies. Then one of them rose and headed toward the garden.

Everyone knows that in dreams one never sees the sun, although one often is aware of a far brighter light. Objects and bodies give off their own luminosity. I found myself in a little park through which ran trellised bowers laden with heavy clusters of white and black grapes; as the lady who was my guide moved beneath these arbors, the shadow of the intertwined trellises seemed to transmute her figure and her clothes. At last she emerged, and we found ourselves in an open space. Traces of the old paths which had cut crosswise through it were barely discernible. It had been neglected for years, and scattered patches of clematis, hops, honeysuckle, jasmine, ivy, and birthwort stretched their long trailing creepers between luxuriant trees. Branches laden with fruit were bowed to the ground, and among clumps of weeds bloomed some garden flowers which had reverted to the wild.

Here and there stood groups of poplars, acacias, and pines, in

the midst of which one had glimpses of statues blackened by time.
I saw before me a pile of ivy-covered rocks from which gushed a
spring of running water; its melodious splashes echoed across a
pool of still water half veiled by the broad leaves of water lilies.

The lady I was following stretched her slender figure in a
movement that made the folds of her taffeta dress shimmer, and
gracefully slipped her bare arm around the long stem of a holly-
hock; then, beneath a bright ray of light, she began to expand in
such a way that gradually the garden assumed her form, and the
trees and flower beds became the rosettes and festoons on her
clothes, while her face and arms impressed their contours upon the
crimson clouds in the sky. I began to lose sight of her as she was
transfigured, for she seemed to be vanishing into her own immensity. "Oh, don't leave me!" I cried. . . . "For nature dies with you!"

As I spoke, I struggled painfully through the brambles, as if
to grasp the widening shadow that eluded me, but I ran against a
fragment of ruined wall, at the foot of which lay a sculpted bust
of a woman. As I picked it up, I had the conviction that it was *of
her*. . . . I recognized certain beloved features, and upon looking
round me, I saw that the garden had taken on the appearance of
a graveyard. Voices were saying, "The Universe is in darkness!"

VII.

This dream, which had begun so happily, threw me into utter
confusion. What did it mean? I did not find out until much later.
Aurélia was dead.

At first I heard only that she was ill. Owing to my state of
mind, I felt only a vague sadness mingled with hope. I believed
that I myself had only a short time to live, and I was now confident of the existence of a world in which loving hearts meet
again. Besides, she belonged to me much more in death than she
did in life. . . . A selfish thought, for which my reason would later
pay with bitter remorse.

I would not wish to attach overimportance to premonitions;
chance works in strange ways; but at that time I was still deeply
preoccupied with a particular memory from the time of our too
brief union. I had given her an old-fashioned ring with a setting of
heart-shaped opal. As this ring was too large for her finger, I had
conceived the fatal idea of having it cut down; I only realized my

error when I heard the noise of the saw. I seemed to see blood
flowing. . . .

Medical care had brought me back to health without yet having restored to my mind the normal operations of human reason.
The building in which I found myself, set upon a hillside, had
an enormous garden planted with exquisite trees. The pure air
of the heights on which it stood, the first breath of spring, the
pleasures of congenial company, brought me many long days of
tranquillity.

The first leaves of the sycamore trees delighted me with the
brilliance of their colors, like the plumes of Pharaoh's cocks.
The view out across the plain offered from morning to evening a
charming panorama, the graduated hues of which captivated my
imagination. I peopled the hills and clouds with heavenly figures
whose forms I seemed to see distinctly. —I wished to give firmer
form to my favorite thoughts, and with the help of some charcoal
and a few bits of brick that I collected, I soon covered the walls
with a series of murals externalizing my impressions. One figure
always stood out among the rest; it was that of Aurélia, depicted
in the guise of a goddess, just as she had appeared to me in my
dream. Beneath her feet a wheel was turning,[12] and the gods
formed her retinue. I managed to color this group by pressing out
the juice of herbs and flowers. —How often did I sink into reverie
before that cherished idol! I went further, I attempted to model in
clay the body of my beloved; each morning I was obliged to begin all over again, for the madmen, jealous of my happiness, took
pleasure in destroying its image.

I was given paper, and for a long time I occupied myself with
creating, in a thousand figurations accompanied by narratives,
verses, and inscriptions in every known language, a sort of history
of the world mingled with recollections from my studies and fragments of dreams which were rendered more vivid by my obsession, or which prolonged its duration. I did not limit myself to the
modern traditions regarding creation. My speculation went further back: I glimpsed, as if in memory, the first pact made by the
genii with the aid of talismans. I tried to put together the stones
of the *Sacred Table*, and to represent around it the first seven *Elohim*
who had divided the world among them.[13]

This system of history, borrowed from the Oriental tradi-

tions,[14] began with the auspicious agreement between the Powers
of Nature, who formulated and structured the universe. —During
the night before I began my work, I had imagined myself transported to a dark planet where the first seeds of creation were
struggling forth. From the bosom of the still soft clay rose gigantic palm trees, poisonous spurge, and acanthus coiling about cacti;
—the barren forms of rocks thrust up like skeletons from this nas-
cent creation, and hideous reptiles wound their way, lengthen-
ing or thickening, through the labyrinthian tangle of unchecked
vegetation. Only the pale light of the stars illuminated the bluish
vistas of this strange landscape; yet, as these creations took form,
a more luminous star drew from them the seeds of light.

VIII.

Then the monsters changed form and, casting off their first
skins, rose up more powerful than before on mammoth paws; the
enormous weight of their bodies crushed the branches and grass,
and in the chaos and confusion of nature they waged battles in
which I myself took part, for I had a body as strange as theirs.
Suddenly an extraordinary harmony echoed within our solitudes,
and it seemed that the mingled cries, roars, and hisses of these
primitive beings were henceforth modulated upon this heavenly
melody. There were infinite variations, one upon the other, the
planet gradually brightened, heavenly forms began to emerge out
of the verdure and the depths of groves, and, henceforth tamed,
all the monsters I had seen were casting off their bizarre shapes
and becoming men and women; others, in their transformations,
were assuming the aspect of wild beasts, fish, and birds.

Who then had performed this miracle? In these new *metamorphoses*, a radiant goddess presided over the rapid evolution of
human beings. Then a new division of species was established,
which, starting with the birds, included beasts, fish, and reptiles.
These were the Divas, Peris, Undines, and Salamanders;[15] each
time one of these creatures died, it would immediately be reborn
in a more beautiful form and would sing praises to the gods.
—However, one of the Elohim had the idea of creating a fifth
race, made up of elements of the earth, and which was called the
Afrites.[16] —This was the signal for a total revolution among the
Spirits who refused to acknowledge the new lords of the world.
I do not know how many thousands of years this fighting lasted,

drenching the world in blood. Three of the Elohim, along with the Spirits of their races, were at last banished to the southern regions of the earth, where they founded vast kingdoms. They had made off with the secrets of the heavenly *cabala* [17] that links the worlds, and drew their strength from the worship of certain stars, to which they ever correspond. These necromancers, exiled to the farthest reaches of the globe, had agreed to transmit their power only among themselves. Surrounded by women and slaves, each of their sovereigns had ensured that he would be reborn in the form of one of his children. Their life lasted a thousand years. As their death approached, powerful cabalists would shut them up in well-guarded sepulchers where they would feed them elixirs and preservative substances. For a long time, they would retain the appearance of life; then, like the chrysalis that spins its cocoon, they would go to sleep for forty days to be reborn in the form of a young child who would later be called to dominion.

Yet the vitalizing powers of the earth were exhausted in feeding these families, whose ever-unaltered blood flowed ceaselessly into new offspring. In vast subterranean passages, hollowed out beneath hypogea and pyramids, they had amassed all the treasures of past races and certain talismans which protected them against the wrath of the gods.

It was in the center of Africa, beyond the mountains of the Moon and ancient Ethiopia, that these strange mysteries took place: for a long time I had languished there in captivity, along with a portion of the human race. The groves that I had once seen so green now bore only pale flowers and withered leaves; an implacable sun devoured the land, and the frail progeny of these eternal dynasties seemed weighed down beneath the burden of life. This majestic and monotonous grandeur, ruled by etiquette and priestly ritual, weighed upon everyone without anyone daring to break free. The old men languished under the weight of their crowns and imperial ornaments, surrounded by doctors and priests whose knowledge guaranteed them immortality. As for the people, forever enmeshed within the divisions of caste, they could be confident of neither life nor liberty. At the foot of trees stricken with death and sterility, at the mouths of dried-up springs, one could see pale, enervated children and young women withering away upon the scorched grass. The magnificence of the royal chambers, the majesty of the porticos, the brilliance of the apparel and jewels was but small consolation for the never-ending tedium of this desolate wasteland.

Soon the population was decimated by illness, the animals and plants died, and the immortals themselves wasted away beneath their splendid attire. —Suddenly there came a scourge, greater than all the rest, to rejuvenate and salvage the world. The constellation of Orion opened the floodgates of the heavens; the earth, overladen with ice at the opposite pole, made a half-turn on its axis, and the seas, spilling over their banks, flooded the plateaus of Africa and Asia; the deluge of water soaked through the sand, filled the tombs and pyramids, and for forty days a mysterious ark drifted about the seas, bearing the hope of a new creation.

Three of the Elohim had taken refuge on the highest pinnacle of the African mountains. Fighting broke out among them. Here my memory clouds, and I do not know the outcome of that supreme struggle. But I can still see, standing upon a flooded peak, a woman whom they had abandoned, crying out, her hair flying, as she wrestled with death. Her plaintive strains rose above the noise of the waters. . . . Was she saved? I do not know. The gods, her brothers, had condemned her to death; but above her head shone the Evening Star, pouring forth its flaming rays upon her brow.[18]

The interrupted hymn of the earth and the heavens rang out harmoniously to consecrate the accord among the new races. And while the sons of Noah toiled painfully in the rays of a new sun, the necromancers, huddled in their subterranean dwellings, ever watched over their treasure and reveled in silence and darkness. Occasionally, emerging timidly from their retreats, they would come to frighten the living or to spread among the wicked the dire teachings of their occult sciences.

Such are the memories that I conjured up by a kind of vague intuition of the past: I shuddered as I recreated the hideous features of those accursed races. Everywhere the suffering image of the Eternal Mother was dying, weeping, languishing. Throughout the shadowy civilizations of Asia and Africa, one could see repeated again and again the same bloody scene of orgy and carnage, which the same spirits recreated under different forms. The last took place at Grenada, where the sacred talisman crumbled beneath the hostile blows of Christians and Moors. How many more years has the world still to suffer—for the vengeance of these

eternal enemies must recommence under other skies! They are the
severed segments of the serpent that encircles the earth. . . . Separated by the sword, they join together again in a hideous kiss
cemented by human blood.

IX.

Such were the images which appeared one by one before my
eyes. Little by little, calm was restored to my mind, and I left that
abode which was for me a paradise. Much later, certain fateful
circumstances laid the groundwork for a relapse, which set in motion once more this interrupted series of strange reveries. —I was
walking in the countryside, absorbed in thought about some work
dealing with religious ideas. As I passed a house, I heard a bird
speaking the few words it had been taught, yet whose confused
babble seemed to me to have meaning; it reminded me of the vision I have recounted above, and an ominous shudder ran through
me. A few steps farther on, I met a friend whom I had not seen for
a long time and who lived in a house nearby. He wanted to show
me his property, and in the course of this visit took me up to a
high terrace from which there was a vast panoramic view. It was
sunset. As we were descending the steps of a rustic staircase, I
tripped and hit my chest on the corner of a piece of furniture.
I had enough strength to get up, and I dashed into the middle of
the garden, thinking I had received a deathblow, but eager to gaze
once more upon the setting sun before breathing my last. Amid
the grief and regret of such a moment, I felt happy to be dying
thus, at this hour, and among the trees, arbors, and autumn flowers. It had been, however, no more than a fainting spell, after
which I still had strength enough to return home and go to bed.
I became ill with fever; recalling the spot where I had fallen, I remembered that the view I had admired overlooked a cemetery,
the very one that held Aurélia's tomb. I had not really thought of
this earlier; otherwise, I could attribute my fall to the emotion
brought on by this sight. —That in itself suggested to me the
idea of a more certain fatality. I felt all the more sorrow that death
had not reunited me with her. Then, upon reflection, I thought
that I was unworthy of it. I bitterly recalled the life I had led since
her death, reproaching myself not for having forgotten her, which
was not at all the case, but for having through vulgar liaisons dis-
honored her memory. The idea occurred to me to seek counsel in

sleep, but *her* image, which had so often appeared to me, returned
no more to my dreams. At first these dreams were confused, inter-
spersed with scenes of bloodshed. It seemed that an entire, fatal
race had been loosed in the midst of the ideal world that I had
seen before, and of which she was the queen. The same Spirit
who had threatened me—when I entered the abode of those pure
families who dwelt upon the heights of the *Mysterious City*—
passed before me, no longer in the white garb that he had then
worn, along with others of his race, but attired like a prince of the
Orient. I leaped toward him, threateningly, but he turned calmly
to face me. O terror! O fury! It was my own face, my whole body,
in idealized and enlarged form. . . . Then I remembered the man
who had been arrested the same night as I and who, in my view,
had been released from the guardroom under my name when my
two friends had come for me. He held in his hand a weapon
which I could scarcely make out, and one of those who accompanied him said, "That is what he struck him with."

I do not know how to explain the fact that in my mind
earthly events could correspond to those of the supernatural
realm; this is easier to *sense* than to state clearly.[19] But who then
was this Spirit who was me and yet outside of me? Was he the
legendary *Double,* or that mystical brother whom Oriental peoples
call *Ferouër?*[20] —Had my imagination not been struck by the story
of the knight who did battle all night long in a forest with a
stranger who was himself? However that may be, I believe that
the human imagination has invented nothing that is not true, in
this world or in others, and I could not doubt that which I had *seen*
so clearly.

A terrible idea occurred to me: "Man is double," I thought.
—"I feel two men within myself," a Father of the Church once
wrote.[21] —The coming together of two souls has placed a composite seed within a body which itself shows two like portions reproduced in every organ of its structure. In every man there is
a spectator and an actor, one who speaks and one who answers.
The Oriental peoples saw in this two antagonists: the good and
the evil genius. "Am I the good, or am I the evil?" I asked myself.
"In any case, *the other* is hostile to me. . . . Who knows if under
certain circumstances or at a certain age these two spirits may not
draw apart? Joined both to the same body by a material affinity,
perhaps one is destined to glory and happiness, the other to an-

nihilation or eternal suffering." Suddenly a fatal flash of light cut through the darkness. . . . Aurélia was no longer mine! . . . I thought I heard someone talking about a ceremony which was taking place somewhere else, and about preparations for a mystical marriage which was my own, and in which *the other* was going to take advantage of my friends' error and that of Aurélia herself. My dearest friends who came to see me and console me seemed plagued by doubt and uncertainty, that is, of a divided mind in regard to me, partly affectionate and trusting, yet looking as though they saw death in my eyes. In everything these people said to me there was a double meaning, although they were not aware of it, since they were not *in the spirit,* as I was. For a moment, indeed, this idea seemed comical to me as I thought of Amphitryon and Sosia.[22] But if this grotesque symbolism were something other—if, as in other fables of Antiquity, it were the fatal truth under a mask of madness? "Well," I thought, "let us wrestle with the fatal spirit, let us wrestle with the god himself, using the weapons of tradition[23] and science. Whatever he may contrive in shadows and darkness, I exist—and to defeat him I have all the time that remains to me upon earth.

X.

How can I describe the strange despair to which these ideas gradually reduced me? An evil genius had taken my place in the world of souls—for Aurélia, he was myself, and the forlorn spirit which animated my body, enfeebled, scorned, unrecognized by her, saw itself forever doomed to despair or annihilation. I gathered all the strength of my will to penetrate still further into the mystery from which I had lifted some of the veils. At times my dreams made a mockery of my efforts, bringing before me only fleeting, grimacing faces. Here I can give only a very peculiar idea of where this mental exertion led me. I felt myself sliding as if on a filament drawn to infinite length. The earth, crisscrossed by colored veins of molten metals, just as I had seen it before, was gradually brightening, lit by its spreading central fire, the whiteness of which blended with the cherry hues upon the sides of the inner globe. From time to time I was amazed to find immense pools of water, suspended in the air like clouds, and yet of such density that one could pull flakes from them; but clearly it was a different sort of liquid from earthly water, doubtless the evaporation of what for the spirit world was the equivalent of the ocean and the rivers.

I arrived within sight of a vast, hilly beach, covered with a greenish-colored sort of reed that was yellowed at the tips as if partially withered by the heat of the sun—but I no more saw the sun now than I had on other occasions. —A castle stood atop the hill which I now began to climb. On the other side of the valley, I saw spread out before me an immense city. Night had fallen while I was climbing the hillside, and I could see the lights of houses and streets. Upon descending the hill, I found myself in a market where they were selling fruits and vegetables like those in the south of France.

I descended a dark flight of stairs and found myself in the streets. Posters were being put up announcing the opening of a casino and listing the theater cast. The printed borders consisted of garlands of flowers, so masterfully drawn and colored that they seemed real. —A section of the building was still under construction. I entered a workshop where I saw workers modeling in clay an enormous animal in the shape of a llama, but which was apparently going to be fitted out with giant wings. This monster was as if infused with a jet of flame which brought it gradually to life, so that it twisted and writhed as it was penetrated by a thousand crimson streaks forming the veins and arteries and fecundating, as it were, the inert matter, which was instantly overspread with a covering of fibrous appendages, pinions, and tufts of woolly hair. I paused to gaze upon this masterpiece, in which one seemed to glimpse the secrets of divine creation. "We have here," I was told, "the primordial fire which brought the first beings to life. . . . At one time, it used to reach all the way to the earth's surface, but its source has since gone dry." I also saw some jewelers' work in which two metals unknown on earth were used: one that was red and seemed to resemble cinnabar, the other a sky blue. The ornaments had been neither hammered nor chiseled, but gradually acquired shape and color, blossoming forth like metallic plants made from the mixture of certain chemicals. "Might one not create men, as well?" I asked one of the workmen, but he replied, "Men come from above, not from below—can we create ourselves? Here, we are merely formulating, by means of the continuous advances in our industries, a substance finer than that which makes up the earth's crust. These flowers which seem real to you, this animal which looks alive, are but the products of an art raised to the summit of our knowledge, and everyone will come to regard them as such."

Those are roughly the words which were spoken to me, or the meaning of which I thought I discerned. I began to wander through the rooms of the casino, and there I found a large crowd, in which I recognized several people I knew, some living, others who had died at various times in the past. The former appeared not to notice me, while the others acknowledged me without seeming to know who I was. I came to the largest of the rooms, which was entirely hung with bright red velvet, embroidered with rich designs of gold braid. In the center stood a couch in the form of a throne. A few passers-by were sitting on it to test its springiness; but, the arrangements not having been completed, they moved off into other rooms. There was talk of a wedding and of the bridegroom who, they said, would shortly arrive to announce the start of the festivities. I was instantly seized by a fit of mad rage. I imagined that the man they were awaiting was my *double*, who was to marry Aurélia, and I made a scene which seemed to shock the assembled company. I began to speak violently, expounding my grievances and appealing for help to those who knew me. An old man said to me, "But one can't behave this way, you are frightening everyone." Then I exclaimed, "I know very well that he has already struck me with his weapons, but I am ready and unafraid, and I know the sign that will defeat him."

At this moment one of the workmen from the shop I had visited appeared, carrying a long rod at the end of which was a red-hot ball. I wanted to hurl myself at him, but he kept holding the ball out before him, threatening my head. The people around me seemed to be jeering at my impotence. . . . Then I drew back as far as the throne, my soul filled with unspeakable pride, and I raised my arm to make a sign which seemed to me to have magical power. A woman's cry, clear and resonant, filled with heart-rending anguish, awoke me with a start! The syllables of an unknown word that I had been about to utter died away upon my lips. . . . I flung myself to the ground and began to pray fervently, weeping a flood of tears. —But what was that voice that had just rung out so harrowingly in the night?

It was not part of the dream; it was the voice of someone living, and yet for me it was the voice and tone of Aurélia. . . .

I opened my window; all was calm, and the cry was not repeated. —I inquired outside; no one had heard anything. —And yet I am still certain that the cry was real and that it had echoed through the air of the living. . . . People will doubtless tell me that it could have been chance alone that made some poor, suffering woman cry out at that very moment, somewhere near my dwelling. —But in my mind, earthly events were linked to those of the invisible world. This is one of those mysterious interconnections which I do not understand myself, and which it is easier to suggest than to define. . . .

What had I done? I had disturbed the harmony of the magical universe from which my soul had acquired the conviction of immortality. I was cursed, perhaps, for having attempted to penetrate an awesome mystery in defiance of divine law; henceforth I could hope for nothing but wrath and scorn! The shades fled in anger, uttering cries and tracing fatal circles in the air like birds at the approach of a storm.

PART TWO

Eurydice! Eurydice![24]

I.

Lost, a second time!

All is finished, all is over! Now it is I who must die, and die without hope! —What then is death? If it were nothingness . . . Would to God it were! But God Himself cannot make death into nothingness.

Why is it that I am thinking of *Him*, for the first time in so long? The fatal cosmology engendered within my mind had no place for that sole sovereignty . . . or rather it was absorbed into the totality of living beings: it was the god of Lucretius,[25] powerless and lost in his own immensity.

She, however, had believed in God, and one day I surprised her with the name of Jesus upon her lips. It flowed from them so sweetly that I wept to hear it. Oh God! Those tears—those tears . . . They have so long been dry! Those tears, oh God! Give them back to me!

When the soul drifts, wavering, between life and the dream, between the mind's disorder and the return of cold reflection, it is in religious thought that one must seek solace; —this I have never been able to find in philosophy, which offers us only maxims of egoism or at best reciprocity, hollow experience, and bitter doubt; —it combats spiritual suffering by annulling sensibility; like surgery, it can only cut out the organ causing the pain. —But for us, born in a time of revolution and turmoil, when all beliefs were shattered—raised, at best, in that faith of sorts which is content with certain external observances, the indifferent adherence to which is perhaps more culpable than impiety and heresy—it is a difficult task to reconstruct at will, the moment we feel the need for it, that mystic edifice which stands fully formed in the consenting hearts of the childlike and the innocent. "The tree of knowledge is not the tree of life!"²⁶ Yet can we cast from our minds all that so many intelligent generations have built up in them, for good or for evil? Ignorance cannot be learned.

I have better hopes of the goodness of God: perhaps we are approaching that long-prophesied age when science, having completed its entire cycle of synthesis and analysis, belief and negation, will be able to purify itself and bring forth from chaos and ruin the marvelous city of the future. . . . One must not hold human reason so cheap as to believe it gains anything from humbling itself completely, for that would be to impugn its celestial origin. . . . God will doubtless value purity of intention; and what father would wish to see his child renounce in his presence all reason and pride! The disciple who had to touch in order to believe was not damned for that!

What have I written? These are blasphemies. Christian humility cannot speak thus. Such thoughts are far from those that soften the soul. On their brow are flashes of pride from Satan's crown. . . . A pact with God Himself? . . . O science! O vanity!

I had collected several books on the cabala. I immersed myself in these studies, and eventually persuaded myself that all that the human mind had accumulated thereupon throughout the centuries was true. The conviction I had acquired of the existence of the outer world conformed too thoroughly with my readings for me to doubt, henceforth, the revelations of the past. The dogmas and rites of the various religions seemed to link up with them in such a way that each contained certain elements of those arcana which comprised its means of proliferation and defense. These forces could weaken, dwindle, and disappear, leading to the invasion of certain races by others, none of which could conquer or be conquered save by the Spirit.

"Nevertheless," I thought, "it is certain that these sciences are fraught with human error. The magic alphabet, the mysterious hieroglyph, have come down to us only in incomplete and distorted form, be it through the workings of time or of those who stand to profit from our ignorance; let us rediscover the lost letter or the vanished sign, let us recompose the dissonant scale, and we will gain strength in the world of the spirits."

It was thus I thought I perceived the connection between the real world and the spirit world. The earth, its inhabitants, and their history were the theater wherein were played out the physical actions which prepared the existence and circumstances of the immortal beings attached to its destiny. Without considering the impenetrable mystery of the eternity of worlds, my thoughts went back to the time when the sun, like the flower that represents it, which turns its head to follow the revolution of its celestial orbit, sowed upon earth the fertile seeds of plants and animals. It was none other than the very fire which, being a composite of souls, instinctively formed the common dwelling place. The Spirit of the God-Being, reproduced and as it were reflected on earth, became the prototype of human souls, each of which was therefore both man and God. Such were the Elohim.

When one is feeling unhappy, one thinks of the unhappiness of others. I had been remiss about visiting one of my dearest friends, whom I had been told was ill. As I headed toward the place where he was being treated, I reproached myself keenly for this negligence. I was sorrier still when my friend told me that the previous day he had been close to death. I entered a whitewashed hospital room. The sun threw cheerful, angular patterns upon the walls, and played over a vase of flowers which a nun had just placed upon the patient's table. It was almost like the cell of an Italian anchorite. —His gaunt face, his yellowed-ivory complexion, accentuated by the blackness of his beard and hair, his eyes aglow with a last trace of fever, —perhaps too, the way his hooded cloak was thrown over his shoulders, made him seem a quite different person from the one I had known. He was no longer the merry companion of my work and leisure; there was something of the apostle about him. He told me how, when the pain of his illness had reached its most acute, he had suffered a final seizure which he thought was his death agony. Immediately, as if by a miracle, his pain had ceased. —What he told me then is impossible to describe: a sublime dream that carried him to the remotest expanses of the infinite, a conversation with a being at once different from and part of himself, whom he had asked, believing himself dead, where God was. "But God is everywhere," replied his spirit. "He is within you and within everyone. He judges you, listens to you, guides you; He is both you and *I*, who think and dream in unison—and we have never parted, and we are eternal!"

I cannot quote anything else from this conversation, which I perhaps heard or understood poorly. I know only that it left a very vivid impression upon me. I will not be so bold as to attribute to my friend the conclusions that I drew, perhaps falsely, from his words. I am even uncertain if the sentiment implied is compatible with Christianity. . . .

"God is with him!" I cried . . . "but He is no longer with me! O misery! I have driven Him from me; I have threatened Him, cursed Him! It was really He, that mystic brother, moving farther and farther from my soul and warning me in vain! That preferred bridegroom, that king of glory, it is He who now judges and condemns me, and who is carrying away to His heaven forever the woman He might have given to me, and of whom I am henceforth unworthy!"

II.

I cannot describe the depression into which these ideas plunged me. "I understand," I thought, "I have preferred the creature to the Creator; I have deified my love and worshipped, according to pagan custom, the woman whose last breath was dedicated to Christ. But if this religion speaks truth, God may yet pardon me. He may give her back to me if I humble myself before Him; perhaps her spirit will return, within me." I wandered aimlessly through the streets, absorbed in this idea. A funeral procession passed, on the way to the cemetery where she had been buried; the idea occurred to me to join the procession and go there as well. "I do not know," I thought, "who this dead man is whom they are ushering to the grave, but I know now that the dead see and hear us—perhaps he will be glad to find himself followed by a brother in sorrow, sadder than any of those accompanying him." This thought brought me to tears, and people doubtless assumed that I was one of the closest friends of the deceased. O blessed tears! For so long, your sweetness was denied me! . . . My head was clearing, and a ray of hope still led me on. I felt strength enough to pray, and did so with rapture.

I did not even attempt to learn the name of the man whose coffin I had followed. The cemetery I had entered was on several accounts sacred to me. Three members of my mother's family had been buried there; but I could not go to their graves to pray, for they had been moved some years before to a distant soil, from whence they came. —I searched a long time for Aurélia's grave, but could not find it. The layout of the cemetery had been changed—perhaps, too, I had had a lapse of memory. . . . It seemed to me that this strange forgetfulness only added to the charges against me. —I did not dare tell the caretakers the name of a dead woman upon whom I had no rights in the eyes of re- ligion. . . . But I remembered that at home I had, written down, the exact location of her tomb, and I hurried back with my heart pounding and my head awhirl. I have already mentioned that I had cultivated strange superstitions in regard to my love. —In a small case that had belonged to *her,* I had saved her last letter. Dare I also confess that I had made of this case a sort of reliquary commemorating certain long journeys during which thoughts of her had been ever with me: a rose plucked in the gardens of Schoubrah, a piece of mummy-cloth brought back from Egypt, some laurel leaves gathered from the Beirut River,[27] two little gilded crystals, some mosaics from Hagia Sophia, a rosary bead, and I don't know what else . . . finally, the piece of paper I had been given the day the grave was dug, so that I would be able to find it. . . . I blushed and trembled as I sifted through this crazy assemblage. I took the two pieces of paper, and as I was about to head once more for the cemetery, I changed my mind. "No," I thought, " I am not worthy to kneel upon a Christian woman's grave; let us not add one more profanation to so many others! . . ." And to quell the tempest raging inside my head, I set off for a

small town several leagues from Paris, where I had spent some
happy days of my youth at the home of elderly relatives, since deceased. I had often enjoyed going there to watch the sunset from
near their house. There was a terrace there, shaded by linden
trees, which also evoked the memory of young girls, relatives of
mine, among whom I had grown up. One of them . . .

But to compare this vague, childish love to that which had
consumed my youth—how could I even think of it? I saw the sun
sink down over the valley which was filling with mist and shadow;
it disappeared, bathing with a reddish glow the tops of the trees
on the slopes of the high hills. The most dismal sadness filled my
heart. —I went to spend the night in an inn where I was known.
The innkeeper told me about one of my old friends, a resident of
the town, who, following some ill-fated speculation, had shot
himself with a pistol. . . . Sleep brought me terrible dreams. I have
only a confused recollection of them. —I was in an unfamiliar
room, talking to someone in the outer world—the friend I just
mentioned, perhaps. A very tall mirror stood behind us. Chancing
to glance at it, I thought I recognized A***.[28] She seemed sad and
pensive, and suddenly, whether she had emerged from the mirror
or whether she had been reflected in it a moment before as she
entered the room, this sweet, beloved figure was at my side. She
held out her hand, cast a sorrowful gaze upon me, and said, "We
shall meet again later . . . at your friend's house."

Immediately I thought of her marriage, of the curse that separated us . . . and I wondered, "Is it possible? Could she be returning to me?" "Have you forgiven me?" I asked in tears. But all had
vanished. I found myself in a secluded setting, a steep hill strewn
with rocks, surrounded by forests. A house that I thought I recognized overlooked this desolate landscape. I wandered this way and
that on winding, labyrinthian paths. From time to time, weary
of trudging among stones and brambles, I tried to find an easier
route along the forest footpaths. "They are waiting for me over
there!" I thought. —A certain hour struck. . . . I said to myself, "*It
is too late!*" Voices answered me: "*She is lost!*" Pitch-black darkness
surrounded me; the distant house was glowing brightly as if lit for
a party and filled with promptly arrived guests. "She is lost!" I
cried, "and why? . . . I understand—she made a last effort to save
me; —I missed the supreme moment when pardon was still possible. There in Heaven, she could entreat the Heavenly Bride-

groom on my behalf. . . . And what does even my salvation matter? The abyss has claimed its prey! She is lost to me and to all! . . ." I seemed to see her as if lit by the gleam of lightning, pale and near death, carried away by dark horsemen. . . . The cry of grief and rage that I uttered in that moment made me awaken, gasping for breath.

"Oh God, oh God! For her, for her sake alone, oh God, have mercy!" I cried, flinging myself to my knees.

It was daylight. Acting on an impulse that I find it difficult to explain, I instantly resolved to destroy the two pieces of paper that I had taken from the case the day before: the letter, alas! that I reread, moistening it with my tears, and the lugubrious document that bore the seal of the cemetery. "Find her grave now?" I thought. "But it was yesterday that I should have returned to it— and my fatal dream is but the reflection of my fatal day!"

III.

The flames devoured these relics of love and death, so intertwined with the tenderest fibers of my heart. I went to walk off my sorrows and my belated remorse in the countryside, seeking to deaden my mind with exercise and fatigue, and hoping perhaps to ensure myself a less harrowing slumber for the following night. With the idea I had conceived of dream as offering man access to and communication with the spirit world, I had hope . . . I still had hope! Perhaps God would be content with this sacrifice. —Here I must stop; it would be too overweening to claim that my state of mind had been brought on solely by a memory of love. I should say rather that I unwittingly cloaked with this idea my deeper remorse for a madly dissolute life, where evil had very often triumphed, and the errors of which I have acknowledged only upon feeling the blows of misfortune. I no longer deemed myself worthy even to think of the woman whom I was tormenting in death after having caused her so much pain in life, and to whose sweet and saintly pity alone I owed a final glance of forgiveness.

The following night I could sleep but little. A woman who had taken care of me in my childhood appeared to me in a dream and reproached me for a very grave offense that I had committed in the past. I recognized her, although she appeared considerably older than when I had last seen her. That very thought caused me to reflect bitterly that I had neglected to visit her in her dying moments. She seemed to be saying to me, "You did not mourn your old relatives as bitterly as you have mourned this woman. How then can you hope for forgiveness?" Then the dream became confused. Faces of people I had known at various times passed rapidly before my eyes. They filed past, becoming brighter, then fading, and falling back into darkness like the beads of a broken rosary. Then I saw some plastic images of Antiquity vaguely taking form; amorphous at first, they acquired firmer outline and seemed to represent symbols that I could only partially comprehend. Yet what I thought they meant was, "All this was intended to teach you the secret of life, and you did not understand. Religions and fables, saints and poets, all worked as one to unveil the fatal enigma, and you have misinterpreted it. . . . Now, it is too late!"

I arose filled with terror, thinking, "This is my last day!" After a lapse of ten years, the same idea that I described in the first part of this narrative returned to me with still more certainty, and more ominous than ever. God had accorded me this time to repent, and I had not availed myself of it. —After the visit of the *stone guest*,[29] I had sat down again to the feast!

IV.

The feeling of deep sadness stemming from these visions and the reflections they gave rise to during my hours of solitude was such that I felt I was lost. All the acts of a lifetime appeared before me in their most unfavorable light, and in the kind of examination of conscience to which I subjected myself, my memory brought back the most remote events with singular clarity. Some sort of false shame prevented me from going to the confessional—fear, perhaps, of committing myself to the dogmas and practices of a formidable religion, against certain elements of which I had retained a philosophical bias. My early years had been only too steeped in ideas born of the Revolution, my education had been too free, my life too vagabond for me to submit easily to a yoke which on many scores would still offend my intelligence. I shudder to think what kind of Christian I would have made if certain principles borrowed from the freethinking of the last two centuries, as well as the study of various religions, had not halted my descent upon that slope. —I never knew my mother, who had decided to follow my father to the wars, like the wives of the ancient Teutons; she died of fever and exhaustion in a cold region of Germany,[30] and my father, for his part, could not influence my early ideas along those lines. The part of the country where I was raised was full of strange legends and odd superstitions. One of my uncles who had the greatest influence upon my early upbringing took an interest, as a pastime, in Roman and Celtic antiquities. From time to time he would find, in his fields or thereabouts, the likenesses of gods and emperors whom his learned admiration taught me to revere, and whose history I gleaned from his books. A certain statue of Mars in gilded bronze, an armed Pallas or Venus, a Neptune and Amphitrite placed above the village fountain, and especially the nice plump, bearded face of the god Pan smiling at the entrance to a grotto, amid festoons of birthwort and ivy, these were the household and tutelary gods of this retreat. I confess that at that time they inspired in me more veneration than did the poor Christian images in the church and the two crudely formed saints on its portal, which certain local scholars claimed were the Esus and Cernunnos of the Gauls.[31] Baffled by all these different symbols, I asked my uncle one day what God was. "God is the sun," he told me. This was the personal conviction of an honorable man who had been a Christian all his life, but who had lived through the Revolution, and who was from a region where many shared this idea of the Deity. This did not prevent the women and children from going to church, and it was owing to one of my aunts that I received some measure of instruction which awakened me to the beauties and glories of Christianity. After 1815, an Englishman who was in our part of the country taught me the Sermon on the Mount and gave me a New Testament. . . . I mention these details only to indicate the source of a certain irresolution which has often coexisted in me with the most profound religious sentiment.

I want to explain how, after having long strayed from the true path, I have felt myself brought back to it by the cherished memory of one who died, and how the need to believe that she still existed has restored to my mind the distinct awareness of certain truths that I had not received into my soul with sufficient firmness. Despair and suicide are the result of certain fatal circumstances in the lives of those who lack faith in immortality, in its torments and its joys; —I believe I shall have accomplished something worthwhile by candidly relating the sequence of ideas through which I have regained peace and serenity, and a new strength to confront life's future misfortunes.

The visions that followed one upon the other while I slept had reduced me to such despair that I could scarcely speak; the company of my friends afforded only a vague distraction; my mind, entirely absorbed by these illusions, rejected any other ideas; I could not read and understand ten lines in succession. Of the most beautiful things, I thought, "What do they matter? They do not exist for me." One of my friends, named George,[32] undertook to vanquish this despondency. He took me to various places on the outskirts of Paris, and was content to do all the talking himself, while I replied with only a few disjointed phrases. His expressive, almost monk-like countenance lent great effect one day to his eloquent declamations against the years of skepticism and political and social demoralization which followed the July Revolution.[33] I had been one of the younger generation of that time, and had tasted its ardent passions and bitter disappointments. Something stirred within me; I reflected that such lessons could not have been imparted without the will of Providence, and that a spirit was doubtless speaking through him. . . . One day we were dining under an arbor in a little village on the outskirts of Paris; a woman came up to our table to sing, and there was something in her worn but pleasant voice that reminded me of that of Aurélia. I looked at her: even her features were not without some resemblance to those I had loved. She was sent away, and I did not dare detain her, but I thought, "Who knows, perhaps *her spirit* is in this woman!" and I felt happy that I had given her alms.

I thought, "I have squandered my life, but if the dead forgive, it is doubtless on condition that we forever refrain from evil and make amends for all the harm we have done. Is that possible? . . . From this moment on, let me strive to do no more wrong, and let me repay in full all that I owe." I had recently wronged someone; it was only an act of negligence, but I began by going to apologize for it. The joy I received from this act of reparation did me enormous good; I now had a reason for living and acting, and I took a renewed interest in the world.

Difficulties arose: events which for me were inexplicable seemed to conspire to thwart my good resolution. The state of my mind made it impossible for me to carry through on some work I had agreed to do. Thinking I was now well, people became more demanding, and as I had renounced duplicity, I found myself being put in the wrong by those who themselves had no such scruples. The mass of reparations to be made was overwhelming to me in my impotence. Political events [34] worked indirectly, by causing me distress and anxiety as well as by depriving me of the means of straightening out my affairs. The death of one of my friends made my grounds for despondency complete. In sorrow I beheld again his house and his paintings, which he had joyfully shown me a month before; I walked past his coffin at the moment when it was being nailed down. As he was of my own age and generation, I thought, "What would happen if I died suddenly like that?"

The following Sunday I arose consumed by grief and despair. I went to visit my father, whose servant was ill, and who seemed to be in a bad temper. He insisted on going himself to fetch wood from his loft, and the only help he would accept from me was my handing him a log that he needed. I left in dismay. In the street I met a friend who wanted to take me to dinner with him in order to distract me a little. I declined and, without having eaten, headed toward Montmartre. The cemetery was closed, which I regarded as a bad omen. A German poet [35] had given me several pages to translate and had advanced me a sum for this work. I set off for his house in order to return the money to him.

As I passed the Clichy tollgate, I was witness to an altercation. I tried to separate the combatants, but without success. At that moment, a lanky workman walked across the very spot where the fight had just taken place, carrying on his left shoulder a child wearing a hyacinth-colored dress. I imagined that he was Saint Christopher carrying Christ, and that I was condemned for my lack of force in the scene that had just occurred. From that moment on, I wandered about in despair through the empty lots which separate the suburb from the tollgate. It was too late to make the visit I had planned. So I started back along the streets leading to the center of Paris. Near the rue de la Victoire I met a priest, and in my confusion tried to make confession to him. He told me that this was not his parish and that he was on his way to spend the evening with friends, but that if I wished to call on him the next day at Notre-Dame, I had only to ask for Father Dubois.

Despairing and in tears, I headed toward Notre-Dame de

Lorette, where I flung myself at the foot of the altar of the Virgin, imploring forgiveness for my sins. Something within me said, "The Virgin is dead and your prayers are futile." I went to kneel in the last row of the chancel, slipping from my finger a silver ring, on the setting of which these three Arabic words were engraved: *Allah! Mohammed! Ali!* Immediately a number of candles were lit in the chancel, and a service began in which I endeavored mentally to take part. When they came to the *Ave Maria,* the priest broke off and began again seven times in the middle of the prayer, without my being able to remember which words came next. Then the prayer was over, and the priest spoke some words which seemed to allude to me alone. When all the lights had been extinguished, I got up and went out, heading for the Champs-Elysées.

By the time I arrived at the Place de la Concorde, I was thinking of taking my own life. Several times I headed toward the Seine, but something prevented me from carrying through with my intention. The stars were shining brightly in the firmament. Suddenly it seemed that they had all gone out at once like the candles I had seen in the church. I thought that time had come to an end, and that the end of the world as foretold in the Apocalypse of Saint John was upon us. I thought I saw a black sun in the empty sky and a blood-red globe above the Tuileries. I said to myself, "The eternal night is beginning, and it is going to be terrible. What will happen when men realize that there is no more sun?" I returned by the rue Saint-Honoré, and pitied the peasants whom I passed as they lingered in the streets. Nearing the Louvre, I walked as far as the square, and there a strange spectacle awaited me. Through swiftly scudding clouds, I beheld several moons moving with great speed. I thought that the earth had left its orbit and was drifting in the firmament like a dismasted ship, moving toward or away from the stars which grew larger or smaller by turns. For two or three hours I gazed upon this confusion, and finally set off in the direction of the city market. The peasants were bringing in their produce, and I thought, "How astonished they will be to see the night continue. . . ." However, dogs were barking here and there, and cocks were crowing.

Overcome with fatigue, I went home and threw myself on my bed. Upon awakening, I marveled to see the light once more. Music from a sort of mysterious choir reached my ears; childish voices were repeating in chorus, "*Christe! Christe! Christe! . . .*" I sup-

posed that a large number of children had been assembled in the
neighboring church (Notre-Dame-des-Victoires) to make invocation to Christ. "But Christ is no more," I thought, "they do not
know it yet!" The invocation lasted about an hour. I finally got up
and went to the arcades of the Palais-Royal. I thought that the sun
probably had enough light left to illuminate the earth for three
days, but that it was depleting its own substance, and indeed I
thought it looked cold and pale. I assuaged my hunger with a
little cake, so that I would have the strength to go as far as the
German poet's house. Upon entering, I told him that all was over
and that we must prepare ourselves to die. He called his wife, who
asked me, "What is the matter with you?" —"I don't know," I told
her. "I am lost." She sent for a cab, and a girl drove me to the
Dubois Clinic.

V.

There my illness returned, assuming various alternating
forms. After a month's time, I had recovered. During the next two
months, I resumed my peregrinations in the vicinity of Paris. The
longest trip I made was to visit the cathedral of Reims. Little by
little I started writing again, and I drafted one of my best tales.[36]
Yet I wrote it with much difficulty, nearly always in pencil on
loose sheets of paper, according to the whims of my reverie or my
rambles. Proofreading was very stressful for me. A few days after I
had published it, I developed a case of chronic insomnia. I would
go and stroll about all night on the hill of Montmartre, and there
I would watch the sun come up. I would have long conversations
with peasants and workers. At other times, I would head for the
market. One night I had supper in a boulevard café and amused
myself tossing gold and silver coins in the air. Then I went to the
market and had an altercation with a stranger, to whom I gave a
hearty slap in the face; I do not know why this had no repercus-
sions. At one point, upon hearing the clock of Saint-Eustache
strike a certain hour, I began to think of the battles between the
Burgundians and the Armagnacs,[37] and I thought I saw the ghosts
of the combatants of that era springing up all around me. I started
a quarrel with a postman who wore a silver badge on his chest,
and whom I said was Duke John of Burgundy. I tried to prevent
him from entering a tavern. For some odd reason that I cannot

explain, when he saw that I was threatening him with death his face became wet with tears. I was moved, and let him pass.

I headed toward the Tuileries, which were closed, and followed alongside the quays; next I walked as far as the Luxembourg, then returned to have lunch with one of my friends. After that I went to Saint-Eustache, where I knelt piously at the altar of the Virgin, thinking of my mother. The tears I shed eased my soul, and as I left the church I bought a silver ring. From there I went to visit my father, and left a bunch of daisies for him, as he was out. From there I went to the Jardin des Plantes. It was crowded, and I lingered a while to watch the hippopotamus bathing in a pool. —Then I went to visit the museum of natural history.[38] The sight of the monsters there made me think of the Flood, and when I went out, a heavy downpour was falling in the gardens. I thought, "What a pity! All these women and children are going to get wet! . . ." Then I thought, "But it's worse than that! The Flood has really begun." The water was rising in the nearby streets; I ran down the rue Saint-Victor, and with the intent of stopping what I believed to be the universal deluge, I threw into the deepest part the ring I had bought at Saint-Eustache. At about that very moment the storm abated, and a ray of sunshine appeared.

Hope returned to my soul. I had arranged to meet my friend George at four o'clock, and I headed toward his house. I passed a curiosity shop and bought two velvet screens covered with hieroglyphic figures. It seemed to me that this was the consecration of Heaven's pardon. I arrived at George's house exactly on time and confided my hope to him. I was wet and exhausted. I changed my clothes and lay down on his bed. As I slept, I had a marvelous vision. I imagined that the goddess[39] appeared to me, saying, "I am the same as Mary, the same as your mother, the same as the one you have always loved in all her forms. At each of your trials I have dropped one of the masks with which I veil my features, and soon you shall see me as I really am. . . ." A delightful orchard emerged from the clouds behind her, a soft, penetrating light illumined this paradise, and all the while I heard only her voice, but felt myself plunged into a delicious intoxication. —I awoke soon afterward and said to George, "Let us be off." As we crossed the Pont des Arts I explained the transmigration of souls to him, and told him, "It seems as if tonight I have the soul of Napoleon in me, urging me on to great things." In the rue du Coq I bought a hat, and while George was still getting change for the gold coin that I had thrown onto the counter, I continued on my way and came to the arcades of the Palais-Royal.

There, I felt as if everyone were staring at me. A stubborn idea had planted itself in my mind—that there were no more dead; I walked through the Galerie de Foy saying, "I have done something wrong," but in searching my memory, which I believed to be that of Napoleon, I could not figure out what it was. . . . "There is something here that I have not paid for!" I entered the Café de Foy with this in mind, and I thought I recognized one of the customers as old father Bertin of the *Débats*.[40] Then I walked through the gardens and watched with interest the little girls dancing in a ring. From there I left the arcades and headed toward the rue Saint-Honoré. I went into a shop to buy a cigar, and when I came out, the crowds were so dense that I was nearly suffocated. Three of my friends extricated me, taking responsibility for me, and had me wait in a café while one of them went to look for a cab. I was taken to the Hospice de la Charité.

During the night my delirium increased, especially in the early hours of the morning, when I saw that they had restrained me. I managed to extricate myself from the straitjacket, and toward morning I walked about the wards. The notion that I had become godlike and was invested with the power of healing made me touch some of the patients with my hands, and going up to a statue of the Virgin, I took off its crown of artificial flowers to bolster the power I attributed to myself. I walked with rapid strides, speaking animatedly of the ignorance of men who think they can work cures with science alone, and spotting a bottle of ether on the table, I emptied it in one gulp. An intern, with a face that I likened to that of the angels, tried to restrain me, but I drew strength from nervous energy, and, just as I was on the verge of knocking him down, I stopped, telling him that he did not understand what my mission was. Then some doctors arrived, and I continued my harangue about the inefficacy of their profession. Then I descended the outside steps, even though I had no shoes on. Coming to a flowerbed, I stepped into it and picked some flowers as I walked about on the grass.

One of my friends had returned to fetch me. So I left the

flowerbed, and while I was talking to him a straitjacket was
thrown around my shoulders; then they put me into a cab and I
was driven to a clinic outside of Paris.[41] I realized, upon finding
myself among the insane, that up until then everything had been
an illusion. Nevertheless, it seemed to me that the promises I attributed to the goddess Isis were being fulfilled through a series
of trials that I was destined to undergo. So I accepted them with
resignation.

The part of the building that I was in overlooked an expan-
sive promenade shaded by walnut trees. In a corner was a little
hillock, where one of the inmates walked around in a circle all day
long. Others, like myself, contented themselves with wandering
about the terrace, which was bordered by a grassy embankment.
On a wall to the west, figures had been traced, one of which represented the shape of the moon with geometrically drawn eyes
and mouth; over this face had been painted a kind of mask; on the
left wall were various drawings of faces in profile, one of which
depicted a kind of Japanese idol. Farther down, a death's-head had
been gouged into the plaster; on the opposite side, two rough-cut
stones had been sculpted by one of the inhabitants of the garden
into little grotesque masks, quite deftly fashioned. Two doors led
to cellars, and I imagined that they were subterranean passages
similar to those I had seen at the entrance to the Pyramids.

VI.

I imagined at first that all the people assembled in this garden had some influence upon the heavenly bodies, and that the
one who walked incessantly around in a circle was regulating the
course of the sun. An old man, who was brought in at certain
hours of the day and who kept making knots and looking at his
watch, appeared to me to be responsible for recording the passage
of time. I attributed to myself an influence upon the course of the
moon, and I believed it had been struck by a thunderbolt from
the Almighty, which had imprinted upon its face the mask I had
observed.

I attributed a mystical meaning to the attendants' conversations and to those of my companions. It seemed to me that they
were the representatives of all the races of the earth, and that together our goal was to establish a new course for the heavenly
bodies and to give greater amplitude to the system. It was my

view that an error had crept into the general scheme of numbers, and that thence came all the ills of mankind. I further believed that the heavenly spirits had assumed human form and were present at this general congress, even while seeming to be absorbed in ordinary concerns. My role seemed to be to reestablish universal harmony by cabalistic art and to seek a solution by conjuring the occult powers of the various religions.

In addition to the promenade, we had another room for our use, the perpendicularly barred windows of which overlooked a green landscape. Looking through these windows to the row of outbuildings, I could see the outlines of the windowed facade forming a thousand pavilions adorned with arabesques and topped with crenelations and spires, which reminded me of the imperial lodges along the shores of the Bosphorus. This naturally led my thoughts to dwell on Oriental themes. At about two o'clock I was given a bath, and I thought I was being attended by the Valkyries,[42] daughters of Odin, who were trying to raise me to immortality by gradually purging my body of all its impurity.

In the evening I strolled serenely in the moonlight, and as I glanced up at the trees it seemed to me that the leaves were tossing capriciously so as to form images of knights and ladies borne by caparisoned steeds. For me, these were the triumphant figures of the ancestors. This thought led me to imagine that there was a vast conspiracy among all living beings to restore the world to its original harmony, and that communication occurred through astral magnetism; that around the earth stretched an unbroken chain of all the intelligences devoted to this universal communication, and that the songs, dances, glances, passing magnetically from one to another, conveyed the same aspiration. The moon was for me the refuge of fraternal souls who, delivered from their mortal bodies, were working with greater freedom toward the regeneration of the universe.

Already the time in each day seemed to me to be increased by two hours, so that I would arise at the hour designated by the hospital's clocks only to wander in the dominion of the shades. My companions seemed to be moving in their sleep and resembled the specters of Tartarus,[43] until the hour when the sun rose for me. Then I would greet that heavenly body with a prayer, and my real life would begin.

From the moment I became certain that I was undergoing the

trials of a sacred initiation, my mind was infused with an invincible strength. I thought myself a hero living under the scrutiny of the gods; all of nature appeared in a new light, and secret voices emanated from plants, trees, animals, the humblest insects, to caution and encourage me. In my companions' speech there were mysterious formulations, the meaning of which was transparent to me; even formless and inanimate objects lent themselves to my mental calculations; —from the groupings of pebbles, the shapes of corners, cracks, or openings, from colors, odors, sounds, the outlines of leaves, I saw emerge hitherto unknown harmonies. "How," I thought, "could I have lived so long outside of nature, and without identifying with it? All is alive, all is in motion, all is connected; the magnetic rays emanating from myself or others pass unimpeded through the infinite chain of creation; it is a transparent network which stretches across the globe, its slender filaments extending by degrees to the planets and the stars. Captive at present upon earth, I converse with the heavenly choir, which shares in my joys and sorrows!"

Suddenly I trembled to think that even this mystery could be unveiled. "If electricity," I pondered, "which is the magnetism of physical bodies, can be subject to a force which imposes laws upon it, all the more reason to believe that hostile and tyrannical spirits can subjugate other intelligences and appropriate their divided strength for the purpose of domination. Thus were the ancient gods conquered and subjugated by new gods; thus," I continued, consulting my memories of the ancient world, "did the necromancers gain mastery over entire nations, who generation after generation languished in captivity under their eternal scepter. O misery! Death itself cannot free them! For we live again in our sons as we lived in our fathers—and the merciless art of our enemies can find us everywhere. The hour of our birth, the point on earth where we first appear, the first gesture, the name, the room—and all the consecrations, all the rituals which are imposed upon us—all this gives rise to an auspicious or fatal series upon which our future entirely depends. But if this is terrible by human calculation alone, think what it must be when linked to the mysterious formulae which govern the order of the worlds. It has rightly been said: nothing is without importance, nothing is without power in the universe; one atom can dissolve everything, one atom can redeem everything!

"O terror! Here is the eternal distinction between good and evil. Is my soul an indestructible molecule, a globule inflated with a bit of air, but which finds its place in nature, or is it emptiness itself, the very image of the nothingness that vanishes into immensity? Or could it be that fatal particle destined to endure, in all its transformations, the vengeance of powerful beings?" Thus I was led to take account of my life, and even of my former existences. By proving to myself that I was good, I proved to myself that I must always have been so. "And if I have been evil," I thought, "will not my present life be sufficient expiation?" This thought reassured me, but did not dispel my fear of being forever numbered among the wretched. I felt myself being plunged into cold water, and an even colder liquid was streaming down my brow. I turned my thoughts to the eternal Isis, sacred mother and spouse; all my aspirations, all my prayers merged in that magical name, I felt myself coming to life again in her, and sometimes she appeared to me in the guise of the Venus of antiquity, sometimes, too, with the features of the Christian Virgin. Night brought this cherished apparition back to me more clearly, and yet I thought, "What can she do, vanquished and perhaps oppressed as she is, for her poor children?" The pale shreds of the crescent moon were growing thinner with every evening and would soon disappear; perhaps we were never to see it again in the sky! However, it seemed to me that this heavenly body was the refuge of all souls kindred to mine, and I saw it filled with plaintive shades destined to be reborn one day upon earth. . . .

My room is at the end of a corridor inhabited on one side by the madmen and on the other by the housekeeping staff. It is the only one favored with a window, overlooking the courtyard, shaded with trees, which serves as a promenade in the daytime. My gaze lingers with pleasure upon the dense leaves of a walnut tree and two Chinese mulberries. Beyond these one has a vague glimpse of a rather busy street, through a trellis fence painted in green. To the west, the view expands; there is a sort of hamlet, with windows covered with greenery or cluttered with birdcages and rags laid out to dry, from which occasionally emerges the profile of a young or old housewife, or the rosy face of a child. One can hear shouts, singing, bursts of laughter; it is either cheerful or sad to listen to, depending on the time of day and on one's state of mind.

I found there all the remains of my various fortunes, the jumbled remnants of several sets of furniture that had been scattered about or sold over the past twenty years. It is a motley agglomeration much like that of Doctor Faust. An antique three-legged table with eagles' heads, a console table supported by a winged sphinx, a seventeenth-century chest of drawers, an eighteenth-century bookcase, a bed of the same period, the oval canopy of which (still unmounted) is covered with red *lampas*,[44] a rustic set of shelves laden with earthenware and Sèvres porcelain, most of it quite damaged, a hookah brought back from Constantinople, a large alabaster cup, a crystal vase, some wood paneling taken from a demolished house I had once lived in on the site of the Louvre and covered with mythological paintings made by now-famous friends, and two large canvases in the style of Prud'hon,[45] representing the Muses of history and drama. For several days I took pleasure in arranging all these, and creating within the cramped attic space a bizarre ensemble that had about it something of the palace and something of the cottage, and which nicely encapsulates my roving existence. I have hung above my bed my Arab clothes, my two painstakingly darned cashmeres, a pilgrim's flask, a hunter's gamebag. Above the bookcase is displayed an enormous map of Cairo; a bamboo console at the head of my bed holds a lacquered tray from India on which I can lay out my toilet articles. I was delighted to find these humble remains of my years of alternating good fortune and misery, which are bound up with all my life's memories. The only things they had put aside for me were a little painting on copper in the style of Correggio,[46] representing *Venus and Cupid*, some panels of huntresses and satyrs, and an arrow that I had kept in memory of the archery societies of the Valois, to which I had belonged in my youth; the weapons had been sold since the new laws were adopted. All in all, I found there nearly everything I had previously possessed. My books, a bizarre assemblage of the knowledge of the ages: history, travel, religion, cabala, astrology, enough to gladden the shades of Pico della Mirandola, the sage Meursius, and Nicolas of Cusa[47]—the Tower of Babel in two hundred volumes—they had left me all of these! There was enough there to make a wise man mad; let us hope that there is also enough to make a madman wise.

With what delight I have been able to file away in my draw-

ers the pile of notes and letters, public or private, important or
obscure, in the order in which they were created, spawned by
chance encounters or my travels in distant lands. In rolls more se-
curely wrapped than the others, I find papers with Arabic lettering, relics of Cairo and Istanbul. O joy! O mortal sorrow! These
yellowed characters, these faded drafts, these half-crumpled letters, this is the treasure trove of my only love. . . . Let me read
them again. . . . Many of the letters are missing, many others are
torn or contain deletions; here is what I find: [48]

. . . .

One night, I was speaking aloud and singing in a kind of ecstasy. One of the attendants came to my cell to fetch me and took
me down to a ground-floor room, where he locked me in. I continued to dream, and although I was standing up, I thought I was
confined in a sort of Oriental pavilion. Examining its corners carefully, I found that it was octagonal. A divan ran around the walls,
and it seemed to me that the latter were made of thick glass, beyond which I could see the glitter of treasures, shawls, and tapestries. A moonlit landscape was visible through a latticed door, and
I seemed to make out the shapes of tree trunks and rocks. I had
lived there already in some other existence, and I thought I recognized the deep caves of Ellora.[49] Little by little a bluish light
filtered into the pavilion, giving rise to strange images. I then
thought that I was in the middle of a vast charnel house where the
history of the universe was written in letters of blood. The body
of a gigantic woman was painted opposite me, but her various
parts had been severed as if by a sword; other women of various
races, whose bodies increasingly predominated, displayed upon
the other walls a bloody jumble of limbs and heads, from em-
presses and queens to the humblest peasant women. It was the
history of all crime, and I had but to fix my gaze upon one spot
or another to see some tragic scene unfolding there. "This," I
thought, "is what has come of power conferred upon men. They
have gradually destroyed and split into a thousand pieces the eternal ideal of beauty, so that the races are, more and more, losing
strength and perfection. . . ." And indeed I could see, on a strip of
shadow that was inching its way through one of the openings in
the door, the descending generations of future races.

I was finally torn from this somber meditation. The kind,
compassionate face of my excellent doctor restored me to the

world of the living. He had me witness a sight which greatly interested me. Among the patients was a young man who had been a soldier in Africa, and who for six weeks had refused to take any food. By means of a long rubber tube inserted into his stomach, he was being made to swallow nutritive liquids. Moreover, he could neither see nor speak, nor, apparently, hear.

This sight made a deep impression upon me. Hitherto lost in the monotonous circle of my sensations or mental sufferings, I now encountered an inscrutable being, silent and long-suffering, seated like a sphinx at the last gates of existence. I began to love him, for he seemed so miserable and forsaken, and I felt myself uplifted by this sympathy and pity. Standing thus between death and life, he seemed to me a sublime interpreter, a confessor predestined to hear those secrets of the soul which words dare not reveal or would be incapable of expressing. He was the ear of God, unalloyed with another's thoughts. I spent hours on end examining myself mentally, my head bent over his and his hands in mine. It seemed to me that a kind of magnetism united our two spirits, and I was overjoyed when for the first time a word issued from his mouth. No one could believe it, and I attributed this beginning of a recovery to my ardent will. That night I had a delectable dream, the first in a long time. I was in a tower, dug so deeply into the earth and rising so high into the sky that it seemed as if my entire life would be consumed going up and down. Already my strength was failing, and I was about to lose heart, when a side door happened to open; a spirit appeared and said to me, "Come, brother! . . ." I do not know why the idea entered my mind that his name was Saturnin. His features were the same as those of the poor patient, only transfigured and intelligent. We were in a stretch of country lit by brightly shining stars; we stopped to contemplate this spectacle, and the spirit laid his hand upon my forehead as I had done the day before in attempting to mesmerize my companion; immediately one of the stars I saw in the sky began to grow larger, and the divinity of my dreams appeared to me, smiling, in a sort of Indian garb, just as I had seen her before. She walked between us, and the meadows turned green, the flowers and leaves sprang up from the ground beneath her feet. . . . She said to me, "The trial you have undergone has come to an end; those countless staircases that you climbed wearily up and down were the very bonds of old illusions which shackled your thought; and now, remember the day when you implored the Holy Virgin, and when, believing she was dead, your mind was overcome by madness. It was necessary that your vow be carried to her by a simple soul, unfettered by the bonds of earth. Such a soul has been found close by you, and that is why it has been granted me to come to hearten and encourage you." The joy which this dream radiated throughout my spirit brought me a blissful awakening. Day was just breaking. I wanted to have some tangible sign of the vision which had comforted me, and I wrote on the wall these words: "You visited me this night."

I record here, under the title of *Memorabilia*, my impressions of several dreams which followed the one just described.

. . . .

Atop a tall peak in Auvergne rang out the shepherds' song. *Poor Mary!* Queen of the heavens! It is you whom they so piously address. This rustic melody has reached the ears of the Corybants.[50] They emerge, also singing, from the secret caves where Love gave them shelter. —Hosanna! Peace on Earth and glory in the Heavens!

On the mountains of *Himalaya*, a little flower was born: forget-me-not! —The shimmering gaze of a star rested upon it for a moment, and an answer was heard in a sweet foreign tongue. —*Myosotis!*[51]

A silver pearl glittered in the sand; a golden pearl sparkled in Heaven. . . . The world was created. Chaste loves, heavenly sighs! Set the holy mountains ablaze . . . for you have brothers in the valleys and timid sisters who are hiding in the depths of the woods!

Fragrant groves of Paphos,[52] you cannot compare to those retreats where one inhales deep draughts of the bracing air of the Homeland. —"High up in the mountains—one dwells so blissfully; —and the wild Nightingale—is happiness to me!"

Oh, how beautiful is my great friend![53] She is so great that she has forgiven the world—and so good that she has forgiven me. The other night, she was sleeping in I know not what palace, and I could not join her. My burnt-chestnut horse was slipping from beneath me. The loosed reins dangled down upon his sweaty rump, and I had to struggle to keep him from lying down on the ground.

That night, good Saturnin came to my aid, and my great friend drew near my side, seated upon her white, silver-caparisoned mare. She said to me, "Courage, brother! For this is the last stage of the way,"—and her large eyes peered avidly ahead, and her long hair, imbued with all the perfumes of Yemen, streamed out behind her in the air.

I recognized the divine features of ***.[54] We were flying to victory, and our enemies were at our feet. The messenger hoopoe led us to the loftiest reaches of the heavens, and the bow of light shone in the divine hands of Apollyon.[55] The enchanted horn of Adonis[56] echoed through the woods.

"O Death, where is thy victory?"[57]—since the victorious Messiah was riding between us! His robe was the color of yellow hyacinth, and his wrists and ankles sparkled with diamonds and rubies. When his light riding whip touched the pearly gates of the New Jerusalem, all three of us were flooded with light. It was then that I descended among men to give them the glad tidings.

I have just awakened from a very sweet dream: I saw again the woman I had loved, transfigured and radiant. Heaven opened in all its glory, and there I read the word *pardon* written in the blood of Christ.

A star suddenly shone forth and revealed to me the secret of the world and worlds. Hosanna! Peace on earth and glory in the heavens!

From the depths of darkness and silence two notes rang out, one low, the other high—and the eternal orb immediately began to turn. Be blessed, O first octave of the divine hymn! From Sunday to Sunday, entwine all our days together in your magical web. The hills sing of you to the valleys, the springs to the streams, the streams to the rivers, and the rivers to the Ocean; the air trembles, and the light harmoniously bursts the budding flowers. A sigh, a shiver of love comes from the swollen womb of earth, and the choir of stars is unfurled in infinite space; it spreads out and draws back upon itself, contracts and expands, and sows far off the seeds of new creations.

On the summit of a bluish mountain a little flower was born. —Forget-me-not! —The shimmering gaze of a star rested upon it

for a moment, and an answer was heard in a sweet foreign tongue.
—*Myosotis!*

Woe to you, god of the North—who with one hammer blow [58]
broke the holy table made from the seven most precious metals!
For you could not shatter the *Rose Pearl* that lay in its center.[59] It
rebounded under the sword—and now we have taken up arms for
its sake. . . . Hosanna!

The *macrocosm*, or greater world, was constructed by cabalistic
art; the *microcosm*, or smaller world, is its image reflected in every
heart.[60] The Rose Pearl was dyed with the royal blood of the Valkyries. Woe to you, god of the forge, who sought to shatter a
world!

Yet Christ's pardon was also pronounced for you!

Be therefore also blessed, O Thor the giant—most powerful
of Odin's sons! Be blessed in Hela, your mother, for often death is
sweet—and in your brother Loki, and in your hound Garm![61]

Even the serpent encircling the World is blessed,[62] for it is
loosening its coils, and its gaping mouth breathes in the anxoka,
the sulphur-colored flower—the dazzling flower of the sun!

May God preserve the divine Balder, son of Odin, and Freya
the beautiful![63]

. . . .

I found myself *in spirit* at Saardam,[64] which I visited last year.
Snow covered the ground. A little girl was walking along, slipping
and sliding on the frozen earth, and was making her way, I think,
toward the house of Peter the Great. Her majestic profile had
something of the Bourbon about it. Her neck, dazzlingly white,
was half-visible above a collar of swans' feathers. With her little
pink hand, she shielded a lighted lamp from the wind, and was
about to knock on the green door of the house when a scrawny
cat came out and entangled itself in her legs, making her fall
down. "Why, it's only a cat!" said the little girl, getting up again.
"A cat is something!" a soft voice replied. I was present at this
scene, and I was carrying on my arm a little gray cat that began to
mew. "It's that old fairy's child!" said the little girl. And she went
into the house.

That night, my dreams took me first to Vienna. —As everyone knows, on each of that city's public squares stand tall columns
called *pardons*. Clusters of marble clouds, representing the order of

Solomon, support globes where seated divinities preside.[65] Suddenly—O wonder!—I began to think of that august sister of the Emperor of Russia, whose imperial palace I had seen at Weimar. —A sweet, tender melancholy conjured up the vision of the colored mists of a Norwegian landscape, lit by a soft gray light. The clouds became transparent, and I saw opening before me a deep abyss into which gushed the raging, icy waters of the Baltic. It seemed as if the whole of the river Neva, with its blue waters, would be engulfed in this rift in the globe. The ships of Kronstadt and Saint Petersburg were tossing at anchor, ready to break loose and vanish into the abyss, when a divine light from above illuminated this scene of desolation.

In the brilliant light of the rays piercing through the mist, the rock which supports the statue of Peter the Great instantly came into view. Above that solid pedestal, clouds began to gather in clusters, rising all the way to the zenith. They held radiant, heavenly forms, among which one could recognize the two Catherines and the Empress Saint Helen,[66] accompanied by the loveliest princesses of Muscovy and Poland. Their gentle glances, directed toward France, compressed the distance with the aid of long crystal telescopes. From this I saw that our country had become the arbiter of the Eastern conflict,[67] and that they were awaiting its resolution. My dream ended in the sweet hope that peace would at last be granted us.

This is how I came to urge myself on to a bold undertaking. I resolved to make fast the world of dream and to lay bare its secret. Why not, I thought, force open at last those mystic gates, armed with all the power of my will, and govern my sensations instead of surrendering to them? Is it not possible to tame this alluring and formidable chimera, to master these spirits of the night who make sport of our reason? Sleep absorbs one third of our lives. It is consolation for the sorrows of our days or payment for their pleasures; but I have never found sleep to bring any repose. After several minutes of drowsy numbness a new life begins, freed from the restrictions of time and space, and doubtless similar to that which awaits us after death. Who knows if there is not some link between these two lives, and if it is not already possible for the soul to bridge them?

From that moment on I devoted myself to probing the meaning of my dreams, and this anxious preoccupation influenced my

waking thoughts. I was persuaded that there existed a link between the outer and inner world; that it was mere lack of attention
or mental confusion that disguised the obvious connection between them—and that this explained the peculiar nature of certain dream scenes, similar to those twisted, grimacing reflections
of real objects tossing upon troubled waters.

Such were the inspirations of my nights; my days were spent
peacefully in the company of the poor patients, with whom I had
made friends. The awareness that henceforth I was cleansed of all
the wrongs of my past life gave my mind infinite delight; the
certitude of immortality and of the coexistence of all those I had
loved had come to me in a tangible fashion, as it were, and I
blessed the brotherly soul who had brought me back from the
depths of despair to the luminous paths of religion.

The poor youth from whom intelligent life had so strangely
withdrawn was receiving care and treatment which, little by little,
overcame his torpor. Having learned that he was born in the
countryside, I spent hours on end singing him old village songs,
which I strove to render with the utmost feeling and expression.
To my joy, I saw that he heard them, and that he repeated certain
parts of the songs. At last, one day, he opened his eyes for a brief
moment, and I saw that they were blue, like those of the spirit
who had appeared to me in my dream. One morning, several days
later, he kept his eyes wide open and did not close them again.
Then he began to speak, though only intermittently, and, recognizing me, addressed me in the familiar form and called me
brother. However, he still could not bring himself to eat. One
day, coming in from the garden, he said to me, "I am thirsty." I
went to get him something to drink; he brought the glass to his
lips but could not swallow. "Why," I asked him, "do you not want
to eat and drink like other people?" —"Because I am dead," he answered; "I was buried in such-and-such a cemetery, at such-and-
such a spot. . . ." —"And where do you think you are now?" —"In
Purgatory; I am undergoing my expiation."

Such are the odd ideas engendered by this sort of illness;
I inwardly realized that I myself had not been far from such a
strange belief. The care that I had received had already restored
me to the affection of family and friends, and I was able to judge
more sanely the world of illusions in which I had lived for a time.
Nevertheless, I feel happy about the convictions that I have ac-

quired, and I liken this series of trials I have undergone to that which the ancients represented as a descent into the underworld.

1855

Translated by Joan C. Kessler

For a recent French edition of this work, see Gérard de Nerval, *Aurélia ou Le Rêve et la vie*, in *Oeuvres complètes*, vol. 3 (Paris: Editions Gallimard, Bibliothèque de la Pléiade, 1993).

Jules Verne

MASTER ZACHARIUS

I. A WINTER'S NIGHT

The city of Geneva is situated at the western point of the lake to which it gives—or owes—its name. The Rhone, which passes through the city as it emerges from the lake, divides it into two distinct sections, and is itself divided, in the center of the city, by an island rising between its two banks. This topography is often to be found in the larger centers of commerce and industry. The earliest inhabitants were very likely seduced by the possibilities of transportation afforded by the rapid arms of the rivers— "those ever-moving roads," in the words of Pascal.[1] In the case of the Rhone, it is ever-rushing.

In the time when regular, modern buildings had not yet appeared upon this island, anchored mid-river like a Dutch galliot, the fantastic agglomeration of houses climbing up one upon the other offered to the eye an image of charming confusion. The island's narrow dimensions had forced a number of these structures to perch upon piles, thrust here and there beneath the violent currents of the Rhone. These solid beams, blackened by time and worn by the tides, resembled the claws of a giant crab, and created a fantastic impression. Several yellowed nets, veritable spiders' webs spread amid these centuries-old structures, stirred in the shadows as if they had been the leaves of these old oaks, and the river, surging amid this forest of timbers, foamed and roared lugubriously.

One of the dwellings upon the island was conspicuous for its singular appearance of age and decrepitude. It was the house of the old clockmaker, Master Zacharius, his daughter Gérande, Aubert Thün, his apprentice, and his old servant Scholastique.

What a singular individual was this Zacharius! His age seemed incalculable. The oldest inhabitants of Geneva could not have told how long his lean, angular head had balanced upon his shoulders, nor when he had first been seen walking down the streets of the city, his long white locks flowing in the wind. This man did not live—he oscillated, like the pendulums of his clocks. His dried and cadaverous features had taken on a somber cast; like the paintings of Leonardo da Vinci, he was darkening.

Gérande occupied the best room in the old house; from a narrow window, her melancholy gaze rested upon the snowy peaks of the Jura. But the old man's bedroom and studio were in a sort of cellar, almost on a level with the river; the flooring was supported by the piles themselves. From time immemorial, Master Zacharius had emerged only at mealtime or when he went out to regulate the various clocks of the city. He spent the rest of the time at a workbench covered with myriad clockmaking instruments, which he had for the most part invented.

For he was a man of talent. His work was held in high esteem throughout France and Germany. The most diligent workers of Geneva freely acknowledged his preeminence, and he brought honor to the people of the city, who pointed to him with the words, "To him belongs the glory of having invented the escapement!"[2]

Indeed, it is from this invention—the importance of which would only later be understood—that we can date the birth of the true science of clockmaking.

After having worked long and masterfully, Zacharius would slowly put back his tools, place the delicate parts that he had been adjusting into small glass cases, and bring the turning of his lathe to a halt. Then he would open a judas hole in the floor, and there, bending over it for hours on end, while the waters of the Rhone crashed and roared beneath him, he would inhale deep draughts of its heady vapors.

One winter evening, old Scholastique was serving supper, a meal in which she and the young apprentice took part, according to longstanding custom. Although Master Zacharius was offered

meticulously prepared dishes served in fine blue and white porcelain, he ate not a thing. He made scarcely any reply to the
gentle words of Gérande, who was visibly troubled by her father's
gloomy silence, and paid no more attention to Scholastique's chatter than to the roar of the river, to which he was now completely
oblivious. After this speechless repast, the old clockmaker left the
table without kissing his daughter or bidding the others the customary goodnight. He disappeared through the narrow door
which led to his retreat, and the staircase creaked and groaned
under his heavy tread.

Gérande, Aubert, and Scholastique remained several moments in silence. It was a dark, gloomy night; heavy clouds moved
slowly across the Alps, threatening rain; the raw chill in the Swiss
air struck despondency into the soul, while the southerly winds
prowled round about, whistling ominously.

"Do you realize, my dear young lady," said Scholastique at
last, "that our master has been withdrawn into himself for several
days now? Holy Virgin! I see why he hasn't been hungry—his
words are stuck in his stomach, and clever indeed would be the
devil who could drag any out of him!"

"My father has some secret grief that I cannot even guess at,"
replied Gérande, as a sad and uneasy expression came over her
features.

"Mademoiselle, do not let sadness invade your heart. You
know Master Zacharius's strange ways. Who can decipher his innermost thoughts? Doubtless he is troubled by some care or
other, but by tomorrow it will be forgotten and he will reproach
himself for having caused his daughter pain."

It was Aubert who spoke thus, as he gazed into Gérande's
lovely eyes. Aubert was the only apprentice whom Master Zacharius had ever allowed into the intimate sanctuary of his labors,
for he valued his intelligence, discretion, and great goodness of
heart, and the young man had attached himself to Gérande with
that mysterious faith which is the mark of heroic devotion.

Gérande was eighteen. Her oval face was like that of the art-
less Madonnas which are still piously hung on street corners
throughout the ancient cities and towns of Brittany. Her eyes radiated an infinite simplicity. She was beloved, like the most exquisite realization of a poet's dream. The clothes she wore were of

the more muted shades and had the characteristic look and odor of church linen. She lived a kind of mystical existence in this city of Geneva, which had not yet succumbed to the sterility of Calvinism.

While, morning and night, she recited the Latin prayers in her iron-clasped missal, Gérande had come to discern a hidden emotion in the heart of Aubert Thün, and to realize what deep devotion the young apprentice cherished for her. And indeed, for him, the clockmaker's old house was the entire world, and all his time was spent at the girl's side when, his labors completed, he left her father's workshop.

Old Scholastique observed this, but said nothing. She preferred to exercise her loquacity upon the cares of the household and the evils of the times. No one tried to check its flow. She was like one of those musical snuffboxes that they made in Geneva, which, once wound up, would need to be broken if it were not to play all its tunes through.

Finding Gérande sunk in a melancholy silence, Scholastique got up from her old wooden chair, placed a candle in her candlestick, lit it, and set it down near a small waxen Virgin sheltered in her niche of stone. It was the custom to kneel before this Madonna, guardian of the domestic hearth, and to pray for her kindly vigilance throughout the night, but that evening Gérande remained seated in silence.

"Well, my dear young lady," said the astonished Scholastique, "supper is over, and now it is bedtime. Why do you tire your eyes by sitting up so late? . . . Ah, Holy Virgin! Better to go to bed and find comfort in sweet dreams! In these wretched times, who can be sure of one day of happiness?"

"Ought we not send for a doctor for my father?" asked Gérande.

"A doctor!" cried the old servant. "Has Master Zacharius ever put any stock in their judgments and fancies? Medicine there may be for watches, but not for human bodies!"

"What are we to do?" murmured Gérande. "Has he gone back to work? Has he gone to bed?"

"Gérande," replied Aubert softly, "some vexing care is troubling Master Zacharius, and that is all."

"Do you know what it is, Aubert?"

"Perhaps, Gérande."

"Tell us," cried the eager Scholastique, thriftily extinguishing her candle.

"For several days, Gérande," said the young apprentice, "something absolutely incomprehensible has been going on. All the watches that your father has made and sold for the past several years have suddenly stopped. Many of them have been returned to him. He has carefully disassembled them; the springs were in good condition and the wheels well set. He has reassembled them more carefully still, but in spite of his dexterity they have refused to run."

"The devil's in it!" cried Scholastique.

"What do you mean?" asked Gérande. "It seems entirely natural to me. Everything here on earth has a limit, and the infinite cannot be fashioned by the hands of men."

"It is true, at any rate," Aubert replied, "that there is, in this, something mysterious and extraordinary. I myself have been helping Master Zacharius search for the cause of this disturbance, but I have been unable to find it, and more than once I have let my tools fall from my hands in despair."

"Then," resumed Scholastique, "why pursue this wicked occupation? Is it natural that a little copper instrument should run and mark the hours of its own accord? We should have kept to the sundial!"

"You would not speak this way, Scholastique," Aubert replied, "if you knew that the sundial was invented by Cain."

"Good Lord! What are you telling me?"

"Do you think," resumed Gérande ingenuously, "that we could pray to God to restore my father's watches to life?"

"Without a doubt," returned the young apprentice.

"Useless prayers," muttered the old servant, "but Heaven will pardon them for their good intentions."

The candle was relit. Scholastique, Gérande, and Aubert knelt down upon the slabs, and the young girl prayed for her mother's soul, for a blessing for the night, prayed for wayfarers and prisoners, for the good and the wicked, and above all for the hidden sorrows of her father.

Then these three devout souls rose with some measure of confidence in their hearts, for they had laid their grief in the bosom of God.

Aubert returned to his room, Gérande sat pensively by the window as the last lights were extinguished in the city of Geneva, and Scholastique, after pouring some water on the glowing brands and securing the two massive bolts on the door, hurried to bed, where she was soon dreaming alarming dreams.

All the while, the dreadful fury of the winter night had intensified. At times the wind rushed between the piles along with the whirling eddies of the river, and made the whole house shudder; but the girl, lost in her sorrow, thought only of her father. Aubert Thün's words had made Master Zacharius's illness take on fantastical proportions in her mind, and it seemed to her that his precious life, grown purely mechanical, now moved only with painful effort upon its worn-out pivots.

Suddenly the shutters, thrust violently inward by the squall, struck the window of the room. With a start, Gérande leaped to her feet, unsure of the cause of the sound which had shaken her from her torpor. When she had regained her calm, she opened the window. The clouds had burst, and a torrential rain was clattering upon the neighboring roofs. The girl leaned out to reach the shutter that was banging in the wind, but she was suddenly afraid. It seemed to her that the river and the rain, blending their tumultuous waters, were engulfing the fragile edifice, whose planks were creaking on all sides. She was about to dash from the room, but then saw below her the reflection of a light that appeared to issue from Master Zacharius's cubbyhole, and during a momentary calming of the elements some plaintive sounds caught her ear. She tried to shut her window, but it was impossible. The wind thrust her violently back, as if it were an intruder breaking into a dwelling.

Gérande thought she would go mad with terror. What could her father be doing? She opened the door, which tore from her hands, banging and rattling under the force of the gale. She then found herself in the dark supper room, groped blindly for the staircase leading to Master Zacharius's workshop, and slipped down the stairs, pale and nearly fainting.

The old clockmaker was standing in the middle of the room, which echoed with the roaring of the river. His bristling hair gave him a sinister appearance. He was talking and gesticulating, deaf and blind to all around him! Gérande hesitated on the threshold.

"It is death!" said Master Zacharius in muffled tones. "It is death! . . . What existence is left for me, now that I have scattered my life throughout the world! For I, Master Zacharius, am indeed the Creator of all the watches I have made! It is part of my soul that I have locked away in each of those boxes of iron, silver, or gold! Each time one of those accursed watches stops, I feel my heart cease beating, for I have regulated them by its pulsations!"

And speaking in this strange manner, the old man glanced toward his workbench. There lay all the parts of a watch that he had painstakingly disassembled. He picked up a sort of hollow cylinder called a barrel, in which the spring is enclosed, and removed the steel spiral which, instead of relaxing according to the laws of its elasticity, remained coiled in on itself, like a sleeping viper. It seemed knotted, like those impotent old men whose blood has congealed over time. Master Zacharius vainly endeavored to uncoil it with his bony fingers, which cast an exaggeratedly elongated silhouette upon the wall, but it was beyond his power, and soon, with a terrible cry of rage, he hurled it through the judas hole into the seething eddies of the Rhone.

Gérande stood breathless and motionless, rooted to the spot. She wanted to rush toward her father, but could not. She felt faint and dizzy, and on the verge of delirium. Suddenly, in the darkness, a voice murmured close to her ear, "Gérande, my dear Gérande! Grief still keeps you awake! Go back to bed, I implore you, the night is cold."

"Aubert," whispered the girl. "It is you!"

"Should I not be troubled by what troubles you?" replied Aubert.

These gentle words sent the blood flowing back into the girl's heart. Leaning upon the apprentice's arm, she said, "My father is very ill, Aubert! You alone can cure him, for this affliction of the soul will not yield to his daughter's comfortings. His mind is beset by a most natural delusion, and by working with him to repair his watches, you will bring him back to reason. Aubert," she went on, "it is not true, is it, that his own life has become one with that of his clocks?"

Aubert did not reply.

"Then is my father's calling one condemned by Heaven?" shuddered Gérande.

"I don't know," returned the apprentice, warming her ice-cold hands in his own. "But go back to bed, my poor Gérande, and let hope return with sleep!"

Gérande slowly made her way to her room and remained there until morning, without her eyes ever closing in sleep, while Master Zacharius, ever mute and motionless, stood gazing at the river as it surged tumultuously beneath him.

II. PRIDE AND SCIENCE

The rigor and severity of the Genevan merchant in matters of business has become proverbial. He is exaggeratedly upright, and unyielding in his integrity. How great, then, must have been Master Zacharius's shame when he saw these watches that he had assembled with such meticulous care returning to him from all sides.

It was a fact that the watches had suddenly stopped, and for no apparent reason. The wheelwork was in good condition and perfectly adjusted, but the springs had lost all elasticity. The clockmaker tried replacing them, but in vain; the wheels remained motionless. These inexplicable disturbances did great harm to Master Zacharius's reputation. His glorious inventions had time and again brought upon him suspicions of sorcery, which were now rearoused. The rumor reached Gérande's ears, and she often trembled in fear for her father when she saw malicious glances directed toward him.

Yet on the day following this night of anguish, Master Zacharius appeared to take up his work again with greater confidence. The morning sun restored some of his courage. It was not long before Aubert came to join him in the shop and was welcomed by an affable greeting.

"I am feeling better," said the old clockmaker. "Heaven knows what strange obsessions were gnawing at my mind yesterday, but the sun has driven them all away with the night mists."

"Well, Master," returned Aubert, "I have no fondness for the night, not for your sake nor for my own!"

"And you are right, Aubert! If you should ever rise to greatness, you will understand that the day is as vital to you as food. The duty of a man of genius is to earn the homage of mankind."

"Master, there is the sin of pride again!"

"Pride, Aubert! Demolish my past, obliterate my present,

squander my future—only then could I live in obscurity! Poor boy, who cannot fathom the sublimities to which my art is wholly bound! Are you not yourself a mere tool in my hands?"

"Yet, Master Zacharius," resumed Aubert, "I have more than once earned your praise for regulating the most delicate mechanisms of your watches and clocks!"

"No doubt, Aubert," replied Master Zacharius, "you are a good worker, whom I prize. But when you work, you think to hold mere copper, gold, and silver in your hands; you do not feel these metals, animated by my genius, throbbing like living flesh! *You* would not die with the death of your creation!"

Master Zacharius fell silent upon these words, but Aubert attempted to renew the conversation.

"Upon my word, Master," said he, "I love to see you labor so unceasingly! You will be ready for the festival of our guild, for I see that the work on this crystal watch is proceeding rapidly."

"No doubt, Aubert," exclaimed the old clockmaker, "and it will be no trivial accomplishment for me to cut and shape this crystal that is hard as diamond! Ah, Louis Berghem did well to perfect the art of diamond cutting,[3] which has enabled me to polish and pierce the most resistant stones!"

Master Zacharius held in his hand several small pieces of cut crystal of exquisite workmanship. The wheels, pivots, and watchcase were of the same material, and he had displayed an uncommon skill in this most difficult task.

"Will it not be wonderful," he went on with flushing cheeks, "to see this watch throbbing beneath its transparent casing, and to be able to count the beatings of its heart!"

"I will wager, Master," replied the young apprentice, "that it will not deviate by one second in a year."

"And you will wager on a certainty! Have I not given it all that is best and purest in me? And does my heart itself ever vary?"

Aubert dared not raise his eyes to his master's face.

"Speak frankly," the old man continued sadly. "Have you never taken me for a madman? Do you not think me at times in the grip of a perilous folly? Yes, 'tis true! In my daughter's eyes and in your own, I have often read my death sentence. —Oh!" he cried in pain, "not to be understood even by those one loves most in the world! But to you, Aubert, I shall prove triumphantly that I am right! Do not shake your head; you shall be astonished! On the day when you shall truly hear and understand me, you shall see that I have discovered the secrets of life, the secrets of the mysterious union of body and soul!"

Speaking thus, Master Zacharius appeared exultant in his vainglory. His eyes shone with an unearthly flame, and pride coursed through his veins. And truly, if ever vanity were justified, it would be that of Master Zacharius!

Indeed, up until his time, the art of clockmaking had scarcely departed from its infancy. Since the day when, four centuries before the Christian era, Plato invented the nocturnal clock, a sort of clepsydra that told the hours of the night by the sound and play of a flute, the science had remained virtually static. The masters gave more thought to aesthetics than to mechanics, and it was the age of exquisite timepieces of iron, copper, wood, and silver that were richly sculpted, like one of Cellini's ewers.[4] They were masterpieces of carving, which measured time very imperfectly, but they were masterpieces nonetheless. When the artist's imagination did not tend toward plastic perfection, it contrived to create clocks with moving figures and melodious chimes, which were made to operate in a most amusing manner. Besides, who troubled himself in those days with regulating the flow of time? Legal time limits had not yet been invented; the physical and astronomical sciences did not yet base their calculations on scrupulously exact measurements; shops did not yet close, nor conveyances depart, at fixed times. In the evening the curfew was sounded, and at night the silence was broken by the crying of the hours. Admittedly men did not live as long, if life is measured by the sum of business achieved, but they lived more fully. The mind grew richer in those noble sentiments born of the contemplation of masterpieces, and art was not created in haste. Two centuries were needed to build a church; a painter would complete only a few canvases in the course of a lifetime; a poet would compose but one great work; but these were so many masterpieces bequeathed to future centuries.

Finally, with the development of the exact sciences, the art of clockmaking received a corresponding impetus, although it was ever hampered by a seemingly insuperable obstacle: the regular and continuous measurement of time.

It was in the midst of this stagnation that Master Zacharius invented the escapement, which made it possible for him to obtain a mathematical regularity by subjecting the movement of the pendulum to a constant force.[5] This invention had gone to the old man's head. Pride, rising in his heart like mercury in a thermometer, had reached the height of transcendent folly. He had let himself be drawn, by analogy, into materialistic conclusions, and as he fashioned his watches he imagined himself to have stumbled upon the secret of the union of body and soul.

Thus it was that on this day, seeing that Aubert was listening to him attentively, he said to him in a tone of naive conviction, "Do you know what life is, my child? Have you fathomed the movement of those springs that give rise to existence? Have you looked within yourself? No—and yet, with the eyes of science, you would have perceived the intimate connection between God's work and my own, for it is from his creation, man, that I have copied the system of wheelwork in my clocks."

"Master," Aubert fervently rejoined, "can you compare a copper and steel machine to that breath of God called the soul, which gives life to our bodies as the breeze animates the flowers? Are there invisible wheels that move our legs and arms? What mechanism could be so well adjusted as to engender thought?"

"That is not the point," Master Zacharius replied gently, but with the obstinacy of a blind man heading toward an abyss. "If you would understand me, you must recall the purpose of the escapement which I have invented. When I beheld the irregularity in the workings of a clock, I realized that its own inner motion did not suffice and must be subjected to the regularity of some independent force. I then perceived that the pendulum might accomplish this, if I were able to regulate its oscillations! Now was it not a sublime insight to restore its lost force by means of the very motion of the clock that it serves to regulate?"[6]

Aubert nodded assent.

"Now, Aubert," the old clockmaker went on, growing more animated, "look within yourself! Don't you see that there are two distinct forces within us, that of the soul and that of the body— that is, a motion and a regulator? The soul is the principle of life: thus, it is motion. Be it engendered by a weight, by a spring, or by some incorporeal influence, it is nonetheless vital. Yet without the body, this motion would be irregular, erratic, impossible! Thus the body regulates the soul, and, like the pendulum, is subject to regular oscillations. It is owing to this simple truth that one grows ill

when food, drink, sleep—in a word, the functions of the body—
are not properly regulated! As with my watches, the soul restores
to the body the force expended in its oscillations. Well then, what
effects this intimate union of body and soul, if not some marvelous escapement, by means of which the wheelwork of the one
meshes with that of the other? This is what I have intuited and
put into application: there are no longer any secrets for me in life,
which is, after all, but an ingenious mechanism!"

Master Zacharius was sublime to behold in his delusion,
which was transporting him to the ultimate mysteries of the infinite. But his daughter Gérande, standing motionless in the doorway, had heard everything. She flew into her father's arms, and he
pressed her convulsively to his heart.

"What is the matter, my daughter?" Master Zacharius asked.

"If I had only a spring here," she declared, putting her hand to
her heart, "I would not love you as I do, father!"

Master Zacharius stared fixedly at his daughter and did not
reply.

Suddenly he uttered a cry, clutched at his heart and collapsed, nearly fainting, upon his old leather armchair.

"Father! What is the matter?"

"Help!" cried Aubert. "Scholastique!"

But Scholastique did not come at once. Someone had
knocked on the front door; she had gone to answer it, and when
she returned to the shop, before she could open her mouth the
old clockmaker, having come to, said, "I suppose, old Scholastique, that you have brought me yet another of those accursed
watches that have stopped!"

"Oh Lord! It is true enough," Scholastique replied, handing a
watch to Aubert.

"My heart could not be mistaken," said the old man with a
sigh.

Meanwhile, Aubert had adjusted the watch with the greatest
of care, but it would not go.

III. A STRANGE VISIT

Poor Gérande would have felt her life ebbing away with that
of her father, had it not been for the thought of Aubert, who was
her only link to the world.

Little by little the old clockmaker was declining. His faculties were obviously growing weaker as he concentrated them exclusively upon a single idea. By a fatal process of association, he brought everything back around to his monomania, and it seemed as if his old earthly life had ebbed away, and a strange, otherworldly power had taken its place. Consequently, certain malicious rivals revived the diabolical rumors that had been spread regarding Zacharius's craft.

The news of the baffling disturbances afflicting his watches sent a shudder among the master clockmakers of Geneva. What did it portend, this sudden apathy of their wheelwork, and wherefore the peculiar mutual exchange between it and the life of Master Zacharius? It was one of those mysteries which cannot be contemplated without a secret terror. In the various classes of the town, from the apprentices to the lords who used the old clockmaker's watches, there was not one who did not perceive the utter singularity of the situation. Everyone wished to gain access to Master Zacharius, but in vain. He fell gravely ill—which was sufficient grounds for his daughter to put an end to these incessant visits, which were degenerating into reproaches and recriminations.

Medicines and physicians were powerless in the face of this organic deterioration, the cause of which eluded detection. At times it seemed as if the old man's heart had ceased to beat, but then the heartbeats would resume with an alarming irregularity.

At that time, the custom existed of submitting the works of the masters to the judgment of the people. The heads of the various guilds sought to distinguish themselves by the novelty or the excellence of their creations, and it was among them that Master Zacharius's predicament excited the most lively commiseration—but one of self-interest. His rivals, fearing him less, pitied him the more readily. They still remembered the old clockmaker's triumphs, when he had exhibited those magnificent clocks with moving figures, those chiming watches, which had attracted universal admiration and commanded such high prices in the cities of France, Switzerland, and Germany.

Meanwhile, owing to the constant care and attention of Gérande and Aubert, Master Zacharius's strength appeared to return somewhat, and in the tranquillity of his convalescence he was able to free himself from his obsessive thoughts. As soon as he could walk, his daughter took him out of the house, which was still besieged with disgruntled patrons. Aubert remained in the shop, fruitlessly adjusting and readjusting those rebel watches; the poor boy, completely mystified, would at times clasp his head in his hands, fearing that he would go mad like his master.

Gérande would escort her father toward the most cheerful avenues of the city. Sometimes, holding Master Zacharius by the arm, she would wend her way along rue Saint-Antoine, from which the view extends out over the hillside of Cologny and across the lake. Sometimes, of a clear morning, they could glimpse the giant peaks of Mount Buet towering on the horizon. Gérande identified by name all these sites, of which her father, in the confusion of his memory, had little recollection, and he absorbed all she told him with childlike pleasure. As they walked along, Master Zacharius leaned upon his daughter's arm, and their white and blond hair seemed to commingle in a ray of the sun.

The old clockmaker came to realize at last that he was not alone in the world. Gazing upon his lovely young daughter, old and broken as he was himself, he reflected how after his death she would be left alone and without support, and he began to cast his eyes about him. Many of the young skilled artisans of Geneva had already sought to woo Gérande, yet none had gained access to the impenetrable sanctuary of the clockmaker's household. It was thus only natural that during this period of lucidity, the old man would fix his choice upon Aubert Thün. Once this idea had taken hold in his mind, he observed that these two young people had been raised with the same ideas and beliefs, and the oscillations of their hearts seemed to him, as he remarked one day to Scholastique, "isochronal."

The old servant, literally charmed with the word, although she did not understand it, swore by her patron saint that the whole town would hear it within a quarter of an hour. Master Zacharius had a difficult time calming her, and finally extracted from her a promise of silence which she never observed.

Consequently, quite without Gérande's and Aubert's knowledge, all Geneva was soon talking of their impending union. But often, in the midst of such gossip, strange snickering laughter could be heard along with a voice that declared, "Gérande will not wed Aubert."

If the gossipers turned round, they would find themselves

face to face with a little old man whom they had never seen before.

How old was this curious being? No one could have told! People guessed that his age could be counted in centuries, but that was all. His large flat head rested on shoulders the width of which was equal to the height of his body, which did not exceed three feet. This odd creature would have figured well on a support for a clock, for the dial would have been naturally situated on his face, and the pendulum would have oscillated quite comfortably inside his chest. One might easily have mistaken his nose for the gnomon of a sundial, so slender and pointed was it; his teeth, widely spaced and with epicycloidal surfaces, resembled the gears of a wheel and made a grinding noise between his lips; his voice had the metallic sound of a bell, and you could hear his heart beating like the tick-tock of a clock. This little man, whose arms moved like the hands on a dial, walked jerkily, without ever turning round. If you followed him you would find that he walked one league an hour, and that his course was nearly circular.

It was only a short time since this strange creature had first been seen wandering, or rather circulating, around the city, but it had already been observed that each day, at the moment when the sun passed the meridian, he would stop in front of the Cathedral of Saint-Pierre, and resume his course after the twelve strokes had sounded. Save for this precise moment, he seemed to loom up amid every conversation dealing with the old clockmaker, and people began to wonder in alarm what possible relation there might be between him and Master Zacharius. Moreover, it was observed that he never lost sight of the old man and his daughter during their daily strolls.

One day, on the Treille, Gérande noticed this monster staring at her and laughing. She pressed closer to her father in fright.

"What is the matter, Gérande?" asked Master Zacharius.

"I don't know," replied the girl.

"But you look changed, my child!" said the old clockmaker. "Are you about to fall ill now, in your turn? Ah well," he added, with a sad smile, "I shall have to look after you, and I shall look after you well."

"Oh, father, it is nothing. I am cold, and I imagine it is . . ."

"What, Gérande?"

"The presence of that man, who is always following us," she answered in a hushed tone.

Master Zacharius turned toward the little old man.

"Indeed, he runs well," said he, with a satisfied air, "for it is just four o'clock. Fear not, my child, for he is not a man, but a clock!"

Gérande stared at her father in terror. How had Master Zacharius managed to read the time upon the face of that queer creature?

"By the by," continued the old clockmaker, paying no more heed to the matter, "I have not seen Aubert for several days."

"Yet he is still with us, father," replied Gérande, her thoughts taking on a sunnier cast.

"What is he doing, then?"

"He is working, father."

"Ah!" cried the old man, "he is working to repair my watches, is he not? But he will never succeed, for it is not repair that they require, but a resurrection!"

Gérande was silent.

"I need to know," added the old man, "if they have returned any more of those damned watches, upon which the Devil has sent a plague!"

With these words Master Zacharius fell into utter silence until he reached the door of his house, and for the first time since his convalescence he descended to his workshop, while Gérande sadly returned to her room.

At the very moment that he entered his shop, one of the many clocks hanging on the wall began to strike five. Ordinarily, the sundry bells of these clocks, admirably regulated as they were, would chime simultaneously, sending joy into the old man's heart; but on this day all the bells rang out one after the other, so that for a quarter of an hour the ear was deafened by their clanging. Master Zacharius suffered torments; he could not keep still, but went from one clock to another, beating time, like a conductor who has lost control of his orchestra.

As the last chimes faded away into silence, the door of the workshop opened, and a shudder passed through Master Zacharius as he saw before him the little old man, who stared at him fixedly and said, "Master, could I not speak with you a few moments?"

"Who are you?" asked the clockmaker curtly.

"A colleague. I am responsible for regulating the sun."

"Ah! You regulate the sun, do you?" said Master Zacharius sharply, without batting an eyelid. "Well, I can scarcely commend you! Your sun runs poorly, and in order to synchronize ourselves with it, we have to keep setting our clocks ahead or behind!"

"And by the Devil's cloven foot," cried the monstrous creature, "you are right, Master! My sun does not always mark midday at the same instant as your clocks, but one day it will be known that this stems from the variations in the earth's translatory movement, and they will invent a mean midday that will resolve this irregularity!"[7]

"Will this be within my lifetime?" asked the old man, his eyes lighting up.

"Without any doubt," replied the little old man, laughing. "Can you think that you will ever die?"

"Alas! But I am very ill."

"Ah yes, let us talk about that. By Beelzebub! It will bring us to what I wish to speak with you about."

And as he spoke, this strange creature leaped up without further ado onto the old leather armchair, crossing his legs beneath him like those fleshless bones that painters of funeral draperies represent beneath skulls. Then he went on in an ironical tone:

"Come now, Master Zacharius, what is happening in this good city of Geneva? They say your health is declining, that your watches have need of a doctor!"

"Ah! So you believe there is an intimate connection between their existence and mine!" cried Master Zacharius.

"Why, I imagine those watches have flaws, even vices. If those hussies do not conduct themselves properly, it is only fair that they should suffer the consequences of their wantonness. They ought to stay in line, so it seems to me!"

"What do you call flaws?" said Master Zacharius, reddening at the sarcastic tone in which these words had been uttered. "Have they not the right to be proud of their origin?"

"Not over much, not over much," replied the little old man. "They bear an illustrious name, and on their faces is inscribed a venerable signature, to be sure, and it is their exclusive privilege to gain entrance to the noblest households; yet for some time they have been out of order, and you can do nothing for it, Master Zacharius—the most bumbling apprentice in Geneva could do better than you!"

"Than me, than me, Master Zacharius!" cried the old man in a terrible upsurge of pride.

"Than you, Master Zacharius, who cannot bring your watches back to life!"

"But it is because I have a fever, and they as well!" replied the old clockmaker, breaking out in a cold sweat from head to toe.

"Very well, they shall die with you, since you are unable to restore any elasticity to their springs!"

"Die! Not I—you told me so yourself! I cannot die, I, the best clockmaker in the world, I who by means of these sundry parts and wheels, have been able to regulate motion with absolute precision! Have I not subjected time to exact laws, and over time do I not reign supreme? Before a sublime genius came to bestow order upon the roving hours, into what a void human destiny was plunged! How could the acts of life be correlated with certainty? But you, whoever you are, be you man or devil, have you never pondered the magnificence of my art, which summons all the sciences to join in its mission? No! No! I, Master Zacharius, cannot die, for since I have regulated time, time would die with me! It would return to the infinite from which my genius has wrested it, and would be swallowed up by the abyss of nothingness! No, I can no more die than the Creator of that universe governed by His laws. I have become His equal, and have partaken of His power! If God created eternity, Master Zacharius has created time."

At this moment, the old clockmaker looked like the fallen angel standing defiant before the Creator. The little old man looked at him fondly and seemed to be prompting him in this blasphemous passion.

"Well said, Master!" he replied. "Beelzebub had less right than you to compare himself to God! Your glory must not perish! Therefore, your servant wishes to provide you with the means of humbling these mutinous watches."

"What is it? What is it?" cried Master Zacharius.

"You shall know on the day you give me your daughter's hand."

"My Gérande?"

"None other!"

"My daughter's heart is already taken," replied Master Zacharius, who seemed neither surprised nor offended by this request.

"Bah! . . . She is not the least beautiful of your clocks . . . but she too will stop at last. . . ."

"My daughter, my Gérande! . . . No! . . ."

"Very well, return to your watches, Master Zacharius. Assemble and disassemble them. Make plans for the marriage of your daughter and your apprentice. Temper the springs made of your best steel. Bless Aubert and the lovely Gérande, but remember that your watches will never run again, and that Gérande will not wed Aubert!"

And thereupon, the little old man took his leave, but not so quickly that Master Zacharius could not hear six o'clock striking in his breast.

IV. THE CHURCH OF SAINT-PIERRE

As time went on, Master Zacharius grew ever weaker in mind and body. Yet a feverish intoxication made him apply himself with greater passion than ever to his work, from which his daughter was unable to distract him.

His pride had continued to swell since that crisis to which his curious visitor had treacherously impelled him, and he resolved to overcome, by sheer force of genius, the accursed influence that hung over himself and his craft. First, he inspected the various clocks throughout the town, which were entrusted to his care. With scrupulous heed, he made certain that the wheelwork was in good condition, the pivots firm, the counterweights perfectly balanced. He even sounded the chime mechanism with the reverence of a doctor listening to a patient's chest. There was not the slightest indication that these clocks were on the verge of a breakdown.

Gérande and Aubert often accompanied the old clockmaker on these visits. He should have taken pleasure in seeing them so attentive at his side, and indeed he might not have been so troubled about his imminent end, had he reflected that his existence would be perpetuated in these cherished beings—that children forever preserve something of their father's life in their own!

Upon returning home, the old clockmaker would resume his

work with feverish industry. Persuaded though he was of the vanity of his effort, he still refused to accept the fact, and ceaselessly assembled and disassembled the watches that were brought to his shop.

Aubert, for his part, struggled in vain to discover the cause of the trouble.

"Master," he would say, "it could only come from wear on the pivots and gears!"

"Do you take pleasure in killing me over a slow flame?" Master Zacharius would vehemently retort. "Are these watches the work of a child? So that I might reproach myself with nothing, have I not smoothed the surfaces of these copper parts with a lathe? Have I not forged them myself, for greater strength? Have these springs not been tempered to perfection? Could they have been steeped in finer oils? You yourself concede that it is impossible, and you admit that the Devil is mixed up in this!"

From morning till night disgruntled customers flocked to the house in ever greater numbers, and managed to gain access to the old clockmaker himself, who hardly knew whom he should listen to first.

"This watch is too slow, and I cannot put it right!" said one.

"This one here," said another, "is truly obstinate, and has stopped, just like Joshua's sun!"[8]

"If it is true," the majority of them repeated, "that your health has an influence on the health of your clocks, Master Zacharius, get well as soon as possible!"

The old man stared at all these people with a wild expression in his eyes, and answered only with a shake of his head or with a few sad words:

"Wait until the first fine weather, my friends! 'Tis the season that rekindles the life in tired frames. We shall be revived by the warmth of the sun!"

"What good is that, if our watches are to be ill through the winter!" said one of the most irate. "You realize, Master Zacharius, that your name is inscribed in full on their dials! By the Holy Virgin! You do little honor to your signature!"

Finally the old man, mortified by these reproaches, took some gold coins from his old chest and began to buy back the disabled watches. At this news, the customers flocked to him in droves, and the funds of the little household were soon exhausted; but the clockmaker's integrity survived unscathed. Gérande heartily approved of this high-mindedness, which was leading her straight toward ruin, and soon Aubert was forced to offer his own savings to Master Zacharius.

"What will become of my daughter?" said the old clockmaker, clutching, as he foundered, at the tender platitudes of paternal emotion.

Aubert dared not reply that he felt confidence in the future and great devotion for Gérande. Master Zacharius, that day, would have called him his son-in-law, and denied those fatal words that were still echoing in his ear: "Gérande will not wed Aubert."

Finally the old clockmaker stripped himself entirely bare. His old antique vases fell into the hands of strangers; he parted with the magnificent, finely carved oak paneling that lined the walls of his abode; several naive canvases by the earliest Flemish painters would soon no longer bring joy to his daughter's eyes; and everything, down to the priceless tools invented by his genius, was sold to reimburse the claimants.

Scholastique alone refused to listen to reason on the subject, but her efforts could not prevent the irksome intruders from making their way to her master and soon emerging afterward with some precious article. Then her chattering could be heard through all the streets of the neighborhood, where she was long known. She went to great lengths to deny the rumors of sorcery and magic which were being spread about Master Zacharius, but since deep down she was persuaded of their truth, she repeated her prayers over and over to redeem her pious falsehoods.

It had been observed that for some time the old clockmaker had neglected his religious duties. In the past he had accompanied Gérande to church and had seemed to find in prayer that intellectual charm that it affords superior minds, being the most sublime exercise of the imagination. The old man's voluntary estrangement from pious observances, combined with the clandestine routine of his existence, had as it were confirmed the accusations of black magic that were being leveled against his occupation. Consequently, with the twofold goal of reclaiming her father for God and for the world, Gérande resolved to summon religion to her aid. She hoped that Catholicism might restore some vitality to this languishing soul, but the doctrine of faith and humility had to contend, in the soul of Master Zacharius, with his insurmountable pride, and ran up against that vanity of science which refers everything to itself, instead of returning to the infinite source from which first principles flow.

It was under these circumstances that the girl undertook her father's conversion, and her influence was so persuasive that the old clockmaker promised to attend high mass at the Cathedral the following Sunday. Gérande was overcome for a moment with ecstasy, as though Heaven had opened before her. Old Scholastique could not contain her joy, and at last had irrefutable arguments against the malicious gossips who accused her master of impiety. She spoke about it to her neighbors, her friends, her enemies, to utter strangers as well as to acquaintances.

"Upon my word, we can scarcely believe what you are telling us, Dame Scholastique," they answered. "Master Zacharius has always been in league with the Devil!"

"Have you not counted," the good woman would reply, "the fine bell towers where my master's clocks chime? How often have they rung out the hours of prayer and the mass!"

"No doubt," they would answer. "But has he not invented machines that run all by themselves and do the work of a real man?"

"Could a child of the Devil," Dame Scholastique would angrily resume, "have possibly executed that fine iron clock in the castle of Andernatt, which the city of Geneva was not wealthy enough to buy? A pious motto would appear at every hour, and a Christian who observed them would have gone straight to Heaven! Now is that the work of the Devil?"

This masterpiece, created twenty years earlier, had in fact carried Master Zacharius to the height of his fame, but even on this occasion he had been widely accused of sorcery. The old man's return to the Cathedral of Saint-Pierre might very well reduce the slanderers to silence.

Master Zacharius, doubtless forgetting the promise he had made to his daughter, had returned to his workshop. Having realized that he was powerless to restore his watches to life, he resolved to see if he might be able to construct new ones. Turning his back upon the lifeless corpses, he focused his efforts once more on the crystal watch that he hoped would be his masterpiece; yet try as he might with his most sterling instruments, and with the most friction-resistant rubies and diamonds for his jewels, the watch fell apart in his hands at his first attempt to assemble it.

The old man kept what had happened a secret from everyone, even his daughter, but from that time forward his health rapidly declined. The life within him was now no more than the last dwindling oscillations of a pendulum deprived of the force that impelled it. It seemed that the laws of gravity, acting directly upon the old man, were dragging him inexorably down into the tomb.

The Sunday that Gérande had so ardently awaited at last arrived. The weather was splendid and invigorating. The residents of Geneva strolled placidly through the city streets, chatting gaily about the return of spring. Gérande, solicitously taking the old man's arm, headed in the direction of Saint-Pierre, while Scholastique followed behind with the prayer books. People stared in curiosity as they passed. The old man allowed himself to be led like a child, or rather like a blind man. It was with an emotion resembling dread that the faithful of Saint-Pierre watched him cross the threshold of the church, and they made as if to draw back at his approach.

The chants of high mass were already echoing through the church. Gérande made her way toward her accustomed pew and knelt down in deepest reverence. Master Zacharius remained beside her, standing.

The mass proceeded with the majestic solemnity of this age of faith; but of faith the old man had none. He did not implore the mercy of Heaven with the anguished cries of the *Kyrie,* nor did he sing the splendors of celestial heights with the *Gloria in Excelsis;* the reading of the Gospels did not rouse him from his worldly reverie, and he forgot to join in the homage of the *Credo.* This proud old man remained immobile, as numb and mute as a stone statue, and even at the solemn moment when the bell rang out the miracle of transubstantiation he did not bow his head but stared directly at the divine host that the priest was holding above the heads of the faithful.

Gérande looked at her father, and a flood of tears moistened her missal.

Just then the clock of Saint-Pierre struck half past eleven.
Master Zacharius turned round with a start toward the old clock
tower that was eloquent still. It seemed to him as if the inner face
were regarding him fixedly, that the figures of the hours were
glowing as if they had been engraved in lines of fire, and that the
sharply pointed hands were shooting forth electric sparks.

The mass was over. It was customary for the *Angelus* to be recited at noon; the priests, before leaving the parvis, waited for the
clock to strike the hour of twelve. In a few moments, this prayer
would ascend to the feet of the Virgin.

But suddenly an ear-piercing sound was heard. Master Zacharius uttered a cry. . . .[9]

The large clock hand, having reached twelve, had abruptly
stopped, and the clock did not sound the hour.

Gérande sprang to the aid of her father, who had collapsed
and had to be carried out of the church.

"It is the deathblow!" sobbed Gérande.

When he had been taken home, Master Zacharius was laid
on his bed in a state of complete prostration. His life seemed to
be confined to the mere surface of his body, like the last puffs of
smoke hovering about a just-extinguished lamp.

When he regained consciousness, Aubert and Gérande were
leaning over him. At these last moments the future took on, for
him, the guise of the present. He saw his daughter alone, with no
support in the world.

"My son," he said to Aubert, "I give you my daughter," and he
stretched out his hand toward his two children, thus united at his
deathbed.

But no sooner had he done this than Master Zacharius sprang
up in a paroxysm of rage. The words of the little old man returned
to his mind.

"I do not want to die!" he cried. "I cannot die! I, Master Zacharius, must not die. . . . My books! . . . My accounts! . . ."

And with this, he leaped from his bed, pouncing upon a book
that contained the names of his customers as well as the articles
which he had sold to them. He greedily turned over the pages of
this book, and his bony finger settled upon one of the leaves.

"There!" he cried. "There! . . . This old iron clock, sold to Pittonaccio! It is the only one that has not been returned to me! It

still exists! It runs! It still lives! Ah, I want it! I will find it! I will take such care of it that death will have no more power over me."

And he fainted away.

Aubert and Gérande knelt by the old man's bedside and prayed together.

V. THE HOUR OF DEATH

Several more days elapsed, and Master Zacharius, this man on the brink of death, rose from his bed and returned to life on the strength of a preternatural excitement. He lived through pride alone. But Gérande had not been mistaken: the body and soul of her father were lost forever.

The old man could be seen gathering together his last reserves, without any concern for his family. He expended enormous energy, walking back and forth, rummaging about, and muttering strange, incomprehensible words.

One morning, Gérande went down to his shop. Master Zacharius was not there.

All that day, she waited for him. Master Zacharius did not come home.

Gérande cried until she had no tears left, but her father did not return.

Aubert scoured the city and gloomily concluded that the old man must have departed its walls.

"We must find him!" cried Gérande, when the young apprentice brought her this painful news.

"Where can he be?" wondered Aubert.

Suddenly he was seized with an inspiration. He remembered Master Zacharius's last words. The old clockmaker now lived only in and through that old iron clock that had not been returned! Master Zacharius must have gone off in search of it.

Aubert confided his thought to Gérande.

"Let us look at my father's book," she replied.

They went down to the shop. The book lay open upon the bench. The records of all the clocks or watches that the old clockmaker had made, and which had been returned to him out of order, had been crossed out, with the exception of one!

"Sold to Lord Pittonaccio, one iron clock, with chimes and moving figures, delivered to his castle at Andernatt."

This was the "moral" clock of which Scholastique had spoken so enthusiastically.

"My father is there!" exclaimed Gérande.

"Let us make haste," Aubert replied. "We may still save him! . . ."

"Not for this life," murmured Gérande, "but at least for the other!"

"It is in God's hands, Gérande! The castle of Andernatt lies in the gorges of the Dents-du-Midi, twenty hours from Geneva. Let us go!"

That very evening Aubert and Gérande, followed by their old servant, were wending their way along the road that skirts the Lake of Geneva. They traveled five leagues that night, stopping neither at Bessinge, nor at Ermance with its famous château des Mayor. They forded, not without difficulty, the torrent of the Drance. Everywhere they went, they inquired about Master Zacharius, and were soon convinced that they were following in his tracks.

The next day at nightfall, after having passed Thonon, they reached Evian, from where they could see the Swiss hills spread out before them across an expanse of twelve leagues. But the betrothed gave scarcely a glance at this magical setting. They went steadily onward, driven by a preternatural force. Aubert, leaning upon a knotty staff, offered his arm by turns to Gérande and to old Scholastique, drawing from his heart boundless energy with which to sustain his companions. The three spoke of their sorrows and their hopes, and so made their way down that beautiful road along the water, on that narrow plateau which lies between the lake shore and the high peaks of Chalais. Soon they reached Bouveret, where the Rhone empties into the Lake of Geneva.

At this point they headed away from the lake, and their exhaustion grew as they traversed the mountainous terrain. The godforsaken villages of Vionnaz, Chesset, Collombay, were soon left far behind them. All the while, their knees sagged, their feet chafed, as they toiled over the sharp ridges that sprang like granite brushwood from the earth. No trace of Master Zacharius!

Yet they must find him, and in their resolve the two declined to seek rest either at the isolated thatched cottages or at the château de Monthey which, along with its dependencies, formed part of the territory of Marguerite de Savoie. At last, toward the end of the day, nearly lifeless with fatigue, they reached the hermitage of Notre-Dame du Sex, at the base of the Dent-du-Midi, six hundred feet above the Rhone.

The hermit received the three as night was falling. They could not have gone a single step more, and there they would needs rest.

The hermit could give them no news of Master Zacharius. They could scarcely hope to find him still alive amid this barren wilderness. The night was dark, the winds of the storm whistled in the mountains, and avalanches thundered down from the summits of the shaken crags.

Kneeling before the hermit's hearth, the two betrothed recounted to him their doleful tale. Their cloaks, covered with snow, lay drying in a corner, and outside the hermit's dog bayed lugubriously, mingling his howls with the howling of the wind.

"Pride," said the hermit to his guests, "was the undoing of an angel created for good. It is the stumbling block against which men's destinies collide. Against pride, that first principle of all vice, all argument is powerless, since by his very nature the man of pride refuses to heed it. . . . All we can do, then, is to pray for your father!"

All four were kneeling down, when the barking of the dog grew louder, and there was a knock on the door of the hermitage.

"Open, in the name of the Devil!"

The door gave way beneath the blows, and a man appeared, wild, disheveled, barely clothed.

"My father!" cried Gérande.

It was Master Zacharius.

"Where am I?" he said. "In eternity! . . . Time has come to an end. . . . The hours no longer strike. . . . The hands have stopped!"

"Father!" repeated Gérande, with such heartrending emotion that the old man seemed to return to the world of the living.

"You here, my Gérande!" he exclaimed, "and you, Aubert! . . . Ah! My dear betrothed, you have come to be married in our old church!"

"Father," said Gérande, clasping his arm, "come back to your home in Geneva, come back with us!"

The old man broke free from his daughter's grasp and darted toward the doorway, where thick drifts of snow were gathering.

"Do not abandon your children!" cried Aubert.

"Why," the old clockmaker replied sadly, "why return to the place from which my life has already departed, and where part of myself is forever entombed!"

"Your soul is not dead!" said the hermit in a solemn voice.

"My soul? . . . Oh, no! . . . Its mechanism is sound! . . . I feel it beating regularly. . . ."

"Your soul is immaterial! Your soul is immortal!" replied the hermit firmly.

"Yes . . . like my fame! . . . But it is shut up in the castle of Andernatt, and I want to see it again!"

The hermit made the sign of the cross. Scholastique was almost fainting. Aubert supported Gérande in his arms.

"The castle of Andernatt is inhabited by a soul that is damned," said the hermit, "one who does not honor the cross of my hermitage!"

"My father, do not go there!"

"I want my soul! My soul is mine! . . ."

"Stop him! Stop my father!" cried Gérande.

But the old man had already dashed across the threshold and plunged into the night, crying, "Mine! Mine, my soul! . . ."

Gérande, Aubert, and Scholastique raced after him. They scrambled over impassable trails, across which Master Zacharius sped like the tempest, impelled by an irresistible force. The snow swirled and raged about them, mingling its white flakes with the foam of overflowing streams.

As they passed the chapel built to commemorate the massacre of the Theban Legion, Gérande, Aubert, and Scholastique hastily made the sign of the cross. Master Zacharius did not even take off his hat.

Finally the village of Evionnaz appeared in the midst of this untilled wasteland. The hardest heart would have been gladdened at the sight of the little town lost amid this awful desolation. The old man continued on, oblivious. Heading left, he plunged into the deepest gorges of the Dents-du-Midi, which far overhead etched their jagged peaks into the sky.

Soon a ruin loomed up before him, as ancient and gloomy as the rocks about its base.

"There! There! . . ." he cried, once more quickening his frenzied pace.

The castle of Andernatt was even at that time scarcely more

than a ruin. A broad, dilapidated, moldering tower rose above it and seemed to threaten the old gabled houses at its feet with its imminent collapse. These vast piles of stones filled one with horror. Amid the debris one had vague intimations of dark halls with caved-in ceilings and of vile vipers' lairs.

A low and narrow postern, opening onto a ditch choked with rubbish, afforded access to the castle of Andernatt. What ancient occupants had passed through there? No one knows. Doubtless some margrave, half-lord, half-brigand, had resided in this place. The margrave was followed by bandits or counterfeiters, who were hanged at the scene of their crime. And legend has it that on winter nights Satan came to lead his wild dances upon the slopes of the massive gorges, which swallowed up the shadows of the ruins within their depths.

Master Zacharius was not intimidated by their sinister appearance. He made his way to the postern. No one barred him from passing. A large, dark courtyard met his eyes. No one barred him from crossing it. He ascended a sort of inclined plane that led to one of the long corridors, the arches of which seemed to snuff out the daylight beneath their massive spans. No one blocked him from passing. Gérande, Aubert, and Scholastique were still close behind him.

Master Zacharius, as if guided by an invisible hand, seemed sure of his way and advanced with rapid strides. He came to an old worm-eaten door that shook beneath his blows, while bats traced oblique circles around his head.

Soon he came to an immense hall, better preserved than the others. Its walls were covered with high sculpted panels, upon which specters, ghouls, and monsters seemed vaguely to stir and commingle. Several long and narrow windows shuddered under the blasts of the storm.

Master Zacharius, upon reaching the center of the hall, uttered a cry of joy.

On an iron support fastened to the wall stood the clock in which his whole life was now contained. This peerless masterpiece was a representation of an old Romanesque church, with its forged iron buttresses and its massive bell tower, which held an entire set of chimes for the day's anthem, Angelus, Mass, Vespers, Compline, and Ave Maria. Above the church door, which opened at the hour of the service, was a rose window, in the center of

which were two moving hands; around the archivolt, the twelve
hours of the clock face were carved in relief. Between the door
and the rose window, just as old Scholastique had described, were
maxims engraved in a copper frame, relating to the employment
of each moment of the day. Master Zacharius had worked out this
succession of mottos with pious care; the hours of prayer, work,
repast, recreation, and repose were arranged according to the religious discipline, and were designed to insure the salvation of
those who scrupulously abided by their commands.

Master Zacharius, beside himself with joy, was about to seize
hold of the clock when he heard a hideous burst of laughter behind him.

He turned round, and by the light of a smoky lamp recognized the little old man of Geneva.

"You—here?" he cried.

Gérande, in fright, pressed closer to her betrothed.

"Greetings, Master Zacharius," said the monster.

"Who are you?"

"Signor Pittonaccio, at your service! You have come to give
me your daughter! You remember my words: 'Gérande will not
wed Aubert.'"

The young apprentice lunged toward Pittonaccio, who
eluded him like a shadow.

"Stop, Aubert!" said Master Zacharius.

"Good night," said Pittonaccio, and disappeared.

"Father," cried Gérande, "let us flee this accursed place! . . .
Father!"

Master Zacharius was no longer there. Down the ruined
stairs and corridors, he was chasing the ghost of Pittonaccio.
Scholastique, Aubert, and Gérande remained in a daze in the
middle of the immense hall. The girl had collapsed onto a stone
seat; the old servant was kneeling beside her in prayer. Aubert
stood watching over his betrothed. Pale gleams of light coiled in
the shadows, and the silence was broken only by those little animals that gnaw on old wood, making sounds that mark the hours
of the "clock of death."

At the first rays of dawn, all three ventured down the endless
staircases which wound beneath this mass of stones. For two hours
they wandered without encountering a living soul, and hearing
only a far-off echo in response to their cries. Sometimes they

would find themselves buried a hundred feet below ground, sometimes they stood upon heights overlooking the desolate mountains.

Chance brought them back again at last to the vast hall which had sheltered them during this night of agony. It was no longer empty. Master Zacharius and Pittonaccio were talking there together, the one standing upright and rigid as a corpse, the other squatting upon a marble table.

Master Zacharius, upon seeing Gérande, went to take her by the hand, and led her toward Pittonaccio, saying, "Behold your lord and master, my daughter. Gérande, behold your husband!"

Gérande shuddered from head to foot.

"Never!" cried Aubert, "for she is my betrothed."

"Never!" replied Gérande, like a plaintive echo.

Pittonaccio began to laugh.

"Then you want me to die?" cried the old man. "There in that clock, the last of all my handiwork that is running still, there my life is contained, and this man has told me: 'When I have your daughter, this clock shall be yours.' And this man will not wind it up again. He can break it and plunge me into nothingness! Ah, my daughter! Then you no longer love me!"

"My father!" murmured Gérande, regaining consciousness.

"If you knew how I have suffered, far from this mainstay of my existence!" the old man went on. "Perhaps no one was tending to this clock! Perhaps its springs were left to wear out, its wheels to become jammed. But now, with my own hands, I can preserve its precious health, for I must not die, I, the great clockmaker of Geneva! Look, daughter, how these hands advance at a steady pace. See, five o'clock is about to strike! Listen carefully, and behold the fine maxim that will appear before your eyes."

The clock struck five with a noise that echoed painfully in Gérande's soul, and the following words appeared in red letters:

You must eat of the fruits of the tree of knowledge.

Aubert and Gérande gazed at each other in astonishment. These were not the orthodox mottos of the pious clockmaker! The clock must have been touched by the breath of Satan. But Zacharius paid no attention, and went on:

"Do you hear, my Gérande? I live, I live still! Listen to my breath! . . . Behold the blood circulating through my veins! . . ."

No, you would not want to kill your father, and you will take this man for your husband, so that I may become immortal and at last attain the power of God!"

At these impious words, old Scholastique made the sign of the cross, and Pittonaccio let out a howl of glee.

"And besides, Gérande, you will be happy with him! Behold this man—he is Time! Your existence will be regulated with absolute precision! Gérande! Since I gave you life, restore life to your father!"

"Gérande," murmured Aubert. "I am your betrothed!"

"He is my father!" replied Gérande, collapsing in a faint.

"She is yours!" said Master Zacharius. "Pittonaccio, you will keep your promise!"

"Here is the key to the clock," answered the hideous creature.

Master Zacharius seized the long key, which resembled an uncoiled snake, and dashed toward the clock, which he proceeded to wind with uncanny speed. The creaking of the spring jarred upon the nerves. The old clockmaker wound and wound the key, without stopping a moment, and it seemed as if this rotating motion continued independently of his will. He wound more and more rapidly, with strange contortions, until he collapsed from sheer exhaustion.

"There, it is wound for a century!" he cried.

Aubert dashed like a madman from the hall. After rushing hither and thither, he found his way out of the infernal structure and made for the open country. He returned to the hermitage of Notre-Dame du Sex and entreated the saintly recluse so desperately that the latter consented to return with him to the castle of Andernatt.

If, during these hours of anguish, Gérande had not wept a tear, it was because she had none left to weep.

Master Zacharius had not left the great hall. Every other minute, he would run to listen to the regular beating of the old clock.

In the meantime, it had struck ten, and to Scholastique's great horror, these words had appeared in the silver frame:

Man can become the equal of God.

Not only was the old man not shocked by these impious maxims, but he was reading them aloud in a delirious frenzy and reveling in these meditations of pride, while Pittonaccio circled about him.

The marriage contract was to be signed at midnight. Gérande, nearly lifeless, was deaf and blind to all around her. The silence was broken only by the old man's words and by the snickering laughter of Pittonaccio.

The clock struck eleven. Master Zacharius shuddered, and in a loud voice read this blasphemy:

> *Man should be the slave of science,*[10]
> *and sacrifice to it relatives and family.*

"Yes," he exclaimed, "in this world science is all!"

The hands slid across the iron clock face with the hiss of a viper, and the clock beat accelerated strokes.

Master Zacharius spoke no longer! He had fallen to the ground, uttering a death rattle, and from his suffocating breast came only these broken words: "Life! Science!"

There were now two new witnesses to the scene, the hermit and Aubert. Master Zacharius lay on the ground. Gérande was praying beside him, more dead than alive. . . .

Suddenly the hard, dry noise of the striking apparatus was heard preparing to sound the hour.

Master Zacharius sprang up.

"Midnight!" he cried.

The hermit stretched out his hand toward the old clock . . . and midnight did not sound.

Then Master Zacharius uttered a cry that must have been heard in the depths of hell, as these words appeared:

> *Whosoever shall attempt to become the equal of God*
> *shall be forever damned!*

The old clock shattered with a noise like thunder, and the mainspring, escaping, bounded across the hall with a thousand fantastical contortions. The old man leaped up and ran after it, trying in vain to grab hold of it, and crying, "My soul! My soul!"

The spring bounded ahead of him, first on one side, then on the other, and he was unable to catch it.

At last Pittonaccio seized hold of it and, uttering a horrible blasphemy, was swallowed up by the earth.

Master Zacharius fell backward. He was dead.

. . . .

The old clockmaker's body was buried among the peaks of Andernatt. Aubert and Gérande then returned to Geneva, and during the long life which God accorded them they strove to redeem through prayer the soul of the outcast of science.

1 8 5 4

Translated by Joan C. Kessler

For a recent French edition of this work, see Jules Verne, *Maître Zacharius*, in *Le Docteur Ox, Maître Zacharius*, . . . (Paris: Librairie Hachette, 1966).

Villiers de l'Isle-Adam

THE SIGN

For Monsieur l'abbé Victor de Villiers de l'Isle-Adam [1]

Attende, homo, quid fuisti ante ortum et quod eris usque ud occasum. Profecto fuit quod non eras. Postea, de vili materia factus, in utero matris de sanguine menstruali nutritus, tunica tua fuit pellis secundina. Deinde, in vilissimo panno involutus, progressus es ad nos,—sic indutus et ornatus! Et non memor es quæ sit origo tua. Nihil est aliud homo quam sperma fœtidum, saccus stercorum, cibus vermium. Scientia, sapientia, ratio, sine Deo sicut nubes transeunt.

> Post hominem vermis; post vermem fœtor et horror;
> Sic, in non hominem, vertitur omnis homo.

> Cur carnem tuam adornas et impinguas, quam, post paucos dies, vermes devoraturi sunt in sepulchro, animam, vero, tuam non adornas,—quæ Deo et Angelis ejus præsentenda est in cœlis!

Saint Bernard: *Meditations*
The Bollandists: *Preparation for the Last Judgement* [2]

O ne winter evening when a few of us writers were drinking tea around a good fire, at the house of a friend of ours, Baron Xavier de la V—— (a pale young man whom prolonged military toils, endured at an early age in Africa, had made physically weak and unusually unsociable), the conversation turned to an extremely gloomy subject: the *nature* of those extraordinary, amazing, mysterious coincidences which occur in some people's lives.

"Here is a story," he said to us, "which I won't burden with any commentary. It is a true story. You may find it impressive."

We lit our cigarettes and listened to the following tale:

"In 1876, at the autumn solstice,[3] about that time when the ever-increasing number of burials performed without due consideration—in too much of a hurry, in fact—was beginning to upset

the Parisian middle classes and plunge them into alarm, at eight
o'clock one evening, coming away from an extremely curious
spiritualist seance, I felt, as I reached home, under the influence
of that hereditary spleen whose black obsession frustrates and re-
duces to naught the efforts of the medical Faculty.

"It is in vain that, at the instigation of the doctors, I have intoxicated myself with Avicenna's beverage;[4] that I have assimilated
hundredweights of iron in accordance with all sorts of formulas;
and that, like a latter-day Robert d'Arbrissel, I have reduced the
quicksilver of my burning passions to the temperature of the Samoyeds,[5] nothing has proved of any avail. I have to resign myself
to the fact that I am a morose, taciturn creature. But beneath a
nervous exterior, I must have what they call an iron constitution,
to be still capable, after so much medical attention, of gazing at
the stars.

"That evening, then, once I was in my bedroom, lighting a
cigar from the candles around the looking glass, I noticed that I
was deathly pale, and I slumped into a roomy armchair, an old
piece of furniture upholstered in garnet-red velvet, in which the
flight of the hours, during my long reveries, strikes me as less te-
dious than usual. My depression was becoming so severe that I felt
ill, even desperate. So, deeming it impossible to shake off this
gloom by means of any kind of social distraction—especially in
the midst of the horrible cares of the capital—I decided, as an
experiment, to leave Paris, to go and take a nature cure far away,
and to indulge in some violent exercise, a few healthy shooting
parties for instance, in order to introduce a little variety into
my life.

"This idea had scarcely occurred to me when, *at the very moment* that I decided on this course of action, the name of an old
friend, forgotten years before, the abbé Maucombe, entered my
mind.

"'The abbé Maucombe!' I said under my breath.

"My last meeting with the learned priest dated back to the
time of his departure for a long pilgrimage to Palestine. The news
of his return had reached me since. He lived in the humble presbytery of a little village in Lower Brittany.

"Maucombe was bound to have some sort of bedroom or attic
available there. No doubt, in the course of his travels, he had collected a few old books and some curiosities from the Lebanon.

And the odds were that the ponds close to the nearby manor houses harbored some wild duck. What could be more convenient? And if, before the cold weather set in, I wanted to enjoy the latter fortnight of the enchanted month of October among the red rocks, if I wished to see once again the splendor of the long autumn evenings over the wooded heights, I would have to make haste.

"The clock struck nine.

"I stood up; I shook off the ash of my cigar. Then, as a man of decision, I put on my hat, my greatcoat, and my gloves; I took my suitcase and my gun; I blew out the candles and I went out, carefully turning the key three times in the secret lock which is the pride of my door.

"Three quarters of an hour later, the Brittany train was carrying me toward the little village of Saint-Maur which was in the abbé Maucombe's spiritual care; I had even found time, at the station, to send off a hurried note in pencil in which I informed my father of my departure.

"The next morning I was at R——, which is only about five miles from Saint-Maur.

"Wanting to have a good night's sleep—in order to be able to go out shooting at dawn the following day—and deciding that a nap after lunch might well impair the perfection of that sleep, I devoted my day, so as to stay awake in spite of my fatigue, to several calls on old school friends. About five o'clock in the afternoon, having carried out these duties, I had a horse saddled at the Golden Sun, where I had taken a room, and, in the light of the setting sun, I found myself in sight of a hamlet.

"On the way I had recalled to mind the priest at whose house I hoped to spend a few days. The time which had elapsed since our last meeting, visits to parishioners, intervening events, and the habits of solitude must have modified his character and personality. I was going to find him gray-haired. But I was familiar with the learned priest's fortifying conversation, and I was looking forward to the evenings we were going to spend together.

"'The abbé Maucombe!' I kept saying to myself. 'What a splendid idea!'

"Asking the old people who were grazing cattle alongside the ditches the way to his house, I discovered that the priest—as a worthy representative of a God of mercy—had acquired the sincere affection of his flock; and, after being told how to reach the presbytery, which is some distance from the huddle of cottages and hovels which constitute the village of Saint-Maur, I set off in that direction.

"I arrived.

"The rustic appearance of the house, the windows with their green blinds, the three sandstone steps, the ivy, the clematis, the tea roses clambering up the walls as far as the roof, where a little cloud of smoke was rising from a revolving chimney cowl, filled one with ideas of meditation, health, and profound peace. The trees of a nearby orchard showed, through a trellis fence, their leaves rusted by the enervating season. The two windows of the single upper storey shone with the fires of the setting sun; a niche containing the statue of a saint had been hollowed out between them. I dismounted silently, tied the horse to the shutter, and raised the door knocker, casting a traveler's glance at the horizon far behind me.

"But the horizon was shining so brightly above the forests of far-off oaks and wild pines where the last birds were flying away into the evening; the waters of a reed-covered pond in the distance were reflecting the sky so solemnly; and Nature was so beautiful, in the midst of that calm air, in that deserted countryside, at that moment when silence falls, that, without letting go of the knocker, I stood there wordless.

"You, I thought to myself, who lack the refuge of your dreams, and for whom the land of Canaan, with its palm trees and its living waters, does not appear in the dawn after you have walked so far beneath the hard stars; traveler so joyful when you set off and now so gloomy; heart made for other exiles than those whose bitterness you now share with evil brethren—behold! Here you can sit on the stone of melancholy! Here dead dreams revive, anticipating the moment of the grave! If you wish to feel a real longing for death, approach: here the sight of the sky thrills to the point of forgetfulness.

"I was in that state of lassitude in which the sensitized nerves vibrate at the slightest excitement. A leaf fell near me; its furtive rustle made me start. And the magical horizon of that region entered into my eyes. I sat by myself in front of the door.

"A few moments later, as the evening air was beginning to turn cool, I returned to an awareness of reality. I jumped to my feet and took hold of the door knocker again, looking at the cheerful house.

"But I had scarcely given it a casual glance when I was forced to stop once more, asking myself this time if I was not the victim of a hallucination.

"Was this really the house I had just seen? What antiquity was revealed to me *now* by the long cracks between the pale leaves? This building had an unfamiliar look; the windowpanes lit up by the dying rays of the evening were burning with a fierce glow; the hospitable door seemed to be welcoming me, with its three steps; but, fixing my attention on those gray flagstones, I saw that they had just been polished and that the trace of carved lettering remained on them; and I realized that they came from the nearby graveyard, whose black crosses now appeared to be very close, a hundred yards away. The house now struck me as having been invested with some bloodchilling quality, and the dismal sound of the knocker, which I dropped in my agitation, echoed through the house like the vibrations of a mourning-bell.

"That sort of *vision*, being spiritual rather than physical, fades rapidly. I did not doubt for a moment that I was a prey to that intellectual depression which I have mentioned. Eager to see a face which would help me, by its human nature, to banish the recollection of it, I lifted the latch, without waiting any longer. I went in.

"The door, moved by a clock weight, closed by itself behind me.

"I found myself in a long corridor at the end of which Nanon, the cheerful old housekeeper, was coming down the stairs, holding a candle in one hand.

"'Monsieur Xavier!' she exclaimed delightedly when she recognized me.

"'Good evening, Nanon, dear!' I replied, hurriedly handing her my suitcase and my gun. (I had left my greatcoat behind at the Golden Sun.)

"I went upstairs. A minute later I clasped my old friend in my arms.

"The tender emotion of our first words and the feeling of the melancholy of the past overwhelmed us, the abbé and myself, for a little while. Then Nanon came in to bring us the lamp and tell us that supper was ready.

"'My dear Maucombe,' I said to him, tucking my arm into his to go downstairs, 'intellectual friendship is something eternal, and I see that we are both of this opinion.'

"'There are Christian minds which enjoy a close divine relationship,' he replied. 'Yes. The world has less "rational" beliefs for which their supporters sacrifice their blood, their happiness, their duty. They are fanatics!' he concluded with a smile. 'Let us choose, for our faith, the most useful, since we are free and we become what we believe.'

"'The fact is,' I answered, 'that it is already extremely mysterious that two and two should make four.'

"We went into the dining room. During the meal, the abbé, after gently scolding me for leaving him without news of me for so long, acquainted me with the spirit of the village.

"He spoke to me about the district, and told me two or three anecdotes concerning the local gentry.

"He recounted his own shooting exploits and fishing triumphs; in short, he displayed the most delightful gaiety and affability.

"Nanon, a fleet-footed messenger, bustled around us, her huge coif flapping like a pair of wings.

"Seeing me roll a cigarette to smoke with my coffee, Maucombe, who was a former officer of the dragoons, followed my example; the silence of our first puffs interrupted our train of thought, and I began to look closely at my host.

"This priest was a tall man of about forty-five. Long gray hair framed within its curls his thin, strong face. His eyes shone with mystical intelligence. His features were regular and austere; his slim figure had resisted the pressure of the years: he wore his long cassock with an air. His words, full of knowledge and gentleness, were uttered in a sonorous voice which came from excellent lungs. Altogether he struck me as being in the best of health: the years had had little effect on him.

"He took me into his little library-cum-drawing-room.

"Lack of sleep on a journey makes one susceptible to the cold; there was a chill in the air, foreshadowing the winter. Consequently, when an armful of twigs blazed up before my knees, between two or three logs, I felt better.

"Ensconced in our brown leather armchairs, with our feet on the firedogs, we naturally started talking about God.

"I was tired: I listened without replying.

"'To sum up,' Maucombe said to me, standing up, 'we are here to show—by our works, our thoughts, our words, and our fight against Nature—*whether we carry the necessary weight.*'

"And he concluded with a quotation from Joseph de Maistre:[6] 'Between Man and God there is nothing but Pride.'

"'All the same,' I said to him, 'we, the spoilt children of Nature, have the honor of living in an age of light.'

"'Let us choose rather the Light of the ages,' he replied with a smile.

"We had reached the landing, with our candles in our hands.

"A long corridor, parallel to the one downstairs, separated my host's bedroom from the one which had been prepared for me, and which he insisted on showing me himself. We went into it; he looked around to see if I was short of anything, and as we shook hands and wished each other good night, a bright gleam from my candle lit up his face. This time I gave a start!

"Was it a dying man standing there beside that bed? The face before me was not, could not be, the same that I had seen over supper! Or at least, if I vaguely recognized it, it seemed to me that I had not really seen it until that moment. A single reflection will explain what I mean: the abbé gave me, humanly speaking, the *second* feeling which, by some mysterious affinity, his house had caused me to experience.

"The face at which I was gazing was solemn and deathly pale, and the eyelids were lowered. Had he forgotten that I was there? Was he praying? Why was he standing like that? His whole person had acquired such a sudden gravity that I closed my eyes. When I opened them again a second later, the good abbé was still there—but now I recognized him. It was all right! His friendly smile dispelled all my anxiety. The impression had not lasted long enough to allow me to ask a question. It had been a shock, a sort of hallucination.

"Maucombe wished me good night a second time and retired.

"'What I need is a good night's sleep!' I said to myself, once I was on my own.

"Straightaway the thought of Death occurred to me; I lifted up my soul to God and I got into bed.

"One of the odd things about extreme fatigue is that it makes

it impossible to go straight to sleep. All sportsmen have had this
experience. It is a matter of common knowledge.

"I expected to fall quickly into a deep sleep. I had built great
hopes on a good night. But after ten minutes I had to admit that
this nervous agitation showed no signs of abating. I heard ticking
sounds and sharp creaks in the woodwork and the walls: presumably death-watch beetles. Each of the almost imperceptible noises
of the night was followed by a sort of electric shock passing
through the whole of my body.

"The black branches brushed together in the wind, outside in
the garden. Every few moments ivy rustled against my window.
My hearing had become as keen as that of people dying from
hunger.

"'I had two cups of coffee,' I thought. 'It must be that!'

"And propping myself up on one elbow on the pillow, I
started staring at the light of the candle on the table beside me. I
gazed hard at it, between my lashes, with that fixed attention
which the complete absence of thought gives to the eyes.

"A little holy-water stoup in colored porcelain, with its twig
of box, hung by the head of my bed. I suddenly moistened my
eyelids with some of the water, to refresh them; then I blew out
the candle and shut my eyes. Sleep approached; the fever abated.

"I was about to fall asleep.

"Three sharp, imperious little knocks were given at my door.

"'What's that?' I said to myself, sitting up with a start.

"Then I noticed that I had already dozed off. I did not know
where I was. I thought I was in Paris. Certain forms of rest produce this sort of ridiculous forgetfulness. Having even lost from
sight, almost immediately, the principal cause of my awakening,
I stretched myself luxuriously, completely oblivious of the
situation.

"'By the way,' I said to myself all of a sudden, 'wasn't somebody knocking just then? Who could possibly be . . . ?'

"At this point in my sentence, a vague, confused notion that I
was no longer in Paris but in a Breton presbytery, the abbé Maucombe's house, entered my mind.

"In a flash I was in the middle of the room.

"My first impression, combined with the feeling that my feet
were cold, was of a bright light. The full moon was shining oppo-

site the window, above the church, and, through the white curtains, was casting its pale, cold flame onto the floor.

"It was about midnight.

"Morbid ideas occurred to me. What was happening? The darkness had an extraordinary quality.

"As I was approaching the door, a patch of light, coming from the keyhole, started moving over my hand and my sleeve.

"There was somebody outside the door: there really had been someone knocking.

"Yet, a few feet away from the latch, I stopped short.

"Something had struck me as surprising: the *nature* of the spot wandering over my hand. It was an icy, blood-red glow, giving off no light. Moreover, how was it that I could see no line of light under the door, from the corridor outside? To tell the truth, what was coming through the keyhole gave me the impression of the phosphorescent gaze of an owl.

"At that moment the church clock struck the hour, outside in the windy night.

"'Who's there?' I asked in a low voice.

"The light went out. I was about to move forward when . . .

"The door swung wide open, slowly, silently.

"In front of me, in the corridor, stood a tall, dark figure: a priest, wearing the three-cornered clerical hat. He was clearly visible in the moonlight, except for his face: all I could see of that was the fire in his two eyes, which were gazing at me with solemn intentness.

"An otherworldly atmosphere surrounded this visitor; his attitude filled me with foreboding. Paralyzed by a fear which instantly assumed the proportions of terror, I looked at the sinister figure in silence.

"All of a sudden the priest slowly raised one arm toward me. He was showing me something vague and heavy. It was a cloak. A big black cloak, a traveling cloak. He was holding it out to me, as if he wanted me to take it!

"I shut my eyes so as not to see it. I did not want to see it. But a bird of night, with a horrible cry, passed between us, and the wind of its wings, brushing against my eyes, made me open them again. I could tell that it was fluttering round the room.

"Then—with a choking gasp of fear, for I could not summon up the strength to cry out—I slammed the door shut with my two clenched, outstretched hands, and frantically turned the key in the lock, my hair standing on end.

"Strangely enough, it seemed to me that all this happened without any noise.

"It was more than my constitution could stand. I awoke. I was sitting up in bed, my arms stretched out in front of me; I was icy cold; my forehead was bathed in sweat; my heart was pounding grimly against the walls of my chest.

"'Ah!' I said to myself. 'What a horrible dream!'

"All the same, my insurmountable anxiety remained. It took me over a minute before I *dared* to move my arm to reach for the matches: I was afraid of feeling a cold hand seize mine in the darkness and give it a friendly squeeze.

"I started as I heard the sound of the matches rolling about under my fingers in the candleholder. I lit the candle again.

"I promptly felt much better: light, that divine vibration, brings variety to dismal surroundings and comforts the worst fears.

"I decided to drink a glass of cold water to revive my spirits completely, and I got out of bed.

"Passing in front of the window, I noticed that the moon was exactly like the moon in my dream, although I had not seen it before going to bed; and, going with my candle in my hand to examine the lock of the door, I found that the key had been turned *from inside,* something which I had definitely not done before falling asleep.

"After making these discoveries I glanced around me. I began to think that the whole affair was very strange. I went back to bed, propped myself up on my elbow, and tried to reason with myself, to prove to myself that all this was just a fit of lucid somnambulism; but I succeeded less and less in reassuring myself. However, fatigue swept over me like a wave, soothed my gloomy thoughts, and suddenly sent me to sleep in my fear.

"When I awoke, the room was full of cheerful sunshine.

"It was a beautiful morning. My watch, which I had hung on the head of my bed, told me that it was ten o'clock. To revive one's spirits, what can compare with daylight and radiant sunshine? Especially when there is a sweet smell in the air, and a fresh breeze blowing through the trees, the spiky thickets, and the flower-covered ditches wet with the dawn!

"I dressed hurriedly, utterly oblivious of the sinister start to my night's sleep.

"Completely revived by repeated ablutions of cold water, I went downstairs.

"The abbé Maucombe was in the dining room, sitting at the breakfast table, reading a newspaper while waiting for me.

"We shook hands.

"'Did you have a good night, my dear Xavier?' he asked me.

"'Splendid!' I replied absentmindedly (out of force of habit and without paying the slightest attention to what I was saying).

"The fact is that I was hungry: that was all.

"Nanon intervened, bringing us our breakfast.

"During the meal our conversation was at once quiet and gay; only the man who lives a holy life knows what joy is and how to communicate it.

"All of a sudden I remembered my dream.

"'By the way, my dear abbé,' I exclaimed, 'I remember now that I had a peculiar dream last night, a dream which was—how shall I put it?—striking? astounding? terrifying? Take your choice! Judge for yourself.'

"And while peeling an apple, I started to give him a detailed account of the grim hallucination which had disturbed my first sleep.

"Just as I came to the *gesture* of the priest offering me his cloak, and *before I had embarked on that sentence*, the door of the dining room opened. Nanon, with that familiarity peculiar to the house-keepers of parish priests, came in, in a ray of sunshine, right in the middle of our conversation, and, interrupting me, handed me a sheet of paper.

"'Here's a letter marked "urgent" that the postman has just brought, this very moment, for Monsieur.'

"'A letter! Already?' I exclaimed, *forgetting my story*. 'It's from my father. My dear abbé, you won't mind if I read it now, will you?'

"'Of course not!' said the abbé Maucombe, likewise losing sight of the story and becoming infected with my interest in the letter. 'Of course not!'

"I unsealed the letter.

"In this way Nanon's arrival had distracted our attention by its suddenness.

"'My good host,' I said, 'this is extremely vexatious: I have scarcely arrived, and I find myself obliged to leave.'

"'But why?' asked the abbé Maucombe, putting his cup down without drinking.

"'This letter asks me to return with all haste, in connection with a lawsuit of the greatest importance. I was expecting that it would not be heard until December; but now I am told that it is due to come up within the next fortnight, and as I am the only person able to put in order the last documents we need to win our case, I must go back! What a nuisance!'

"'That really is annoying!' said the abbé. 'Most annoying! . . . At least promise me that as soon as it is over . . . The great thing is salvation: I was hoping to be able to do something to achieve yours—and here you are slipping out of my grasp! I was already convinced that God had sent you to me. . . .'

"'My dear abbé,' I exclaimed, 'I shall leave my gun with you. Before three weeks are out, I shall be back, and this time for a few weeks, if you wish.'

"'Then go in peace,' said the abbé Maucombe.

"'You see, nearly the whole of my fortune is at stake,' I murmured.

"'A man's fortune is God!' Maucombe said simply.

"'And tomorrow, how should I live if . . .'

"'Tomorrow, one stops living,' he replied.

"Soon we left the table, finding some consolation for our parting in this formal promise to return.

"We went for a stroll in the orchard and looked round the dependencies of the presbytery.

"All day long the abbé showed me, not without a certain pride, his poor rustic treasures. Then, while he read his breviary, I walked round the neighborhood alone, delightedly breathing in the pure, refreshing air. On his return Maucombe talked for a while about his travels in the Holy Land; all this brought us to sunset.

"Evening came. After a frugal supper, I said to the abbé Maucombe:

"'The *express* coach leaves at nine o'clock sharp. From here to R—— will take me about an hour and a half. I need half an hour to pay my bill at the inn when I return the horse: a total of two hours. It is seven o'clock now: I must leave you straightaway.'

"'I will come part of the way with you,' said the priest. 'The walk will *do me good*.'

"'By the way,' I went on, preoccupied with my own thoughts, 'here is my father's address, where I stay in Paris, in case you need to write to me.'

"Nanon took the card and slipped it into the frame of the mirror.

"Three minutes later, the abbé and I had left the presbytery and were making our way along the highroad. I was naturally holding my horse by the bridle.

"We had already become a couple of shadows.

"Five minutes after our departure a penetrating drizzle of thin, icy rain, driven by a horrible gust of wind, started lashing our hands and faces.

"I stopped short.

"'My dear old friend,' I said to the abbé, 'I really cannot allow this. Your life is precious and this icy shower is anything but healthy. Go back home. Once again, this rain could give you a dangerous soaking. Do go back, I beg you.'

"After a moment's thought, the abbé, thinking of his faithful, gave in to my reasons.

"'I have your promise, my dear friend, haven't I?' he said. And, as I held out my hand to him, he added:

"'Just a moment! You have quite a way to go, and this drizzle, as you say, is penetrating.'

"He gave a shudder. We were close to one another, motionless, looking hard at each other like two travelers in a hurry.

"At that moment the moon rose over the firs, behind the hills, lighting up the moors and the woods on the horizon. It bathed us in its dismal, livid light, its pale, empty flame. Our shadows and that of the horse were silhouetted hugely on the roadway. And in the direction of the dilapidated old stone crosses which, in that Breton village, stand in the thickets in which perch the birds of evil omen from Dead Men's Wood, I heard, in the distance, a horrible *cry*, the shrill, terrifying falsetto of the rookery. A screech owl with phosphorescent eyes, the glow of which was flickering above the great arm of the holly-oak, took flight and passed between us, prolonging that cry.

"'Come now!' the abbé Maucombe went on. 'I shall be home in a minute, so take . . . *take this cloak!* I insist!' he added in an unforgettable voice. 'I insist! You can send it back to me by the waiter at the inn, who comes to the village every day. . . . *I beg you to take it.*'

"Uttering these words the abbé held out his black cloak to me. I could not see his face, on account of the shadow cast by his broad three-cornered hat; but I could see his eyes *which were gazing at me with solemn intentness.*

"He threw the cloak around my shoulders and fastened the clasp with affectionate concern, while I, drained of strength, closed my eyes. And taking advantage of my silence, he hurried off toward his presbytery. At the bend in the road he disappeared from sight.

"Out of presence of mind—and also partly without thinking—I vaulted onto my horse. Then I sat motionless.

"Now I was alone on the highroad. I could hear the countless noises of the countryside. Opening my eyes, I could see the desolate spectacle of the huge, pale sky, across which dull clouds were scurrying, hiding the moon. In the meantime I sat still and erect, although I must have been as white as a sheet.

"'Come now,' I said to myself, 'take it easy. I have a touch of fever and I walk in my sleep. That's all.'

"I tried to shrug my shoulders: a mysterious weight prevented me.

"And then, coming from the far horizon, from the depths of the woods, a flock of ospreys passed over my head with a great noise of wings, crying horribly mysterious syllables. They went and settled on the roof of the presbytery and the steeple in the distance; and the wind carried mournful cries to my ears. Upon my word, I felt frightened. Why? Who will ever be able to tell me? I have seen action; I have crossed swords several times; my nerves are steadier than most; and yet I maintain, very humbly, that I was frightened here—and in earnest. I even felt a certain intellectual esteem for myself. Not everybody can be frightened of these things.

"I therefore silently pressed my spurs into the poor horse's sides, and, my eyes shut, the reins hanging loose, my fingers clutching the mane, and the cloak floating behind me, I could feel that my horse was galloping as fast as it could; every now and then my quiet muttering in its ear must have imparted to it, instinctively, the superstitious horror with which I was trembling in spite of myself. The result was that we arrived in less than half an hour. The noise of the paving stones in the suburbs made me raise my head—and give a sigh of relief.

"At last! I could see houses, lighted shops, the faces of fellow human beings behind the windowpanes! I could see passersby! I had left the realm of nightmares!

"At the inn, I settled down in front of the blazing fire. The conversation of the carriers put me in a condition not far removed from ecstasy. I had left Death behind. I looked at the flame between my fingers. I drank a glass of rum. I finally regained control of my faculties.

"I felt that I had returned to real life.

"I was even—I must admit it—a little ashamed of my panic.

"And how calm I felt when I carried out the abbé Maucombe's commission! What a supercilious smile I gave as I examined the black cloak when I handed it over to the innkeeper! The hallucination had dissipated. I would willingly have played, in Rabelais's words, 'the boon companion.'

"The cloak in question struck me as having nothing extraordinary or even special about it—apart from the fact that it was very old and even patched, darned, and mended with a sort of strange tenderness. No doubt a profound sense of charity led the abbé Maucombe to give away as alms the price of a new cloak: at least that was how I explained it.

"'You couldn't have picked a better time,' said the innkeeper. 'The waiter's due to go to the village about now. He'll be off any minute. He'll take the cloak back to Monsieur Maucombe on the way, before ten o'clock.'

"An hour later, in my compartment, with my feet on the footwarmer, wrapped in the greatcoat of which I had regained possession, I said to myself, lighting a good cigar and listening to the whistle of the train:

"'There's no doubt about it, I prefer that noise to the hooting of the owls.'

"I must admit that I rather regretted having promised to return.

"At that point I fell at long last into a deep sleep, completely forgetting what I would henceforth dismiss as an insignificant coincidence.

"I had to stay at Chartres for six days, to collect some documents which later on brought about a favorable conclusion to our lawsuit.

"Finally, with my mind full of ideas of papers and pettifoggery, and in the grip of my sickly boredom, I returned to Paris on the evening of the seventh day after my departure from the presbytery.

"I went straight home, arriving on the stroke of nine o'clock. I went upstairs and found my father in the drawing room. He was sitting next to a little table, in the light of a lamp, and he was holding an open letter in his hand.

"After a few words he said to me:

"'I'm sure you don't know the news this letter brings me: our dear old friend the abbé Maucombe has died since you left him.'

"These words gave me a profound shock.

"'Yes, he died the day before yesterday, about midnight—three days after you left his presbytery—from a chill caught on the highroad. This letter is from old Nanon. The poor woman seems to be so distracted that she repeats twice over an odd phrase . . . about a cloak. . . . But read it for yourself!'

"He held out to me the letter in which the saintly priest's death was announced to us—and in which I read these simple lines:

"'He was very happy—so he told us in his last words—to draw his last breath and be buried in the cloak which he had brought back from his pilgrimage to the Holy Land, *and which had touched The Sepulchre.*'"

1867 — 1868

Translated by Robert Baldick

Villiers de l'Isle-Adam

VÉRA

For Madame la Comtesse d'Osmoy [1]

The form of the body is more *essential* to it than its substance.
Modern Physiology [2]

L ove is stronger than Death,[3] said Solomon; and it is true that
its mysterious power knows no limits.

It was dusk one autumn evening, some years ago, in Paris. A
few carriages, with their lamps already lit, were rolling along toward the darkened Faubourg Saint-Germain, returning from the
Bois de Boulogne later than the rest. One of them stopped in front
of the entrance to a huge mansion surrounded by age-old gardens;
the stone shield over the archway bore the arms of the ancient
family of the Comtes d'Athol, namely, *a silver star on a blue ground*,
with the motto *Pallida Victrix*,[4] under the ermine-lined coronet of a
prince. The heavy doors swung open. A man of thirty-five,
dressed in mourning, with a deathly pale face, got out of the carriage. On the staircase silent servants raised torches into the air.
Without seeing them, he climbed the steps and went into the
house. It was the Comte d'Athol.

Reeling slightly, he climbed the white stairs leading to the
bedroom where, that very morning, in a velvet coffin, covered in
violets and wrapped in folds of batiste, he had laid his pale wife,
his lady of joy, Véra, his despair.

Upstairs, the door opened softly over the carpet; he drew the
curtain aside.

Everything was where the countess had left it the previous
evening. Death had struck swiftly. The night before, his beloved
had fainted away in such profound joys, had abandoned herself in
such exquisite embraces, that her heart, bursting with delight, had

274

failed her: her lips had suddenly become moist with a mortal crimson. She had scarcely had time to give her husband a farewell kiss, smiling wordlessly; then her long lashes had fallen like mourning veils over the splendid darkness of her eyes.

The indescribable day had passed.

About noon, after the horrible ceremony in the family vault, the Comte d'Athol had dismissed his black-clad escort at the cemetery. Then, shutting himself up alone with the dead woman, between the four marble walls, he had pulled-to the iron door of the mausoleum. Incense was burning on a tripod before the coffin: a bright crown of lamps shone around the young woman's head.

He had stood there all day, dreaming, conscious of nothing but a tenderness bereft of hope. At six o'clock, as dusk was falling, he had left the sacred spot. After closing the vault, he had pulled the silver key out of the lock, and, standing on tiptoe on the topmost step of the threshold, he had gently tossed it into the tomb. He had thrown it through the trefoil over the door, onto the flagstones inside. Why had he done this? Undoubtedly in response to some mysterious resolution never to return.

And now he stood once more in her death chamber.

The window, draped with huge curtains of purple cashmere brocaded in gold, was open: the last ray of the evening sun lit up, in its frame of old wood, the large portrait of the departed. The count looked around him at the dress thrown onto an armchair the evening before; and at the jewels on the mantelpiece, the pearl necklace, the half-open fan, the heavy bottles of perfumes which *She* would never breathe again. On the unmade ebony bed with the twisted columns, beside the pillow on which the impression of her divine, beloved head was still visible in the midst of the lace, he caught sight of the bloodstained handkerchief in which her young soul had flown on one wing for a moment; the open piano, holding a piece of music which would never be finished now; the Indian flowers which she had picked in the conservatory and which were withering in old Dresden vases; and, at the foot of the bed, on a black fur, the little Oriental velvet slippers, on which there gleamed a whimsical motto of Véra's, embroidered in pearls: *Qui verra Véra l'aimera.*[5] His beloved's bare feet had played in them the morning before, kissed at every step by the swansdown lining. And over there, in the shadows, stood the clock, whose spring he had broken so that it should strike no more hours.

So she had gone. . . . But *where?* . . . And why should he go on living ? . . . It was impossible, absurd.

And the count gave himself up to his thoughts.

He looked back over the whole of his past life. Six months had elapsed since his marriage. Had it not been abroad, at an embassy ball, that he had seen her for the first time? . . . Yes. That moment was resuscitated very clearly before his eyes. She appeared before him, a radiant vision. That evening their eyes had met, and they had realized, deep in their hearts, that they were of similar natures and destined to love each other for ever.

The discouraging remarks, the watchful smiles, the insinuations—all the obstacles which the world raises to delay the inevitable happiness of those who belong to one another—had vanished in the face of the tranquil confidence in each other which they felt at that very moment.

Véra, weary of the insipid formalities of her circle, had come to see him at the first difficulty which had arisen, thus simplifying in august fashion the commonplace exchanges in which the precious substance of time is wasted.

At their first words the futile comments of other people on their score struck them as a flight of night birds disappearing into the darkness. What a smile they exchanged! What an indescribable embrace!

Yet the fact was that their natures were most extraordinary. They were two creatures endowed with wonderful senses, but of a wholly earthly character. Feelings were prolonged in them with an alarming intensity. They forgot themselves in the joy of sensation. On the other hand certain ideas, such as those of the soul, of Infinity, of *God Himself,* were so to speak hidden from their understanding. The faith of a great number of human beings in things supernatural was simply a source of vague astonishment to them, a closed book to which they paid no attention, not being qualified either to condemn or justify. Consequently, recognizing that the world was foreign to them, they had isolated themselves, as soon as they were married, in this dark old mansion, whose thickly planted gardens deadened the sounds from outside.

Here the two lovers plunged into the ocean of those languid

and perverse pleasures in which the spirit mingles with the mysteries of the flesh. They exhausted the violence of desire, the thrill of tender passion. They became the beat of one another's heart. Their minds penetrated their bodies so perfectly that their forms assumed an intellectual character, and their kisses, the meshes of a burning chainmail, bound them together in an ideal fusion, a prolonged ecstasy. But all of a sudden the charm was broken; the terrible accident parted them; their arms untwined. What shadow had taken his dead love from him? Dead? He could not believe that. Did the soul of a cello disappear in the cry of a broken string?

The hours passed.

Through the window he looked at the darkness spreading across the heavens; and Night took on a *personality* in his eyes. He saw her as a queen walking sadly in exile, and the diamond clip of her mourning tunic, Venus, shone all alone above the trees, lost in the depths of the sky.

"It is Véra," he thought.

At this name, spoken in an undertone, he started like a man awakening; then, standing up, he looked around him.

The objects in the room were now lit by a hitherto indistinct glow, that of a night light which was tinting the darkness blue, and to which the night sky gave the appearance of another star. It was the incense-scented flame of an iconostasis, a family heirloom of Véra's. The triptych, made of precious old wood, was hanging by its Russian esparto between the mirror and the picture. A quivering gleam of light from the gold inside fell on the necklace, among the jewels on the mantelpiece.

The halo of the Madonna, clad in sky-blue garments, shone brightly, tinged with pink by the Byzantine cross whose delicate red outlines, melting in the glow, streaked the gleaming orient of the pearls with blood. Ever since childhood Véra had gazed pityingly with her great eyes at the pure, motherly face of the hereditary Madonna, and, since by her nature she could give her only a *superstitious* love, she offered her that sometimes, when she passed, innocent and thoughtful, in front of the night light.

The count, moved to the depths of his soul at this sight by painful memories, stood up, hurriedly blew out the holy light, and, groping in the darkness for a bell rope, gave it a tug.

A servant appeared: an old man dressed in black. He was holding a lamp which he put down in front of the countess's portrait. When he turned round, it was with a shudder of superstitious terror that he saw his master standing smiling as if nothing had happened.

"Raymond," the count said calmly, "*the countess and I are tired out this evening; you will serve supper about ten o'clock.* . . . Incidentally, we have decided to isolate ourselves even more here, as from tomorrow. None of my servants, except yourself, is to pass the night in the house. You will give each of them three years' wages and tell them to leave. Then you will bar the door and light the candelabra downstairs, in the dining room. You will be able to look after us by yourself. We shall do no entertaining in the future."

The old man trembled and looked at him attentively.

The count lit a cigar and went down to the gardens.

The servant thought at first that his master's grief, too keen and overwhelming for him to bear, had unhinged his mind. He had known him since childhood, and realized at once that the shock of too sudden an awakening could be fatal to this sleep-walker. His first duty was to keep the secret entrusted to him.

He bowed his head. Was he to give his loyal support to this pious dream . . . to obey . . . to go on serving *them* without taking Death into account? What a strange idea! Would it last a single night? . . . Tomorrow, tomorrow, alas! . . . Oh, who could tell? . . . Perhaps! . . . After all, it was a sacred undertaking. And by what right was he reflecting on it?

He left the bedroom and carried out his orders to the letter; that very evening, the strange existence began.

It was a question of creating an awe-inspiring mirage.

The awkwardness of the first few days quickly disappeared. Raymond, first of all in a daze, then out of a sort of tender deference, made such an effort to be natural that before three weeks had passed he occasionally felt almost taken in himself by his goodwill. His mental reservations disappeared. Now and then, feeling a kind of giddiness, he had to remind himself that the countess was definitely dead. He was caught up in this funereal game and kept forgetting the reality. Soon he needed more than a moment's thought to convince himself and take hold of himself.

He saw that he would end up by abandoning himself entirely to the terrifying magnetism with which the count was gradually imbuing the atmosphere around them; and he was filled with fear, a vague, sweet fear.

D'Athol was in fact living in complete oblivion of his beloved's death. He could not help but feel that she was perpetually present, the young woman's body was so closely linked to his. Sometimes, on sunny days, on a bench in the garden, he would read aloud the poems she loved; sometimes, in the evening, by the fireside, with the two cups of tea on a little table, he would chat with the smiling *Illusion* whom he could see sitting in the other armchair.

The days, the nights, the weeks flew by. Neither of the two men realized what they were doing. And strange phenomena now started occurring in which it became difficult to distinguish the point at which real and imaginary coincided. A presence was floating in the air; a form was trying to break through, to weave itself on what had become an indefinable space.

D'Athol was living two lives, like a visionary. A pale, gentle face, glimpsed like a flash of lightning between two flickers of an eyelid; a faint chord suddenly struck on the piano; a kiss which closed his lips just as he was about to speak; *feminine* affinities of thought which awoke in him in response to what he said; a division of himself so profound that he could smell, as in a fluid mist, the sweet, heady scent of his beloved beside him; and, at night, between wakefulness and sleep, the sound of whispered words; all these were signs of a negation of Death, raised to a power never known before.

Once D'Athol felt her and saw her so clearly beside him that he took her in his arms; but this movement dispelled her.

"Child!" he murmured with a smile.

And he went back to sleep like a lover playfully rebuffed by his sleepy mistress.

On *her* birthday, by way of a joke, he placed an immortelle in the bouquet which he tossed on to Véra's pillow.

"Seeing that she thinks she is dead," he said.

Thanks to the profound and omnipotent determination of Monsieur d'Athol, who, by the sheer power of his love, created the life and presence of his wife in the house, this existence ended up by taking on a sombre, persuasive charm. Raymond himself no longer felt any fear, having gradually become accustomed to these impressions.

A black velvet dress glimpsed round the bend of a path; a laughing voice calling to him from the drawing room; a ring on the bell when he awoke, as in the old days; all this had become familiar to him. It was as if the dead woman were playing at being invisible, like a child. She felt so deeply loved that it was perfectly *natural.*

A year had passed.

On the evening of the Anniversary the count, sitting by the fire in Véra's room, had just finished reading her a Florentine fable: *Callimaco.* He closed the book, and then, pouring himself some tea, he said:

"*Douschka*, do you remember Rose Valley, the banks of the Lahn, the castle of the Four Towers ? . . . That story reminded you of them, didn't it?"

He stood up, and saw in the bluish mirror that he was looking paler than usual. He took a pearl bracelet out of a bowl and examined it closely. Had not Véra removed it from her arm just now, before undressing? The pearls were still warm and their orient softened, as if by the warmth of her flesh. And what of the opal in that Siberian necklace, which, like the pearls, loved Véra's beautiful breasts so much that it turned sickly pale in its gold trellis-work when the young woman forgot it for a little while? In the old days the countess used to love the faithful stone because of that. . . . This evening the opal was shining as if it had just been taken off, and as if it were still imbued with the dead woman's exquisite magnetism. Putting down the necklace and the precious stone, the count accidentally touched the batiste handkerchief on which the drops of blood were as wet and red as carnations on snow. . . . There, on the piano, who had turned the last page of the music she had been playing? And the holy light must have re-kindled in the reliquary, for its golden flame was casting a mystic glow over the Madonna's face and closed eyes! And those newly picked Oriental flowers, blossoming in the old Dresden vases— what hand had just placed them there? The room seemed gay and full of life, in a more intense, significant way than usual. But nothing could surprise the count. It seemed so normal to him that he did not even pay any attention when the hour struck on the clock which had been stopped for a year.

Yet this evening anybody would have sworn that the countess was trying in an adorable way to come back into this room which was scented with her presence. She had left so much of herself in it! Everything which had formed her life drew her here. Her charm hung in the air; the prolonged assaults made by her husband's passionate will must have loosened the vague bonds of the invisible around her. . . .

She was *forced* to come back. Everything she loved was here.

No doubt she wanted to smile once more at her reflection in this mysterious mirror in which she had so often admired her lily-like face. The sweet creature must have shuddered, over there, among her violets, under the extinguished lamps; the divine creature must have shivered, all alone in the vault, looking at the silver key which had been tossed onto the flagstones. She wanted to come to him, too. And her will dwelt on the idea of incense and isolation. Death is a final circumstance only for those who hope for something from Heaven; but, for her, Death and Heaven and Life were all contained in their embrace. The solitary kiss of her husband attracted her lips in the darkness. And the bygone sound of melodies, the intoxicated words of former times, the materials which covered her body and preserved its perfume, those magic jewels which *summoned* her to them in their obscure sympathy, and above all the overwhelming, absolute impression of her presence—an impression which objects themselves had come to share in the end—everything was calling her there, and had been drawing her there for so long and so imperceptibly that, finally cured of the sleeping Death, *She alone* was missing.

Ideas are living creatures; and since the count had hollowed out in the air the shape of his love, that space had to be filled by the only creature which was homogeneous with him, or else the Universe would have collapsed. The impression was created at that moment, final, simple, and absolute, that *She must be there in the room.* He was as calmly certain of this as of his own existence, and all the objects around him were saturated with this conviction. It could be seen in them. And *since Véra alone,* tangible and visible, *was missing, it was essential that she should be there* and that the great Dream of Life and Death should open its infinite doors for a moment. Faith extended the road of the resurrection to her tomb. A gay, musical laugh lit up the marriage bed with its joy; the count turned round. And there before his eyes, created out of will and memory, languidly lying with one elbow on the lace pillow, her hand supporting her heavy black tresses, her lips deliciously parted in a smile of paradisaical delight, beautiful beyond compare, the countess was looking at him with eyes which were still a little drowsy.

"Roger!" she said in a faraway voice.

He came over to her. Their lips met in a divine, oblivious, immortal joy.

And they realized *then* that they were in fact *one and the same being.*

The hours brushed with impassive wings this ecstasy in which, for the first time, earth and heaven were united.

Suddenly the comte d'Athol gave a start, as if struck by a fatal reminiscence.

"But now I remember!" he said. "What is the matter with me? You are dead!"

The moment he uttered this last word, the mystic flame of the iconostasis went out. The pale light of morning—a grayish, rainy, commonplace morning—filtered into the room through the gaps between the curtains. The candles turned pale and guttered out, their red wicks giving off an acrid smoke; the fire disappeared under a layer of warm ash; the flowers faded and withered in a few moments; the pendulum of the clock gradually regained its previous immobility. The *conviction* of all the objects vanished abruptly. The opal had died and lost its gleam; the bloodstains had faded too on the batiste next to it; and effacing herself between the desperate arms which were trying in vain to hold her tight, the passionate white vision withdrew into the air and was lost from sight. A farewell sigh, faint but distinct, penetrated to Roger's very soul. The count stood up; he had just realized that he was alone. His dream had dissolved all of a sudden; he had broken the magnetic thread of its radiant texture with a single word. The atmosphere was now that of a death chamber.

Like those glass tears which are illogically shaped and yet so solid that a blow with a mallet on their thick end would not break them, but which shatter immediately into an impalpable dust if the needle-thin tip is broken off, everything had vanished.

"Oh!" he murmured. "So it's all over! . . . I have lost you! . . .
You are all alone! . . . What road must I take now to reach you?
Show me the path which leads me to you!"

Suddenly, like a reply, a shining object fell with a metallic
sound from the marriage bed onto the black fur. A ray of the sinister earthly dawn lit it up. . . . The lonely man bent down and
picked it up; and a sublime smile illumined his face as he recognized this object. It was the key to the tomb.

1876

Translated by Robert Baldick

Guy de Maupassant

THE HORLA

May 8. What a glorious day! I spent the whole morning lying on the grass in front of my house, under the enormous plane tree that provides it with complete shelter and shade. I love this part of the country; I love living here, for it is here that I have my roots—those deep and delicate roots that bind a man to the soil on which his forefathers were born and died, to traditional ways of thinking and eating, to local customs, dishes, idioms, to the lilt of the peasants' voices, to the smell of the earth, the villages, and even the air itself.

I love this house where I grew up. From my windows I can see the Seine flowing alongside my garden, on the other side of the road, almost in my yard—the great, wide Seine, which flows between Rouen and Le Havre, dotted with passing ships.

Away to my left is Rouen, that vast city of blue roofs, beneath its host of pointed Gothic steeples. They are innumerable, some slender, others broad, dominated by the iron spire of the cathedral, and filled with bells that ring out on fine mornings in the limpid air, sending forth their gentle, far-off iron hum, their metallic chimes that are wafted to me, now louder, now fainter, as the breeze swells or falls.

What a lovely morning it was!

Toward eleven, a long line of ships sailed past my gate, drawn by a tugboat the size of a fly, which groaned under the strain and spewed forth thick clouds of smoke.

Behind two British schooners, with their red flags fluttering against the sky, came a magnificent Brazilian three-master, spot-lessly white and gleaming all over. I waved to it, I hardly know why, except that the sight of it gave me such pleasure.

May 12. For several days now I have had a bit of a fever; I feel somewhat ill, or rather, I feel depressed.

Whence do they come, these mysterious influences which turn our happiness into dejection and our confidence into misery? It is as if the air, the invisible air, were filled with unknown Forces, whose mysterious proximity acts in some way upon us. In the morning I wake full of joy, my throat swelling with a desire to sing. —Why? —I go down to the river bank, and suddenly, after a short stroll, I turn homeward with a heavy heart, as if some misfortune awaited me there. —Why? —Is it a shiver of cold which, passing over my skin, has shaken my nerves and filled my soul with gloom? Is it the shape of the clouds or the shades of light, the ever-changing hue of things which, entering through my eyes, has disrupted my thought? Who can tell? Everything around us, everything we look at without seeing, everything we brush past without noticing, everything we touch without feeling, everything we encounter without truly perceiving, has sudden, astonishing, and inexplicable effects upon us, upon our senses, and through them, upon our thoughts and our very hearts.

How profound it is, this mystery of the Invisible! We cannot fathom it with our paltry senses, with our eyes that can distinguish neither what is too tiny nor too large, neither what is too close nor too far, neither the inhabitants of a star nor those of a water droplet . . . with our ears that deceive us, for they transmit the vibrations of the air to us only in sonorous form—they are fairies who by a miracle transform movement into sound, and by this metamorphosis give birth to music, turning the silent rhythms of nature into song . . . with our sense of smell, weaker than a dog's . . . with our sense of taste, that can scarcely tell the age of a wine!

Ah, if only we had other senses to perform other miracles for us, how much more we could discover in the world around us!

May 16. There is no doubt about it, I am ill! And yet I felt so well last month! I have a fever, a terrible fever, or rather a feverish irritation of the nerves which afflicts my mind as much as my body. I have a continuous, dreadful sensation of lurking danger, a feeling of imminent misfortune or approaching death, a premonition which is doubtless the sign of some as yet unknown disease germinating in the flesh and in the blood.

May 18. I have just been to see my doctor, for I could no longer sleep. He said that my pulse was rapid, my pupils dilated, and my nerves highly strung, but that there were no alarming symptoms. I was told to take showers and drink potassium bromide.

May 25. Still no change! My condition is certainly most peculiar. As evening draws on, an inexplicable anxiety comes over me, as if the night concealed some terrible menace. I eat dinner in haste, then try to read, but I can make no sense of the words; I can scarcely distinguish the letters. So I pace up and down my drawing room, gripped by a vague and overwhelming fear, the fear of sleep, fear even of my bed.

About ten o'clock, I go up to my room. No sooner have I entered it than I double-lock and bolt the door; I am afraid . . . of what? . . . I never had any fears until now. . . . I open my wardrobes, I look under my bed, I listen . . . I listen . . . for what? . . . Is it not strange that a simple malaise, a disorder of the circulation, perhaps, or an irritation of a nerve ending, a slight congestion, a minute perturbation in the delicate and imperfect functioning of our living machine, can make a victim of melancholia out of the most cheerful of men, and a coward out of the bravest? Then I get into bed, and I wait for sleep as if it were an executioner. I wait, dreading its approach, with pounding heart and trembling limbs, and my entire body lies shuddering in the warmth of the bedclothes, until the moment when I slip all at once into slumber, as one might fall into a pit of stagnant water to drown. I never feel it coming, as I used to, this treacherous sleep which lies in wait for me, ready to pounce upon my face, force my eyes shut, and destroy me.

I sleep—a long time—two or three hours—then a dream—no—a nightmare seizes me. I am fully aware that I am lying in bed and asleep. . . . I feel it, I know it . . . and I am also aware that someone is approaching me, looking at me, touching me, climbing onto my bed, kneeling on my chest, taking me by the throat and squeezing . . . squeezing with all his might, so as to strangle me.

And I struggle to break free, weighed down by that awful helplessness and paralysis of dreams. I try to cry out—I cannot; I try to move—I cannot; with a horrible effort, gasping for breath, I try to turn over and throw off this being who is crushing and choking me—but I cannot!

And suddenly I awaken, frantic, drenched in sweat. I light a candle. I am alone.

After this attack, which recurs every night, I am at last able to sleep peacefully until dawn.

June 2. My condition has worsened. What is the matter with me? The bromide does no good; neither do the showers. This afternoon, in order to tire out my body, which is already exhausted enough, I went for a walk in the Roumare Forest. At first I thought that the fresh air, the sweet, mild air, full of the fragrance of grass and foliage, would infuse new blood into my veins and new vigor into my heart. I turned into the broad hunting trail and took the narrow path leading toward La Bouille, which runs between two rows of immensely tall trees whose branches form a thick, green, almost black roof between me and the sky.

All at once a shiver ran down my spine, not a shiver of cold, but a strange shudder of dread.

I quickened my pace, anxious and uneasy at being all alone in this wood, stupidly and irrationally alarmed by my utter solitude. Then suddenly I had the impression that I was being followed, that someone was walking at my heels, quite close, close enough to touch me.

Abruptly I turned around. I was alone. Behind me I could see nothing but the straight, broad path, lined with high trees, and empty, terrifyingly empty. On the other side, the path stretched out endlessly before me, just as empty and just as frightening.

I shut my eyes. Why? And I began to spin round on one heel, very quickly, like a top. I almost fell; I opened my eyes again; the trees were dancing, the ground was swaying; I had to sit down. Then, ah!—I could no longer remember from which direction I had come. A peculiar sensation! Peculiar! Peculiar indeed! I no longer had any idea. I started off to the right, and soon found myself back in the trail that had led me into the heart of the forest.

June 3. I had a horrible night. I am going to go away for a few weeks. A little trip will surely put me right again.

July 2. Home again. I am cured. And I had a delightful holiday. I visited Mont Saint-Michel, which I had never seen before.

What a sight, when you arrive in Avranches, as I did, toward the end of day! The town stands on a hill, and I was taken to the public gardens just on its outskirts. When I got there, I uttered a cry of astonishment. An enormous bay stretched out before me as far as the eye could see, between two widely separated coasts which dissolved into mist in the distance. In the middle of this vast yellow bay, beneath a brilliant, golden sky, there rose amid the sands a strange, dark, pointed mountain. The sun had just set, and on the horizon, still aflame, appeared the outline of that fantastical rock, with a fantastical structure upon its summit.

The following morning, as soon as it was light, I made my way toward it. It was low tide, as it had been the evening before, and as I drew near I saw the extraordinary abbey rising up before me. After several hours of walking, I reached the enormous mass of stone which serves as foundation for the little town and the church which towers above it. Having climbed the steep, narrow street, I entered the most magnificent Gothic temple that was ever built for God upon earth, vast as a city, with innumerable low halls hollowed out beneath vaulted roofs, and lofty galleries supported by frail columns. I entered that gigantic jewel of granite, as delicate as lacework, covered with towers and slender pinnacles where twisting stairways wind their way upward, towers that thrust into the blue sky of day and the black sky of night their curious heads bristling with chimeras, demons, fantastical beasts, and monstrous flowers, all linked together by finely sculpted arches.

When I reached the summit, I said to the monk who was my guide, "Father, you must be very happy here!"

He replied, "It is quite windy up here, Monsieur." And we began to converse, looking down upon the incoming tide which raced across the sand, covering it with a breastplate of steel.

And the monk told me stories, all the old stories belonging to the place, one ancient legend after another.

One of them particularly struck me. The local people, those of the Mont, claim that at night you can hear voices on the sands, and that you can hear the bleating of two goats, one loud, the other fainter. Skeptics say that it is nothing but the cry of the sea birds, which at times sounds like goats' bleating, at times like human moans. But fishermen out late at night swear to have seen an old shepherd roaming about on the dunes between tides, near the little town which has sprung up so far from civilization. They say no one has ever seen his face, which is hidden in his cloak, but they have seen him leading a he-goat with the face of a man and a she-goat with the face of a woman, both with long white hair, chattering incessantly and quarreling in a strange tongue, then suddenly interrupting themselves to bleat with all their might.

"Do you believe all that?" I asked the monk.

"I don't know," he murmured.

I went on, "If there are other beings than ourselves living on this earth, how is it that in all this time we have never come into contact with them? How is it that you have never seen them; how is it that I have never seen them?"

He answered, "Can we see even a hundred thousandth part of what exists? Take the wind, the greatest force in nature, which can knock men down, shatter buildings, uproot trees, make the sea swell into watery mountains, destroy the cliffs, and toss great ships onto the reefs—the murderous wind, that shrieks, and moans, and roars. . . . Have you ever seen it, *can* you see it? Nevertheless, it exists."

This simple logic reduced me to silence. This man was either a seer or a fool. I was not entirely sure which—but I said not a word. What he had just uttered, I myself had often thought.

July 3. I did not sleep well. Clearly there is some fever about, for my coachman is suffering from the same illness as myself. When I came home yesterday, I noticed how unusually pale he was, and asked him, "What is the matter with you, Jean?"

"The trouble is I can't get any sleep, Monsieur, my nights seem to eat up my days. Since you went away, Monsieur, it's been hanging over me like a spell."

The other servants are all right, but I am deathly afraid of falling ill again.

July 4. There is no doubt about it; I am ill. My old nightmares have come back. Last night I felt someone squatting on top of me, with his mouth against mine, sucking my life out through my lips. Yes, he was sucking it from my throat like a leech. Then, having had his fill, he got off me and I awoke, so bruised, shattered, and exhausted that I could scarcely move. If this continues many days longer, I will surely have to go away again.

July 5. Have I lost my mind? What happened last night, what I saw, is so strange that my head reels at the thought of it.

I had locked my door, as I do now every evening; then, feeling thirsty, I drank half a glass of water, and I happened to notice that my decanter was filled up to the crystal stopper.

Then I went to bed and soon dropped off into one of my dreadful slumbers, from which I was roused a couple of hours later by an even more horrible shock.

Imagine a man murdered in his sleep, who awakens with a knife through his lung, with the death rattle in his throat, covered in blood, unable to breathe, on the verge of death, without understanding a thing—there you have it.

Having at last regained my senses, I felt thirsty again. I lit a candle and went over to the table where I had left my decanter. I lifted it and tilted it over my glass; nothing came out. —It was empty! It was completely empty! At first I was mystified; then all at once such a dreadful sensation came over me that I had to sit down, or rather, I collapsed into a chair. Then I leaped up again, peering round me. Then, beside myself with astonishment and fear, I sat down once more in front of the transparent vessel. I stared fixedly at it, trying to piece together the puzzle. My hands were trembling. Had someone been drinking this water? Who? I? It must have been I. It could only have been I. So I was a somnambulist; without knowing it, I was living that mysterious double life that makes us wonder if there are two beings within us, or if an alien being, invisible and unknowable, momentarily animates (when our soul is benumbed) our captive body which obeys the other as it does our own self, more than our own self.

Ah! Who can understand the frightful agony I felt? Who can understand how a man must feel when, wide awake, rational and sane of mind, he stares in terror through the glass of a decanter, looking for the water that has vanished while he slept! I stayed there until daybreak, not daring to go back to bed.

July 6. I am going mad. Someone drank all the water from my decanter again last night—or rather, I drank it!

But was it I? Was it I? Who else could it have been? Who? Oh, my God! I am going mad! Will nobody help me?

July 10. I have just performed the most astonishing experiments.

Surely, I am mad! And yet . . . !

On July 6, before going to bed, I placed some wine, milk, water, bread, and strawberries on my table.

Somebody drank—I drank—all the water, and some of the milk. The wine, bread, and strawberries were left untouched.

On July 7, I repeated the same experiment, with the same result.

On July 8, I omitted the water and the milk. Nothing was touched.

Finally, on July 9, I placed only water and milk on the table, taking care to cover the decanters in white muslin, and to tie the stoppers with string. Then I rubbed my lips, beard, and hands with black lead, and lay down.

The same invincible sleep took hold of me, followed soon after by the horrible awakening. I had not moved at all; there were no lead marks on my sheets. I rushed over to the table. The muslin around the decanters had remained intact. Trembling with fear, I untied the string. All the water had been drunk! And so had the milk! Oh, my God! . . .

I am leaving for Paris at once.

July 12. Paris. I really must have been out of my mind these last few days! I must have been the victim of my excited imagination, that is, unless I really am a somnambulist, or have fallen under one of those well-documented but so far unexplained influences that we call hypnotic suggestion. In any case, the turmoil of my mental state was bordering on insanity, but twenty-four hours in Paris have been enough to restore my equilibrium.

Yesterday, after some errands and visits, which invigorated me and seemed to breathe new life into my soul, I rounded off my evening at the Théâtre Français. They were performing a play by Alexandre Dumas the younger, and his keen and powerful wit completed my cure. Solitude is certainly a danger for people with an active intelligence. We need thinking and talking beings around us. When we are alone for long periods, we people the void with phantoms.

I returned along the boulevards to my hotel in excellent spirits. Jostling through the crowds, I thought, not without irony, of my terrors and speculations of the previous week, when I had believed—yes, actually believed—that an invisible being was living under my roof. What a frail thing our mind is, and how easily it is thrown into distraction and alarm whenever it is confronted with some little fact beyond its comprehension!

Instead of simply concluding, "I do not understand because the cause escapes me," we are quick to imagine all manner of fearful mysteries and supernatural powers.

July 14. Bastille Day. I strolled through the streets. The fireworks and the flags filled me with childish delight. Still, it is ridiculous to rejoice on a fixed date, by government decree. The populace is an ignorant herd, at times stupidly docile, at times fiercely rebellious. When it is told, "Be merry," it is merry. When it is told, "Go and fight your neighbor," it goes to fight. When it is told, "Vote for the Emperor," it votes for the Emperor. Then it is told, "Vote for the Republic," and it votes for the Republic.

Those who lead it are also fools, but rather than obeying men, they obey principles, which can only be inane, barren, and false by the very fact that they are principles, that is to say, ideas thought to be certain and immutable in a world where one can be sure of nothing, since light and sound alike are but illusions.

July 16. Yesterday I witnessed some things that deeply disturbed me.

I was dining with my cousin, Madame Sablé, whose husband commands the 76th Regiment of Chasseurs at Limoges. There were two young women there, one of whom is married to a medical doctor, Dr. Parent, who specializes in nervous disorders and in the extraordinary phenomena uncovered recently through experiments on hypnotic suggestion.

He told us at length about the remarkable results obtained by English scientists and by medical doctors of the School of Nancy.[1]

The facts that he related struck me as so odd that I professed myself utterly incredulous.

"We are," he declared, "on the point of discovering one of the most important secrets of nature, that is to say, one of the most important secrets on this earth, for there are surely others far more important out there in the stars. Ever since man began to think, ever since he learned to express and record his thoughts, he has felt himself in the palpable presence of a mystery that is impenetrable to his crude and imperfect senses, and he has tried to compensate for the feebleness of his sense organs by the force of his intelligence. When this intelligence was still in its rudimentary stages, the obsession with the invisible took more banal forms of fear. Thus was born the popular belief in the supernatural, the legends of wandering spirits, fairies, gnomes, ghosts, I might even say the legend of God, for our notions of the workman-creator, from whatever religion they may derive, are certainly the most mediocre, stupid, and unacceptable inventions that ever sprang from man's fear-ridden brain. Nothing is truer than Voltaire's maxim: 'God made man in His own image, but man has returned the favor in kind.'[2]

But for a little over a century now, we seem to have had an intuition of something new. Mesmer and others have opened up for us an unexpected path, and, during the last four or five years in particular, we have truly arrived at some remarkable results."

My cousin, who was as skeptical as I, was smiling. Dr. Parent said to her, "Would you like me to try to put you to sleep, Madame?"

"Yes, do."

She seated herself in an easy chair, and he began to stare at her fixedly, so as to hypnotize her. I suddenly felt rather uneasy, my heart beat faster, my throat went dry. I saw Madame Sablé's eyes grow heavy, her mouth contract, her bosom heave.

Ten minutes later, she was asleep.

"Sit down behind her," the doctor told me.

And I took a seat behind her. He put a visiting card in her hand and said to her, "This is a mirror; what do you see in it?"

"I see my cousin," she replied.

"What is he doing?"

"He is twirling his moustache."

"And now?"

"He is taking a photograph out of his pocket."

"Whom is it of?"

"Of himself."

It was true! The photograph had been given me that very evening, at my hotel.

"What is he doing in this picture?"

"He is standing with his hat in his hand."

Obviously she could see into that card, into that white piece of cardboard, as if it had been a mirror.

The young women were frightened, and exclaimed, "Stop, that's enough! Enough!"

But the doctor ordered, "You will get up tomorrow at eight o'clock; then you will call on your cousin at his hotel, and you will beg him to lend you five thousand francs which your husband will expect to receive from you on his next leave."

Then he awakened her.

On my way back to the hotel, I thought about this curious seance and was beset by doubts, not regarding the absolute and unquestionable good faith of my cousin, who had been like a sister to me since childhood, but rather regarding the possibility of trickery on the doctor's part. Had he not perhaps concealed a mirror in his hand and held it in front of the sleeping young woman at the same time as his visiting card? Professional magicians do far stranger things.

I returned to my hotel and went to bed.

This morning at half-past eight, I was awakened by my valet.

"It's Madame Sablé," he said. "She wishes to speak to Monsieur at once."

I dressed hurriedly and had her shown in.

She sat down, looking very distressed and keeping her eyes lowered. Without raising her veil, she said, "My dear cousin, I have a great favor to ask of you."

"What is it, cousin?"

"I am terribly embarrassed to have to tell you this, and yet I must. I need, desperately need, five thousand francs."

"Surely not! You?"

"Yes, me—or rather my husband, who has asked me to get it for him."

I was so astonished that I could only stammer in reply. I began to wonder whether she and Dr. Parent were not having a little fun at my expense, whether it were not simply a well-planned and well-acted practical joke.

But as I looked at her closely, all my doubts vanished. She was trembling with emotion, so painful was the step that she had taken, and I could see that sobs were rising in her throat.

I knew that she was very rich, and said, "How is it that your husband does not have five thousand francs at his disposal? Come now, think a moment. Are you sure that he told you to ask me for it?"

She hesitated a few seconds as if searching hard for something in her memory, and then replied, "Yes . . . yes . . . I am sure."

"Did he write to you?"

Again she hesitated, reflecting. I could sense the tortured workings of her mind. She did not know. All she knew was that she had to borrow five thousand francs from me for her husband. So she plucked up the courage to tell a lie.

"Yes, he wrote to me."

"When? You didn't mention it yesterday."

"I received his letter this morning."

"Can you show it to me?"

"No . . . no . . . it was very personal . . . too personal . . . I . . . I burned it."

"Then your husband must be in debt."

She hesitated once more, then murmured, "I don't know."

Brusquely, I declared, "The fact is, right now I have not five thousand francs to give you, dear cousin."

She uttered a cry of pain.

"Oh! Please, I beg of you, I beg of you, get it for me. . . ."

She was working herself into a frenzy of agitation, clasping her hands as though she were praying. Her tone of voice changed; she was now sobbing and stammering, in thrall to the inexorable command she had received.

"Oh! I beg of you . . . if you knew how I am suffering . . . I must have it today."

I took pity on her.

"You shall have it without delay," I said. "I promise you."

"Oh, thank you, thank you!" she cried. "How good you are."

"Do you remember," I went on, "what happened at your house yesterday?"

"Yes."

"Do you remember that Dr. Parent put you to sleep?"

"Yes."

"Well, he ordered you to come to me this morning to borrow five thousand francs, and now you are obeying that suggestion."

She thought for a few moments, then said, "But it is my husband who needs the money."

For a whole hour I tried to convince her, but to no avail.

When she had gone, I rushed to see the doctor. He was just leaving, and he listened to me with a smile. Then he said, "Do you believe me now?"

"Yes, how can I not believe you?"

"Let us go to your cousin's house."

She was already half asleep on a chaise longue, overcome with fatigue. The doctor felt her pulse and looked at her for some time with one hand lifted toward her eyes, which slowly closed under the irresistible compulsion of that magnetic power.

When she was asleep, he said, "Your husband does not need the five thousand francs any longer. So you will forget that you asked your cousin to lend it to you, and if he mentions it to you, you will not understand."

Then he awakened her. I drew a wallet from my pocket: "Here, my dear cousin, is what you asked me for this morning."

She was so astonished that I dared not insist. Nevertheless, I tried to jog her memory, but she denied it all vigorously, thought that I was making fun of her, and finally almost lost her temper.

. . . .

There you are! I have just returned to my hotel without eating any lunch, so shaken was I by that experience.

July 19. Many people to whom I have told this story have laughed at me. I no longer know what to think. The wise man says: Perhaps.

July 21. I dined at Bougival, then spent the evening at the boatmen's ball. There is no doubt that everything depends on one's place and environment. To believe in the supernatural when one is on the island of La Grenouillère would be the height of folly . . . but on the summit of Mont Saint-Michel? . . . Or in India? We are frightfully influenced by our surroundings. I am returning home next week.

July 30. I got back yesterday. All is well.

Aug. 2. Nothing new; the weather is splendid. I spend my days watching the Seine flow by.

Aug. 4. Quarrels among my servants. They claim that someone is breaking glasses in the cupboards at night. The valet accuses the cook, who accuses the linen maid, who accuses the two others. Who is the culprit? It would take a clever man to tell.

Aug. 6. This time I am not mad. I saw . . . I saw. . . . I saw! . . . I can no longer doubt it. . . . I saw! . . . It left me chilled to my fingertips . . . to the very marrow of my bones. . . . I saw! . . .

At two o'clock, in broad daylight, I was walking in my rose garden . . . in the path where the autumn roses are starting to bloom.

As I stopped to look at a *géant des batailles,* which bore three magnificent flowers, I saw—I saw very distinctly, right before my eyes—the stem of one of the roses bend as if an invisible hand had pulled it forward, then break as if the hand had plucked it! Then the flower rose, following the curve that a hand would have made carrying it toward a mouth, and remained suspended in thin air, lone and motionless, a frightful splotch of red only a few feet from my eyes.

I lunged at it frantically, trying to get hold of it. There was nothing there; it had disappeared. Then I was seized with a furious rage at myself; it is impermissible for a reasonable, serious-minded man to have such hallucinations.

But was it really a hallucination? I turned round to look for the stem, and immediately found it lying upon the bush, freshly broken, between two other roses that remained upon the branch.

Then I came back to the house, completely distraught. For I am certain now, as certain as that day follows night, that there is an invisible being living close by me, who feeds on milk and water, who can touch things, pick them up and move them about, and who therefore is endowed with a material nature, although invisible to our senses, and who is living as I do under this very roof. . . .

Aug. 7. I had a peaceful night. He drank the water from my decanter but did not disturb my sleep.

I wonder if I am mad. As I was walking in broad daylight this afternoon along the river bank, I began to have doubts about my sanity, not vague doubts like before, but distinct, unqualified doubts. I have seen madmen, and I have known some who remained intelligent, lucid, even clear-sighted, in all but one detail. They could talk on any subject with clarity, ease, and depth, until suddenly their thought, striking against the reef of their mania, would splinter into pieces, scatter, and sink in that fearsome, raging ocean full of leaping waves, fogs, and squalls, that we call "madness."

Surely I would think myself mad, absolutely mad, if I were not conscious of it all, fully cognizant of my mental state, if I did not probe and analyze it with the utmost lucidity. So all in all I must be a rational man, subject to delusions. Some strange disturbance must have taken place within my brain, one of those disorders which physiologists are now attempting to observe and define, and this disturbance must have caused a serious rupture in the sequence and logic of my ideas. Similar phenomena occur in dreams, which carry us through the most improbable phantasmagoria without causing us the least surprise, since our inner mechanism of verification and control is dormant, whereas our imaginative faculty is awake and active. Might it not be that one of the imperceptible keys in my psychic keyboard has become stuck? Following an accident, a person can lose his memory for proper nouns, verbs, numbers, or simply dates. It has now been established that different mental operations are localized in different parts of the brain. Why is it surprising, then, that my ability to verify the reality of certain delusions should be temporarily impaired?

Such were my thoughts as I strolled along the river. The sunlight cast a brilliant sheen over the water, and a charm over the countryside, filling me as I gazed with a love for life—for the swallows, whose lightness and grace is a delight to the eye, for the grasses on the river bank, whose gentle rustling is rapture to the ear.

Little by little, however, an inexplicable feeling of malaise crept over me. I felt as if some force, some occult force, were numbing my limbs, impeding my movements, pulling me back. I felt that aching desire to return that a person feels when he has left behind someone he loves who is ill, and is seized by a premonition that the illness has taken a turn for the worse.

So in spite of myself I turned back, certain that I would find some bad news, a letter or telegram, waiting for me at home. But there was nothing, and I was left feeling more surprised and uneasy than if I had had yet another fantastic vision.

Aug. 8. Yesterday I spent a horrible evening. He has not shown himself again, but I can feel him near me, spying on me, observ-

ing me, probing me, controlling me, more formidable when he
conceals himself like this than if he were to betray by supernatural
signs his constant, invisible presence.

However, I managed to sleep.

Aug. 9. Nothing, but I am afraid.

Aug. 10. Nothing; what will tomorrow bring?

Aug. 11. Still nothing. I cannot stay at home any longer with this
fear and these thoughts in my mind; I am going to leave.

Aug. 12, ten o'clock at night. All day I wanted to leave but could not. I
tried to perform this extremely simple act of free will—to go
out—to get into my carriage to drive to Rouen—but I could not
do it. Why?

Aug. 13. When a person is afflicted by certain diseases, all the
springs of his physical being seem broken, all his energies sapped,
all his muscles limp, his bones as soft as flesh and his flesh as fluid
as water. This is what I am experiencing, in a strange and distress-
ing fashion, in my spiritual being. I have no strength left, no courage, no control over myself, no power even to exercise my will. I
can no longer will; but someone else wills for me—and I obey.

Aug. 14. I am lost! Someone has taken possession of my soul and is
master of it! Someone is commanding all my acts, all my movements, all my thoughts. I am no longer anything in myself, I am
no more than an enslaved and terrified spectator of everything I
do. I want to go out; I cannot. He does not wish me to; so, frantic
and trembling, I remain in the armchair where he keeps me
seated. I desire no more than to get up, to raise myself up, in order to prove to myself that I am still my own master. I cannot! I
am riveted to my chair, and my chair riveted to the floor, such
that no power in the world could budge us.

Then, all of a sudden, I feel I must, I must, I must go to the
far end of my garden, pick some strawberries, and eat them. And
off I go. I pick some strawberries and I eat them! Oh, my God!
My God! My God! Is there a God? If there is a God, deliver me,
save me, help me! Oh, forgive me! Have pity on me! Save me! Oh,
what suffering! What torture! What horror!

Aug. 15. This is surely how my poor cousin was possessed and controlled when she came to borrow five thousand francs from me. She was under the power of an alien will that had infused itself into her like another soul, another parasitic, tyrannical soul. Is the world coming to an end?

But who is he, this being who rules over me, this invisible, unknowable, prowling creature from a supernatural race?

So Invisible Beings do exist? Why is it, then, that since the beginning of time they have never manifested themselves as clearly as they are doing for me now? I have never read about anything remotely like what has been happening in my house. Oh, if only I could get away from it, if I could only leave, escape, never to return. Then I would be saved—but I cannot.

Aug. 16. I managed to escape today for two hours, like a prisoner who finds the door to his cell accidentally open. I suddenly felt that I was free and that he was far away. I ordered the horses to be harnessed in haste, and I drove to Rouen. Oh, what a joy it was to be able to say to someone, "To Rouen!" and be obeyed!

I stopped at the library and asked if I could borrow the long treatise by Dr. Hermann Herestauss[3] on the unknown inhabitants of the ancient and modern world.

Then, just as I was getting back into my carriage, and about to say, "To the station," I heard myself shout—not say but shout, in a voice so loud that passersby turned to look at me—"Home," and beside myself in agony, I collapsed onto the cushion of my carriage. He had found me and taken possession of me once more.

Aug. 17. Ah, what a night! What a night! And yet I suppose I ought to be glad. I read until one o'clock in the morning. Hermann Herestauss, doctor of philosophy and theogony, has written a history of the manifestations of all the invisible beings that haunt men in their waking life and in dreams. He describes their origin, their power, their sphere of control. But not one of them resembles the being that haunts me. It would seem that ever since man began to think, he has had a dread and foreboding of some new being, stronger than himself, who would be his successor upon the earth; and feeling his presence imminent, and unable to foresee the form this master would take, he created out of his ter-

ror a whole fantastical race of occult beings, dim phantoms born
of fear.

Having read until one o'clock in the morning, I went to sit
by the open window in order to cool my brow and collect my
thoughts in the calm night air.

It was pleasant and mild! How I would have loved such a
night, in the old days!

There was no moon. The twinkling stars were atremble in the
black depths of the sky. Who inhabits those worlds? What forms
of life, what living beings, what animals and plants do they contain? The thinking beings of those distant universes, what do they
know that we do not? What can they do that we cannot? What
things, unknown to us, do they see? Will not one of them, someday, ford the abyss of space and appear on our earth to conquer it, just as the Normans of old crossed the sea to vanquish
weaker races?

We are so frail, so helpless, so ignorant, so tiny and insignificant upon this revolving speck of mud and water.

So musing, I drowsed off in the cool night air.

I slept for about forty minutes; then, still motionless, I
opened my eyes, roused by some odd and obscure sensation. At
first I saw nothing; then all at once I thought I saw a page of the
book that I had left open on the table turn over of its own accord.
Not a breath of air had entered by the window. Surprised, I sat
and waited. After about four minutes had passed, I saw, I
saw—yes, I saw with my own eyes—another page flip onto the
previous one, as if a finger had turned it over. My armchair was
empty, or appeared empty, but I realized that he was there, sitting
in my place and reading. With a furious leap, the leap of an en-
raged beast turning to gore its tamer, I lunged across the room to
seize him, strangle him, kill him! . . . But before I reached my
chair, it tipped over as though someone had jumped up and run
away. . . . My table shook, my lamp toppled and went out, and my
window slammed shut as though a burglar, taken by surprise, had
leaped through it into the night, grabbing hold of the shutters as
he went.

So he had fled! He had been frightened, frightened of me!

Then . . . then . . . perhaps tomorrow . . . or the day after . . .
or some day or other, I will be able to lay my hands upon him

and pound him into the ground. Do not dogs at times bite and strangle their masters?

Aug. 18. I have been thinking about it all day. Oh yes, I will obey him, yield to his impulses, carry out his every will, make myself humble, submissive, cowardly. He is the stronger one. But the hour will come. . . .

Aug. 19. I know . . . I know . . . now I know all! I have just read the following in the *Revue du Monde scientifique:* "A rather curious report has reached us from Rio de Janeiro. An epidemic of madness, comparable to the contagious waves of insanity which swept through the populations of Europe in the Middle Ages, is at this moment raging in the province of São Paulo. The frantic inhabitants are fleeing their homes and villages, abandoning their farms, claiming to be pursued, possessed, controlled like human cattle by invisible yet tangible beings, vampires of some kind who feed upon their vitality while they are asleep, and who also drink milk and water without appearing to touch any other kind of food.

"Professor Don Pedro Henriquez, accompanied by several other medical authorities, has left for the province of São Paulo in order to study on location the origin and symptoms of this strange madness, and to suggest to the Emperor such measures as he thinks necessary to restore the demented population to sanity."

Ah! Ah, I remember, I remember the fine Brazilian three-master that sailed past my windows on the 8th of May, on its way up the Seine. I thought it so pretty, white, and bright. The Being was on board, on his way from over the sea, where his race was born. And he saw me! He saw my house, which was also white, and he leaped ashore. Oh, my God!

Now I know, now I understand. The reign of man is ended.

He has come, He who was feared by primitive peoples, He who was exorcised by anxious priests, summoned by sorcerers in the darkness of night, without ever appearing to them, He to whom the momentary masters of the world attributed, in their forebodings, all the monstrous or graceful forms of gnomes, spirits, genies, fairies, and elves. After these crude conceptions of primitive terror, more insightful men intuited him more clearly. Mesmer had an inkling of him, and for ten years now doctors

have known quite precisely the nature of his power, even before
he began to exercise it. They have been playing with this weapon
belonging to the new Lord of the universe: the tyranny of a mysterious will over the enslaved human soul. They called it magnetism, hypnotism, suggestion . . . whatever. I have seen them playing with this horrible power like careless children! Woe upon us!
Woe upon man! He has come, the . . . the . . . what is he called? . . .
The . . . it is as if he were shouting his name to me, and I can not
hear it . . . the . . . yes . . . he is shouting it. . . . I am listening . . . I
cannot hear . . . tell me again . . . the . . . Horla. . . . I heard it . . .
the Horla . . . it is he . . . the Horla . . . he has come!

Ah! The vulture has eaten the dove; the wolf has eaten the
sheep; the lion has devoured the sharp-horned buffalo; man has
killed the lion with arrow, sword, and gun; but the Horla will do
to man what man has done to the horse and the ox: he will make
him his creature, his servant and his sustenance, by the mere
power of his will. Woe upon us!

And yet sometimes an animal will rebel and kill the man who
tamed it. . . . I too want to . . . I could . . . but for that I must know
him, touch him, see him! Scientists tell us that animals' eyes, being
different from ours, do not perceive things as ours do. . . . And
likewise, my eyes are unable to perceive my new oppressor.

Why? Oh, now I remember the words of the monk of Mont
Saint-Michel: "Can we see even a hundred thousandth part of
what exists? Take the wind, the greatest force in nature, which can
knock men down, shatter buildings, uproot trees, make the sea
swell into watery mountains, destroy the cliffs and toss great ships
onto the reefs—the murderous wind, that shrieks, and moans, and
roars, have you ever seen it, *can* you see it? Nevertheless, it exists!"

And I pondered further: my eye is so weak, so imperfect, that
it cannot even perceive solid bodies if they happen to be transparent, like glass! . . . If a two-way mirror were placed in my way, I
would run right into it, just as a bird that has flown into a room
will bang its head against the windowpanes. There are myriad
other things which delude and deceive the eye. Is it surprising,
then, that it is unable to perceive a new kind of body through
which light can pass?

A new being! Why not? Surely he was bound to come! Why
should we be the last? Why are we unable to see him, as we see all

the other beings that were created before us? Because he is more perfect than we are, his body finer and more consummate than ours—ours which is so frail, so clumsily designed, encumbered with organs that are always tired and strained like taut springs, ours which lives like an animal or vegetable, drawing its sustenance painfully from air, grass, and meat, a living machine subject to disease, deformity, and decay, short-winded, ill-regulated, artlessly grotesque, ingeniously ill-made, at once a crude and delicate construction, the rough outline of a being who might someday become intelligent and noble.

There are so few classes of creatures in the world, from the oyster up to man. Why not one more, when the time period separating each successive appearance of the different species has elapsed?

Why not one more? Why not other trees as well, bearing gigantic flowers, blazing with color and perfuming the earth for miles around? Why not other elements besides fire, air, earth, and water? —Are there only four father elements, sources of all life? What a shame! Why are there not forty, four hundred, four thousand! How paltry, meager, and pitiful life is! How sparingly apportioned, how poorly conceived, how crudely constructed! Ah, the elephant or the hippopotamus—what grace! The camel— what elegance!

But, you will say, the butterfly! A winged flower! I can imagine one the size of a hundred universes, with wings whose shape, beauty, color, and sweep are beyond expression. But I see it . . . it flutters from star to star, refreshing and perfuming them with the light, harmonious breath of its flight! . . . And the inhabitants of those upper worlds watch it flutter past, in an ecstasy of delight! . . .

. . . .

What is the matter with me? It is he, he, the Horla, who is haunting me, filling my mind with all this nonsense! He is within me, he has become my soul; I will kill him!

Aug. 19.[4] I will kill him. I have seen him! Last night I sat down at my table and pretended to be absorbed in writing. I knew very well that he would come prowling round me, close to me, close enough for me to touch him, or grab him. And then! . . . Then, I would have the strength of despair; I would use my hands, my knees, my chest, my forehead, my teeth, to strangle him, crush him, bite him, tear him to pieces.

And I lay in wait for him with all my senses in anxious vigilance.

I had lit my two lamps and the eight candles on my mantelpiece, as though in this bright light I might actually have been able to see him.

In front of me stood my bed, an old oak four-poster; on my right was the fireplace; on my left was the door, which I had carefully locked after leaving it open for some time in order to lure him inside; behind me was a very tall wardrobe with a full-length mirror which I used every day for shaving and dressing, and into which I was in the habit of looking each time I passed it.

I pretended to be writing, in order to fool him, for he too was spying on me —when all at once I sensed, I felt certain, that he was reading over my shoulder, that he was there close by my ear.

I stood up, my arms outstretched, turning round so quickly that I almost fell. And do you know? . . . The room was as bright as daylight, and yet I could not see myself in the mirror! . . . It was empty, clear, and deep, filled with light! But my reflection was not there . . . and I was facing it! I could see the whole limpid expanse of glass from top to bottom. I stared at it with panic-stricken eyes, not daring to step forward, not daring to make a move, sensing that he was there but that he would elude me once more, he whose immaterial body had swallowed up my reflection.

How frightened I was! Then suddenly my reflection began to appear in the misty depths of the mirror, as though I were seeing it through a layer of water. This water seemed to flow from left to right, slowly, so that with each second my reflection became more distinct. It was like the passing of an eclipse. Whatever was concealing me did not appear to have a sharply defined outline, but rather a sort of opaque transparency which grew clearer by degrees.

Finally I was able to see my reflection perfectly, just as I do every day when I look in the mirror.

I had seen him! The horror of it has remained with me, and even now makes me shudder.

Aug. 20. Kill him—but how? How, if I am unable to get hold of him? Poison? But he would see me putting it in the water, and besides, would our poisons have any effect on his immaterial body? No . . . no . . . of course not. Then how? . . . How? . . .

Aug. 21. I have sent for a locksmith from Rouen, and ordered iron shutters for my room, the kind they have on the ground floor of certain private residences in Paris, to keep out burglars. He is going to make me a similar kind of door as well. I made myself out to be a real coward, but what do I care? . . .

. . . .

Sept. 10. Rouen, Hotel Continental. I have done it . . . I have done it . . . but is he dead? I am shattered by what I have seen.

Yesterday, after the locksmith put up my iron shutters and door, I left them wide open until midnight, even though it was starting to get cold.

All at once I sensed he was there, and a feeling of joy, mad joy, came over me. I got up slowly and began to walk up and down the room, continuing for some time so that he should not suspect anything. Then I took off my boots and with a casual air put on my slippers. I closed my iron shutters, and sauntering back toward the door, I double-locked it. Returning to the window, I fastened it with a padlock and pocketed the key.

Suddenly I realized that he was hovering restlessly around me, that it was his turn to be afraid, that he was ordering me to open the door for him. I came close to giving in, but did not; with my back against the door, I opened it a little, just wide enough for me to back through, and as I am very tall, my head touched the lintel. I was certain that he could not have escaped, and I locked him in alone, all alone. What joy! I had him! Then I ran downstairs; from the drawing room, which is below my bedroom, I took both my lamps and emptied the oil over the carpet and the furniture—everywhere. Then I set it alight and fled, after having carefully double-locked the heavy entrance door.

I went to hide at the far end of my garden, in a clump of laurels. What a long time it took—what a long time! Everything was black, silent, motionless; not a breath of air, not a star, only mountains of clouds that I could not see but which weighed so heavily, oh so heavily, upon my heart.

I watched my house, and waited. What a long time it took! I

was beginning to think that the fire had gone out, or that *He* had put it out, when one of the lower windows shattered under the pressure of the fire, and a tongue of flame, a great red and yellow tongue of flame, long, soft, and caressing, climbed up the white wall, licking its way to the roof. A glow of light spread over the trees, along the branches and through the leaves, and along with it, a shudder of fear. The birds were waking; a dog began to howl; I felt as if dawn were breaking. The next moment, two more windows shattered, and I saw that the whole lower storey of my dwelling was now one frightful, blazing inferno. But then a cry, a horrible, piercing, heartrending cry, a woman's cry, rang out into the night, and two attic windows flew open! I had forgotten about the servants! I saw their terror-stricken faces, and their arms waving in the air! . . .

Then, frantic with horror, I began to run toward the village, yelling, "Help! Help! Fire! Fire!" I met some people who were already on their way to the house, and I went back with them to see what was happening.

The house was now no more than a horrible and magnificent pyre, a monstrous pyre that lit up the face of the earth, a funeral pyre in which human beings were being burned alive, and in which *He* was burning too—He, my prisoner, the New Being, the new master, the Horla!

Suddenly the entire roof fell in, and a volcano of flames shot up sky-high. Through every window opening into the furnace I could see the cauldron of fire, and I thought of him there in that oven, dead. . . .

Dead? Perhaps. . . . But what about his body? His body, through which light could pass, was it not invulnerable to those methods of destruction which to us are fatal?

What if he were not dead? . . . Perhaps only time has any power over the Invisible, Terrible Being. Wherefore this transparent, unknowable body, this body of the Spirit, if it too must fear sickness, wounds, infirmities, untimely death?

Untimely death? The source of all human terror! After man, the Horla. —After he who may die on any day, at any hour, at any minute, through any kind of accident, comes he who shall die only at his appointed day and hour, when he has reached the limit of his existence!

No . . . no . . . there is no doubt, not the slightest doubt. . . .
He is not dead. . . . Then . . . then . . . then I shall have to kill
myself! . . .

. . . .

1887

Translated by Joan C. Kessler

For a recent French edition of this work, see Guy de Maupassant, "Le Horla," in
Contes et nouvelles, vol. 2 (Paris: Editions Gallimard, Bibliothèque de la Pléiade,
1979).

Guy de Maupassant

WHO KNOWS?

I.

My God! My God! At last I am going to write down what has happened to me! But how can I? How do I dare? It is all so bizarre, so inexplicable, so incomprehensible, so absurd!

If I were not certain of what I have seen, certain that there were no weak points in my logic, no flaws in my construction, no gaps in the rigorous sequence of my observations, I should imagine myself a simple lunatic, the victim of some strange hallucination. After all, who knows?

I am now in an asylum, but I entered voluntarily, out of caution, out of fear! Only one living soul knows my story—the doctor here. I am going to write it down. I hardly know why. Perhaps to rid myself of it, for it weighs upon me like an unbearable nightmare.

Here it is:

I have always been a loner, a dreamer, a sort of solitary philosopher, kind-hearted, content with little, bearing neither bitterness toward men nor resentment toward heaven. I have always lived alone, owing to a kind of malaise that steals over me when I am with others. How can I explain it? I don't think I can. It is not that I refuse to see people, to chat, to dine with friends, but when they are around me for any length of time, even the ones I know best, they begin to weary me, to get on my nerves, and I experience a growing, tormenting desire to have them go away, or to go away, myself—to be alone.

This desire is more than a need, it is an overpowering compulsion. And if I had to remain in the presence of other people, if I had to listen to—or simply hear—their conversations much longer, some mishap would surely befall me. What exactly? Ah, who knows? A simple fainting fit, perhaps? Yes, very likely.

I crave solitude so much that I cannot even endure the presence of other people sleeping under the same roof. I cannot live in Paris, for there I suffer untold agonies. I die a kind of spiritual death—and my body and nerves are tortured by the vast, teeming crowds living and breathing all around me, even as they sleep. Ah, the sleep of others is even harder for me to bear than their talk. And I can never rest when I know, when I sense, that on the other side of the wall there are other lives suspended in these periodic eclipses of human reason.

Why am I like this? Who knows? Perhaps there is a simple explanation: I very quickly tire of everything that does not take place within me. And there are many people who share my predicament.

There are two separate races on this earth. There are those who have need of others, whom others amuse, engage, soothe, and whom solitude exhausts, depletes, overwhelms, like climbing a formidable glacier or crossing a desert. And there are those, on the other hand, whom others weary, bore, exasperate, pain, while isolation calms them, fills them with peace in the autonomy and fantasy of their mind.

In short, we have here a normal psychic phenomenon. Some people are constituted to live outside themselves, others to live within. As for me, my attention to external affairs is short-lived, and once it reaches its limit I am overcome body and soul with an unendurable malaise.

The result of all this is that I become—or had become—deeply attached to inanimate objects, which for me take on the importance of living beings. My house has become—had become—a world in which I pursued a solitary yet active existence, surrounded by physical things—furniture, familiar knickknacks—which in my eyes had all the warmth and benevolence of human faces. I had filled my house with them, adorning it little by little, and when I was inside, I felt as content, as satisfied, as truly happy as in the arms of a loving woman whose familiar caress has come to be a gentle, soothing necessity.

I had had this house built in a beautiful garden that sheltered it from the public roads, on the outskirts of a town which offered all the resources of society that I might now and then desire. All my servants slept in a separate building a little distance away, at the far end of the kitchen garden, which was surrounded by a high wall. The dark veil of evening, as it descended silently upon my secluded dwelling, buried beneath the foliage of large trees, was so calming and comforting that every evening I would delay going to bed for several hours so as to savor it a little longer.

That day there had been a performance of *Sigurd*[1] at the theater in town. It was the first time I had heard this magical opera, and it had given me much pleasure.

I made my way home on foot, walking briskly and cheerfully, my head abrim with sonorous melodies and charming visions. It was dark, very dark, so dark that I could barely see the road, and several times I came close to tumbling into the ditch. The distance from the tollgate to my house is about a kilometer, perhaps a little more—that is to say, a leisurely walk of about twenty minutes. It was one o'clock or one-thirty in the morning; the sky ahead of me began to grow a little lighter, and a crescent moon appeared, the sad, wan crescent of its last quarter. The crescent of the first quarter, the one that rises at four or five o'clock in the evening, is bright, cheerful, burnished with silver, but the one that rises after midnight is reddish, doleful, sinister—a real Witches-Sabbath moon. Every late-night walker has made the same observation. The first crescent, be it as slender as a thread, gives off a cheerful light that gladdens the heart, and traces crisp, clear shadows upon the ground; the latter sheds at best a feeble glimmer, so dull that it hardly casts any shadows.

I saw from a distance the dark, massive shapes of my garden, and was suddenly gripped by an unaccountable malaise at the thought of entering it. I slackened my pace. The night was mild. The heavy mass of trees had all the appearance of a grave in which my house was entombed.

I unlatched my gate and entered the long avenue of syca-mores which led up to the house. It was arched overhead like a great tunnel, and ran through dense clumps of shrubbery, along grassy lawns where, in the moonlit darkness, the flower baskets stood out as oval patches of indefinite hue.

As I neared the house, I was gripped by a strange feeling

of agitation. I stopped. Not a sound was to be heard, not the slightest rustle of leaves upon the trees. "What is the matter with me?" I thought. For ten years I had returned home like this without the slightest anxiety. I had not been afraid. I have never felt afraid at night. The sight of a prowler or a burglar would have filled me with rage, and I would have hurled myself upon him without hesitation. Besides, I was armed. I was carrying my revolver. But I did not touch it, so determined was I to resist the fear which was germinating within me.

What was it? A premonition? That mysterious premonition that takes possession of a man's senses when he is about to encounter the inexplicable? Perhaps. Who knows?

As I went forward I felt shudders running across my skin, and when I reached the wall of my vast house, with its closed shutters, I felt I must wait a few minutes before I could open the door and go inside. So I sat down on a bench, beneath my drawing-room window. There I waited, trembling slightly, my head leaning against the wall and my eyes fixed upon the shadowy foliage. For the first few moments, I noticed nothing out of the ordinary. There was a humming noise in my ears, but that is a frequent occurrence with me. At times I think I hear trains passing, or the ringing of bells, or the tramping of crowds.

But soon these humming noises became more distinct and more recognizable. I had been mistaken. It was not the usual throbbing of my veins that I was hearing in my ears, but a very particular, though confused, sound which without a doubt was emanating from inside my house.

I could make it out through the wall—this steady noise, more a stirring than a noise, the confused sound of a multitude of moving objects—as if someone were displacing, gently dragging about, all my furniture.

For a while I doubted the evidence of my senses. But when I had pressed my ear to a shutter, so as better to discern the nature of this strange disturbance, I became persuaded, absolutely convinced, that something abnormal and incomprehensible was taking place inside my house. I was not afraid, but I was . . . how should I put it . . . aghast with astonishment. I did not cock my revolver—knowing full well that there was no need to use it. I simply waited.

I waited for quite a while, unable to decide what to do, my mind lucid, but distraught with anxiety. I stood there waiting, listening to the noise which was growing louder, at times taking on a violent intensity, and which seemed to have become a rumble of impatience or anger, the rumble of a mysterious rebellion.

Then suddenly, ashamed of my cowardice, I grabbed my bunch of keys, chose one, thrust it into the lock, turned it twice, and pushing upon the door with all my strength, sent it banging against the inner wall.

The noise rang out like a gunshot, and as if in reply to this explosion, a tremendous din rang out from top to bottom of the house. It was so sudden, so awful, so deafening, that I recoiled a few steps, and though I still knew it to be useless, drew my revolver from its holster.

I waited a little while longer. Now I could make out an extraordinary stamping noise on the stairs, on the floors, on the carpets—a stamping, not of human shoes, but of crutches, wooden and iron crutches that reverberated like cymbals. And then I suddenly observed, upon the threshold, an armchair, my large reading armchair, waddling out of the front door. It went out through the garden. Others followed, my drawing-room chairs, then the low sofas, dragging themselves along on their short legs like crocodiles, then all the rest of my chairs, leaping and bounding like goats, and the little footstools, scurrying like rabbits.

Oh, what a fright! I slipped into the shrubbery and crouched down, still staring at the procession of my furniture, for it was all filing past, one behind the other, quickly or slowly according to its weight and size. My piano, my large grand piano, went by, galloping like a bolted horse, with a murmur of music in its belly; the tiniest objects slid like ants across the gravel—brushes, glasses, goblets, gleaming in the moonlight with the phosphorescence of glowworms. The rugs and hangings slithered by, stretching themselves like octopuses as they went. I saw my writing desk appear, a rare antique of the last century, which contained all the letters I have ever received, the entire history of my heart, an ancient story which has caused me much suffering! And there were photographs inside it, too.

Suddenly I was no longer afraid; I hurled myself upon it, grabbing hold of it as one would a burglar, or a fleeing woman.

But it continued on its relentless course, and in spite of my efforts, in spite of my anger, I could not even slow it down. As I wrestled desperately with this terrible force, I was thrown to the ground, still struggling. Then it rolled me over, dragging me along the gravel, and already the furniture following behind it had begun to trample over me, treading roughly upon my legs and bruising them. When I let go of the desk, the other furniture passed over my body like a cavalry charge over a soldier thrown by his horse.

At last, mad with terror, I was able to drag myself from the drive and hide again among the trees, only to watch all my possessions, from the lowliest, the tiniest, the most modest objects, the ones I had taken least notice of, vanish before my eyes.

Then I heard in the distance the tremendous crash of slamming doors, echoing sonorously from the now empty house. They slammed shut from top to bottom, until finally the door to the front hall, which in my folly I had opened myself only to unleash this exodus, was flung shut last of all.

I fled as well, in the direction of the town, and only when I had reached the streets, where there were still a few people about, did I regain my composure. I went and rang the bell of a hotel where I was known. I had shaken the dirt off my clothes, and I told them that I had lost my bunch of keys, which also contained the key to the kitchen garden where my servants slept in a separate house behind the surrounding wall, which protected my fruit and vegetables from prowlers.

Once in the bed they had given me, I pulled the sheets up over my eyes. But I could not sleep, and with a beating heart I lay waiting for daybreak. I had left word for my servants to be notified as soon as it was light, and at seven o'clock in the morning my valet knocked on my door.

I could see from his face that he was distraught.

"Something terrible happened last night, Monsieur," he said. "What is it?"

"Someone has stolen all of Monsieur's furniture—everything, absolutely everything, down to the smallest items."

This news pleased me. Why? Who knows? I was in complete control of myself, certain of my ability to dissemble, to conceal from everyone what I had seen, to bury it in my innermost being like some dreadful secret.

I replied, "Then they must be the same people who stole my keys. We must inform the police immediately. Let me get ready, and I will join you in a few moments."

The investigation lasted five months. Nothing was ever un-covered; the police could not turn up even the smallest knick-knacks, nor find the slightest trace of the thieves. Naturally! If I had revealed to them what I knew. . . . If I had told them . . . they would have locked me up—not the thieves, but me, the man who could have seen such a thing.

Oh, I knew how to keep quiet. But I did not refurnish my house. It would have been futile. The whole thing would have be-gun all over again. I did not want to return. I never did return. I never saw it again.

I moved to a hotel in Paris, and consulted with doctors upon the state of my nerves, which had been worrying me a good deal ever since that awful night.

They urged me to travel. I followed their advice.

II.

I began with a trip to Italy. The sunshine did me much good. For the next six months I wandered from Genoa to Venice, from Venice to Florence, from Florence to Rome, from Rome to Naples. Then I traveled through Sicily, a land admired for its scenery and its monuments, relics from the days of the Greeks and Normans. I crossed over to Africa and journeyed peacefully across that great, serene, yellow desert, where camels, gazelles, and nomadic Arabs roam, and where by day or by night, no haunting visions cloud the translucent air.

I returned to France by way of Marseilles, and despite all its Provençal gaiety, the diminished radiance of the sun dampened my spirits. Returning to the continent, I experienced the strange emotions of a sick man who had thought he was cured, before a dull pain alerts him that the root of the disease has not yet been eliminated.

Then I returned to Paris. After a month had passed, I was bored there. It was autumn, and before winter came I was eager to take a trip through Normandy, which I had never visited before.

I began, of course, with Rouen, and for a week I wandered,

rapt and enthralled, through that medieval city, that amazing museum of extraordinary Gothic monuments.

One evening around four o'clock, I turned into an odd little street along which flowed an ink-black stream called the "Eau de Robec," and was staring up at the curious, ancient physiognomy of the houses when my attention was suddenly captured by a row of secondhand furniture shops, one right after the other.

Ah, they had chosen a fitting location, those sordid traffickers in outworn trinkets, in this uncanny alleyway overlooking this sinister stream, beneath the pointed tile and slate roofs upon which still creaked the weather vanes of a bygone age!

In the depths of these dim shops, I could see an agglomeration of sculpted chests, pottery from Rouen, Nevers, and Moustiers, painted and oaken statues, Christs, Virgins, saints, church ornaments, chasubles, copes, even sacred vessels and an old, gilded, wooden tabernacle from which the spirit of God had departed. Oh, what cavernous depths lay within these tall houses, these great houses, filled from cellar to attic with objects of every imaginable kind, objects whose lives seemed long ended, and yet which have outlived their original owners, their time, their century, their fashion, to be acquired as curios by new generations.

My fondness for antiques was reawakened in this city of antiquaries. I went from shop to shop, crossing in two strides the rotting four-plank bridges that lay across the foul-smelling water of the Eau de Robec.

God have mercy! What a shock! There before me was one of my finest wardrobes, at the side of an archway cluttered with objects, and which looked like the entrance to the catacombs of a cemetery of ancient furniture. I went up to it, trembling all over, trembling so that I dared not touch it. I reached out my hand, hesitating. Yet it was indeed mine, a priceless Louis XIII wardrobe, recognizable by anyone who had seen it even once. Suddenly, glancing a little further into the somber depths of the gallery, I beheld three of my armchairs, upholstered in petit point tapestry, then, further still, my two Henry II tables, so rare that people used to come all the way from Paris to see them.

Just imagine! Just imagine my state of mind!

And on I went, paralyzed and almost lifeless with fear, but on I went bravely, like a knight of the Dark Ages entering a realm of black magic. At each step I found more of what had belonged to me, my chandeliers, my books, my paintings, my rugs and hangings, my weapons, everything, except the writing desk full of my letters, which was nowhere to be seen.

On I went, descending to dark galleries, then climbing to upper floors. I was alone. I called out; no one answered. I was alone; there was not a soul in this house, vast and tortuous as a labyrinth.

Night fell, and I had to sit down in the darkness on one of my chairs, for I was resolved not to leave the place. From time to time I called out, "Hallo! Hallo! Is anybody there?"

I had been there for more than an hour at least when I heard footsteps, faint, measured footsteps coming from somewhere nearby. My first instinct was to flee, but bracing myself, I called out again, and I saw a light appear in the next room.

"Who's there?" said a voice.

I answered, "A customer."

"It is very late to be entering a shop," was the reply.

I rejoined, "I have been waiting for you for more than an hour."

"You can come back tomorrow."

"Tomorrow I shall have left Rouen."

I dared not go toward him—and he was not coming to me. I could still see the gleam from his lamp, illuminating a tapestry in which two angels were hovering above the dead upon a field of battle. It, too, belonged to me.

I said, "Well? Are you coming?"

He replied, "I am waiting for you."

I rose and went toward him.

In the middle of a large room stood a tiny little man, very short and very fat, phenomenally fat, like a hideous freak.

He had a sparse, straggly, yellowish beard, and not a hair on his head! Not a hair! As he held his candle up at arm's length to see me, his skull looked like a little moon in that vast room cluttered with ancient furniture. His face was wrinkled and bloated, and his eyes could barely be seen.

I bargained with him for three chairs which belonged to me, and paid him a large sum of money on the spot, giving him only the number of my room at the hotel. The chairs were to be delivered the next morning before nine.

Then I left. He saw me to the door with much politeness.

I went next to the police inspector and told him of the theft of my furniture and of the discovery I had just made.

Forthwith, he sent a telegram to the prosecutor's office which had been investigating the burglary, asking for information about the case, and invited me to wait in his office until he had received an answer. An hour later the reply came back, confirming my story.

"I am going to have this man arrested and question him at once," he told me, "for he may have gotten suspicious and had your belongings removed. If you would care to go and dine somewhere and return in two hours, I will have him in my custody and will interrogate him once more in your presence."

"Gladly, Monsieur. I cannot thank you enough."

I went to dine at my hotel, and ate with greater appetite than I would have thought possible. I was really quite pleased. We had him.

Two hours later I returned to the police inspector, who was waiting for me.

"Well, Monsieur," he said upon seeing me. "We have not found your man. My agents have not been able to get their hands on him."

Ah! I felt as if I were about to faint.

"But . . . you did find his house, at least?" I asked.

"Certainly. We are even placing it under surveillance until he returns. But as for him—disappeared."

"Disappeared?"

"Disappeared. He usually spends his evenings at the home of a female neighbor, who is also a secondhand dealer—a queer old witch, the widow Bidoin. She has not seen him tonight, and cannot provide us with any clues as to his whereabouts. We shall have to wait until tomorrow."

I left the station. Ah, how sinister, disturbing, haunted the streets of Rouen now seemed to me!

I slept very badly that night, for my sleep was continually interrupted by nightmares.

Not wishing to appear too anxious or too much in a hurry, I waited until ten o'clock the next morning before going to the police.

The dealer had not reappeared. His shop remained closed.

The inspector told me, "I have taken all the necessary steps. The prosecutor's office is being kept informed of the progress of the case. We will go together to the shop and have it opened, and you can show me what belongs to you."

We drove there in a carriage. Several policemen were standing in front of the shop door, along with a locksmith, and the door was opened for us.

Upon entering, I could see neither my wardrobe, nor my armchairs, nor my tables, nor anything at all that had once furnished my house, nothing whatsoever, whereas the evening before I had been unable to take a step without coming upon one of my possessions.

The inspector, surprised, looked at me at first with suspicion.

"My God, Monsieur," I told him, "the disappearance of this furniture oddly coincides with that of the dealer."

"That is true," he said with a smile. "You were wrong to buy and pay for those articles of yours yesterday. It aroused his suspicions."

"What is incomprehensible to me," I went on, "is that every one of the places that were occupied by my own furniture are now filled by others."

"Oh," the inspector replied, "he had all night, and probably accomplices as well. This house must communicate with its neighbors on either side. But have no fear, Monsieur, I will attend to this case very diligently. The thief will not elude us for long, since we are keeping watch on his hideaway."

. . . .

Ah, my heart, my heart, my poor heart, how it was beating!

. . . .

I stayed in Rouen for a fortnight. The man did not return. Naturally! Naturally! Whoever could have foiled this man, or caught him unawares?

Then, on the morning of the sixteenth day, I received from my gardener, who had been left as caretaker of my empty and pillaged house, the following strange letter:

Monsieur,

I am writing to inform you that last night something

occurred which no one has been able to understand, not even the police. All the furniture has returned, all of it, without exception, down to the smallest articles. The house now looks exactly the same as it did the day before the burglary. It's enough to make you lose your mind. It happened during the night between Friday and Saturday. The paths are all torn up, as if everything had been dragged from the gate to the front door. It looked just like this on the day of the disappearance.

We await Monsieur's return. I remain,

Your humble servant,

Raudin, Philippe

Ah, no! No! No! I will not go back!

I took the letter to the Rouen inspector.

"It was a very clever restitution," he said. "Let us lie low for the time being. We will catch the man one of these days."

. . . .

But they have not caught him. No, they have not caught him, and I am scared of him now, as if he were some ferocious beast unleashed behind my back.

Undiscoverable! He is undiscoverable, this monster with the moon-shaped skull! They will never catch him. He will never come back to his shop. What does it matter to him? I am the only one who could find him, and I don't want to.

I don't want to! I don't want to! I don't want to!

And if he returns, if he goes back to his shop, who could prove that my furniture was ever there? He has only my word against him, and I sense that it has begun to be regarded with suspicion.

Ah, no! I could no longer endure that kind of existence. But neither could I keep silent about what I had seen. I could not go on living like everyone else with the nagging fear that the same events might begin all over again.

I came to see the doctor in charge of this asylum, and told him the whole story.

After questioning me for a long time, he said, "Monsieur, would you consent to remain here for a time?"

"Willingly, Monsieur."

"Do you have means?"

"Yes, Monsieur."

"Do you wish to have private rooms?"

"Yes, Monsieur."

"Do you care to receive friends?"

"No, Monsieur, no, nobody. The man from Rouen might try to hunt me down here, out of revenge."

. . . .

And I have been alone, entirely alone, for three months. I am at peace, more or less. I have only one fear. . . . If the antique dealer were to go mad . . . and if he were to be brought into this asylum . . . Even prisons are not safe.

1890

Translated by Joan C. Kessler

For a recent French edition of this work, see Guy de Maupassant, "Qui sait?" in *Contes et nouvelles*, vol. 2 (Paris: Editions Gallimard, Bibliothèque de la Pléiade, 1979).

Marcel Schwob

THE VEILED
MAN

O f the combination of circumstances that have been my undoing I can say nothing; certain accidents of human life are
as artistically contrived by chance or by the laws of nature as the
most demoniacal invention: one cries out in wonder before them
as before a painting by an impressionist who has captured a singular and momentary truth. But if my head should fall, I trust that
this narrative will survive me and that in the history of human
lives it might be a true oddity, as it were a lurid opening onto the
unknown.

When I entered that terrible carriage, two people were occupying it. One facing away from me, enveloped in a traveling-rug,
was fast asleep. His covering was flecked with spots on a yellowish ground, like a leopard skin. Many such are sold in travel-goods
departments: but I can say at once that, touching it later, I realized that this was really the skin of a wild animal. Likewise the
sleeper's bonnet, when I observed it with the especially acute
power of vision that came to me, seemed to me to be of an infinitely fine white felt. The other traveler, who had a pleasant face,
appeared just into his thirties. Beyond that he had the insignificant appearance of a man who readily sleeps on railway trains.

The sleeper did not show his ticket, nor did he turn his face
while I was installing myself opposite him. And once I was seated
on the bench I ceased to observe my fellow travelers so as to reflect upon the various matters that preoccupied me.

The movement of the train did not interrupt my thoughts, but it directed their current in a curious fashion. The song of the axle and the wheels, the grip of the wheels on the rails, the crossings of the points with the juddering that periodically shakes badly suspended carriages transformed itself into a mental refrain. It was a species of vague thought that broke in regular intervals upon my other ideas. After a quarter of an hour the reiteration bordered on the obsessive. By a violent effort of will I rid myself of it; but the vague mental refrain took on the form of a musical notation which I anticipated. Each jolt was not a note, but it was the echo in unison of a note conceived in advance, at once feared and desired; to such an extent that these eternally similar shocks ran the most extended gamut of notes corresponding, in truth, in its superimposed octaves beyond the compass of any instrument, to the layers of suppositions that are often piled up by the mind in travail.

In the end, to break the spell, I took up a newspaper. But, once I had read them, entire lines detached themselves from the columns and, with a sort of plaintive and uniform sound, reintroduced themselves to my view at intervals I anticipated but could not modify. I leaned back against the seat, experiencing a singular sensation of disquiet and of emptiness in my head.

It was then that I observed the first phenomenon that plunged me into the realms of the uncanny. The traveler on the far side of the carriage, having raised his bench and adjusted his pillow, stretched out and closed his eyes. Almost at the same moment the sleeper facing me silently rose and drew about the globe of the lamp the little spring-loaded blue shade. In this operation I should have been able to see his face—*and I did not see it.* I caught a glimpse of a confused blur, the color of a human face, but of which I could not distinguish the least feature. The action had been accomplished with a silent rapidity that stupefied me. I had not had the time to take in the sight of the sleeper standing erect when, already, I saw only the white crown of his bonnet above the speckled cover. It was a trifling matter, but it disturbed me. How had the sleeper so quickly been able to grasp that the other had closed his eyes? He had turned his face in my direction and I had not seen it; the rapidity and the mysterious quality of his motion were inexpressible.

A blue obscurity now hung between the upholstered benches, now and then barely broken by the veil of yellow light projected from without by an oil lamp.

The circle of thoughts that haunted me closed in as the train's pulsations increased in the silence. The uneasy quality of the motion had fixed it; and, slowly modulated like a monotonous chant, stories of murderers on trains welled up out of the gloom. A cruel fear contracted my heart, all the more cruel since it was vague, and incertitude augments terror. Visible, palpable, I sensed the image of Jud starting up—a thin face with cavernous eyes, prominent cheekbones and a filthy goatee beard—the face of Jud the murderer, who killed at night in first-class carriages and who, after his escape, had never been recaptured. The darkness helped me to paint with the features of Jud the confused blur I had seen in the lamplight, to imagine beneath the speckled covers a man crouched, ready to spring.

I was violently tempted to hurl myself to the far end of the carriage, to shake the sleeping traveler, to cry aloud to him my peril. A sense of propriety held me back. Could I explain my disquiet? How could I respond to that well-bred man's astonished glance? He was sleeping comfortably, well wrapped-up, his head on the pillow, his gloved hands crossed on his chest: by what right was I to awaken him because another traveler had shaded the lamp? Was there not already a symptom of madness in my mind, which persisted in linking the man's action with the consciousness he must have had of the other's sleep? Were these not two different events, belonging to different series, linked by a simple coincidence? But at this point my fear became insistent; so much so that, in the train's rhythmical silence, I felt my temples throbbing; a tumult in my blood, which contrasted painfully with my outward calm, set things swirling round me, and events vague and still to come, but with the conjectured precision of things that are about to happen, marched through my brain in endless procession.

And suddenly a profound calm established itself within me. I felt the tension of my muscles relax in a complete abandon. The swirling of my thoughts was stilled. I experienced the inward fall that precedes sleep and swooning, and, with eyes open, I was in fact swooning. Yes: with eyes open and endowed with an infinite power of which they availed themselves without effort. And this relaxation was so complete that I was incapable of governing my senses, or of making a decision, or even of representing to myself any thought of action of my own devising. Those superhuman eyes were of themselves directed upon the mysterious-faced man and, while seeing through obstacles, at the same time saw them. Thus I *knew* that I was looking through a leopard skin, and through a flesh-colored silken mask, a *crépon* covering a swarthy face. And my eyes immediately met with other eyes, eyes that shone with an insupportable blackness: I saw a man dressed in yellow, with buttons seemingly of silver, enveloped in a brown overcoat; I knew he was covered in a leopard skin, but I saw him. I also heard (for my hearing had just taken on an extreme acuity) his breathing, urgent and panting, like that of a man making a considerable effort. But it must have been an inward effort, for the man was moving neither arms nor legs; it was indeed such—for his will annihilated my own.

One last resistance manifested itself in my being. I was aware of a struggle in which, in reality, I played no part, a struggle carried on by that deep-seated egoism of which one is never aware and which governs one's self. Then ideas came drifting into my mind—ideas that were not mine, that I had not created, in which I recognized nothing in common with my substance, perfidious and alluring as the black waters over which one leans.

One of these was murder. But I no longer conceived it as an act filled with dread, accomplished by Jud, as the issue of a nameless terror. With a certain glimmer of curiosity and an infinite prostration of everything that had ever been my will, I experienced it as possible.

Then the veiled man rose and, regarding me fixedly through his flesh-colored veil, went with gliding steps toward the sleeping traveler. With one hand he seized him by the nape of the neck, firmly, and at the same time he stuffed a silken pad into his mouth. I felt no distress, nor had I any desire to cry out. But I was there, and dull-eyed I watched. The man drew a narrow, sharp-pointed Turkestan knife, the hollow-ground blade of which had a central channel, and he cut the traveler's throat as one would bleed a sheep. The blood spurted up to the luggage rack. Drawing it sharply toward him, he had thrust in his knife at the right side. The throat gaped open. He uncovered the lamp and I saw the red gash. Then he emptied the man's pockets and dabbled his hands in the bloody pool. Next he came toward me and, unresisting, I endured his smearing my inert fingers and my face, of which not a wrinkle twitched.

The veiled man rolled up his traveling-rug and threw on his overcoat, while I remained next to the *murdered* traveler. The terrible word made no impression upon me—until suddenly I found myself desolate of support, without the will to make up for the lack of my own, empty of ideas, befuddled. And coming to myself by degrees, gummy-eyed, phlegmy-mouthed, my neck stiff, as if held in a leaden grip, I found I was alone, in the early gray dawn, with a corpse that tossed about like a bundle. The train was threading its way through an intensely monotonous stretch of open country dotted with clumps of trees—and when, after a long-drawn-out whistle that echoed on the clear morning air, it stopped, I appeared stupidly at the carriage door, my face striped with clotted blood.

1891

Translated by Iain White

From Marcel Schwob, *The King in the Golden Mask and Other Writings*, translated by Iain White (Manchester: Carcanet New Press Limited, 1982). Reprinted with permission.

Notes

Introduction

1. "Le merveilleux," in French, refers to the realm of the supernatural and to literary works (or elements of such) which draw upon this realm.

2. Tzvetan Todorov, in *The Fantastic: A Structural Approach to a Literary Genre* (Cleveland/London: Press of Case Western Reserve University, 1973), sees this hesitation on the part of the reader as essential to a definition of the fantastic.

3. A modern translation of this work was recently published (Jacques Cazotte, *The Devil in Love*, ed. and trans. Stephen Sartarelli [New York: Marsilio, 1993]).

4. Marquis de Sade, *Idée sur les romans* [1800], ed. O. Uzanne (Paris: Rouveyre, 1878), 32–33.

5. "Apothéose de Joseph Barra et d'Agricola Viala," 1774 (Cornell University Library, Division of Rare and Manuscript Collections; photocopies of printed material by Charles Nodier). This and subsequent translations in the Introduction and Notes are my own, unless otherwise specified.

6. Charles Nodier, *Oeuvres complètes*, 12 vols. (Genève: Slatkine Reprints, 1968), 8:52–53.

7. Ibid., 8:45–46.

8. Laurence M. Porter, "The Forbidden City: A Psychoanalytical Interpretation of Nodier's *Smarra*," in *Symposium* (1972): 331–348. This essay appears in slightly altered form as the chapter "Absorption by the Terrible Mother: Nodier's *Smarra*," in Porter's *The Literary Dream in French Romanticism* (Detroit: Wayne State University Press, 1979).

9. Ernest Jones, *On the Nightmare* (New York: Grove Press [1931], 1951).

10. "The Sandman," in *Selected Writings of E. T. A. Hoffmann*, vol. 1, *The Tales*, ed. and trans. Leonard J. Kent and Elizabeth C. Knight (Chicago and London: University of Chicago Press, 1969), 146.

11. For a detailed analysis of this phenomenon, see Robert Darnton, *Mesmerism and the End of the Enlightenment in France* (Cambridge, Mass.: Harvard University Press, 1968); and Maria M. Tatar, *Spellbound: Studies on Mesmerism and Literature* (Princeton, N.J.: Princeton University Press, 1978).

12. *Spellbound*, 29.

13. *Physiologie du mariage*, in Honoré de Balzac, *La Comédie humaine*, 12 vols. (Paris: Editions Gallimard, 1976–80), 11:107.

14. Ibid., 10:52–53.

15. Ibid.

16. Nathaniel Hawthorne, *The Centenary Edition*, 13 vols. (Columbus, Ohio: Ohio State University Press, 1962–77), 9:225–226 ("Fancy's Show Box").

17. Alan William Raitt, *Prosper Mérimée* (New York: Charles Scribner's Sons, 1970), 182.

18. Ivan Nagel, "Gespenster und Wirklichkeiten: Prosper Mérimées Novelle 'La Vénus d'Ille,'" *Neue Rundschau* 68 (1957): 419–427, specif. 423–425.

19. See Theodore Ziolkowski's chapter on the Venus and the Ring legend in *Disenchanted Images: A Literary Iconology* (Princeton, N.J.: Princeton University Press, 1977).

20. Ibid., 18.

21. Prosper Mérimée, *Correspondance générale*, 17 vols., ed. Maurice Parturier (Paris: Le Divan; and Toulouse: Privat, 1941–1964), 5:238.

22. Raitt, *Prosper Mérimée*, 185 (trans. Raitt).

23. Jean Pierrot, *Merveilleux et fantastique: Une Histoire de l'imaginaire dans la prose française du romantisme à la décadence (1830–1900)* (Lille: Service de Réproduction des Thèses, Université de Lille III, 1975), 77.

24. Frank Paul Bowman, *Prosper Mérimée: Heroism, Pessimism, and Irony* (Berkeley and Los Angeles: University of California Press, 1962), 17 and 35.

25. Georges Poulet, *Etudes sur le temps humain* (Paris: Plon, 1949), chap. 14 ("Théophile Gautier").

26. Johann Wolfgang von Goethe, *Faust et le second Faust*, trans. Gérard de Nerval (Paris: Editions Garnier Frères, 1962), 204.

27. Charles Baudelaire, "Théophile Gautier," *Oeuvres complètes* (Paris: Editions du Seuil, 1968), 464.

28. Sigmund Freud has commented on the importance of archeological symbolism in a psychoanalytic context: "There is no better analogy for repression, which at the same time makes inaccessible and conserves something psychic, than the burial which was the fate of Pompeii and from which the city was able to rise again through work with the spade." (*Delusion and Dream and Other Essays*, ed. and with an intro. by Philip Rieff [Boston: Beacon Press, 1956], 61.)

29. Pierre-Jean-Georges Cabanis, *Oeuvres complètes*, 5 vols. (Paris: Bos-

sange Frères, 1823), 2:165. Dumas would later note in his memoirs, "I have read this whole discussion in connection with my *Mille et un Fantômes*, and attest to having taken a lively interest in it." (*Mes Mémoires*, 5 vols. [Paris: Editions Gallimard, 1954–1968], 5:401.)

30. Nicolas Wagner, Introduction to Alexandre Dumas, *Les Mille et un Fantômes* (Genève: Slatkine Reprints, 1980), iv.

31. Raymond Bellour, "Dumas, l'homme d'une image," *Magazine Littéraire* 258 (October 1988): 54.

32. Ibid.

33. Dumas, *Les Mille et un Fantômes*, 18–19.

34. Ibid., 32.

35. Dumas, *Mes Mémoires*, 3:315–317.

36. This idea is developed by Nicolas Wagner in his introduction to Dumas, *Les Mille et un Fantômes*, vi.

37. Dumas, *Mes Mémoires*, 2:110–131.

38. Ibid., 5:59–60.

39. Dumas, *Les Mille et un Fantômes*, 10–11.

40. Gwenhaël Ponnau explores the complex relationship between the literary fantastic and nineteenth-century psychiatry in *La Folie dans la littérature fantastique* (Paris: Editions du Centre National de la Recherche Scientifique, 1987).

41. Alexandre Jacques François Brierre de Boismont, *Hallucinations: or, The Rational History of Apparitions, Visions, Dreams, Ecstasy, Magnetism, and Somnambulism* (New York: Arno Press, 1976); this edition is a reprint of the original American edition (1853).

42. Jacques Moreau de Tours, *Du Hachisch et de l'aliénation mentale* (Paris: Fortin, Masson et Cie., 1845), 31. Cited in Michel Jeanneret, "La Folie est un rêve: Nerval et le docteur Moreau de Tours," *Romantisme* 27 (1980): 64.

43. Jacques Moreau de Tours, "De l'Identité de l'état de rêve et de la folie," in *Annales Médico-psychologiques* (July 1855): 402. Cited in Jeanneret, 65.

44. Jacques Moreau de Tours, *La Psychologie morbide* (Paris: Masson, 1859), 429. Cited in Jeanneret, 69–70.

45. The name "Aurélia" is taken from the heroine of E. T. A. Hoffmann's novel *Die Elixiere des Teufels* (*The Devil's Elixirs*), one of the primary literary influences upon Nerval's tale.

46. *Selected Writings of E. T. A. Hoffmann*, 1:161.

47. Jules Verne, *Le Tour du monde en quatre-vingts jours* (Paris: Garnier-Flammarion, 1978), 47, 85–86.

48. See p. 264 of this volume; Villiers's translator renders the word as "affinity."

49. The Song of Solomon, 8:6.

50. Edgar Allan Poe, *The Complete Tales and Poems* (New York: Random House, 1938), 654.

51. This work was translated into English as *Transcendental Magic: Its Doctrine and Ritual*, rev. ed., trans. Arthur Edward Waite (London: Rider [1923], 1984).

52. Eliphas Lévi, *Dogme et rituel de la haute magie*, 2 vols. (Paris: Baillière, 1861), 1:53, 61.

53. Ibid., 184–187.

54. Alan William Raitt, *Villiers de l'Isle-Adam et le mouvement symboliste* (Paris: Librairie José Corti, 1965), pt. 2, chaps. 3 and 4 ("L'Hégélianisme" and "L'Illusionnisme," 217–264).

55. Villiers's novel has been rendered into English as *Eve of the Future Eden*, trans. Marilyn Gaddis Rose (Lawrence, Kans.: Coronado Press, 1981), and as *Tomorrow's Eve*, trans. Robert Martin Adams (Urbana: University of Illinois Press, 1982).

56. Michel Picard, "Notes sur le fantastique de Villiers de l'Isle-Adam," *Revue des Sciences Humaines* 95 (July–September 1959): 326.

57. Villiers de l'Isle-Adam, *Tribulat Bonhomet*, in *Oeuvres complètes* (Paris: Mercure de France, 1922), 3:48–49.

58. Guy de Maupassant, *Contes et nouvelles*, 2 vols. (Paris: Editions Gallimard, 1979), 2:464.

59. Ponnau, 67–71.

60. Maupassant, 2:310.

61. Eduard von Hartmann, *Philosophy of the Unconscious: Speculative Results according to the Inductive Method of Physical Science* (Westport, Conn.: Greenwood Press, 1972). This translation is a reprint of the 1931 edition issued in the series International Library of Psychology, Philosophy, and Scientific Method.

62. Albert-Marie Schmidt, *Maupassant par lui-même* (Paris: Editions du Seuil, 1982), 136.

63. Ibid.

64. Poe, 238–239.

65. Monique Jutrin, *Marcel Schwob: "Cœur double"* (Lausanne: Editions de l'Aire, 1982), 12.

66. George Trembley, *Marcel Schwob: Faussaire de la nature* (Genève: Librairie Droz, 1969), 10.

67. Marcel Schwob, *The King in the Golden Mask and Other Writings*, trans. and intro. Iain White (Manchester: Carcanet New Press Limited, 1982), 9.

68. Jutrin, 43.

69. Ibid., 50.

70. Ibid., 42.

71. Trembley, 36. Trembley draws upon Georges Buraud, *Les Masques* (Paris, 1948).

72. Ibid.

Smarra, or The Demons of the Night

1. "Dreams boldly play with us in the illusion of night / And inspire false fears in the timorous mind." Nodier is mistaken in his attribution. The quotation is traditionally included in the corpus of the first century B.C. Roman poet Tibullus (*Elegies*, III, 4, verses 7–8); however, the third book of the *Elegies* is now recognized as the work of a minor poet of Tibullus's circle, Lygdamus.

2. *The Tempest*, II, 3.

3. A town on Lago Maggiore in Italy.

4. The Latin writer Lucius Apuleius (c. A.D. 124–170), author of the novel *The Golden Ass*, which narrates the adventures of a young man changed by magic into an ass. In Book 1, the narrator, Lucius, visits Thessaly, a region of northern Greece associated with sorcery and black magic, and hears a lurid tale of witchcraft and murder.

5. One of the Borromean Islands, in Lago Maggiore.

6. "O faithful witnesses of my deeds, Night and Diana, who command silence when sacred mysteries are performed; now, now come to my aid." (Horace, *Epodes*, V.)

7. *The Tempest*, II, 2.

8. See note 4, above.

9. The chief city of ancient Thessaly, on the Peneus River.

10. In antiquity, the district of Ceramicus lay in the northwestern sector of Athens, Ceramicus exterior (outside the walls) being adjacent to the Sepulcra Publica, the city's largest necropolis.

11. Nodier is referring to the Jews' harp, a small, lyre-shaped instrument placed between the teeth, which gives tones from a metal tongue struck by the finger.

12. One of the largest and richest cities of ancient Greece, Corinth was often involved in political and military conflict. Nodier may be referring to the siege of 243 B.C., when the Achaean League freed the city from Macedonian occupation. The Romans destroyed Corinth in 146 B.C.

13. Nodier uses the term "aréopage," from "Areopagus," the supreme tribunal of Athens, which met, usually at night, on a hill consecrated to Ares, the god of war. In French, "aréopage" can be used more generally to designate any solemn assembly.

14. In Greek mythology, the lamiae were female monsters who, vampire-like, preyed on the blood of young men. They were the namesakes of Lamia, a Libyan queen who, after being robbed of her children by Hera, stole others' children and ate them.

15. In the original (Renduel) edition of Nodier's works, the author provides a "Translator's Note" (Nodier's first preface to *Smarra* presented his tale as an authentic text from Illyria, the land of vampires): "I believe this does not refer to ancient Corcyra [Corfu] but to the [Dalmatian] island of Curzola [Korčula] which the Greeks call *Dark Corcyra*, because of the appearance given it at a distance by the vast forests which cover it."

16. The reference to Apollo's son Asclepius (Aesculapius), Father of Medicine, draws attention to Apollo's role as god of healing, and sender and stayer of plagues.

17. Ancient Greek city in the northeastern Peloponnese. One of the most famous shrines of Asclepius was located here.

18. One is surprised that Nodier describes the hexagonal cell of the honeycomb as five-sided.

19. The Vale of Tempe, narrow valley in northeastern Thessaly.

20. In the Renduel edition, Nodier's note refers the reader to the Dal-

matian poem, "La Luciole" ("The Firefly"), included in the same volume. (Nodier's free translation of the poem was made through the intermediary of an existing Italian translation.)

21. The *stadion*, an ancient Greek unit of measurement, was equivalent to about 180 meters; "twenty and a half *stadia*" equal more than two miles.

22. *Elegies*, I, 2, verses 43–46 and 49–50. "I have seen her drawing down the stars from heaven. / Her chanting can reverse the river's flow. / Her spells can split the ground, lure ghosts from graves / and pluck the bones from smoldering pyres. / . . . / When she pleases she can drive the clouds from sullen skies; / when she pleases muster snow in summer's dome." (Tibullus, *Elegies*, 2d ed., trans. Guy Lee [Liverpool: Francis Cairns, 1982].)

23. *The Tempest*, I, 2.

24. "In Shakespeare's *Tempest*, an inimitable model of this type of writing, the *human monster* who is given over to the evil spirits also complains of unbearable cramps that precede his dreams. It is odd that this physiological induction regarding one of the cruelest maladies that has ever tormented humankind has been grasped only by poets." (Nodier's note.)

25. A wheel-shaped instrument, thought to have been used from ancient times in operations of magic. In the two-page "Note on the Rhombus," which follows *Smarra* in the Renduel edition, and to which Nodier refers the reader in a footnote, he gives a lexicographical exposition of the use of the word by writers of antiquity. He also links the rhombus with a modern child's toy known as a "diable" or "devil."

26. In Latin, "Saga" signifies sorceress or soothsayer, also a procuress. Nodier here uses the word as a proper noun.

27. A word coined by Nodier. It was borrowed by Victor Hugo in his early poem "La Ronde du Sabbat," in which he also mentions the demon Smarra.

28. Another word coined by Nodier, from the Greek "chronos" modified by the prefix a-, thus "timeless, without age." It is also linked to the Greek "akronia" ("amputation, mutilation").

29. One of the meanings of this word, "snake charmer," derives from the name of a Libyan people who, in ancient tradition, charmed serpents and were immune to their venom. Nodier also plays on the entomological meaning of "psylle": a tiny, plantsucking insect (in English, "psylla" or "psyllid").

30. From the Greek "morphosis" ("process of forming"). Patrick Berthier observes that Saint Paul uses the word to designate illusory external appearances or forms, and that Nodier probably means to suggest a kind of specter. (Charles Nodier, *La Fée aux miettes, Smarra, Trilby* [Paris: Editions Gallimard, 1982], 377.)

31. "In ancient Slavic, *Ogoljen* ('stripped bare'), either because they are naked like specters or, ironically, because they strip the dead. I say *ghouls* because this word, customary in the translations of *Arabian Tales*, is not foreign to us and is obviously formed from the same root." (Nodier's note.)

32. *The Aeneid*, VI, verses 739–42. "Therefore they are punished for their ancient sins / and they are schooled with suffering. Some hang suspended / to the empty winds; from others the sins are washed away / by huge gurgling whirlpools, or burned away with fire." (Vergil [*sic*], *The Aeneid*, trans. James H. Mantinband [New York: Frederick Ungar Publishing Co., 1964].)

33. *The Tempest*, III, 2.

34. An important theme in Aeschylus's tragedies is the transmission of sin and guilt from one generation to another.

35. Claudius Claudianus, usually referred to as Claudian, *Against Rufinus*, I, verses 126–28: "There is heard the mournful weeping of the spirits of the dead as they flit by with faint sound of wings, and the inhabitants see the pale ghosts pass and the shades of the dead." (Claudian, vol. 1, trans. Maurice Platnauer [London: William Heinemann, 1922].) The first word of the quotation is actually "Illic," and not "Hic."

36. *A Midsummer Night's Dream*, V, 1.

37. Saint Charles Borromeo, Counter-Reformation churchman. He worked to alleviate suffering during the pestilence of 1576. In the seventeenth century, a huge statue of Saint Charles was erected at Arona, his birthplace.

The Red Inn

1. Astolphe de Custine (1790–1857), friend of Balzac and author of several works of fiction and nonfiction, among them *Russia in 1839*.

2. Johannisberg is a village on the Rhine.

3. Marie-Antoine Carême (1784–1833), who served as master chef for Talleyrand and some of the crown heads of Europe.

4. The *Gymnase dramatique*, vaudeville and musical theater founded in Paris in 1820. The word "gymnase" can also refer to a German secondary school, and Balzac plays on both meanings.

5. Anthelme Brillat-Savarin (1755–1826), author of a witty gastronomical treatise published in 1825.

6. An illusionistic exhibit utilizing a large, partly translucent painting, placed to be viewed from a distance through an opening. It was developed by Louis-Jacques-Mandé Daguerre, inventor of the daguerreotype, who opened his Diorama in Paris in 1822.

7. In Latin, "contemptible soul."

8. The revolutionary calendar instituted by the National Convention in 1793 reckoned its starting point from the founding of the first French Republic (September 22, 1792). Balzac's narrator has erred in matching the month *Vendémiaire* of Year VII with October 1799; it actually falls within Gregorian calendar year 1798.

9. The names of General Augereau and other historical figures of the period are mentioned by Balzac to add verisimilitude to his tale.

10. The assignat was the paper currency issued by the French Revolutionary government. The increasing issuance of the assignats resulted in inflation.

11. The territory of an elector, one of the princes who had the right to elect the Emperor of the Holy Roman Empire. Balzac is referring specifically here to the territory of the elector of the Rhine Palatinate.

12. Balzac is inexact here; the region of Swabia lies south of the Rhine provinces, within which the cities of Mainz and Cologne are located.

13. Henri de la Tour d'Auvergne, vicomte de Turenne (1611–1675), military commander under Louis XIII and Louis XIV.

14. "Wilhem," in Balzac's idiosyncratic adaptation of the German.

15. "This was my wish." (Horace, *Satires*, II, 6, 1.)

16. The Treaty of Amiens (1802), signed by Britain with France, Spain, and the Batavian Republic (the Netherlands), achieved a peace in Europe for fourteen months during the Napoleonic wars.

17. The Battle of Wagram (1809), one of Napoleon's most brilliant victories.

18. Moxa treatment, a medical practice that originated in China, is performed by burning small cones of dried leaves on certain designated points of the body.

19. The supreme council and tribunal of the Jews during postexilic times.

20. Maximilien-Sébastien Foy (1775–1825) was a military leader who emerged as a popular spokesman of the liberal opposition following the Bourbon Restoration (1815).

21. Racine, *Phèdre*, IV, 2.

22. The Edict of Nantes (1598), which granted religious liberties to the French Huguenots, was revoked by Louis XIV in 1685.

23. The "doctrinaires" were a small group of politicians, partisans of a constitutional monarchy, who came on the French political scene during the Bourbon Restoration. They wished to lift their political formulations to the level of a philosophical system, an endeavor which led to the somewhat sardonic tone of their appelation (and Balzac's satirical characterization in the next paragraph).

24. From the Hebrew "Aceldama" (field of blood), the name given to the field that Judas bought with the sum he had acquired by betraying Jesus (Acts of the Apostles, 1:18–19).

25. By the seventeenth-century Spanish Jesuit theologian, Antonio Escobar y Mendoza.

26. Jeanie (not Jenny) Deans, a character in Sir Walter Scott's novel, *The Heart of Midlothian* (1818).

The Venus of Ille

1. "May the statue, I said, be kind and gentle, for it is so like a man." (Lucian, *The Lover of Lies*, 19.)

2. Highest mountain in the eastern Pyrenees.

3. A ruined Augustinian priory notable for its fine Romanesque sculpture.

4. The words used by Mérimée ("ne bougeait pas plus qu'un Terme") are taken nearly exactly from La Fontaine's *Fables*, IX, 19. In antiquity, such

a pillar ("terminus"), often shaped as a standing figure, was commonly fixed in the ground as a marker and venerated as sacred to Terminus, god of boundaries.

5. In the French, "from the cedar to the hyssop," an expression that originates in the Bible (1 Kings 4:33).

6. Coustou is the name of a family of French sculptors active at the time of Louis XIV and later. Mérimée is most likely referring to Nicolas Coustou (1668–1733), the author of several statues in the Tuileries.

7. Mérimée is playing on the lines from Molière's *Amphitryon*, II, 2: "How irreverently of the gods / This rogue is pleased to talk!"

8. Myron, fifth century B.C. Greek sculptor, a worker in bronze, whose "Discobolus" (Discus Thrower) is well known through Roman copies. Later in the story, Monsieur de Peyrehorade will claim only that the statue is a work of Myron's school, made by one of his descendants.

9. "You know not the rewards of Venus." (Virgil, *The Aeneid*, IV, verse 33.)

10. In the game of Morra, a person must guess the number of fingers that his opponent is extending on a hand in rapid motion. The statue in the Louvre known as Germanicus, which seems to predate the famous Roman general of that name, represents a Roman official with arm raised in the stock gesture of the orator.

11. Racine, *Phèdre*, I, 3.

12. In Latin, "Beware the one who loves."

13. In Latin, "What say you, learned colleague?"

14. In the French, "à grand renfort de besicles," an expression taken from Rabelais, *Gargantua*, chap. 1.

15. "Eutyches Myron made Venus Turbul . . . at her command."

16. Jan Gruter (1560–1627) and Johan Caspar von Orelli (1787–1849), humanists, scholars, and philologists, authors of learned works on the inscriptions of antiquity.

17. Diomedes, said by Homer to have wounded Aphrodite (Venus) during the siege of Troy. As later narrated in Ovid's *Metamorphoses* (XIV, verses 496 ff.), one of Diomedes' companions gave renewed offense to the goddess with his reckless insults, in consequence of which he and his fellows were punished by being changed into birds.

18. "Give me lilies in handfuls." (Virgil, *The Aeneid*, VI, verse 883.)

19. Article five of the French Constitutional Charter (1814, modified in 1830) guarantees freedom of religion.

20. Ancient Macedonian seaport, on the Adriatic coast. Near here in 48 B.C., Caesar suffered a temporary military reverse at the hands of Pompey.

21. In Spanish, "You'll pay for this."

22. The Sabines were an ancient people living in central Italy, to the east of Rome. According to legend, the founders of Rome supplied their lack of women by raiding their Sabine neighbors.

23. Mérimée is alluding to the "misfortune" of psychosomatic impotence, which was often imputed to sorcery; the subject is discussed by

Michel de Montaigne in "Of the Power of Imagination" (*Essais*, I, 21), and by Madame de Sévigné in her letter to Madame de Grignan (*Correspondance*, April 8, 1671). The quote is from Madame de Sévigné.

The Dead in Love

1. Semi-legendary ruler of Assyria, notorious for his sybaritic life, the sensational end of which is the subject of Delacroix's huge canvas, *The Death of Sardanapalus* (1826).

2. See Job 31:1; "I have made a covenant with my eyes; how then could I look upon a virgin?"

3. Gautier alludes to Belshazzar as "Balthazar," an alternative rendering of the name of the last ruler of Babylon, who according to the Bible (Daniel, 5) receives dramatic warning of his imminent doom while carousing with his retinue. The Egyptian queen Cleopatra, one of history's most celebrated femmes fatales, is the central figure in Gautier's story, "Une Nuit de Cléopâtre."

4. An apple-green variety of chalcedony, valued as a gem.

Arria Marcella

1. Daniel-François-Esprit Auber (1782–1871) was the composer of *La Muette de Portici* (1828).

2. In Italian, "inn" or "public house."

3. Shakespeare, *Hamlet*, V, 1: "To what base uses we may return, Horatio! Why may not imagination trace the noble dust of Alexander till 'a find it stopping a bunghole? . . . Imperious Caesar, dead and turned to clay, / Might stop a hole to keep the wind away . . ."

4. In ancient Roman times, a tavern serving warm drinks.

5. The first of April (or the Kalends). In the Roman calendar, the Nones designated the seventh day in March, May, July, and October, the fifth in the other months. The days were counted before, not after, the Kalends, Nones, and Ides.

6. In Latin, "They will be in the morning."

7. High, laced boots common in antiquity.

8. Probably Fabio has in mind Pliny the Elder, the famous Roman naturalist, who died investigating the eruption of Vesuvius.

9. Boileau, *L'Art poétique*, IV, verse 50.

10. Gautier couples Lucullus, the Roman general of the first century B.C., with the fictitious Trimalchio, the crass upstart in Petronius's novel *Satyricon*, who comically presides over a vulgarly ostentatious banquet.

11. The French "le néant" signifies "nothingness, non-being."

12. The Roman practice was to designate the year by reference to the name or names of the consul(s) in office for that year. L. Munatius Plancus was twice consul, in 42 B.C. and again in a year not definitely known.

13. The allusion is to the triumphal procession, with an escort of torch bearers and flute players, given the Roman consul Duilius after he defeated the Carthaginians in a sea battle off Mylae in 260 B.C.

14. Of Gades (Cádiz), in Spain.

15. The *Journal des Débats*, Parisian daily newspaper founded in 1789. The *Débats* was moderately liberal in its viewpoint and one of the most influential publications of the French press in the nineteenth century.

16. Second century B.C. Greek statesman and historian of the growing power of Rome. Machiavelli is said to have been strongly influenced by the "pragmatic" outlook of Polybius.

17. Charles Albert Demoustier (1760–1801), author of the affected but once popular *Lettres à Emilie sur la mythologie*.

18. French historical painters active in Gautier's time.

19. In part 2 of Goethe's great dramatic poem, Faust is permitted to return to a phantasmal antiquity and to steal away the shade of the fabulous Helen of Troy.

20. Semiramis, mythical Assyrian queen noted for her beauty and wisdom; Aspasia (fifth century B.C.), Greek courtesan, witty and beautiful mistress of the Athenian ruler Pericles; Cleopatra (first century B.C.), alluring queen of Egypt, noted for her romantic relations with Julius Caesar and Mark Antony; Diana of Poitiers (1499–1566), mistress of Henry II of France, a woman of cold yet seductive elegance depicted in several distinguished works of art of the sixteenth century; Giovanna d'Aragon (1500–1577), Italian-born princess linked by blood to the house of Aragon, subject of a portrait in the Louvre painted by Raphael.

21. Titus reigned from A.D. 39–81; Pompeii was destroyed in A.D. 79.

22. A medium common in antiquity, employing melted beeswax and resin, which after application was fixed with heat.

23. In Latin, "Beware of the dog."

24. Ancient Italic language spoken in central Italy, displaced by Latin by the end of the first century A.D.

25. A name commonly given to slave characters in ancient comedy.

26. The most famous painter of the French neoclassical school.

27. See *The Red Inn*, note 6.

28. In Latin, "here happiness lies."

29. Italian for "evil eye," from the verb "gettare," "to throw" (a spell).

30. In Latin, "Hail, stranger."

31. *De Viris Illustribus*, a collection of brief, anecdotal biographies of famous men, by the first century B.C. Roman historian Cornelius Nepos; *Selectae e Profanis Scriptoribus Historiae*, a Latin reader popular in the eighteenth and nineteenth centuries.

32. Lutetia Parisiorum was the Gallo-Roman precursor of the city of Paris.

33. In Gautier's pun, "mais il y perdit son latin, et à vrai dire ce n'était pas grand'chose." "Perdre son latin" (literally, "to lose one's Latin") is an idiomatic expression meaning "to understand nothing, to be at a loss."

34. In classical mythology, Pollux was one of the Dioscuri, his twin Castor being mortal, he immortal.

35. Plautus was a third/second century B.C. Roman author of comedies, twenty-one of which survive and have had a great influence on later comic theater.

36. Ceremonies honoring the goddess Athena, celebrated in ancient Athens, and represented in the Panathenaic frieze of the Parthenon. It is unclear whether Gautier is referring to the sky as background for the Panathenaea, or to the painted blue that once formed the background of the Panathenaic frieze.

37. Artemis (Diana) in her role as moon goddess.

38. From the sculptural compositions associated with the exterior of the Parthenon (perhaps designed by Phidias but presumed to have been executed by his assistants), one receives an impression of mastery in the representations of the draped human form. However, Gautier's reference to Cleomenes, a rather obscure Greek sculptor who has been linked to the "Venus de Medici," seems inappropriate insofar as the well-known statue in the Uffizi in Florence is totally without drapery.

39. The most famous mosaicist of antiquity, Sosos, worked at Pergamum in Asia Minor.

40. Paris, the mythical Trojan whose abduction of Helen ignited the Trojan War, is here set on the same plane of reality (or ideality) as the historical Egyptian queen, who sailed up the Cydnus River to Tarsus when summoned by Mark Antony for their momentous first meeting.

41. Helen of Troy was actually the daughter of Zeus, who visited Leda, Tyndareus's wife, in the form of a swan. (The twins Castor and Pollux also issued from this union of the human with the divine.)

42. When Ixion attempted to seduce Hera, her husband Zeus substituted for the goddess a cloud-like semblance, by which Ixion became the father of the centaurs.

43. Monsters of Greek mythology; among the Empusae were reckoned the Lamiae, who feasted on the blood of their human lovers.

44. "Vox faucibus haesit." (Virgil, *The Aeneid,* 2:774, 3:48, 4:280, 12: 868.)

The Slap of Charlotte Corday

1. Written after the Revolution of 1848, the comment betrays the author's nostalgia for his youth and his more wholehearted sympathy for the Revolution of 1830. The earlier revolution, in which he had enthusiastically taken part, had ushered in the July Monarchy of Louis Philippe. It was during the reign of the "Citizen King" that Dumas rose to fame and in general most flourished. Though he supported the Republic proclaimed in 1848, his deepest sympathies were with an age now passed.

2. The last tale in Dumas's collection will be told by this young woman, later revealed to have been a victim of vampirism.

3. In an earlier chapter of *Les Mille et un Fantômes*, Dumas's narrator had been one of several witnesses to a murder confession on the part of Jacquemin, a stone quarrier who had severed his wife's head with a sword.

4. The murderer had placed the head upon a sack of plaster after the crime.

5. Dr. Sömmering, a Frankfurt scholar of surgical anatomy, his disciple

Dr. Oesler (not Oelcher), and Dr. Jean-Joseph Sue, librarian of the Paris School of Medicine, all argued for the continuance of sensation after execution on the guillotine. The French public was made familiar with the terms of the debate through Dr. Sömmering's famous letter in the form of a dialogue, written in 1793 but published in the Paris *Moniteur* in 1795. Sömmering is the major source for the arguments made in Dumas's tale by M. Ledru.

6. The French physician Joseph-Ignace Guillotin (1738–1814), elected to the National Assembly in 1789, was instrumental in having a law passed requiring executions to be carried out by means of a machine, so that they might be as "painless" as possible. This machine soon became known as the "guillotine."

7. Albrecht von Haller (1708–1777), Swiss physiologist, author of *Elementa Physiologiae Corporis Humani* (Physiological elements of the human body)— not, as Dumas claims, *Elements of Physics*.

8. Melchior Adam Weikard (1742–1803), German physician. Dumas has mistranslated Weikard's *Der philosophische Arzt* (The philosophical physician). Both Haller and Weikard are mentioned in Dr. Sömmering's letter to the *Moniteur* (see note 5, above).

9. Nicolas Philippe Ledru (1731–1807), French physician known by the name of Comus, who acquired the title of King's Physician in 1783.

10. The Italian physicist Alessandro Volta (1745–1827), famous for his early work in electricity, invented the voltaic pile (electric battery); the Italian physician Luigi Galvani (1737–1798) conducted electrical experiments on animal tissue, research which focused attention on the concept of electric currents; the German physician Franz Anton Mesmer (1734–1815) popularized the notion of animal magnetism and devised a system of treatment supposed to effect "magnetic cures."

11. "The Mountain," a term designating the most radical members of the National Convention (who occupied benches high up against the wall) during the French Revolution. Among the *Montagne* were the Jacobins, who ruled France during the Reign of Terror (1793–1794).

12. Georges Danton (1759–1794), French Revolutionary leader and orator, and Camille Desmoulins (1760–1794), influential journalist and pamphleteer of the Revolution.

13. Jean-Paul Marat (1743–1793), French physician and prominent champion of the Revolution through his inflammatory journalism.

14. Charlotte Corday (1768–1793), the assassin of Jean-Paul Marat.

15. Literally, "without knee breeches"; this term was used to refer to the radical democrats of the French Revolution, for the most part men of the poorer classes or their leaders.

16. François-Séverin Marceau (1769–1796), a young military hero of the French Revolutionary wars.

17. Jean-Baptiste Kléber (1753–1800), French Revolutionary general who suppressed the counterrevolutionary uprising in the Vendée in 1793.

18. "It is not for the sake of flirting with horror that we dwell at length upon such a subject, but it seemed that at a time when the abolition of the

death penalty is a matter of great concern, such commentary is not without profit." (Dumas's note.)

19. 1793.

Aurélia, or Dream and Life

1. Nerval published the first ten chapters of his tale in the January 1, 1855, issue of the *Revue de Paris*. Although without the heading "Part One," it was "to be continued" in the next issue. During the night of January 25, 1855, the homeless and penniless Nerval hanged himself in the rue de la Vieille-Lanterne. The remaining portions of his manuscript (which did not yet contain final revisions) were published posthumously in the February 15 issue of the *Revue de Paris*, under the heading "Seconde Partie."

2. In Book XIX of *The Odyssey*, Homer distinguishes between two kinds of dreams: those that come through gates of ivory and are mere illusion, and those that come through gates of horn and foretell truly, if properly understood.

3. Emanuel Swedenborg (1688−1772), Swedish scientist and religious philosopher turned mystic and visionary, who attempted to interpret the Scriptures in the light of the "correspondence" between the spiritual and physical worlds.

4. *The Golden Ass* of Apuleius (see *Smarra*, note 4) treats of the ignoble imprisonment within the body of an animal of an aware and observant human being, who is eventually released from his condition through his spiritual initiation into the mysteries of the Egyptian goddess Isis.

5. Dante's *Divine Comedy*, a poem in one hundred cantos, recounts the narrator's spiritual pilgrimage through Hell, Purgatory, and Paradise.

6. *La Vita nuova* (*The New Life*) is a collection of poems written by Dante celebrating his ideal love for the woman he called Beatrice.

7. See Jean-Jacques Rousseau, *Emile*: "If it were here the place to do so, I would try to show how the first voices of conscience arise from the first movements of the heart, and how the first notions of good and evil are born from the sentiments of love and hatred." (Rousseau, *Oeuvres complètes*, vol. 4 [Paris: Editions Gallimard, 1969], 522.) This connection is noted in Gérard de Nerval, *Oeuvres complètes*, vol. 3 (Paris: Editions Gallimard, 1993), 1339 note 4.

8. Laura played a role in the work of the Italian poet Petrarch (1304−1374) analogous to that which Beatrice played for Dante.

9. Dürer's famous engraving, *Melancholia*, is a learned yet powerfully expressive interpretation of the Saturnine personality type, the type of imaginative genius, as formulated by Marsilio Ficino and other Renaissance humanists.

10. Nerval refers here to Paul Chenavard, a history painter whose large-scale drawings and sketches for an ambitious but unrealized mural project, illustrating his mythic vision of the story of humanity as an epic progression of heroes and beliefs, are preserved in the *Musée des Beaux-Arts* in Lyon.

11. "Seven was the number of Noah's family: but one of the seven was mysteriously related to the previous generations of the Elohim! . . .

". . . Imagination, like a lightning-flash, showed me the multiple gods of India as symbols of the family, as it were, primitively concentrated. I tremble to go further, for in the Trinity there also resides an awesome mystery. . . . We were born under Biblical law . . ." (Nerval's note.)

"Elohim," the usual name for God in the Hebrew scriptures, is actually a plural form and is commonly so used in the esoteric tradition, which Nerval appears to be following.

12. The wheel is a symbol associated with the idea of fortune or destiny, as emblematized by the Tarot card designated *Fortune*, or *Wheel of Fortune*. Nerval's image of a goddess, beneath whose feet a wheel is turning, suggests the famous engravings of Albrecht Dürer depicting the goddess Fortuna, who stands in similar fashion on a globe.

13. According to Pierre-Georges Castex (*Aurélia* [Paris: SEDES, 1971], 167), the author associates this "Sacred Table" with the biblical King Solomon: in his notes to *Voyage en Orient*, Nerval makes reference to "the emerald table of Solomon, bordered with precious stones." More importantly, perhaps, Castex describes the sacred table as being (in the esoteric tradition) a "symbol of the union of the macrocosm and the microcosm."

For Elohim, see note 11, above.

14. For Nerval and his contemporaries, "Oriental" was usually taken to refer to the lands and traditional cultures of the Near East.

15. Divas and Peris are Persian genies of evil and good, respectively. Undines and Salamanders, spirits of water and fire, are two of the four elementary spirits described in the abbé de Villars's *Le Comte de Gabalis* (1670), a repository of occultist lore.

16. In Arabian legend, one of a class of demonic spirits.

17. Tradition of Jewish esoteric mysticism, based on the supposition that man is linked to God through a chain of ten immaterial emanations or manifestations. Strongly affected by Neoplatonic concepts, medieval cabalists sought to interpret Scripture by means of a system that assigned hidden symbolic significance to words, letters, and numbers.

18. This imagery has been linked by Jean Richer (*Nerval: Expérience et création* [Paris: Hachette, 1963], 476) to the emblematic image of the Tarot card designated *The Star*. This card, which depicts below the star or stars a young woman pouring water into a lake or sea, is associated with the idea of hope, renewal, and salvation.

19. "To me, this referred to the blow that I had received in my fall." (Nerval's note.)

20. According to Jean Richer (see note 18, above), Nerval found this term in books on Near Eastern mythology, but through a slight confusion applies it to the notion of the double; in his sources, it has more the meaning of "prototype" or "archetype" (Richer, 478–479).

21. The author is likely referring to Saint Paul, who proclaims the dichotomy between soul and body in his Epistle to the Romans. Nerval also

draws on a line from his own translation of Goethe's *Faust*: "Two souls, alas, are lodged within my breast."

22. In Greek mythology, Amphitryon's wife Alcmena became pregnant by the god Zeus, who visited her disguised as her husband. In the dramatizations of this myth by Plautus (second century B.C.) and by the French playwright Molière in the seventeenth century, Sosia is Amphitryon's man-servant, whose identity is temporarily assumed by the god Mercury.

23. Nerval is alluding to the hermetic tradition.

24. In ancient Greek legend, Pluto permitted Orpheus to recover his wife Eurydice from the underworld, provided that he not turn and look back at her. Nevertheless, Orpheus did look back, thus losing Euridice forever. It has also been noted that Nerval's epigraph comes from a line of an aria in Gluck's opera *Orfeo ed Euridice* (*Orpheus and Euridice*). (Nerval, *Oeuvres complètes*, 3 : 1353.)

25. Lucretius Carus (c. 98–55 B.C.), Latin poet and philosopher. In his *De rerum natura* (*On the Nature of Things*), Lucretius sets forth his vision of an atomic and mechanistic universe, in which the gods, who neither created nor can change the world, are remote and unconcerned with the lives of men.

26. From Lord Byron's poetic drama *Manfred* (1817): "The Tree of Knowledge is not that of Life." (I, 1)

27. Nerval is referring to the Nahr-Beyrouth, a river channel that is dry most of the year.

28. It is unclear why Nerval uses the ellipsis here.

29. The allusion is to the Don Juan legend, more specifically to Molière's drama, *Dom Juan* (1665). The title character invites the statue of the Commander, a man he had killed in a duel, to dine with him; the "stone guest" in fact arrives, and returns the invitation. The play ends as the unremorseful libertine descends to his perdition.

30. Nerval's father served as a doctor in Napoleon's Rhine army; his mother, who had accompanied her husband, died of a fever when Nerval was two years old.

31. Primitive Celtic deities; Esus was a god of vegetation and war, Cernunnos a deity of the underworld.

32. George Bell, one of Nerval's closest friends in his last years, and author of a biography of the writer.

33. The insurrection of 1830 brought Louis Philippe to the French throne and inaugurated the political and social ascendancy of the bourgeoisie in France.

34. These were the events leading up to Louis Napoleon's *coup d'état* in 1851.

35. Nerval's friend, Heinrich Heine (1797–1856).

36. *Sylvie* (1853).

37. Two contending factions in the struggle for political power in early fifteenth-century France.

38. In the French, "les galeries d'ostéologie."

39. Isis; see Introduction, p. xxxvi.

40. Louis-François Bertin (Bertin the Elder), founder of the *Journal des Débats*. Bertin had died twelve years earlier, in 1841.

41. The private clinic of Dr. Emile Blanche, at Passy.

42. In Nordic mythology, the Valkyries were maidens who were sent to the battlefields by the sovereign god Odin to select among the slain those worthy of a place in Valhalla.

43. In classical mythology, Tartarus was the dim, remote, underground realm of the dead.

44. A patterned silk fabric.

45. Pierre-Paul Prud'hon (1758 – 1823), a proto-Romantic painter of historical, allegorical, and amorous subjects.

46. Antonio Allegri da Correggio (1494 – 1534), Italian painter of religious themes, erudite allegory, and many mythological subjects involving nudes whose voluptuousness is enhanced by his characteristically soft and subtle play of light and color.

47. Giovanni Pico della Mirandola (1463 – 1494), Italian humanist and synchretistic philosopher, chief exponent of Florentine Neoplatonism, who sought to reconcile Christianity with Platonic philosophy, and who was also the first Christian scholar to use cabalistic doctrine in support of Christian theology; Johannes Meursius (1579 – 1639), Dutch professor and historiographer, author of a commentary on the Alexandrian poet Lycophron; and Nicholas of Cusa (1401 – 1464), German churchman, humanist, and "Renaissance man," who favored mystical intuition over reason as a path to knowledge.

48. Nerval here leaves a lacuna, which his first publishers (after his death in 1855) filled with the author's *Letters to Aurélia*, but which most subsequent editions have retained.

49. Village in India, famous for its ancient temples excavated out of rock cliffs.

50. The attendants of the Greek nature goddess Cybele, who were supposed to have accompanied her with wild dances and music.

51. The name of the star-shaped flower, "forget-me-not."

52. Ancient town on the island of Cyprus. A celebrated temple of the goddess Aphrodite is located here.

53. This sublime "friend" is Nerval's composite figure of the eternal and redemptive feminine—at once the narrator's lost love Aurélia, the goddess Isis, the Christian Virgin (mediator for those who seek divine forgiveness), and the Queen of Sheba, whom Nerval also associated (more explicitly in *Voyage en Orient*) with his feminine ideal. The Queen of Sheba can be connected with the figure in Aurélia through the reference to "the perfumes of Yemen" (the ancient kingdom of Sheba, or Saba, included present-day Yemen), and, in the next paragraph, the allusion to "the messenger hoopoe," a bird described in *Voyage en Orient* as attending the Queen of Sheba.

54. Nerval had crossed out a word identifying this female figure as Sophia, the personification of divine wisdom in the Gnostic tradition.

55. The "Destroyer" or the "angel of the bottomless pit" in Revelation 9 : 11. Nerval appears to be merging this figure with Apollo, the

sun-god of Greek mythology, one of whose attributes is the bow. Thus it would seem that Apollyon has been symbolically included in the universal pardon.

56. In the Greek myth, Adonis's death (he was killed while hunting) and resurrection were symbolic of the death and rebirth of plant life.

57. From 1 Corinthians 15:55.

58. Presumably the reference is to Thor, the Nordic god of thunder, and his magic hammer.

59. Castex (see note 13, above) makes a connection between the "sacred" or "holy" table and the wisdom of Solomon, and, following Richer, associates the Rose Pearl with the Queen of Sheba: in a fragment of an earlier version of *Aurélia*, the narrator had identified the divinity of his dreams (part 1, chapter 7) as the Queen of Sheba and pictured her as wearing a necklace of "rose pearls." Castex assumes Thor to represent the Germanic peoples who invaded the Roman world, and sees the breaking of the sacred table by Thor as symbolic of the shock of the barbarian invasions upon "Judeo-Christian civilization"—which, however, survived the fall of the Empire to become the Christendom of medieval and modern times.

60. In the language of theosophy, the words "macrocosm" and "microcosm" are often used to refer to the universe and man. (Nerval, *Oeuvres complètes*, 3:1370 note 8.)

61. In Nordic mythology, Odin is the father and chief of the gods; Loki is the crafty, disturbing spirit of evil; Hela rules the realm of the dead; Garm is the hound that guards Hela's gate. (Hela was more traditionally the daughter of Loki.)

62. The Midgard Serpent, like the Homeric ocean, encompassed the earth and stirred up storms.

63. Balder was a Nordic god of light, purity, beauty, and perfect justice, who suffered death through Loki's wicked cunning; Freya was a goddess of love and fertility.

64. Zaandam, city in Holland. It was dubbed Saardam ("worthy of the czar") in memory of Peter the Great, who had stayed there in 1697 to learn shipbuilding. Nerval visited the house of Peter the Great at Zaandam in 1852.

65. Nerval refers to the monument on the Graben in Vienna, dedicated to the Holy Trinity, which was erected by order of Emperor Leopold I to commemorate Vienna's deliverance from the plague of 1679. It takes the form of a pillar of billowing cloud supporting angels and leading up to the Trinity at the top. Sculpture on the base shows the demon of the plague overthrown by Faith. There is but one such monument in Vienna (although there are others in other towns in Austria), and they are actually known as Pestsäule (plague columns). Frank Paul Bowman, in his article "'Mémorables d'*Aurélia*: Signification et Situation Générique" (*French Forum* 11, no. 2 [May 1986]: 169–181), discusses the thematic and intertextual processes at work in Nerval's designation of these columns as "pardons" (Bowman, 176–177).

66. Catherine I (1684–1727), wife of Peter the Great; Catherine II (Catherine the Great, 1729–1796); and Saint Helen (c. 248–328), Roman empress and mother of Constantine the Great.

67. The Crimean War (1853–1856), which pitted the Russians against the British, French, and Ottoman Turks. With the hope for peace in Europe, Nerval's dream of personal and cosmic salvation takes on a historical dimension.

Master Zacharius

1. Blaise Pascal, French philosopher and mathematician (1623–1662). I am unable to trace this quotation.

2. "The heart of any mechanical clock is its escapement, the device which through a repetitive mechanical motion regulates the running down of the motive power." (Samuel L. Macey, *Clocks and the Cosmos* [Hamden, Conn.: Archon Books, 1980].) The invention of the earliest form of escapement, which first made the mechanical clock a possibility, actually considerably predates Zacharius's time, which the story indicates as being pre-Calvin (see page 227) but subsequent to the introduction, in 1476, of Louis de Berquem's new diamond-cutting technique (see page 232).

3. Verne is referring to the fifteenth-century Flemish diamond cutter, Lodewyk van Berken, also known as Louis de Berquem (not Berghem).

4. Benvenuto Cellini (1500–1571) was an Italian Renaissance sculptor and goldsmith.

5. The innovation that revolutionized the design of the mechanical clock was the introduction, in the seventeenth century, of the pendulum. Verne takes substantial poetic license here, as the new precision in timepieces actually came from connecting a pendulum to the preexisting escapement, not adding an escapement to clocks already using the pendulum. The seventeenth-century innovation is associated with two important names in the history of science: using Galileo's discovery of the pendulum's regular periodicity, the Dutch scientist Christiaan Huygens designed the first successful pendulum clock in 1657, thus inaugurating the "horological revolution." Verne would seem to have credited his fictional protagonist with the invention of the escapement because the identity of the mechanical genius (of an earlier, medieval time) who actually introduced it is unknown.

6. Verne refers to the fact that if a pendulum is used in a clock to control and regularize its ticking (that is, the time interval between beats), then a force is needed to keep the pendulum in motion. This force is supplied by the motion of the wheelwork that is being regulated. In other words, there is a reciprocity and interdependence between the wheelwork (which keeps the pendulum moving) and the pendulum (which controls the pace of the wheelwork).

7. Zacharius is referring to variations in the earth's velocity along the path of its slightly eccentric, elliptical orbit. Therefore, actual "sun time" runs either faster or slower than "mean time," except for four times in the year (four places in the orbit) when they coincide.

8. The biblical Joshua, successor to Moses, led the Hebrews into the Promised Land. At one point, he commanded the sun to stand still while the men of Israel took vengeance upon their enemies (Joshua 10:12–14).

9. Zacharius's cry is not the "sound" just mentioned; rather, it is apparently in response to the clangorous whirring sound of the clock's breakdown and expiration.

10. In French, "la science" can be translated, depending on the context, as "knowledge" (as in the biblical "tree of knowledge of good and evil") or as "science." In the context of the blasphemous clock mottos in this tale, both meanings are present.

The Sign

1. Villiers's uncle, who was a priest.

2. "Observe, man, what you were before you came into being and what you will be until your death. Undoubtedly there was a time when you did not exist. Then, made from vile matter, nourished in your mother's womb with menstrual blood, your raiment was the placenta. Then, wrapped in a vile rag, you came toward us, —thus clothed and adorned! And you have no memory of your origin. Man is nothing other than fetid sperm, a sack of excrement, food for the worms. Knowledge, wisdom, reason, without God, pass like the clouds.

"After the man, the worm; after the worm, stench and horror;

So every man is transformed into that which is not human.

Why do you adorn and paint your flesh, which, after only a few days, will be devoured by worms in the tomb, while yet you do not adorn your soul,—which will appear in Heaven before God and his Angels!"

The Bollandists were a group of Jesuits in seventeenth-century Belgium who, under the direction of Father John Bollandus, compiled an authoritative edition of the lives of the saints, the monumental *Acta Sanctorum*. Saint Bernard of Clairvaux (1090[?]–1153), here quoted by the Bollandists, was a French churchman and mystic.

3. Villiers seems to have meant the autumn equinox, although a page later he alludes to the latter half of October.

4. According to Alan Raitt and Pierre-Georges Castex (Villiers de l'Isle-Adam, *Oeuvres complètes* [Paris: Gallimard, 1986], 695), this is an expression for a solution of the drug "senna," a purgative. If there is no connection between the name of the drug, Arabic in origin, and that of the famous Arabian physician, then the term would appear to have originated as a pun.

5. The French monk and ecclesiastical reformer, Robert d'Arbrissel (1047–1117), founder of the Order of Fontevrault, was the advocate of a strict discipline among the regular clergy. Villiers may be alluding to a story, rather in the style of Boccacio (cited by Raitt and Castex from Baldric's biography of Robert d'Arbrissel), concerning the monk's personal efforts to temper his libido.

The Samoyeds are a nomadic people who live in regions of northern Siberia, above the Arctic circle.

6. Joseph de Maistre (1754–1821), French writer and diplomat, was a monarchist and ultramontane who vigorously opposed the tenets of the Enlightenment.

Véra

1. Villers's friend, the Count d'Osmoy, supported the production of his play, *Le Nouveau Monde*, with funds for the lease of a theater.

2. According to Raitt and Castex, p. 1346 (see note 4 of "The Sign," above), Villiers here paraphrases A. Véra (*Introduction à la philosophie de Hegel*), as he had already done in *Claire Lenoir* when he wrote: "As for the physiologists, are they not compelled to affirm that the *form* of the body is more essential to it than its *matter?*"

3. These are the words spoken by Clarimonde in Gautier's "The Dead in Love"; the biblical quotation is "love is as strong as death" (Song of Solomon, 8:6).

4. In Latin, "Pale but victorious."

5. "Whoever sees Véra shall love her."

The Horla

1. Maupassant is referring to the hypnotism research of James Braid in England (c. 1840), and that of the School of Nancy in France, founded in 1866 by Auguste Liébault and continued in Maupassant's day by Hippolyte Bernheim. This school considered itself a rival to the hypnotism research which Jean Charcot was conducting at the hospital of La Salpêtrière in Paris.

2. Voltaire, *Le Sottisier*, 32 (see Maupassant, *Contes et nouvelles*, vol. 2 [Paris: Gallimard, 1979], p. 1630 note 4 bottom).

3. Invented name that draws loosely upon the German; "Her(r)" (the man, or the master) "ist" (is) "aus" (out, outside). The word for "outside" in French is "hors"—part of the etymology of the "Horla."

4. Readers may note the anomaly in the dating of this and the previous journal entry.

Who Knows?

1. Opera (1884) by the French composer Ernest Reyer (1823–1909), based on the same sources in Nordic mythology that were employed by Wagner in his opera *Siegfried*.